A BLACK FOX RUNNING

BRIAN CARTER

With a Foreword
by Melissa Harrison

BLOOMSBURY
LONDON · OXFORD · NEW YORK · NEW DELHI · SYDNEY

Bloomsbury Publishing
An imprint of Bloomsbury Publishing Plc

50 Bedford Square
London
WC1B 3DP
UK

1385 Broadway
New York
NY 10018
USA

www.bloomsbury.com

BLOOMSBURY and the Diana logo are trademarks of Bloomsbury Publishing Plc

First published in Great Britain by J. M. Dent 1981
This edition first published in Great Britain 2018

Every reasonable effort has been made to trace copyright holders of material
reproduced in this book, but if any have been inadvertently overlooked
the publishers would be glad to hear from them.

This is a work of fiction. Names and characters are the product of the author's imagination
and any resemblance to actual persons, living or dead, is entirely coincidental.

No responsibility for loss caused to any individual or organization acting on
or refraining from action as a result of the material in this publication
can be accepted by Bloomsbury or the author.

British Library Cataloguing-in-Publication Data
A catalogue record for this book is available from the British Library.

Library of Congress Cataloguing-in-Publication data has been applied for.

ISBN: HB: 978-1-4088-9613-6
          EPUB: 978-1-4088-9615-0

2 4 6 8 10 9 7 5 3 1

Typeset by Integra Software Services Pvt. Ltd.
Printed and bound in Great Britain by CPI Group (UK) Ltd, Croydon CR0 4YY

To find out more about our authors and books visit www.bloomsbury.com.
Here you will find extracts, author interviews, details of forthcoming
events and the option to sign up for our newsletters.

09/08/19

A BLACK FOX
RUNNING

Fiction
Lundy's War
The Moon in the Weir
Jack
In the Long Dark
Nightworld

Non-fiction
Where the Dream Begins
Dartmoor: The Threatened Wilderness
Yesterday's Harvest
Walking in the Wild
Carter's Country

To every fox who ran before the hounds and to my children, Christian and Rebecca, that they may know and love the wild places.

FOREWORD

A Black Fox Running is not a children's book, but I first encountered it as a child. I must have been seven or eight when my mother first read it to me, the Devon landscape it so vividly described thrillingly familiar to me as the beloved country of our summer holidays. The story of the Dartmoor hill foxes entered my imagination and put down roots far deeper than anything else I've since read about the natural world, and its unsentimental depiction of both animals and humans and rhapsodic, protean prose has become a yardstick for all other descriptive writing, and a beacon for my own.

Since then I've reread *Black Fox* at least a dozen times – probably more. I took it with me to university, and then to a series of rented London flats; when at last the pages fell out of my copy I tracked down a replacement online, and was delighted when it arrived signed. In my early twenties I wrote to its author, the Devon artist, poet, columnist, children's writer, naturalist and broadcaster Brian Carter, telling him how important his book was to me; sadly, it didn't reach him. Now, though, to be able to introduce his extraordinary novel to a new readership feels like the fulfilment of a promise, and the repayment of a long-held debt.

A Black Fox Running opens *in medias res*, with a simple exchange that encapsulates much of what is to come:

> *'Yes, I can smell him,' said Stargrief. The old dog fox raised his muzzle.*
> *'And the lurcher,' Wulfgar said.*

Wulfgar is the black fox of the novel's title; Stargrief his friend, a seer at nearly nine winters old. 'Him' is the trapper Leonard Scoble, fifty-eight in 1946. 'His face carried the blotches of burst blood vessels and across his rutted baldness he had laid a few strands of grey hair. On his right cheek was a mole as black as an ash bud. There was about his shabby bulk a suggestion of real strength but alcohol had sapped his stamina.' Carter writes with a subtle mixture of pity and disgust that persists throughout the book. Far more than the red-coated riders of the South Devon Hunt, Scoble and his dog Jacko are the foxes' true nemeses, and Carter's novel tells the story of their conflict, and of their lives – which are one and the same thing.

Scoble is a man who kills not just for food or even for sport, but in anger. His hatred of foxes is absolute, a function not only of his view of them as 'vermin' – a different category to 'animal' – but rooted in genuine nightmare: a dead mule, three foxes and a ditch near the River Somme. He suffers from what we would now call PTSD, and the horrors of the Great War, not to mention his violent and deprived childhood, bleed uncontrollably into his present, feeding his misogyny, misanthropy and cruelty in a viscerally believable way. His lurcher, Jacko, is no better, a dog deformed by madness, a creation entirely of Scoble whose bloodthirstiness and unpredictability – now loving, now vicious; a tragic mirror of his own father – has fatally unmoored his charge. Carter paints Jacko as irredeemable in a way that Scoble is not; he is the darkest side of the man made flesh.

We are less used, these days, to novels in which wild animals talk, although in 1981 when *Black Fox* was first published they were, of course, hugely popular. But Carter takes great care not to further anthropomorphise his subjects: they kill everything from beetles to baby rabbits to lambs frequently, bloodily and with no compunction; urinate and leave scats; mate, groom, and suffer sometimes from worms, ticks and mange, Carter inhabiting their unfamiliar vulpine bodies – their sensitive noses, the pads of their paws, their brushes – with shamanistic ease. The sounds they make, when overheard by humans, are the sounds foxes really do make, and there is something deeply convincing about Carter's side-note that when stoats or otters communicate in what he dubs the 'canidae argot' it is with the 'unpleasant nasal twang' common to all mustelids.

But the fact that the animals in this book speak serves a deeper purpose than it does for the rabbits in *Watership Down*, for example, or the moles of *Duncton Wood*. *A Black Fox Running* is unique in being just as much a story about humans as it is about animals; people are neither centre-stage, as they are in most writing about the natural world, nor banished to the sidelines in favour of wild creatures, as in most talking animal books, and glimpsed only as some kind of inexplicable force for destruction. In *Black Fox*, humans and animals are named and treated equally, as highly differentiated subjects, each individual the centre of its own universe. It is necessary to this even-handedness that the foxes speak; to have made them mute, as Henry Williamson did Tarka, would have allowed only the humans in the book to demonstrate their agency and destroyed what is, for me, the most important aspect of the novel: the creation of a world in which the utterly divergent viewpoints of mankind and animals co-exist for us as readers, challenging our anthropocentric point of view and extending our imaginative sympathies. Here, Dartmoor is neither the foxes' flawed paradise, a trapper's grim larder nor the Hunt's fiefdom, but all those things at once; similarly, humans are not selfish and harmful, nor benevolent custodians, but both, because our nature is motley and complex. Indeed, Carter's writing insists on complexity, however discomfiting it is – and in that subsists the moral truth at the heart of this wise and compassionate book. For any conclusion we draw or decision we make about our relationship with the natural world is flawed and unsustainable if it insists on simplicity where there is none.

To the foxes, to be killed by the Hunt is 'the good death': challenging to some modern sensibilities, perhaps, but understandable when you consider that the alternatives are Scoble's snares, poison bait, buckshot or gin traps. Although he never reconciled himself to the hunting of wild creatures for sport, in his beguiling childhood memoir *Yesterday's Harvest* – part *Cider with Rosie,* part *Portrait of the Artist as a Young Dog* – Carter writes:

> *My sympathies like those of the other children I knew were with the fox, and I was deeply suspicious of those well-breeched men and women braying over my head in light saloon bar accents. Wherever they gathered I smelt violence of a dark, pagan kind... I could not understand why posh grown-ups were allowed to hunt an animal to death. Later... I learned that the hounds dealt death swiftly, not like the snare, the gin or the badly aimed buckshot. I shed many prejudices when I got to know Claude Whitley, Master of the South Devon Hunt... but at the age of nine everything registered in black and white. The sleek, red fox was born to freedom and I loved him... his enemies were my enemies and because they came from another class they were easy to misunderstand and dislike.*

The boy Brian, with his deep love of Dartmoor and fascination for the natural world, has a cameo in *Black Fox* as 'Stray', a fair-haired child sent to Dartmoor to recuperate from illness, who roams the moor collecting birds' eggs, opening the moorland gates for tips and tracking the foxes and other wildlife. Brian suffered from bronchial pneumonia as a child and the illness, and its then-rudimentary treatment, left him with night terrors and St Vitus's Dance (now known as Sydenham's chorea). Kept home from school for long periods and encouraged to spend as much time as possible out of doors, he took to the moors and found healing in nature, becoming, in adulthood, a robust and inveterate hiker and rock-climber, a walk leader and talented footballer, as well as an artist, novelist and poet.

The partial model for Scoble the trapper can also be found in *Yesterday's Harvest*, as well as a wealth of other details from *Black Fox*: we meet Carter's larger-than-life father, shades of whom are surely to be found in the 'thicky girt romancer' Bert Yabsley; there's the 'great ammil' of March 1947, when the record-breaking snows of the previous winter partially melted and then refroze to cover the moor in verglas; a visiting snowy owl with 'a beak like a five-ton grass hook'; a fox dancing on its hind legs at sunset, snapping craneflies from the air – all incidents that found their way into *Black Fox*. I suspect that the sense of a lost arcadia that imbues the entire book – even underlying its most shocking and brutal passages – is due not only to the fact that Carter was writing about the world of forty years before, one which had, by the early 1980s, changed a great deal, but because in writing *A Black Fox Running* he was inhabiting again the golden years of his own boyhood and experiencing again 'the glory and the freshness of a dream'. 'Sure, the kid would change but childhood was a separate lifetime anyway,' Richard, the American visitor to Dartmoor, thinks of the boy Stray in *Black Fox*. 'It wasn't just the stifling of the pastoral instinct that dulled the vision. You couldn't endure that intensity day after day.'

In Carter's memoir, too, can be found the seeds of the richly mystical landscape of his novel: the Celtic mythology his Welsh mother teaches the young Brian, taken straight from the pages of the *Mabinogion*. The foxes' deity is Tod – which means 'death' in German – and they believe in an afterlife in the Star Place. There are hints that their religion has passed through varying stages of practice and belief, but as it's experienced by Wulfgar, Stargrief and the rest of the High Tor Clan of the Hill Fox Nation it has more than a touch of Zen Buddhism and even existentialist philosophy alongside its Celtic flavours, charged with immanence and saturated with the sanctity of living things. It's clear that this sense of transcendence – beyond cant, beyond empty ritual – was central to Carter's own experience of nature, and while it's not something I share, the spiritual passages in *Black Fox* have, for me, an unarguable depth and sincerity.

They're also leavened with earthiness, humour and the exacting observations of a true naturalist, and at every re-reading I'm bowled over anew by the facility with which Carter can switch register – not just in terms of dialogue (the rich Devon dialect of the working men contrasted with the upper-class tones of the Shewtes; the naturalistic speech of the foxes set against the spivvy slang of the stoats) – but in tone, perspective and subject-matter. Again and again he undercuts an elevated passage with something much more down to earth: a fox twisting irritably to nip fleas from its fur; a buzzard shooting its mutes onto a gatepost; labouring men making blue jokes over pints of rough cider. Passages of limpid, matchless description break up more straightforward sections focusing on Scoble, Stray or Wulfgar, while the narration slips between the third person and free indirect speech with ineffable fluidity. In Carter's hands the point of view, too, can shift in a single passage from fox to human to sparrowhawk in a way that should be disorientating, but never is. This isn't simply a stylistic trick but a cornerstone of his imagination, for the world he creates is one in which everything that is occurring at any given moment has equal significance, whether it's a leaf drifting downstream or a man setting a snare.

Passages like this occur every few pages, and the way they enlarge the imagination made me fall in love with *A Black Fox Running*, and are the reason I love it still:

> *The harvest had been sung home in village churches all over Dartmoor: Widecombe, Ilsington, North Bovey, Holne, Chagford, Lustleigh, Manaton, Peter Tavey – names like a peal of bells. Gifts had been brought to the Barley Man. Bonfires burnt in cottage gardens and the smoke climbed softly blue into thinner blue. Across the in-country the shires plodded, dragging the plough through dark soil. Browns and golds had crept into the woods, and rowan and silver birch were at their loveliest among the heather by the brook where Wulfgar lay.*
>
> *He tested the breeze with his nose. The night was brilliant under the Hunter's Moon. A tawny owl hooted and received a sharp reply from his mate. The fox ran with the stream to the Manaton-Beckaford lane and singled out a strong thread of coney scent. He killed the buck swiftly on the lawn of Aish Cottage. There were no lights on in the*

building, for the American had gone home. While Wulfgar skinned the rabbit he dozed in the airliner high above the Atlantic.

Or:

The tawny owl dropped off the crag called Lover's Leap and released a tremulous cry. It sailed over the river and flopped down into the nettles and gripped the vole, pinching the little creature's scream into silence. Then it entered the darkness beneath the oaks and winged off to the Iron Age fort on the hilltop. A star left the Milky Way and slid across the sky.

Throughout the book Carter's focus is simultaneously close and universal, and although in *Black Fox* he tells one story, we're never allowed to forget that there are other animals, other perspectives, other stories playing out at the same time – like the merlin tiercel hunting a meadow pipit that spots Wulfgar, but 'only as an unimportant peripheral object'. Each change of register and viewpoint, each switch from macro to wide-angle and back is a reminder to us that the world is various and teeming – incorrigibly plural – and most of all, that humans are just one element of an interconnected whole. This challenge to our habitual, egocentric perspective anticipated twenty-first-century intellectual movements such as post-humanism and object-oriented ontology by more than thirty years, and has never been more vital than it is today.

But more than all of this, *A Black Fox Running* is a book about place. Carter fell in love with the wild beauty of Dartmoor when he was a boy growing up fifteen miles or so away in the seaside town of Paignton, and he came to know it with the overwhelming intensity of childhood, tramping its windswept moors and sunken lanes, exploring the newtake fields with their drystone walls, climbing tors, catching butterflies, following rivers and streams and always, always, watching its wildlife. Animating every passage of his novel is a deep cartographic and ecological knowledge of and tangible love for 'the good unspoilt place': an intensely sacred landscape, the landscape of his childhood.

Much has changed in Devon since the 1940s when *A Black Fox Running* was set. Traffic has increased, while rural poverty, agricultural modernisation and second home ownership have hollowed out many communities; upland and farmland birds have gone into steep decline; hunting with dogs was banned in 2005 and wildflower meadows have all but vanished, hay no longer being made the traditional way but wrapped in plastic for silage. But Dartmoor itself endures almost unaltered, and visitors to Hound Tor, Wistman's Wood, Trendlebere Down or the Becka Brook will find themselves even now walking through the luminous landscapes of the book. It is an extraordinary feeling.

In 2005, *A Black Fox Running* was nominated as one of the classics of British nature writing by readers of the *Guardian*. "I couldn't believe it when the book appeared on the *Guardian* list," Carter said in an interview. "It is an honour to be among those other writers." It came as no surprise to me to see *Black Fox* on the list, and when I became a writer myself I took every opportunity to mention it, surprised to find that it wasn't better known; in 2015 I wrote about it in a piece for the *Guardian*, and was thrilled to receive a letter from Brian's widow, Patsy.

Brian Carter – 'Bri' – died in 2015, at the age of seventy-eight, having contributed to every edition of weekly West Country newspaper the *Herald Express* since the early 1980s. As well as Patsy, he left two children, Christian and Rebecca, and three grandchildren. Sadly, he and I never met, but to me he remains a true inheritor and disseminator of the passionate love of wild places that has animated so many of this country's greatest writers on the natural world.

'Now, again, I was in the good unspoilt place alone, crouching in one of twilight's blue hollows. A full and golden moon was rising out of Torbay, cutting a furrow across the meadow. What I absorbed then was not built of words. The shaping of it would come later as the need to write grew out of despair for the vanishing splendour,' he writes in his memoir. 'How long the summer of my ninth year seemed but that Friday dusk beside the stream has never faded. I find echoes of it in Wordsworth's poetry and in all the great verse whose beauty has been harvested from the human spirit and the open air.'

It's my hope that this new edition of *A Black Fox Running* will inspire more lovers of the natural world to find their own echoes, just as I did, in Carter's breathtakingly beautiful book.

Melissa Harrison, 2018

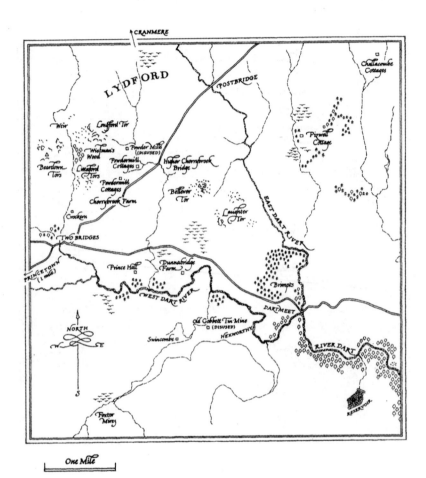

Wulfgar's Country
DARTMOOR

Part One

'Nature teaches beasts to know their friends'

Coriolanus

WULFGAR

'Yes, I can smell him,' said Stargrief. The old dog fox raised his muzzle.

'And the lurcher,' Wulfgar said.

They came out of the trees to drink at Lansworthy Brook. Wulfgar led the way, stepping gingerly through the reeds. His paws crunched into frail ice where it silvered the hoofprints of cattle. He was a large, dark fox with a brush almost as black as the peaty Dartmoor soil, and even his underfur and lower limbs were black. The wind and rain of three summers had lent his coat a pale sheen and the tip of his brush was whiter than wild parsley. His eyes gleamed against the grey December afternoon and pointed ears deciphered the faintest sounds which the wind could not mask.

'They were here last night,' said Stargrief. Two inches of tongue moistened his nose and he read the air long and carefully. His head moved a little from side to side and he seemed to lean on the wind, each quiver of his nostrils bringing him a detailed account of what lay in the field and far beyond. Presiding over everything was the smell of gin-metal spiced with the scent of passing birds. The earth smelt of ice and moss and nibbled grass, cattle, men and dogs, then the rank odour of the trapper alerted all his senses.

Stargrief was slight and inconspicuous. His coat was the colour of winter woodland. He placed his paws carefully in Wulfgar's tracks, for gin traps had been tilled amongst the reeds to catch wild duck.

'That mad dog isn't far off,' Wulfgar said. The smell of fieldmice lofted in a white plume as he yawned.

'This is a bad place in broad daylight,' said Stargrief. 'There's a disused sett in the wood up ahead. I don't know about you but I'm on my last legs. I could really do with a sleep.'

Running beside the stream they came to the ford. Stargrief's heart no longer raced but he found it difficult to match his young friend's speed through the wooded valley of the River Sig.

The sett was warm and dry. The badger boar and sow had been dug out and clubbed to death by the man who owned the lurcher. Wulfgar licked a paw and rubbed it over his face.

'The bottoms of my pads are freezing,' said Stargrief. 'Winter seems to last for ever. What a penance age can be!'

He groaned and laid his tail across his nose.

'Maybe the lurcher could do you a favour,' Wulfgar said cheerfully.

'I won't make it easy for him,' said the old dog fox. His thin angular body was shaking.

'Winter has sharp teeth,' Wulfgar said. 'Curl up against me, old mouse. There's more flesh on a seagull. After all these seasons are you afraid of death?'

'No. Dying doesn't trouble me — but you're so damned stiff the next day.'

Wulfgar chuckled in the darkness.

Now hunger eclipsed everything.

The path was less than a foot wide, and where it mounted the hedge of blackthorn, hazel and bramble behind Bagtor Cottages, the grassy surface was trampled but not worn away. Here and there were crumbs of snow.

Delicately Wulfgar flattened out over the top of the hedge and the wind passed, leaving a sudden hush. He squinted up the valley. Thrushes flashed among the leafless trees. The Sig glittered through distances speckled with white smudges that moved and bleated. Wulfgar narrowed his eyes. Above the blur of Saddle Tor clouds left little room in the sky for the sun of the winter solstice. His paws scuffed the crisp bramble leaves and he heard the shrew scream. It was not a scream of fear, for the shrew was even hungrier than the fox. Standing on tiny hind feet it menaced the fieldmouse amongst the stems of bramble and hemlock, then it was on the mouse's back and the struggle was over before the wind returned.

The hunting foxes trotted up the coomb of half-frozen sphagnum moss and lichen to the birth place of the River Sig. The world was bounded by the slow heave of horizons ending always in cloud. Powder snow lifted and smoked on the easterly wind, hissing through grass and furze to drift against drystone walls and clumps of heather.

Wulfgar stalked mallard and snipe but caught nothing. Soon it became necessary to cross the Widecombe Road under the scrutiny of Swart the crow and his mate Sheol who were scavenging among a flock of Scottish Blackface sheep.

The wind brooded on its melody. Despite the ache in the air the sheep gave off a warm, damp smell. Back from the road the heather grew thick and deep, and Galloway cattle stood in it up to their hocks. The foxes passed among them and found the sheep path. Presently the heather gave way to turf and they came upon some cowpats. Flicking them over one by one with their paws they greedied on the beetles lodged in the soft under-sides.

'Must the soul tread the same stony track as the body,' Stargrief said wearily.

'Is that a question?' asked Wulfgar.

'If it is, who can answer it? I was only making noises – like a sick cub.'

Wulfgar licked the old fox's muzzle.

'I wish I was the first fox standing in the brand new world,' Stargrief went on.

'You'd get your coney then.'

'I wouldn't need conies.'

'Even Holy Tod visited the rabbit runs.'

'Yes, I'm sorry. I've lived on dreams for too long.'

'Didn't the beetles help?'

'Of course, of course! But I see a fox lying dead on the cold hillside and it makes me sad.'

'Perhaps it is yourself you see.'

'Perhaps. Winter is like a long illness.'

'Don't forget you have been sick,' Wulfgar said briskly. 'You were out of your mind for two sunsets. We all thought you were going to die. You should have died.'

'Better dead than ga-ga,' Stargrief smiled.

'Life would be easier if you'd stop thinking about yourself.'

He was tired of company and Stargrief could see it in his eyes.

North-east of where they stood Hay Tor was bursting out of cloud. Dartmoor was the colour of a hen kestrel. Beside water the grass was green and stiff, and the wind keening through the heather sounded like the stricken shrew. Scent lay breast high. Wulfgar jerked up his head and sniffed the invisible contours of what lay before them. Instantly he was aware of fox.

'How did the hunting go, Ashmere?' he said.

The sheep path, which was one of the main highways for most moorland creatures, brought them to the scenting post. At first they failed to see the young dog fox Ashmere, who was crouching low and facing them with ears pricked. Then the twitching of his brush caught Wulfgar's eye.

'Have the crows got your tongue?'

Ashmere rolled onto his back and presented his throat to the dark fox. The gesture was not wasted.

'Come on,' Wulfgar said. 'Get up and go about your business. You're not a cub any more.'

'And you must learn to live with your greatness,' said Stargrief.

Wulfgar strutted around the grey tooth of granite where three paths met before cocking his leg and depositing his own strong smell. The odour of the post contained much gossip, telling him not only how many foxes had visited it but also their names and condition.

After luxuriating in the ritual he sat on his haunches and thrust a stiff hindleg into the air and cleaned his belly.

'The hunting wasn't so good,' said Ashmere. 'In fact it was terrible. This morning the hounds came to the Great Down and ran me close to death. They killed a vixen.'

'What was her name?' asked Stargrief.

'Fernsmoke.'

'I knew her,' said Stargrief. 'She was very young,'

Nothing lives long, he thought, only the valleys and tors.

This morning she saw the sunrise and was part of it.

Brambles were knotting his guts but his eyes remained blank.

'They broke her up under the beeches,' said Ashmere.

'It was a clean death,' said Wulfgar.

His companions nodded.

'The Good Death,' said Stargrief. 'And what about you, Ashmere?'

'I'm still a bit stiff and tired. I'll probably kennel in the woods below.'

'Watch your step,' said Wulfgar. 'The trapper was down by the mill yesterday. His dog's on the loose again.'

'I'd rather have the hounds breathing on my arse than that creature trailing me,' Ashmere said. 'The lurcher never gives up. Never.'

Wulfgar and Stargrief went down the path keeping their heads high to avoid the spikes of gorse. The wind sang in their chest fur. Beneath Saddle Tor were four small frozen ponds. A heron paced the margins, but despite his slowness he flapped into the sky before the foxes could strike. The bird was called Scrag. Behind the ice he had seen tangles of grass lying motionless in the water gloom like sleeping eels.

'Herons aren't good eating, anyway,' Stargrief said.

Wulfgar nuzzled the texture of the day, sifting rabbit smell from the scores of other scents which showered his knowing.

'Maybe we'll find a coney old enough for you to catch,' he said.

'If he's that old he won't be worth catching,' said Stargrief.

'Would you like me to stun an earthworm for you?'

'Eat your grandmother's scats!' Stargrief growled. 'I may be groggy but I'm not stupid. When I'm really fit I'll grab conies by the warrenful.'

Brightness flooded the sky around Holwell Tor and further on Greator Rocks and Hound Tor were shadows in shifting haze. Beyond Wulfgar's vision Stormbully the buzzard sailed across the Leighon Ponds to take up his station above the slopes.

The foxes trotted past the hawthorn where Swart lived. Three shrivelled red berries had eluded the songbirds and woodpigeons and they guided the eye to the crow's nest less than twelve feet from the ground. Swart and Sheol had raised many youngsters here, for the tree was old but sound. Ponies and cattle had rubbed the bark off the middle of the trunk with their flanks, leaving wisps of black hair clinging to the wood. Stargrief snapped at these as he eased his scat onto the roots, sniffed at it and loped away.

'What do the stars say about the coney hunting?' Wulfgar asked.

'They say Wulfgar comes to the runs with all the speed and guile of a legless pig.'

Wulfgar smiled the lazy smile of an animal who was completely aware of his strength and power, and Stargrief basked in his good humour. No other fox of the Hay Tor Clan was permitted to take such liberties.

They skirted the bog above the glint of running water. The murmur of jackdaws' wings overtook them and crept back into the hush. Here and there the track was flooded and they trotted alongside it. The smell of rabbit was strong now and they clapped down in the heather and Wulfgar began to stalk.

Near the ruins of the quarryman's cottage was a hawthorn tree and a lawn of turf. Under the tree sat a rabbit. Although he was a first season buck he had learnt the lessons of his kind. There were movements in the heather which had nothing to do with the wind. Upright on his haunches he watched the dog fox rippling towards him, eyes flashing green and bright, mouth smiling. Instinct urged him to bolt but curiosity rooted him to the spot.

The fox advanced slowly and smoothly. He flowed out of the heather and turned three somersaults on the lawn, then he stood on his hindlegs and twirled and swayed until the rabbit lost his fear. Two more somersaults brought Wulfgar almost within striking distance. He rolled over and bit at the tag of his brush. The rabbit smell pulsed in the pit of his stomach and he held the buck with his slumberous eyes, gathering himself to pounce. But even as his muscles hardened, the blackbird slammed into the hawthorn and let loose its scolding chatter. At once the rabbit was up and gone, his flight leaving Wulfgar scrabbling among the fallen stones of the cottage where there were many burrows. One bolt-hole was large enough for him to crawl into but the passage soon narrowed and he retreated backwards feeling angry and foolish.

Stargrief did not laugh.

Other foxes came to mind as they walked up the slope of dead bracken to Holwell Tor. Light was ebbing from the sky and the wind had dropped to a gentle breeze.

'How has Wendel survived for two whole winters?' Wulfgar said. 'He's such a bloody idiot.'

'Thorngeld says he's taken fowls from the trapper's coops.'

'He'll end up on a wire. Pity the hounds didn't get him instead of Fernsmoke.'

And instantly he regretted his peevishness. In the beauty of day's end he felt close to Tod, for life was sweet. Season lapped over season, animals died, others came into the world. The stream never stopped flowing.

'I'll come as far as the tor with you,' said Stargrief.

Near the hilltop a herd of Dartmoor ponies grazed, their coats thick and shaggy, their manes long. They tugged at the grass and ignored the foxes. Wulfgar paused to sniff the trunk of a rowan tree. Rabbits had been gnawing the bark and Ashmere had left his scat on one of the roots. He had also eaten dung beetles and his scat had a bluish tinge. Wulfgar ran his nose over it and continued up the sheep path to the brow of the tor.

From the highest granite outcrop he looked up at Black Hill. In the coomb at his feet was the old granite tramway that long ago had carried wagons loaded with granite blocks from the rock face to the road and thence to waiting ships at Teignmouth. Stone from Haytor Quarries had been used to rebuild London Bridge in the reign of Queen Victoria, but the business had failed and the moors had crept back to hide most of the scars.

'Where will you lie tonight, old friend?' said Wulfgar.

'On that hill – close to the stars, close to Tod.'

'Put in a good word for me.'

'I always do.'

'Then I'll leave a rabbit by Crow Thorn.'

'And you will run with Tod in the golden fields.'

'Like a legless pig?' Wulfgar smiled.

'As Wulfgar of the High Tors – proudly. And they will tell your saga in the Star Place.'

'What if I leave two rabbits at the tree?'

Stargrief laughed and trotted down through the bracken to the tramway.

After he had satisfied himself that the air was free of the taint of man, Wulfgar went to his kennel on the west-facing side of the hill, under the tor. It was a sheltered spot in the heather and furze above a great clitter where he often sat and swam on the tide of his thoughts into drowsiness.

For the fox, evening was a time of mystery. Wulfgar settled down and laid his chin on outstretched fore-paws. The Becca Brook rushed through the dusk to shining ponds that mirrored the sky. Greator Rocks and Hound Tor sailed out of cloud but the head of the Leighon Valley was lost in mist. Daws jangled into the beeches of Holwell as lights were coming on in the old house. The sky on the horizon where Blackslade Down nudged the West was grey and gold.

The pupils of Wulfgar's eyes narrowed to vertical slits and he gazed at the sun until clouds hid it and filled the valley with darkness. A hundred thousand years before his birth another fox had lain under Holwell Tor watching the same sun go down. Stargrief had spoken of such a past as if the blurring of countless seasons was of no more significance than the fall of hawthorn blossom.

Wulfgar winkled balls of ice and snow from between his toes. The sky was deepening grey, then darkness swelled and the night became a vast map of scents. The daws no longer made a din in the beech trees but the crisp air amplified the sound of the river.

MOONLIGHT AND FOG

In the stealth of a frosty night the barn owls quartered vole runs close to Jay's Grave, white of moonlight on white wings, the glaring moors racing to the sky. Kitty Jay had hanged herself in some forgotten winter of man's history. Her grave was a simple mound of grass and stones with a jam jar of flowers at the head. It lay at the crossroads and was visited by tourists.

The owls knew nothing of suicide or wrong of any sort, for their purity was of the moonlight through which they sailed. Every so often they screeched at each other as though the silence were too much to endure, but the voles died noiselessly in the grip of talons that squeezed the breath out of them. Each pellet on the barn floor at Hedge Barton contained the bones and fur of six or seven of these tiny animals.

Wulfgar heard the owl cries and checked for a moment in the grass at the foot of Hound Tor. He stood and assayed the distances with ears and nostrils, then he sniffed at a dead whortleberry leaf, brushing the twig with the tip of his nose so gently he failed to disturb the frost. It was nearly dawn and he had yet to make a good kill. Back in Leighon Woods the bank voles had proved hard to catch, and the owls had not helped. Trotting down the slope to Swallerton Gate he saw the halo round the moon above Hameldown Beacon. A vixen barked in the copse near Beckaford and he answered without urgency.

Two nights later Wulfgar came to the stand of beech trees at Holwell called the Rookery. The weather had changed. A mild west wind washed away the frost and the sky vanished. There was before him a shifting greyness like his own breath, the moisture beading his whiskers and fur. He walked along the path of beech leaves with the exaggerated delicacy of a cat. Among the trees on the ground above him Thorgil the badger was rooting for grubs. The great, one-eyed boar grunted as he dug and scratched. His sett in Leighon Woods had been occupied by badgers long before the Norman conquest, and in one direction the galleries and tunnels ran for a hundred yards.

Another creature had heard the badger and was fleeing down the slope as fast as his short legs would carry him. He was a hedgehog named Earthborn, who during the cold spell had dozed in a pile of dry leaves against a field wall. Now he scuttled across the woodland path and almost collided with Wulfgar. Immediately the muscles along his sides and back contracted and he curled into a ball. Wulfgar strode around him stiff-legged, brush twitching, and gingerly touched the spines with the pad of a forefoot. The ball of prickles tightened and the fox cocked his leg and doused the hedgehog. Snuffling and sneezing Earthborn uncurled and the life was crunched out of him.

After he had eaten the hedgehog Wulfgar came up through the beeches to a drystone wall. With the light of the new day brightening the fog, he leapt the wall and landed in the wet grass. It was good to be among the rabbit runs, gulping the exciting smell of conies. The fog thinned and the world emerged from darkness; trees walked out of shadow, cattle grew legs, and a slow flood of colour brought things alive. But for the rabbits leaping in the wires the fox-smell added a new dimension to their fear. Since dusk of the previous day they had fought the snares, sinking through exhaustion and despair to a place where misery whirlpools.

The trap line ran from the field towards the crossroads under Bonehill Down. Wulfgar killed the first rabbit he came to and left only a foot in the snare. He skinned and ate the carcass on rough ground surrounded by ponies who were rising from beds of heather. The morning was opening up, but fog in a milky mass covered the river, which threaded noisily through the valley bottom. Rain began to fall and the wind freshened and veered north-westerly, carrying on a gust the faint cry of the vixen. This time Wulfgar made no reply for he had smelt man.

The fox showed his teeth and broke cover. Halfway across the patch of cotton grass he put up a flock of lapwings, and the birds pursued him, wheeling and keening until he was among the gorse and scrub rowan. Wulfgar trotted on at hunting pace, down into the valley bed, over the Becca Brook and up through the bracken to Holwell Clitter. Among the boulders the wind spoke in slow, deep hoots … .

The trapper loosened the wire and tossed the rabbit's foot into the trees, while the lurcher danced around his legs.

'Down, Jacko – you bleddy fool,' he snarled.

Jacko laid back his ears and whimpered. His master stared absently through his thoughts and dropped the snare into the sack.

'Fox,' he said. 'Smell him, Jacko? We missed him, but only just.'

He rammed his fists in his pockets. Along the shoulder of downland the lapwings darted and called. Breasting the sere grasses Wulfgar stood out like a dark, heraldic device.

'It's that sly black bugger,' the trapper said quietly. 'You had a couple of fowls from Yarner Wells last night, didn't you, boy. But I'll have you – by Christ I will. I'll have you if it's the last thing I do.'

As he reached down and fondled the dog's ears, the lurcher yawned and raked its belly with a rigid hind foot.

THE BOXING DAY MEET

Wulfgar was born in the earth at Mountsland Copse with the sound of gunfire in his ears. For nine seasons he had passed along the picket lines of tent encampments and had heard the convoys of lorries on the moorland roads while he came and went like a cloud shadow. Towards the end of the war the army had been busy around Haytor Rocks, but few men had seen the dark fox slinking to the garbage heap at dusk. Now the war was over and the soldiers had gone, although there was still the occasional crackle of rifles from the Rippon Tor range.

Time passed as imperceptibly as a face ages. Wulfgar came often to Black Hill in search of Stargrief but the ancient dog fox had retreated into his dreams and did not seek company. Alone on the hilltop in the twilight, which Devonians call dimpsey, Wulfgar would catch the flicker of Bovey Tracey's lights and hear the trains puffing up to Lustleigh. Then the owls would send their cries floating on the stillness and the stars would tremble and wink around him. The Plough, the constellations of the Great Bear and the Little Bear, the bright cluster of Cassiopeia, Capella and Vega, Sirius and Orion danced in the margins of his consciousness, and sitting there drinking the night sky he thought about the countryside that lay beyond death. All foxes knew of the place where creatures were absorbed into god's love. Here light was made magnificent, a spiritual aurora borealis beyond the reach of men.

Stormbully was alone. His mate had died hideously in a pole trap set by the man who kept the lurcher. The pole trap was a kind of circular gin that the trapper had placed in the fork of a pine tree on the edge of Mill Wood when the North Eastern moors were red with rowan berries. Swart the crow had tried to take the bait of rabbit flesh but the old hen buzzard had driven him off. Caught by the legs she had hung upside down throughout the night until the trapper ended her misery at daybreak. Stormbully's grief endured after the last leaves had fallen from the birches in the goyals close to Bag Tor, and even now as he tacked across the great westerly storms of year's end he sometimes felt her winging beside him and heard her cat-call rising from the spring of their first mating. There was little joy in his flight. He disliked the rain that rolled off the hills like smoke from an oil fire. Planing down through scudding cloud, he circled Haytor Rocks and windsurfed over the horses and riders who were congregating outside the Moorland hotel.

Dartmoor is not easy country to ride over but the Boxing Day Meet at Haytor Vale was popular among hunting folk. Despite the rain a good field had assembled to follow the South Devon. For nearly a century and a half packs of mainly black and tan hounds had chased the big, tough hill foxes who were as wild as the country they ranged over. In 1892 several horses went in a bog and almost perished before they were dragged clear.

The mastership of the South Devon pack had been in the hands of a Whitley since the outbreak of the First World War. Claude Whitley was a tall man with craggy features and a wry sense of humour, and he wore the hunting pink that had belonged to his father. He could read the countryside almost as well as the fox he hunted and loved.

'Well, Scoble,' he said to the trapper. 'I hope you're not bagging any of my foxes. I'm told they're fetching seven and six a pelt these days.'

'You know me better than that, maister.'

'The pheasants are keeping you busy, then.'

'Rabbits, maister. Me and Jacko's playin' 'ell with the conies. Wouldn touch a pheasant – no zur.'

Claude Whitley smiled and tapped the side of his nose with a forefinger. Scoble gazed blankly up at him. Last night's rough cider broke from his face in beads and mingled with the raindrops.

'Mind you keep that animal on a leash,' the master said in parting.

Scoble touched the peak of his cap and unclenched his fist for Jacko to lick the nicotine-stained fingertips.

Returning from Strelna and Yarner Wood early in the morning of the meet Wulfgar had smelt man. The rain was falling in grey swaths but the taint of the trapper and his dog had soured the air coming off Holwell Quarry. Heavy fox gins had been tilled near the clitter but remained empty.

The episode was enough to disturb Wulfgar, who took himself off to kennel in the hawthorn scrub of Seven Lords Lands. Torrential rain had fallen throughout the night and continued unabated as the first horseboxes rattled through Emsworthy Gate. The River Dart burst its banks at Salmon's Leap weir under Buckfastleigh and at Hoods Bridge further downstream. The Bovey also rose and flooded the railway line at Bovey Tracey. It was poor hunting weather, for heavy rain can kill scent.

Wulfgar would have been content to sleep among the woody stems of heather and whortleberry all day. From his hiding place he heard the sparkling song of a black-bird, which seemed to be singing at the storm from the top twig of a rowan tree. Wulfgar curled deeper into his thoughts and recalled the wise things Stargrief had said during their last meeting. Stargrief had survived eight winters and although he could never have matched Wulfgar in combat he was as brave as he was sagacious. All foxes are valiant but there are degrees of valour. Stargrief was small and slight but he had more heart than Wendel and Ashmere put together. And he under-stood the world. He had told them about the all-loving Tod and the Star Place, and had explained the desires and tastes and instincts that had flowed down genera-tions of blood into Wulfgar's veins. The law was kill or be killed, but behind it lay the summer country and the comradeship of the foxes who had gone before him into the golden haze.

'Yoi – yoi, leu-in, leu-in.'

The cry whipped Wulfgar to his feet, and he left a warm pocket of air in the hollow, rank with the odour secreted by his anal scent gland and the glands on his pads. The dog fox snaked between the furze clumps until he came to a tributary stream of the Becca. His ears and nose had located the pack. They were feathering the lawn at Quarryman's Cottage where Wulfgar had run after Scoble's visit to the clitter. Then the hounds spoke and above their cry rose the cavernous belling of Lancer, the greatest hound to come out of Denbury kennels. The pack had found Wulfgar's line and thirty couple of dogs poured down the slope towards Saddle Tor.

The horn sang out and the field came at the burst over one of the few places on the North Eastern moors where riding was not really hazardous. The huntsman who had told the pack to 'leu-in' – which was his way of encouraging them to smell out the fox – stood in his stirrups and watched the animals with pride. To find so quickly in foul weather was a good omen.

Wulfgar ran in the stream where it glided amongst bell heather into the Leighon Valley. He was swift but not as fast as a bolting rabbit, and there was about his dark, graceful form an aura of confidence.

The thrushes hit the trees like bullets. The noise of the wind and water blended in a dull roar, and to the east and west cloud fumbled the hilltops. Distances were dark under rain. Wulfgar ghosted through the scrub birch and sedges, and plashed along the Rookery path. The rain hissed through branches that writhed and flailed. The ground heaved in places as the beech roots lifted. He was still running flat-out, carrying his fur close to his body, wet and spiky.

The pack lost the scent at the brook and ranged about the undergrowth. Lancer and Captain – a tan-coloured dog – took to the water. The huntsman regarded them placidly and walked his horse downstream until he gleaned a whiff of fox.

'Leu-in, leu-in,' he cried. 'Yoi – yoi. Come on my beauties. Leu-in, leu-in.'

The pack settled on the line and gave tongue. Their body-steam mixed with the spray raised by their feet. Lancer was in the forefront, his great lolloping stride gobbling up ground. He was unaware of the excitement and confusion behind him. A horse slipped and crashed on its side, then other horses fell, but the rest of the field surged irresistibly into the neck of the valley.

Wulfgar trotted with a flock of sheep until they huddled under the newtake wall. He jumped the wall and crossed the Becca Brook. His heart had slowed and his nostrils no longer gaped but he was releasing a sharp, heavy smell. Although he did not take the hounds for granted he moved with a kind of arrogant unconcern down the river to the ponds.

Wind exploded in the tops of the trees, bending the dead flags and reeds, lifting the water in waves. The stinging rain filled Wulfgar with joy and he ran swiftly again, the world blurring around him, along water-bright ditches, runnels and guts onto a rough stone track. He had taken the line of least resistance, giving a virtuoso performance of cunning for its own sake. Where he paused to drink, a little downstream of the stone footbridge, he left his print in soft mud beside the Becca. The river was brim full of flood water.

Wulfgar traced the shape of his lips with his tongue and walked briskly up the hill. On the wind the belling pack sounded as remote as yesterday. He loped into the wild sky, pressing under the gate to breathe the air of real moorland again, and the sweep of turf brought him to a hollow littered with the debris of a medieval village. Instinct took over and he fled for Thorgil's sett, but a party of farm labourers out ferreting turned him and he ran along the treeline to the scattered buildings of Great Houndtor. Emerging from a copse of young oaks he stood making up his mind which way to go. Then he departed leisurely, leaving in his wake, a long way behind, sixty dogs and a field of drenched, grim-faced riders.

The hunted fox who knows his ground runs in a rough circle, but being wise to his game the foot-followers had parked their cars and vans on the roadside with a clear view of Hayne Down. Rain, driven horizontally by the gale, rattled like grit on side windows and bonnets.

Wulfgar was among the boulders behind a thirty-foot column of granite called Bowerman's Nose, where he squelched over sumptuous brown mosses and dull green lichens that completely covered many of the rocks. In the crevices ferns and rowan saplings grew, and pipits found shelter. The fox ran low onto open ground, crossed the Manaton Road and turned by Blissamoor Cottage. Scoble switched on his windscreen wipers and made sure it was the 'black bugger'. A woman in a head-scarf and oilskins tapped on the side door.

'Which way, Mr Scoble?' she said.

'Natsworthy, ma'am. I'd bet money on it.'

As the fox crept out of Heatree Plantation, a wood-cock whirred up from the brambles and the wind smacked it away. Behind him a pheasant alarmed and sounded like a fat man choking on a plum stone. He crossed to Hamel Down pursued by the cry of the pack.

Lancer led the rest of the hounds past Ford Farm, holding the weak line marvellously with his nose. Wulfgar bounded up through furze and bracken to the head of Woodpit and the clouds. The rain drove hard into his back. When he breasted patches of ling there was a remarkable change in scent, a pungent muskiness that the deluge could not obliterate. Slithering down the steep slope of bearded thistle into the brush and bristling stumps of a felled larch wood he remembered Fernsmoke. Among the tangle of brambles and branches he rested and groomed his chest. He could smell Lancer half a mile away. The hound had checked where a herd of Galloways had foiled the line. Huntsman and master watched him work and once it was necessary for the whipper-in to stop the pack from running back over ground they had already covered. While they cast, the hounds moved their sterns quickly to and fro. They were feathering.

Wulfgar pushed deeper into the thicket. Under a larch bough he discovered the tiny brown body of a wren and ate it in one gulp. The bird had been killed by a clap of thunder two days before.

Near the centre of Bagpark he encountered the faint stink of fox. His nose brought him to the root tangle of a fallen tree. Large green eyes stared back into his own.

'So I did hear the hounds,' said the stranger. 'Sometimes I can't tell if I'm dreaming or not.'

Wulfgar went up to him and sniffed his face. The old dog fox's nose was warm and dry. He had a belly full of tapeworm and had not eaten for three nights.

'My name is Runeheath,' he said. 'I live in the woods where the two great rivers meet. The pain in my gut is giving me hell, so last night I walked with the storm and finished up here.'

'Where are you heading?' Wulfgar said, as if he did not know.

'The Star Place,' Runeheath grinned. 'I've had it. Still, to live through six summers is enough. Are the hounds pushing you?'

'Tod no!' Wulfgar said. 'They couldn't run down a three-legged hedgehog on a straight road.'

'What about a sick old fox?' said Runeheath quietly. 'Would they do for him?'

'It's not necessary,' Wulfgar said. 'I could take them round in circles till dark and leave them chasing moonbeams.'

'Would you deny me the Good Death?'

Wulfgar shook his head.

'No more words, then,' said Runeheath, and he got to his feet and stretched.

There was a heavy coldness in the air. Wulfgar turned and left the old dog fox to his destiny. The hounds spoke again, and above the din of the storm Lancer's baying filled the valley. Wulfgar came out of the ruined larch wood and ran down to the River Webbum where it was narrow enough for a horse to jump. He let the current carry him to the spinney by Stouts Cottages, and was climbing the hill to Chinkwell Tor when the hounds, running at full cry, saw Runeheath.

Though I may die
the grass will grow,
the sun will shine,
the stream will flow.

Runeheath recalled the first time his mother had chanted the prayer in the earth under the ash saplings. He felt curiously weightless, and it was not an unpleasant sensation. The hot ache in his stomach had vanished and he ran easily with the suppleness of a yearling. Brown horizons swam out of the rain that darkend the sky, while his past dropped behind him and vanished in mist. Then the sky tilted and the hills were flying in slow disarray, and it was as if his nerve-ends fused and all the power rushed inwards to charge the spirit for its release. Numbness cancelled out the sudden flash of fear and beyond the black silence of Lancer's jaws the country of abundant game and eternal summer moonlight opened to receive him. The crash of hound clamour ended as the beasts milled around the body Runeheath had left behind.

THE TRAPPER AND HIS DOG

The woodpeckers wobbled away like green flares in the coppice oak. Scoble stood at the kitchen door and lit a cigarette. Jacko whined briefly from the centre of a yawn and sniffed the frosty air. Beyond the vegetable garden of Yarner Cott glittering hedges wandered into dusk. There was a whisper of ferrets in the straw of the hutches down by the chicken run. Scoble let the smoke drift from his nostrils. A fortnight of driving rain had at last given way to brighter weather, and the evening smelt faintly of rotting leaves and soil. It was a good time, when all the noise of living was turned down and a man could put his thoughts together.

Dragonflies' wings of ice covered the hollow parts of the turnip leaves. A blackbird said chink-chink! and shook the cold out of its feathers, and behind the ferret hutches the teazels bent under the weight of gold-finches. Daylight leaked from the sky that showed over Haytor Down. The treetops were black against the stars. Vega twinkled with blue fire. From the depths of Yarner Wood the tawny owls began to cry and that saddest of all evening sounds, the hooting of a steam train, echoed along the cleave.

'Get in, dog,' Scoble said, and Jacko returned happily to the warm kitchen.

The darkness came suddenly to life as fieldfares skirmished in the trees for roosting places. Scoble shut the door and settled the fire with the toe of his boot. He had scrounged a wagonload of logs from an old cider apple orchard that had been grubbed-out at Liverton. The cheerful flames made orange puddles on the hearth and flickering shadows on the walls. Scoble flopped down in his armchair and worked at the wires for a new batch of snares. All over the kitchen were many engines for taking wild animals, but he had hidden the pole traps in a chest under the table. The big, heavy fox gins lay beside the cabinet where Scoble kept his guns. These gins had served him well. Three fox pelts were pegged to the stretching board, good pelts that would soon be ready to join the bundle in the bedroom, and nailed along the oak beams were the tails of squirrels and foxes. Smaller gins used against rabbits and wild-fowl, net-traps for crows, a couple of claptraps, long nets and snares stood in a heap near Scoble's chair.

The lurcher enjoyed browsing through the trapping gear, where there were enough smells to fuel his madness. The blood-smell always made his own blood sing behind his eyes and he liked nothing better than to be among the conies, wrenching the life out of them. 'Kill-killy-kill,' he crooned to himself as the warm blood flowed. 'O Killy-killy-killy and Jacko do cracko the old coneyo!' How the moments blurred in the humming ecstasy of deeds which liberated him from the agony of thinking. Sometimes ideas burnt like acid into his brain, but chopping a rabbit or, better still, a lamb brought glorious release. Only as a pup burrowing into his mother's warmth had he known such peace. Jacko's kingdom was full of victims, who waited for his coming and welcomed his embrace.

'I come from sky,' Jacko thought. 'My head full of fire.'

He had looked into a pool once and had seen his eyes twinkling among the stars.

'What you thinkin' about, dog?' Scoble said. He went to the nine-gallon barrel by the window and drew off a pint of scrumpy, the real farmhouse rough cider of Devon. The lurcher's tail thumped the floor.

'You'm a prapper ornament – damn me if you idn,' Scoble said. 'But you knows yer trade, boy. You'm like a four-legged gin.'

He sat down again and ate his beef dripping, while twigs crackled and blazed on the fire. Jacko stared up at him, strange images churning in his skull. The primrose-coloured scrumpy vanished into the trapper's face. He would drink nine or ten pints before crawling off to bed, but often he drank more. It had been so since 1918 – cider and whisky, occasionally at the pub but usually alone. He was fifty-eight but looked older. His face carried the blotches of burst blood vessels and across his rutted baldness he had laid a few strands of grey hair. On his right cheek was a mole as black as an ash bud. There was about his shabby bulk a suggestion of real strength but alcohol had sapped his stamina.

During the First World War Scoble had fought on the Somme where he had been wounded in the legs. The memory of lying in long, wet grass beside a dead mule for a day and a night would return on a wave of nausea. Poor old Charlie the mule. It wasn't his war. The shell seemed to explode under the animal and spill out its tripes. Scoble emptied his tankard and fetched a refill, and the apple log spat and flared white, like a Very light. That was when the foxes came, in the darkness, under the arcing flares, three of them, snapping and growling and worrying the mule's carcass, there in that ditch in France. 'Christ!' Rifleman Leonard Scoble of the Devonshire Regiment cried. 'Christ, it'll be me next! The bastards are goin' to eat me.' And he yelled obscenities at the foxes but they just kept on gnawing at the mule. All night they were at it. Gradually he had slid into unconsciousness and when he came to he was in a field hospital. For the rest of the war he dreaded the lonely death and the foxes who always seemed to be lurking on the edge of darkness.

'They idn animals, Jacko,' he said, fishing between the cushion and the arm of the chair for his tobacco tin. 'They'm bleddy vermin. And that black bugger is the maister of 'em all. But I'll have him. Blackie will take a vixen and bring 'er to they old rocks. Then us wull have him – won't us, boy. Yaas, you'm a good dog.'

He lit the Woodbine and sighed smoke. Above the muslin half-curtain of the kitchen window he could see the moon edging into the sky, rising slowly from the trees.

VIXEN

Just before dusk Wulfgar left Hook's Copse, walking with his customary soft step among the oaks and ashes. Red squirrels were busy in the treetops where there was still enough light to give the plum-covered twigs a sheen. The branches bent under the weight of the squirrels who flung themselves across canyons of shadow to flit through one tree after another until the dreys were reached.

For a little while Wulfgar sat and watched the small, dark shapes sailing overhead. The treetops rocked against a cloudless sky, then settled into stillness.

Trollgar the brown owl crooned gently to his mate from his perch in the tallest ash. His flat face glared down at nothing in particular and his talons closed like a vice on a dead vole. Using the tip of his hooked upper mandible he tenderly preened the breast feathers of the hen bird while the faint, bubbling notes caressed the silence.

Wulfgar ranged over ground that men had once mined, and below Owlacombe Farm, in one of the tiny wooded valleys that Devonians call goyals, he killed a rat. The rat came from a ruined linhay buried under a tangle of elderberries. Wulfgar ate it down to the scaly tail and sat among the vole runs in the hedge beside the Sigford Road. The waxy greenness of the first celandines smelt of cat, for the farm tom had recently been out watering his territory.

Cattle slithered and stumbled down the lane, harried by a labourer with a stick and a couple of dogs. Fear brimmed the animals' eyes, for they were treated as things, not creatures. From birth to death they bowed to Man's tyranny and were used carelessly as if such mute calmness could not house a soul.

The dog fox ran up the tree-dotted hill with the last dregs of sunset on his left shoulder, over ground called Owlacombe Beams. The crisp pallor of frost lay on the fields. Dusk bloomed and a huge golden moon lit the sky above Bur-changer Cross. Flocks of redwings and fieldfares dropped into the copses, and the Dogstar twinkled from constellations paler than the frost.

Wulfgar carried an emptiness in his stomach that had nothing to do with hunger. For nearly a week the ache had grown, pulling him out of sleep and disturbing his thoughts. He had covered a lot of countryside trying to shake off his restlessness, and a black fox had been seen at places as far apart as Two Bridges and Holne. Once he had even taken a pet rabbit from the lawn of Mearsdon Manor in Moretonhampstead.

He came over the hedge of ivy, granite rocks, holly and ferns and glided down the Bagtor Road. In the coombe where Lansworthy Brook was a thread of moonlight beneath alders and hazels he caught a moorhen, and before eating it clipped the pinion feathers tight to the base with his teeth.

The night was clear and the frost too slight to stifle scent. The reek of wet swedes lifted from the fields of West Horridge. Sandwiched between the hedgerows was the warm shippen smell of cattle and to the south-east the land slipped away into the vast plain of South Devon. Blackness, blurred here and there with yellow lights, was seen from grass level, from loops and snarls of bramble.

He stood on the bracken bank above the roofs of West Horridge's barns and the vixen's scream tore the darkness. The weird owl-like screech rose and fell and trailed off into silence. Wulfgar trotted forward and paused for a moment, and again the cry rang from the moonlit distance, three screams long drawn-out and shrill. Wulfgar gave a yelping bark and sounded like a tomcat going into battle. From the surrounding coombs and hills came the answering cries of other dog foxes on their way to the clicketing. Deep in Wulfgar's gut the vixen's scream corkscrewed and he cruised along on the floodtide of his lust, the shrill insistent keening passing through him like a knife.

Beyond East Horridge he overtook a noble dog fox named Briarspur, but no words were exchanged. Briarspur's lips were drawn back in a silent snarl and his brush swished from side to side.

Soon the brakes of ash and alder gave way to a hanger of ancient beech trees, where the vixen's music was loud and the barking of dogs seemed to rise from the shadows all around.

She was there, ghosting through the trees into his senses, no flesh and blood creature but a phantom of soft fire. The dog foxes circled her cautiously, giving off a strong musky odour. The screaming stopped, but the suitors continued to bark insults at each other while the vixen rolled on her back in the dead leaves. Seven foxes had obeyed her call.

Among the younger dogs was Wendel the chicken-killer whose arrogance and stupidity were well known. He strutted up to the vixen on stiff legs.

'What do they call you?' he said.

'Teg,' she replied.

'Well, Teg – I'm Wendel the Fearless. My name is spoken with respect from Black Mere to the wide road. In combat I'm unbeatable. Before the hounds I'm smoke. Grown foxes are like cubs when they come up against me.'

'Cluck, cluck, cluck,' sneered Brackenpad. 'The Terror of the Chicken Runs isn't fit to eat the scats of real dog foxes.'

'I disagree,' said Briarspur. 'Wendel is welcome to my scat anytime he fancies it. But if I were Wendel the Fearless I'd get my arse out of here – now, while it's intact.'

Brackenpad sniffed and pretended to nip a flea from his belly fur. He had seen Wulfgar and was in no hurry to fight for a prize he could never hope to win. Of all the dogs who knew Wulfgar only Wendel was reckless enough to challenge for the vixen. He was two years old and had never mated.

'I don't run,' he said, puffing out his brush and expelling his breath across his teeth in the clicketing sound.

'He flies – like a hen,' Briarspur said.

The dog foxes were still restless and noisy but although they snapped at each other the tomcat growling lacked malice. Teg sat on her hindlegs and gazed about her. Beyond the jostling males she saw the black, motionless shape of Wulfgar. The blaze of her eyes held the moonlight.

'Wendel,' Wulfgar barked. 'You have the heart of a rabbit and the brains of a mouse. The night is a big place. Go and hide in it.'

'Make me – Scat-eater.'

A surge of anger lifted Wulfgar's hackles. He trotted forward with murder in his belly, nursing a hatred too thick for words. The vertical ovals of his eyes were full and dark, his tail twitched and his lips were screwed back in a terrible snarl. The explosive firework noise climbed to a venomous yaraow of passion. Wendel came in sideways, his teeth bared, and Wulfgar savaged him with a frenzy born of an emotion more profound than hatred. The last leaf broke from the tree above them and before it reached the ground the contest was over. Dazed and bleeding Wendel crouched at the great dog fox's feet. His whimpering roused pity in the hearts of those who watched.

'Get him out of my sight,' hissed Wulfgar, and Ashmere helped Wendel into the trees to lick his wounds. The other dog foxes stared at Wulfgar as they would have stared at an immortal animal who had descended from the Star Place. Moonlight flickered about his swarthy body so that he looked like a true creature of the night. His ears were cocked and his nose quivered. The beauty of the vixen's face played on his senses and the painful hunger of wanting her cut off his breath. But before he could lead her away another challenger entered the glade, large and reddish-grey and moving lazily in the manner of a seasoned veteran.

'Thornblood will fight all present for the vixen,' he said. The words came out in a chattering torrent, which to human ears would have sounded like the staccato screeching of a jay.

'She is mine,' said Wulfgar.

'I've come too far to chat, friend,' said Thornblood. 'This is fang and claw business. Talk's cheap.'

'Then let's do a little business,' Wulfgar grinned.

They circled each other, humpbacked and bristling. Puffed-out brushes swished and twitched and the peculiar clicking sound punctuated the caterwauling. Many of the onlooking dogs joined in and the hollow depths of Bagtor Woods amplified the chorus. Thornblood was braver than most of his kind but he had never met an animal like Wulfgar. They fought in the classic manner of the Hill Fox Nation – darting under the opponent's jaws to snap at his throat. There was no holding or worrying, but whenever the fangs struck they drew blood. Wisps of hair danced around their heads and the pungent smell of their bodies lingered for a week afterwards.

Gradually Wulfgar's ferocity wore Thornblood down but he refused to give in. Sometimes the snarling animals stood on their hindlegs and tried to deliver the good clean bite that would end the contest. Wulfgar bled about the nose, his upper lip was torn and his forelegs were injured, yet his strength seemed limitless.

Dismay registered in Thornblood's eyes. He carried a dozen bad wounds and had lost his nimbleness. Only pride kept him snapping at the black shadow that swelled from the smoke of their bodies and breath to deliver pain in sharp spasms.

'He's had enough, Wulfgar,' said Brackenpad.

'Well, Thornblood?' Wulfgar said, sitting back on his haunches.

'The vixen is yours,' Thornblood gasped. 'Fighting you is like grappling red-hot barbed wire.'

His lips were drawn back in a grin of exhaustion. Brackenpad and Briarspur went over to him and started to clean his wounds with their tongues.

'Look after him,' Wulfgar said. 'And now if there is no more of this fang and claw business …'

The dog foxes lowered their eyes.

'Good,' he said, and turned his back on the gathering and walked slowly down towards the road.

Teg followed him with short, swift steps, and when she drew level she said, 'Are we to go together?'

'Yes,' Wulfgar said gently, and the little vixen leaned against him as they went out into the moonlight.

COURTSHIP

He had taken many vixens before but had never loved one as much as he loved Teg. Quietly they ran through the tiny hamlet of Bagtor and on down the lane, and the starry night broke around them in sweet-smelling waves. The River Lemon falling from pool to pool under the trees of Crownley Parks was part of the silence and never disturbed it. Sometimes she spoke but they were words that soon faded from the knowing. The joy of living within the moment took them beyond themselves. For there is a state of grace that all wild creatures discover where the spirit makes its secret assignation with the seasons.

None of this belongs to us, Wulfgar thought. We belong to it. We live with it and in the end it claims us.

The river rushed under the bridge and on past the mill. Teg's coat had been groomed by the wind and the rain and seemed to spark moonlight. He drew his tongue along the warm white fur of her chin and the shift of their blood was a surf-sound in the night. Coming out of her love he wondered where time had gone. To curl into warmth while she licked his head was fine. Their sleep was unclouded by bad dreams or pangs of conscience.

The ash tree moving across the sun made the light flicker. For several days Wulfgar and Teg had ranged over the moors and the in-country and the bond between them had strengthened. At the shippen by the road at Kelly's Farm they had eaten rats and mice. The rats had whispered across the beams and Wulfgar had scattered them for Teg to catch. A farm labourer setting snares near Yarner Wood had seen a big dark fox and a small red-grey vixen creeping round the keeper's gibbet. Wulfgar had stood on hindlegs to sniff at the corpses that swung gently in the wind. Two sparrowhawks, a kestrel, a pair of stoats, a weasel, crows, magpies, jays and a feral cat hung from the strand of barbed wire. The labourer had tried to shoot the foxes but fumbled the safety catch.

'He was as black as coal and as big as a pony,' he told his mates that evening. They stood at the bar of the Rock Inn and drank scrumpy. Scoble sat by the fire, stroking Jacko's ears with a twig.

'He had a vixen with 'im,' the labourer went on. 'They was closer to me than that dartboard, but before I could blast 'em they'm off.'

'Blackie was down round Mountsland back along,' someone else said. 'My uncle seen un cross the sheep field below Halsanger.'

Scoble lidded his eyes and bent the twig slowly until it cracked.

A flock of hen chaffinches broke across the morning. Stormbully had shot his mutes on the gatepost at Holwell before sailing above the roof of the wood. He watched the foxes with interest, for their stealthy progress along the drystone wall meant rabbits.

The buzzard's globose eyes were eight times keener than a man's and from three hundred feet he detected the small group of feeding conies. He fell in a swift rush and hit the doe from the rear, putting her burrow-mates to flight and halting the foxes in their tracks. Then Stormbully was lifting again on long, broad wings whose tips were splayed-out like fingers, with the dead rabbit hanging from his talons. In great flaps he flew into a beech tree and butchered the carcass.

Teg sat back on her haunches and growled.

'Do you ever get the feeling that Tod is poking fun at you?' she said.

Wulfgar could not help laughing. She looked so comical with her tail whisking and the tip of her tongue hanging over her bottom teeth.

'I've never thought of Tod having a sense of humour,' he said.

'Why not – he's fox, isn't he?'

'Yes, but very special fox.'

He smiled at her and licked the fine inner-hair of one of her ears.

'He's supposed to loosen snares and trick the hounds and perform all sorts of miracles,' Teg said.

'Cub stuff,' Wulfgar said. 'Stargrief says it's too simple.'

'How does Stargrief know?'

'He has visions.'

'Anyway, Holy Tod let the hawk snatch the coney from this vixen's jaws,' Teg sighed. 'And he didn't loosen the wire that choked the life out of my mother.'

'It's a daft idea, Teg. Tod speaks to foxes like Stargrief in dreams and visions. He doesn't interfere with individual lives. Loosen one snare and you've got to loosen the lot.'

'My mother said we just had to pass through the seasons and we would come to the Star Place without any fuss. I'm not sure I want all the answers before I get there.'

'Maybe there aren't any questions,' Wulfgar said.

Teg frowned. 'Yes, I see what you mean,' she said. 'Loving is enough.'

A mysterious felicity burnt in her eyes. Trotting beside her onto the heath of Holwell Down he was aware of how her moods and emotions affected his life. To be alone now seemed unimaginable. This was living in the sacred manner, and surely Tod understood. Even he had loved a vixen. Wulfgar glanced at Teg. She had such delicate features: slender muzzle, chocolate-brown eye patch sloping in a line to the corner of her mouth, white bib. His whole existence centred on her being; nothing else mattered. That night as he slept with his chin on her neck he felt the world rolling under him.

The days passed and dog and vixen became bolder and more mischievous. It was bright spring morning in Wulfgar's heart. He felt he could jump up and catch the stars that hovered above Hay Tor like moths. When he stood on his hindlegs and twirled around Teg, the tomcat yell of love pouring from his gape, she laughed helplessly and lost her breath. Then they would lie together and nibble each other's fur in the bliss of mutual grooming.

And often he was weak with happiness, scampering over Hamel Down behind her. His yikkerings and barks were heard in the village of Widecombe, but they were the sounds of Dartmoor winter nights and caused little comment. Other dog foxes avoided Wulfgar. Suddenly his territory had become dangerous. Only Stargrief, whose mating instinct was as blunt as his fangs, was permitted to roam within sight of Hay Tor. Teg's blood-chilling screech kept vagrant dogs on edge, but Wulfgar's spoor was enough to douse the fiercest desire.

The moors belonged to the kestrels and buzzards, to the merlin and the lark; they were in constant attendance. Foxes came and went, rarely lingering. The grey smell of the twilight hills would often make them whimper like cubs with the ache to journey to far horizons. Distance promised so much and there was always the chance that something amazing lay under the skyline.

One evening while they waited in the heather for darkness to mantle Blackslade Mire, Mordo the raven brought his mate Skalla to a nearby rock. The cawing of rooks carried up the cleave and at Chittleford woodcocks darted and twisted in courtship flight. It was a soft, Westcountry evening. Coltsfoot had pushed through the frail skeleton of the shrew Wulfgar had killed at Bagtor Cottages, and deep in the goyals of the Webbum Valley alder catkins hung motionless above the river.

Mordo caressed his mate's neck, the great wedge of his bill lifting black feathers to reveal grey down. With strange purring cries he urged her into the air, and called his deep 'cronk-cronk' and rolled and swooped. Side by side dog and vixen leapt the stream at Grey Goose Nest and read the darkness all the way to Emsworthy. The aerobatics of Mordo and Skalla continued against the stars. It was not yet Candlemas but the mild weather brought a touch of spring to the uplands.

A fieldmouse eating haws it had stored in the last year's nest of a blackbird nearly fainted as it peered down through the cracked mud into Wulfgar's eyes. The dog fox was sniffing a wisp of black fur left by a gone-wild farm cat. The fur was hooked on a twig near the base of the hawthorn. Steelygrin, the tom who had deserted the kitchen range of Whisselwell Farm for a swashbuckling life, had nearly caught the fieldmouse half an hour before but Trollgar had intervened. Cat and owl had quarrelled briefly and departed to hunt elsewhere, so the fieldmouse lived.

Wulfgar and Teg killed a hare on the slopes of Rippon Tor. The dog fox chased the animal along its favourite run to a gap in the wall where the vixen lay in ambush. Despite the swiftness of her pounce and bite the hare had time to scream before it died. The foxes carefully skinned it and ate all except the pads and head.

'I'm still hungry,' Teg said, cleaning her face with a forepaw.

'There are rabbits at the rocks by Four Ponds,' Wulfgar said. 'They aren't easy to catch. Their burrows go under the stones of a ruined house.'

'Rabbits are stupid,' Teg said.

'But some aren't so stupid as others,' Wulfgar said patiently. 'Their tunnels are narrow. It would take ages to dig them out.'

She grinned and showed her small white canine teeth.

'Dog and vixen can do anything, Wulfgar.'

Foxes are creatures of few words, like most hunters. Moving silently up the sheep path they came to the newtake wall of Emsworthy. Rabbits scattered and fled, and a slight breeze set the blackthorn squeaking.

It comforted Wulfgar to hear the Becca singing from the invisible valley bed to his left. He stopped and drew a cold draught of air. The rabbits had left a little of their fear on the night.

'Fitch,' Teg said, wrinkling her nose.

'Yiss,' said a thin voice. 'Fitch – and a fitch wot's not too happy because a couple of bloody foxes have ruined his work.'

Chivvy-yick the stoat spoke Fox with the odd nasal accent of the mustelid tribe. He darted out of the drystone wall then back again, peeping at them from a chink.

'Maybe you're just too thick to chop conies,' Wulfgar smiled.

'Sod off! I've forgotten more about drummers than you'll ever learn. You're as nimble as that bloody tor.'

'Why don't you crunch him, Wulfgar?' said Teg. Her brush twitched.

'Because he can't catch me, maggot face,' the stoat hissed, retreating deeper into the Crevice.

He had spent the best part of the evening lulling the rabbits into a stupor, so from the safety of his labyrinth he mocked the foxes and cursed them. But Teg and Wulfgar being wise to the ways of a fitch in a drystone wall left him and climbed the hillock to Saddle Tor.

A farm labourer came whistling along the main road on his bicycle into darkness that swam away below them to the far-off sea and the flash of Berry Head lighthouse.

'Bloody foxes,' Chivvy-yick fumed. He jigged up and down in rage and spat through his fangs.

Several stoats rippled along the wall towards him.

'Foxes,' he hissed. 'We've been robbed by stinkin' foxes. O I hate 'em. I hate 'em.'

His relatives exchanged baffled looks and licked their lips.

'OK, you worm brains,' Chivvy-yick snarled. 'What about our grub? Sittin' on your butts gawping at the stars won't grab us a drummer. Git into them burries – sharpish.'

Teg and Wulfgar took the pony track to Four Ponds and drank at their leisure. The water broke from the biggest flood pool in a silver lip and tinkled across the night.

TWO GREEN LEAVES

The mild weather showed no signs of breaking. A little after St Valentine's Day Teg discovered she was with cub. Dog and vixen were still joyful wanderers but their hunting games had become serious exercises in cunning. Twice they had robbed Scoble's trap lines and on one memorable occasion Teg had snatched a guinea fowl from the roadside at Canna while a couple of labourers were hanging a gate less than twenty yards away.

'It's not worth taking so many risks,' Wulfgar said.

'But it's fun,' Teg replied. 'Men are like rabbits.'

'They're not,' said Wulfgar firmly. 'Start believing that and you're dead. Your mother taught you to fear Man above all creatures. She didn't tell you to watch out for rabbits.'

'I meant they're stupid.'

'I know what you meant, Teg, but once they decide to destroy you they don't give up. They come after you with dogs and guns or they set traps. Stay invisible and live. Leave Man's things alone.'

'We'll find a safe den for the cubs, won't we?' she said.

'The safest place there is.'

'The only really safe place for foxes', Teg said, 'is death.'

'You're beginning to sound like Stargrief.'

'It's your fault. You've always got to poke around under the surface of things.'

She smiled to soften her words.

'Come on,' Wulfgar said. 'I'll race you to the top.'

He led her to the broad summit of Conies Down Tor. Flocks of starlings and lapwings darkened the sunset. The valley head where the Cowsic River began was a reedy bowl streaked by narrow streams, and on the opposite side of the river a herd of almost a hundred Dartmoor ponies cropped the thicker grass among the hut circles. The air was full of the music of water running off the hills.

When Tod trotted into the first dusk of creation the Dartmoor wilderness was as it is today. Wulfgar and Teg could cross vast tracts without glimpsing a human being.

The moors were not old with Man's history. Civilisations had come and gone, but little of their glory remained. A few hut circles, some megaliths, pounds, lynchets, terraces and the odd Clapper bridge did not add up to much. All were weathered down to anonymity. Stargrief understood such things. On those special occasions when he had emerged from his meditation he had spoken to small gatherings of the Haytor Clan, using the bardic phrases of his ancestors. He was the great survivor. Foxes regarded him with reverence and few doubted that he was under the personal protection of Tod.

Wulfgar and Teg sat in the lee of a boulder. Masses of pink cloud blotted the sky behind them. The vixen pressed a forepaw on her brush and cleaned the tag, while Stargrief's words sang behind Wulfgar's eyes:

'I speak of the Now and the What Has Been and the What Will be, to the foxes who will go through death to the Star Place. I think of the time before Man came and I look to the time of Man's going from the beloved country.

'We are no more than shadows flickering briefly on the moors. But the flickering is beautiful. Through falls of hawthorn blossom we pass. We drink the seasons and the seasons take us. The seasons are hounds. No earth or clitter can keep that pack at bay.'

At night the hunting kept him busy, for he could think with his body in the thrill of pursuit and capture.

They left the North Moor late one afternoon and trotted over tilting fields to Cator Court. There was a sudden gleam of lamplight in an upstairs window that checked the foxes for a moment. The moist smell of watercress bruised by the hooves of cattle lofted from the ford.

'I was chased by a dog near here when I was no more than a cub,' Teg said. 'Didn't he give me a fright! He was all legs and teeth – like the bogeywolf my mother used to go on about.'

'Sounds like the lurcher,' Wulfgar said. 'How did you get away?'

'I climbed a tree and hid in the ivy. The dog made a lot of noise.'

'Dogs always do. The lurcher's mad. He's killed foxes. Last summer he took a piece out of Wayland's ear.'

Teg shivered.

As darkness fell the countryside became silent and the barn owls appeared. Although they swept with a noise-less beating of wings down West Shallowford goyal, they screamed to scare small creatures into movement. The rustlings in the hedge betrayed voles and shrews. Sometimes earth dribbled over dry leaves. The night was prickled with faint squeaks and screams, many of which ended abruptly.

The sun was lifting a little higher above the southern hills every day. Wulfgar and Teg crossed a countryside of apple-green coombs and brown hills. The drystone walls were held together by gravity and they marched into the haze of high ground, and where they joined in right angles there were sheltered pockets of bracken. On warm afternoons the foxes slumbered here, burrowing into the dead fronds while the larks sang above them and gnats danced round their heads.

With day crumbling into smoke they talked of love and the good life they shared. Fox is a raw language, wrung from rock and heather, but for Wulfgar and Teg it was a musical celebration of their togetherness. They flickered on the margins of dusk above the farmsteads, and their cries set the work dogs whimpering,

A rising easterly wind brought a cold snap and there was a brief, vicious return of winter with light snowfalls on ground above a thousand feet. Running over patches of whiteness dog and vixen left a double line of small oval prints that other foxes noted. At Hedge Barton the sparrows pressed tightly together against the barn wall, behind the ivy. The earth became firm again, but not with the killing frost that breaks a gardener's heart.

Wulfgar and Teg enjoyed walking over white fields. The ponies had retreated from the heights to coombs where water always flowed even under the thickest snow. They lay in field corners nibbling the grass thawed out by their body warmth and their breath climbed into the air like mist from the bogs. With the coming of the foxes they knelt and got up in a strange, clumsy way as if the cold had stiffened their muscles.

The snow lay for a couple of days and vanished. Rain fell gently and calm mornings became warm afternoons.

Blackbirds and thrushes sang in the village gardens at sunset. On the lawn of the Moorland Hotel were drifts of snowdrops, and beneath the rosebeds chrysalides and caterpillars waited for the real spring. In the banks of the deep lane by Easdon Farm the celandines were full and golden, and among the roots primroses were budding. The grass was very green along the ditchside.

'Why the old cottage?' Teg said.

They had journeyed to the Leighon Ponds at the end of a day spent dozing in a copse.

'Pride, I suppose,' Wulfgar said. 'I've never been able to take a rabbit from that warren.'

Teg narrowed her eyes.

'You mean there's such a thing as a clever coney?'

'Lucky coney,' he said. 'A lucky animal doesn't need brains. Anyway, what would a rabbit do with intelligence? They lead such dull lives. If they thought about it it would drive them crazy.'

'It's all that grass,' said Teg, mysteriously.

Beside the Becca Brook they found a dead trout. Romany the otter had killed several that evening and he had taken a single bite out of the fish's shoulder. Wulfgar let Teg eat the trout and afterwards they climbed up to Holwell Tor and made their way through twilight to Quarryman's Cottage.

'O no!' Teg whispered. 'Not fitch again!'

They clapped down in the furze and lifted their heads to read the wind. There was enough light to reveal what was going on below in front of the ruins.

A gang of stoats, including Chivvy-yick, were wrangling over a coney. Chivvy-yick had one forepaw raised and the other resting on the carcass, his lips twisted back to show the tiny white thorns of his fangs.

'Will you leave off!' he snarled. 'I eats first and when I've had enough Shiv can get stuck in. It's fitch law.'

'Me and Flick-Flick caught the bloody drummer,' Shiv said. 'We should get the first helping.'

'Mind you don't get my fangs in yer throat, dung beetle,' Chivvy-yick said, glaring at him.

'There's four of us,' Shiv said.

'But it's your throat I'll go for, my bucko. So why not join the queue? There's plenty for everyone. This is a very plump drummer.'

'OK – OK,' Shiv said. 'Just make sure you don't scoff the lot.'

'You're family,' Chivvy-yick grinned. 'Would I cheat my own flesh and blood?'

'Yiss,' said Flick-Flick. 'You'd eat granny if she smelt like a drummer. And you wouldn't share 'er either.'

Chivvy-yick laughed through his nose and sounded like a wet blade of grass being drawn between forefinger and thumb.

'Keep laughing, fitch,' Wulfgar snarled. 'But get your paws off my rabbit.'

The dog fox leapt from the bracken and confronted the stoats. He was humpbacked and bristling, and his puffed-out tail spoke volumes.

In Chivvy-yick's vocabulary there was no word for fear, but he understood the meaning of discretion. A dog fox weighing twenty-four pounds and standing sixteen inches tall at the shoulders is worthy of respect, especially if you are a seven-ounce mustelid. Chivvy-yick withdrew, swearing horribly, and chivvied his relatives.

'Five fitches could chop a fox,' he hissed. 'Now if Flick-Flick and Shiv was to come at old Canker Head from this side, and Slickfang and Snikker did likewise from the other side, yours truly would be free to attack that bit of fur under Canker Head's chin.'

'And this vixen would crunch the funny little fitch like a dry stick,' said Teg.

She had crept up behind the fitch patrol to within easy pouncing distance. Chivvy-yick squeaked. There was a flurry of snakelike bodies and the stoats shot down the nearest burrows where they lingered to toss insults. Five pairs of tiny green eyes pinpricked the darkness.

'Maggot Face and old Canker Head will regret this,' Chivvy-yick yelled. 'I don't forget. I never forget. Never. Stinkin' foxes! Never!'

Wulfgar carried the rabbit to the top of Holwell Tor and they ate it under the rowan trees beyond the reach of the stoats' yikkering.

There were dark days and days of great luminosity. All along the Becca yellow tassels hung from the hazel bushes. A thousand feet above the valley Stormbully mewled on his thermal. He had taken another mate. She had come from Hexworthy and was called Fallbright. The bulky nest of twigs and sticks in the oak tree in Mill Wood had received her approval. With wings angled against the wind she carved her own circle in the sky and called to Stormbully like a cat speaking to its kittens.

Wulfgar glanced up and three clear drops of water fell from his chin into the Becca Brook. The stillness of the afternoon made him uneasy. The trapper's smell clung to the docks beside the path and Wulfgar's nose quivered as he picked up the rich scent of rabbit. He looked for Teg but she had gone a little way ahead and in a flash he understood.

'Teg,' he barked. 'Teg – stay where you are.'

He darted over the stone bridge and followed her trail down the Becca into scrub oak.

'Teg,' he cried again.

'Over here,' she replied. 'There's a dead coney.'

His mouth went dry and like some garish episode from a nightmare he heard the clang of the trap snapping shut. Then Teg was screaming. He breasted the ferns feeling her agony clenching in his stomach. The gin held her by the front paw. It was one of three Scoble had tilled around the rabbit carcass. Teg's eyes were big with fear. She fidgeted and twisted in the gymnastics of her terror.

'Teg, please keep still,' Wulfgar said. 'I can't help you if you don't keep still.'

The screaming stopped. Teg crouched and licked the mangled paw. She gazed at him from some distant, private world of pain. Her ears were flattened to her head and her brush swished and jerked. A stong acrid odour escaped from her fur.

'What can you do?' she gasped,' – kill me? Well, do it – do it.'

Wulfgar moved cautiously, stepping in her footprints. He sniffed at the gin and tugged at the chain with his teeth. Teg was whimpering now.

'Forget that,' she said, 'I can't go round with this thing on my leg.'

They stared helplessly at each other through their misery.

'You must bite off her foot,' said a calm voice. 'It must be done quickly. The trapper will return at sunset.'

'But a three-legged vixen …' Teg said in horror.

'Three-legged vixens have cubs and some have been known to live to my age,' said the voice.

And Stargrief appeared like a conjurer's trick in the bramble thicket. He was gaunt and grey and his brush was no longer bushy, but he had the brightest eyes Teg had ever seen. Very gently he licked the trapped paw.

'Is it bad, Teg?' Wulfgar said.

'No – there's hardly any pain now. Please get on with it, and do it quickly.'

'Look into my eyes, Teg,' said Stargrief. 'Forget everything else. Come – do as I say.'

In the pool were the bright unmoving reflections of green leaves. The cub vixen peered down from the alder root. 'Teg,' her mother cried. 'Where are you, Teg?' Like underwater flames the leaves blazed and winked at her. Her body had floated away. She was merely an idea in someone else's mind. Was death like this? Was this death? Now there were just two green leaves and her eyes printed upon them. Numbness spiralled into peace ...

'It's done,' Wulfgar said.

Teg lay on her side and Stargrief and Wulfgar licked the stump of her leg until the bleeding had stopped and the wound was clean. Then they helped her to her feet and supported her body with their own, one each side of her.

'O Tod,' the little vixen panted. 'I can't hobble around like this. I can't.'

'You'll get used to it,' Stargrief said. 'Wulfgar will look after you. Everything heals in time, Teg. You mustn't give up.'

But the unborn life stirring inside Teg had already strengthened her resolve.

They took her to Thorgil's sett and laid her in a chamber deep under the oak wood.

'I'll wait outside,' said Stargrief.

Once they were alone Wulfgar curled up beside her and made her snuggle into his body. Tenderly he licked the wound while she tried to sleep.

'You will court another vixen,' she whispered. 'What use am I? You'll get fed up looking after a cripple.'

'Please, Teg – don't hurt me,' Wulfgar said. 'I love you. How can you talk like that?'

She fetched up a long, shuddering sigh and let exhaustion sweep everything out of her mind.

Wulfgar left the sett several hours later but Stargrief had gone; so had the rabbit carcass and the gins. The trapper's taint fouled the night air. A brown owl spoke, but the fox found no beauty in its cry, then coming to the Becca to drink he discovered Thorgil grooming himself on a rock.

'How is Teg?' said the badger.

'Very ill,' said Wulfgar. 'She left a paw in the trap.'

'I'm sorry,' said Thorgil in his deep, quiet voice. 'You are welcome to use my sett for as long as you like. The entrance under the boulders by the dead tree is safest. It's hard to hide gins there.'

'I'll remember this kindness,' said the fox.

'We are friends, Wulfgar. If you find a gin near here let me know and I'll roll on it. Gins I can deal with. It's the wires that bother me. Last spring I lost a cub in a snare.'

Wulfgar sealed his eyes and lapped the dark water.

'The lurcher doesn't come here very often,' Thorgil said a little later, sensing the fox's anxiety.

'He had a go at me once, but I left my mark on him. Didn't he yelp! He went over Black Hill like the wind, his tail between his legs. He may be mad but he's not mad enough to bother me twice.'

The dog fox went to the vole runs at Hedge Barton and hunted mechanically. There was a bleakness round his heart that persisted until Teg hobbled out into the sunshine on the morning of the third day.

WISTMAN'S WOOD

The harrows were raising red-brown clouds of dust in the lowland fields. A chill wind blew from the North, bending the crocuses and unopened daffodils from Haytor Vale to Trumpeter and on to Stover Park. In woods all over Devon cock pheasants were gathering their harems.

Teg lay up for a week in Thorgil's sett. She refused food and when she was not sleeping she spent hours licking her maimed leg, but every so often she struggled down to the brook and ate grass and drank the pure water.

'It's a dead loss,' she sighed after a longer trip to the ponds. 'I couldn't chop a sleeping frog. I'd be better off dead.'

'Nonsense,' Wulfgar said. 'Hunting's not everything. I can easily catch enough for us both, but you are really very good on three legs. Look – do you feel strong enough to make a journey?'

'Where to?'

'Rocky Wood. It's not exactly just over the hill but if we take it easy we could be there in three or four sunsets.'

'Why is it so important?' said Teg.

'Well, you can't have the cubs here. Foxes have been dug out of this sett before and in any case it's not fair on Thorgil. Rocky Wood is safe. I've never smelt gin steel anywhere near it. The trapper isn't likely to bother us there.'

'When do we start?'

'Tonight,' said Wulfgar. 'Stargrief has promised us a full moon.'

'Stargrief is a beautiful old animal,' said Teg.

Even on three legs she was a nimble creature, but she could not execute the fox pounce that ends with the forepaws clamping the prey to the ground. It galled her to have to lie under cover while Wulfgar ranged around for conies and mice. She ate sullenly, making sure there was more than enough left for him. But his love and kindness gradually won her over and the old passion for life returned. The moon was still the moon and night the true, thrilling place of labyrinthine scents.

The foxes followed the pony paths over Hameldown Tor to Challacombe. March showers made the high ground glitter. The sheep huddled together wherever there was shelter, for lambing time was near and they were nervous. Crows were in constant attendance, waiting to feed on misfortune, and they craarked at Wulfgar and Teg. Light glinted blue on their plumage. Wobbling on the air they looked like black rags, but when they flew too close to Teg she leapt and snapped a mouthful of feathers from the hen bird's tail.

Wulfgar's pace was slow, but moving as they did between sundown and daybreak the foxes never had to hurry. Below Pizwell Cottage the Walla Brook crept through a marsh where curlew nested. In the mud of the flood pools common frogs had buried themselves, absorbing oxygen through their slack skin. They were more dead than alive. Herons came to the marsh to feast on them when the warm weather made them kick for the sun.

'Oor-li, oor-li,' sang the curlews, adding their own melancholy to the sadness of twilight. The cock bird flew in circles, dropping chains of short notes, and whenever the hen settled among the reed clumps he pursued her in a curious hunchbacked walk. They were the colours of dusk and their song was as soft as the evening air.

Through lengthening shadows Wulfgar and Teg crossed the clapper bridge at Bellever and wandered up Lakehead Hill. Teg was very weary, her tongue was flopped over her chin and only courage kept her on her feet. Wulfgar sniffed out a kennel where the ling was tall and bushy, and the foxes lay side by side watching the lights of Powdermill Cottages twinkle in the clarity of early night. A bus crawled along the road towards Postbridge, boring into the blackness with its head-lamps, but when the silence returned it was profound.

'I think I'll wait here while you hunt,' Teg yawned. 'I'm so tired I could sleep till summer.'

'But will you be all right?'

'Of course – go on, you must be hungry.'

She smiled but her voice was sad.

'Am I much of a burden?' she asked.

Wulfgar swallowed his misery and licked her muzzle.

'Whenever I look at you,' he said, 'I see a countryside where there are no men like the trapper. There are no guns turned on us and no traps set to crush our limbs and no hounds to worry us into the Star Place.'

'That sounds like the Star Place,' Teg said.

'No – it's closer. It's this side of death.'

'There's no such place, Wulfgar.'

The dog fox sat up and scratched his side.

'Maybe not,' he said. 'But lately I've had glimpses of a land that looks like the moors. The same bit of coun-tryside always fills my dreams. And it never changes.'

'Tell me about it.'

He gazed down at her from unseeing eyes.

'The hills are much higher than the tors. Their peaks are like knives poking into the clouds. Great rivers rush down the hillsides in rapids and falls. And there are huge birds in the sky, and the valley is carpeted with rabbits.

'Where the snow lies on the high ground the hares are white and there are white grouse. The hunting is good and no man wants to kill us.'

'How do you know?'

'I can feel it as strongly as I feel your love.'

'It must be very comforting to have such dreams.'

'Perhaps they are visions,' Wulfgar said.

Her eyes widened.

'But you're not like Stargrief,' she said.

'Maybe I'm becoming like him. Does that sound conceited?'

Teg shook her head.

'You are Wulfgar,' she said, as if it were sufficient.

From Longford Tor the sunset was too magnificent merely to be looked at. Religions are born out of such experiences – beginnings and endings, dawn and sundown. His thoughts swept and danced across the deathless countryside, ideas swooping into despair.

Wulfgar turned away. The vixen raised her eyes to meet his own.

'It goes beyond love of fox for fox, doesn't it?' she said. 'But why must we grope around in darkness?'

'There's Rocky Wood,' he said stiffly, and she felt she had trespassed on some forbidden area of his being.

Below Beardown Tors, the West Dart passed quickly over shallows of rock and grit. Moonlight shivered on the water like beads of mercury vibrating on a drum. The reef of oaks known to men as Wistman's Wood and to foxes as Rocky Wood lay on the hillside at their feet, and the sound of the river grew louder as they descended.

From a great jumble of boulders the dwarf oaks grew close together, gnarled branches entwined. Moss, lichens and ferns sprouted from the bark, and bracken clogged the roots where the leaves of many seasons were rotting down to humus. The wood had come into being as a handful of acorns spilled from the crop of a pigeon. The bird had fallen victim to a peregrine falcon, long before the men of bronze had made their lynchets and terraces. Teg's nose quivered.

'Songbird, rabbit, mouse, squirrel – but no trapper,' she said.

'We aren't the first foxes to use Rocky Wood,' Wulfgar smiled.

They trod gingerly on the dead leaves and twigs, and wherever it was possible went over the low branches for fear of snares. Wulfgar let Teg lead and waited patiently for her to select the earth.

'This will do,' she said eventually, poking her head out of a hole that was partly concealed by a boulder. 'There are two bolt-holes at the back and a den big enough to raise a dozen cubs. I like the way it's hidden by the ferns and brambles. No man could dig us out, it's solid rock. When the trees come into leaf we'll be invisible. A buzzard wouldn't know we were around.'

Wulfgar ranged as far afield as Huntingdon Warren in the South and Cranmere Pool to the North. Around Dunnabridge Farm on the West Dart there were good pickings – fieldmice, conies, rats and chickens. When the sheep dropped their lambs there was afterbirth and the odd stillborn scrap of wool and mutton. Close to Crockern one dawn he found the bodies of a sheep and two lambs. The ewe had successfully dropped the first but had struggled and died having the second. Wulfgar buried the heavier lamb for future use and carried the other back to Teg.

For long hours he ran wild with the hunting fever. Full of bravado he stalked a cock red grouse in the heather above Huntingdon Warren and killed the bird as its mating call crescendoed to a harsh 'go-bek-bek, go-bek-bek'. On the outskirts of Holne he was spotted with a baby rabbit in his jaws. A boy with fair hair, who had cycled all the way from Paignton because he loved Dartmoor and its creatures, saw Wulfgar lope off into the furze. The boy had spent the afternoon opening and closing the moorland gate for tips, but he valued the sight of the dark fox above the coppers and threepenny bits that bulged his trouser pocket.

Along the stone walls blackthorn was in blossom, its frail white flowers traced against a cloudswept sky. The glare of sunlight gilded the grassmoor. Wulfgar drank at the Wheal Emma Leat and ate a salmon that he found wedged between rocks below the weir on the River Swincombe. A ring ouzel flew away crying 'tac-tac-tac'. The bird's bib was whiter than the water that rushed past the round, polished rocks to feed the pools under the Old Gobbett Tin Mine.

JACKO RUNNING

Scoble came home drunk from Newton Abbot market. His face was redder than usual and he breathed heavily through his mouth. The cider barrel tap squeaked as he turned it on and the level of the scrumpy rose to his thumb. Scoble swayed and took half a dozen swift backward steps to regain his balance, like a lunatic learning the tango. Jacko regarded him apprehensively from under the table. Cider gushed out of the barrel to form a golden puddle on the floor.

'Bloody hell!' roared Scoble, fumbling with the tap. The eyes of dog and master met, and Jacko licked his lips and tried to look lovable.

'What you starin' at, bone bag?' Scoble said. 'I'll beat some sense into your thick head. Yaas – I will.'

He staggered to the grate and reached down to pick up a stick. Scrumpy slopped over his trouser front. He collapsed on his knees and found his mouth with the pint pot. By the time he had finished drinking he had forgotten what he was doing. Like a child surrendering to weariness at the end of a long day, he curled up and laid his head on the fender and passed dizzily into unconsciousness.

The door rattled gently, swung wide, and let the remains of a sunny afternoon flood the kitchen. With hardly a click of his claws Jacko departed, taking the garden wall in his stride, running elegantly down the road to Yarner Wells. The ruddy sky drew all the soft inner parts of his head up tight against his skull. At first there was a churning agony of heat, then numbness and light-headed bliss.

'Jacko run the red race,' said a voice very similar to his own. Sheep broke away from him in sumptuous panic and he rolled a mad bloodshot eye at them.

'Too close to home,' said the voice.

He sniggered.

'Jacko sly. Jacko know all tricks. O kill-killy-kill, but over the hill. Yes yes O yes! Over the hill.'

Another shock-wave of sheep, ewes fat with lamb, eyes like fear-tinted marbles. He smashed into them, nipping a leg, tearing out a tuft of wool, blindly, playfully, holding the throbbing desire in check. At Yarner Wells some chickens were scratching the gravelly wayside. He killed two and would have had a third, but an upstairs window flew open and a woman squawked. It was old Mrs Lugg whose sight was failing.

'What be it, mother?' her daughter called up the stairs.

'Fox, I think,' said the old lady. 'It's after they fowls.'

But Jacko was streaking up the hillside out of sight, spitting small feathers from between his teeth. On the top of Black Hill he lay panting beside the cairn and gazed westward. There was rain in the air and distances were clearly etched. Jacko's chest heaved. His eyes were redder than the sun. Thoughts quaked like lava and he whimpered, waiting for the pain to pass. Slowly the sunset opened and admitted him to the gold and scarlet kingdom, where golden sheep paraded before him in glorious slow motion. A river of blood flowed into golden ponds, and blood-red birds and black birds sailed silently overhead. Then the sun was gone and the magic was draining out of the landscape as swiftly as the pain faded from his mind. The ground seemed to tilt and fall from under him. He closed his eyes and somersaulted into black-ness …

There was a late rising of the moon above the trees. Jacko woke up shivering. It was a windless night with sound carrying immense distances, and clouds moving low across the tops of the western tors. The lurcher struggled to his feet and lifted his muzzle and howled. The goods train that was gathering speed below Pullabrook answered with a long drawn out hoot.

'Night belong to me,' Jacko growled. 'I kill other dog. Yes yes! Killy killy killy.'

And he ran off to find the goods train dog.

The dark, decaying wood was haunted by owls of Trollgar's family. Whenever they screeched Jacko showed his teeth and lifted his hackles. The merciless light of the moon was splintered by the branches of Yarner's trees. Needles of light pierced his brain. He ran hard to drive the pain out, down the stream past Reddaford Water and on to the River Bovey. The train had gone. His body quivered with madness and the need to kill set his nerves on fire.

'Jacko great. He come from stars. Stars love Jacko. They say, "Send us animals to play with. We lonely, Jacko. Send us sheep, lambs, rabbits, foxes, squirrels. Kill 'em quick and they fly up to us.'"

The lurcher stopped babbling and lapped at the stars that dappled the surface of the river.

'Drink stars. Put out pain. Fire go out in my head.'

He went through the sepulchral coombs of the cleave, beneath roots shaped like gargoyles. But he was too noisy and did not encounter any victims until he reached Parke. Here he stumbled upon a blind rat who was crossing a woodland ride gripping the tail of a companion. The blind rat died and its friend lived.

Jacko ran on. The stars sang to him and when they suddenly fell silent he looked up and saw clouds filling the sky.

At Bovey Tracey he took the road that brought him once again onto the moors. By Kiln Brake the pain drove through his head in a fiery wave, and he crawled into the ash trees and blacked-out – almost on top of a fox. Wendel sprang up from his kennel of brambles and ran very quickly from the spinney. The lurcher had fallen on his brush and Wendel had dribbled scats in his haste to depart. Darting across the road he nearly met death under the wheels of a motorbike. Lacing the air with the musk of fear he headed for the oak coppice on the edge of Haytor Down, wondering why he was still alive.

Dawn filtered through mist and the moon had faded to transparency. Behind the eastern spur of Dartmoor the sun rose. Jacko opened his eyes onto the ball of burning gold and yawned. For him there were no yesterdays. The sun was his father, the stars were his masters and friends. In the hedge bordering the cottage gardens of Ullacombe a yellow-hammer trilled, and the robin who ruled the vegetable patch of the Rock Inn broke into song. All winter he had sounded like a rusty iron gate swinging on its hinges, but now he warbled loud and passionately to warn other cock birds off his territory. Many earthworms had been swallowed to fuel his performance. Behind him the remoteness of quiet, deserted farmland materialised from the mist.

Jacko's long legs brought him to Haytor Quarry Ponds. Mordo the raven sat in the top of a rowan tree above the quarry and watched the lurcher. Every so often Mordo thought of his mate who was sitting on four eggs and he bowed and chuckled. Long ago ravens had nested on Hay Tor, but boys from Widecombe had taken the eggs. Mordo and Skalla had built a nest of sticks lined with sheep's wool, moss and ponies' hair in a 100-foot-tall oak at Pullabrook Wood. The eggs, were pale green, blotched and freckled with dark brown markings.

'Big black bird know Jacko,' the lurcher said. 'He bow to me. He know I friend of stars. One day I chew off his head and he fly up to stars. Jacko good dog. Stars say so.'

He cocked his leg and watered the handle of a rusty iron winch. Mordo laughed quietly to himself, and a swish and flap of black wings announced the arrival of Swart.

'Is it the dog?' said the crow.

'It's a dog, right enough,' the raven grinned.

'That one's special,' Swart said. 'He's cracked, addled; nutty as a hazel bush. He goes round killing everything that moves – for fun. It's obscene.'

The rowan branch bent under the weight of the two corvids.

'He don't bother me,' Mordo said, regarding his cousin cheerfully.

'The corvid that is born to be hanged need never fear the mad dog,' Swart said.

'Ah well,' Mordo laughed. 'We all run the risk of the keeper's gibbet. What a bundle of bad weather you are, Swart.'

Swart frowned and waggled his beak in his breast feathers to disturb the fleas.

'I was born crow and have been ever since,' he said.

'That's a fact,' said the raven.

Jacko flashed him a look of utter desperation and began to bark.

'He's talking to himself again,' said Swart.

'And why not?' cronked Mordo. 'I do it.'

'Ah yes,' the crow said slyly. 'Well, I'm not surprised.'

'It's because I enjoy talking to intelligent corvids,' Mordo said, refusing to relinquish his good humour. 'There aren't many about.'

Swart ruffled his feathers and quizzed the raven with a bright, black eye. He had never laughed in his life and he had no intention of beginning now.

'Funny – you never see ravens till the best part of the day's gone,' he said.

'We sleep slowly,' Mordo grinned.

'Cra-ark,' said Swart and he flew away.

An idea crumbled in Jacko's head and gusted through his brain like sparks from a furnace. Daws floated down into the silence and started to chatter. A pair of wood-pigeons rose in a slow concave curve, paused with a clap of wings and swooped – only to begin their upward glide again. From the reedy margins of the pond came the clucking of moorhens, and the surface was divided for a moment by the blue flight line of a kingfisher. Jacko sighed. The raven preened the coverts of a great, black wing, whose feathers held and bent the light.

The lurcher drank noisily and set off towards the sun. Pain swelled behind his eyes like organ music and he raced down to Emsworthy, hurdling the furze clumps, dodging in and out of the rocks. Clouds drifted by, a shower fell and the road glistened. Jacko sat by the gate and fought the giddiness. The word 'KILL' was branded on the dome of his skull in fiery capitals. He grinned and sniffed the air. The smell of death leaked from a passing cattle truck. Round, terror-stricken eyes were pressed to chinks in the slats. Liquid excrement splatted onto the road and Jacko whimpered. The truck was a mirage wobbling on the red horizon. With a snakelike action the lurcher turned and bounded into the Leighon Valley, and under Holwell Tor he found Ashmere sleeping in the heather. The young fox leapt up but Jacko caught him by the neck and wrenched the life out of him with a twist of his powerful shoulders. From the corner of his eye he saw another fox slinking away but he had to linger and savage the carcass. By the time he was ready to kill again Stargrief had slipped into the clitter and quietly placed himself beyond the reach of the lurcher's jaws.

'I get you,' Jacko barked. 'You there. Jacko get you. Tonight he come and –'

He gnashed his teeth and snapped at invisible foxes. For a long while he barked into the hollow places of the clitter and he loved the way they made his voice sound deep and menacing.

'Old grey fox I get you,' he panted. 'Yes – Jacko do cracko old foxy-o. Bloody quick.'

Madness lifted him out of himself and he was running again towards the clean expanse of water, when the birdlike whistle of Romany brought him back into the morning. Rooks left the nests they were patching in the beechtops and mobbed him, but Jacko laughed wildly, lifting his head high and rolling his eyes.

'One day Jacko grow wings,' he barked. 'Then flap-flap he go and he kill all black birds in sky. All caw-caw birds get sent to stars. And stars say, "Good dog, Jacko", and Jacko get best place at fireside.'

From the dam at the end of the ponds Romany called again to his mate, and Moonsleek's reply fluted down the Becca Brook. Something was wrong. The otter bitch swallowed the frog she had caught and made for the river, but Jacko hurtled out of an explosion of rooks and bowled her over. She spat at him like a fire cracker and gave a sharp yikker of rage. No wild creature had ever stood up to Jacko before, and the lurcher stared down at her in wonder. Moonsleek uncoiled and bit his nose. Jacko screeched and brushed her off with flailing forepaws. The otter wriggled under the alder roots and melted into the river.

'Caw caw caw,' laughed the rooks.

Jacko splashed through the shallows. The dark flickering shape of the otter sped away from him but he was fast and never lost sight of it. Beneath the alders a dipper was striding along underwater, upstream, held down by the current washing over his slanting back. Every now and then he lifted a pebble with his beak and winkled out tiny crustaceans, but when Jacko's shadow fell upon him he burst from the water and dashed over the marsh on short, brown wings.

Moonsleek swam into the deep water of the ponds and Romany joined her. A trout leapt high and fell back with a splash. The lurcher scampered up and down the bank whimpering at the otters as they glided among the drowned branches of sallows. At last he could bear it no longer and with a loud snarl he dived in and savaged the water. Romany closed his jaws on one of Jacko's hindlegs and bit him to the bone.

It was a very wet and subdued dog that hobbled up to Holwell Tor.

'Jacko kill they water fitches,' he growled. 'Yes – killy killy killy. But not in water. Water not good. Stars say so.'

There was a nest of small hot stars in his head. What was he going to do? He licked his wound and tried to remember. Then it dawned on him. He was a mighty lurcher running across a red world, reaping a red harvest. In the dream of his pain he killed a sheep and two newborn lambs. Red drizzle drifted down from the red sky.

'No more, no more, please,' he whined.

The stars laughed at him and he ran for home dragging his stiff and bloody hindleg.

CONFRONTATION

'Ashmere is dead,' Stargrief said.

Wulfgar silently waited for him to elaborate.

'It happened in a flash. He was asleep. The lurcher just shook him by the neck and that was that. One moment he was alive and then he wasn't.'

The old dog fox lowered his eyes.

'The lurcher killed a sheep and some lambs as well,' he went on.

'That's bad,' said Wulfgar. 'When sheep are killed, men come with dogs and guns.'

'We take and are taken,' Stargrief said.

'Yes, well, maybe we accept too much. We aren't stupid like rabbits. We are hunters.'

Stargrief smiled.

They were sitting under a chin of rock on Longford Tor. The wind of the vernal equinox was combing the deer grass in the valley by the derelict powder mill. Blossom lifted from the blackthorns. The north-easterlies had brought a fresh snowfall, forcing the ewes and lambs down from the high ground to the roadsides. Snow lay thinly in patches on the north-facing sides of walls and buildings.

'I'm finding it difficult to make long journeys,' said Stargrief.

'I hope I'll live to enjoy such difficulties,' Wulfgar said.

'A long life doesn't necessarily mean happiness,' said Stargrief.

'Ashmere would disagree.'

'It was a good, clean death.'

'Always death – good, bad, Tod's will, the wire, the gin, a blast from a gun. We accept and die, or run and cringe. It isn't a hunter's philosophy.'

'The world has changed since Tod's day. It belongs to Man.'

'But we aren't stupid.'

'So what do you suggest?'

'I don't know,' Wulfgar said. 'I only know we accept too much as inevitable.'

Stargrief nodded and extended his forelegs in a luxurious stretch. A sunny morning broke though the river mist. The silver-green tufts of thread moss were stiff and cold between the animals' toes. Both foxes sniffed the air that smelt faintly of running water, furze and sheep, as clouds swept across the open moor bringing a flood of darkness.

'I think I ought to go back to the clitter and the ponds,' Wulfgar said.

'You're asking for trouble,' Stargrief said.

'If the trapper sees I'm not around he'll start looking elsewhere. You know what he's like. And Teg's in no condition to run or do anything.'

'How long will you be gone?'

'A couple of sunsets.'

'I could provide the odd rabbit or a nestful of field-mice if Teg would accept such gifts from a worn-out old dog.'

Wulfgar smiled and nodded.

'The state I'm in,' Stargrief continued, 'she'll probably have to look after me.'

Under Broad Barrow he found Thornblood and Briarspur trailing a sickly pony foal. The mare kept nudging the little creature with her nose, snuffling gently, but the foal carried the heaviness of death and could not be roused. Every so often its mother showed her teeth and charged the foxes who separated and waited patiently for her anger to subside. The murky start to the day suited the occasion. Hail fell and rattled off the bare hillside. The foxes bowed their heads and let the squall wash over them.

'So it was Ashmere's turn,' Thornblood said rhetorically.

Wulfgar squinted at him while the hailstones beat a sharp tattoo on his skull.

'That bloody lurcher's as hard to shake off as the Itching Sickness,' said Briarspur.

The shower passed and the sky above Hay Tor brightened. A shimmering flock of rooks lifted from Natsworthy Spinney and fell and rose again. The foxes turned as one and stared into the valley. Their movements were unhurried, for they knew that once the oaks were in bud the hounds would not come to the moors. The hunting season on Dartmoor was over and the riders who had whooped and spurred their way across the wilderness were now preparing for the point-to-point races. Pheasants, partridges, grouse and foxes were safe from all save the poachers' guns.

'How long have you been following this scent?' Wulfgar asked when they had finished reading the wind.

'Two sunrises,' Briarspur said. 'It should have dropped ages ago.'

He placed his nose briefly on a hailstone and regarded Wulfgar from the corner of his eye.

'I'll join you at sundown,' the dark fox said.

He ran through the cuckoo pints and ramson that carpeted the floor of the spinney. Once he was alone it was possible to absorb Mind-self in Body-self so that no thoughts raced ahead of the moment. The soft yellow blaze of hazel catkins lit the trees as they roared and danced. Many branches had been ripped and broken by the equinoctial gales. Stormbully and Fallbright rode the turbulence high above the valley, but they saw Wulfgar leave the hazels and ashes and marked his progress up the steeps to Honeybag Tor.

At Hedge Barton a sparrowhawk snatched a cock chaffinch from the bramble thicket behind the great barn. The little bird screamed in the predator's talons and a rook came flapping out of the treetops cawing loudly to taunt the hawk. For a hundred beats of the chaffinch's heart, rook and sparrow hawk jostled each other in mid-air. Then the sky overhead was suddenly black with rooks who continually stooped on the hawk until the songbird was released.

Wulfgar lingered on the edge of the brambles in case there were any casualties. The wind in the beech trees sounded like a giant blowlamp.

He trotted in the lee of the wall down to Swallerton Gate. Between the clouds over Hay Tor there were rich seams of silver that broadened as Wulfgar skirted the cottage and came stealthily to the roadside. The grassy verge and the road were alive with toads who had been treading ancestral paths all through the night, seeking the Leighon Ponds. Some mysterious force had guided them across the darkness with no visible landmark to give them bearings. But foxes do not eat toads and there was nothing excitable in their actions to rouse Wulfgar's killing lust. He went up the slope of furze and heather to the tor that cut the sky raggedly at the base.

Scoble had wasted a good hour casting March Browns across the shallows where the Becca ran into the Leighon Ponds. Moodily he squatted among the alders while the wind thumped the water and bent the reeds. It was an impossible day for fly fishing but between gusts down in the valley bottom there were periods of tranquillity. At such times the bailiff busied around the salmon pools and left the open stretches to poachers of genius. Scoble knew of easier ways to land a feed of trout but fly fishing was his passion. He had no diffi-culty in exchanging fish for whisky or petrol coupons. When he had finished he would hide the tackle and collect it after dark.

Sitting on a fallen tree the trapper considered the situ-ation. Fish were rising and feeding but March Browns were not doing the job. He picked at his wart and drew his eyebrows together in a frown. The unlit Woodbine had stuck to the sensitive tissue of his lower lip and had to be freed with the tip of his tongue. Swearing softly he put a match to the cigarette and began to tie on a nymph. His big fingers were surprisingly nimble as they knotted the silk. The cigarette smoke stung his eyes, and he pawed at them and blinked. Then he glanced up and waited for the landscape to settle back into clarity.

Among the birch trees at the water's edge on the far side of the brook stood the big dark fox. Scoble froze and let out his breath in a shuddering sigh of excitement. His stomach heaved and quaked with a sensation akin to lovesickness.

Wulfgar did not flinch. His nose had already told him the lurcher was absent, although the taint of the trapper filled his nostrils. He lifted his head slightly and decoded the wind's other messages. Scoble could not take his eyes off him. The fox seemed to grow larger and brighter like an image on a negative. Then something clicked in Scoble's mind and the lantern slide dropped neatly into place: field-corner, groundsel, ladies' smocks, tall grass, brambles – everything starkly white and the phosphorescent carcass of the mule teeming with foxes where light dilated and contracted.

'You black devil,' Scoble roared, but the rifle in his hand turned into a fishing rod and he was staring across the river while the thunder of heavy artillery receded into a past that refused to die. Wulfgar had gone, but when the trapper came to the mud under the birches he found the oval spoor.

'Good, good,' he said. The words were forced through clenched teeth.

A toad hopped over his boot and sat looking up at him like a dog. Scoble inhaled deeply and teased his wart with a fingernail. Nausea welled up in his guts. Other toads were emerging from the grass and plopping into the water. Down by the dam at the Hound

Tor end of the ponds Scrag the heron was filling his crop with them. The trapper shivered and tugged the collar of his greatcoat up round his ears.

Dusk stooped swiftly as it does in early spring, but an illusion of sunlight remained in the smudges of sulphur tuft fungus on the rowan stump close to the dead foal. The mare lay beside the little body and licked it and nudged it with her nose. Sometimes she spoke to it softly from the depths of her love. The hard fact of death had not registered in her simple brain, but the three foxes sitting on the boundaries of her grief had attended such rituals before.

EARLY SPRING

Bert Yabsley grinned and said, 'I saw 'em with my own eyes – two red ones and Old Blackie. They was fierce enough to scare off the mare and pull down the foal.'

The farmer folded his arms on the bar and gazed pensively into his Guinness. He was a small, honest little man with a nose like a partridge's beak and bow legs encased to the knees in polished gaiters.

'I've never heard of 'em hunting in packs,' he said.

'It's that black sod,' said Scoble. 'He's more wolf than fox.'

'Dang me if you idn right, Len,' Yabsley agreed. 'I came up on 'em smartish and gave 'em both barrels but they was away through that furze like a dose of salts. Then Old Blackie trots back as bold as brass and gives me that cold-blooded stare – the "gull-eye" my missus calls it – and I'm buggered if I didn go all goosepimply.'

Farmer Lugg sipped his Guinness and smiled.

'You should have used a silver bullet, Bert,' he said.

'That's as maybe,' Scoble said. 'But he got your ewe and a brace of lambs.'

His pale eyes remained expressionless while the smoke-yellowed tip of a forefinger rolled the wart on his cheek. Lugg nodded and the humour left his face as the corners of his mouth dropped.

'It didn look like no fox job,' he said. ''Twas messy. Foxes kill neat, and they usually chew the heads off lambs.'

'I told 'ee, maister,' Scoble said quietly. 'That fox is different. My Jacko disturbed him and the two had a scrap. You've seen the dog chomp foxes before but he met his match in Blackie. Look at his leg – look, to the bloody bone that is.'

'We'd best sit in the corner out the way,' said the farmer.

Bert Yabsley called his dogs to heel and transferred his tankard to the table under the window. His face was redder than Scoble's but there was a cheerfulness too that went well with his Falstaffian appearance. When he was not labouring for Farmer Lugg he dug out badgers and stopped earths. Throughout that part of the moor he was acclaimed as a great liar – 'thicky girt romancer' the locals called him. Yabsley told lies as easily and with as much relish as mediocre men tell dirty jokes. A good, heavily embroidered untruth flushed from his mouth brightened the dull lives of his drinking companions.

But the big, bluff public bar jester did not have to 'romance' about his terriers. They were called Billy, Tacker and Jan, and they were the bravest Jack Russells on Dartmoor. Tacker was the star performer. Once he had taken a chin-grip on a big dog or a fox, he was hell to dislodge. Jacko hated him, for the terrier had made the lurcher yelp many a time.

'I got 'im from a gypo at Ashburton Pony Fair,' Yabsley said, crumpling one of Tacker's ears gently in a huge fist.

''Im and your Jacko idn exactly bosom pals, Len.'

Scoble frowned and swallowed half a pint of scrumpy.

'Blackie's back round Holwell Clitter,' he said slowly, like a man surfacing from some dark thought.

'Then us will have to get 'im out,' said Yabsley.

'No terrier has ever got a fox out of that clitter,' the farmer said. The Jack Russells sniffed at the soles of his boots and Jan cocked a leg against Scoble's wellington.

'Tacker could winkle a mouse out of a woodpile,' Yabsley said. He made a soft, smacking sound with his lips and Jan came running to receive the caresses.

'I've seen 'im work clitters the wind couldn't get through. He's had a fox belting round like a fart in a collander. Dang me if that poor beast didn die of giddiness!'

'Holwell Clitter's as tangled as a cow's guts,' the farmer said. He glanced over his shoulder and lowered his voice.

'Emsworthy Gate before daybreak on Saturday and for Christ's sake keep your trap shut, Bert. I idn going to be too popular with the hunting folk if they gets to hear about this shoot.'

'They don't have sheep to worry about,' said Scoble. 'Foxes idn no better than rats. If I had my way I'd shoot the bloody lot.'

'You can't trap 'em, then?' said Lugg.

'If I tilled gins at Holwell the toffs would have my guts for garters.'

'If they had a living to make they woudn be so keen to do it by the book,' Yabsley said.

Farmer Lugg blew his nose.

'You're wrong, boy,' he said. 'Gentry always does it by the book. It's bred into 'em.'

'And I idn sorry,' Yabsley laughed, picking up Tacker and crushing a kiss on the dog's head.

Scoble lidded his eyes like a tired bantam and stared at him through the lashes.

'There's nort better than a lady's arse filling a nice tight pair of jodphurs,' Yabsley went on.

His hand traced the shape of an invisible buttock in the air before him.

'I idn surprised you're the father of eight kids,' Farmer Lugg said wrily.

'Soon it'll be nine,' Yabsley roared. 'Joan's expectin' again.'

Wulfgar took pleasure in the loneliness of bog and tor. It was satisfactory to think of Teg waiting for him under the oaks, by the river, although at times the sadness in her voice as she questioned him about the night's hunting made him feel guilty. But with the lengthening of the shadows he went eagerly to the rabbit runs. The realisation that he was a traveller shuttling between two lives added to the inner conflict.

Once or twice he kennelled elsewhere. Brush laid across nose encouraged reverie. He would spend half the night lying close to the stars, not quite wide awake, letting the dreams run their course. What if Teg had become a convenience and was no longer a necessity? Full of self-hatred he dismissed the thought.

'I love Teg.' He spoke calmly. Blurred with trees the horizon squirmed in a tear, broke free and stood breathless again. He fumbled blindly along the thread of clan instinct. Beyond the screech and wail of owls was the half-heard whisper of dead foxes. The tor drifted somewhere between ideas but the distance was swelling into a shout of shapes.

'I am here,' Wulfgar said. The wind lifts my fur. I am printed on the mists of gone-forever seasons, like Tod.

Only in the absence of other foxes do pure thoughts fly from the heart. Stream, heather, sky – to soothe all pain. I drink the sky.'

And floating there close to sleep he saw the vision.

The mountain tops were snowy, and white rivers poured swiftly into lakes fringed with oak and pine. Rabbits were eating seaweed among red deer, hares and wild goats on the shore. The rabbits were as numerous as autumn leaves under beech trees, and their warm, delicious smell clung to the breeze.

He told Stargrief of the experience the next day. The ancient dog fox had taken to kennelling permanently on a mossy ledge near the top of Longford Tor.

'Yes,' he said. 'That sounds like a vision.'

'But what does it mean?'

'I don't know – but you'll find out when Tod wants you to.'

'Have you had many visions, Stargrief?'

'A few; nothing grand. Small visions, I suppose. I even had a vision with you in it once – long before you were born.'

'Tell me about it.'

'There isn't much to tell. It was always the same – the dark fox running before a whole pack of foxes over countryside no moorland dog or vixen has ever visited. I saw the high tors covered with snow.'

'And did you feel the happiness?'

'Yes.'

The hills were hardening in sunlight and all down the valley the grass glinted. The morning air was keen but the purity of light meant real spring. By the powder mill the fields were as bright and green as a fox's eye.

'Teg must be very close to having the cubs,' Stargrief continued. 'What you did by the ponds was good for your family, but men are sure to come to the home-lands. Many foxes will die.'

'The clever ones will survive.'

'Of course. It has always been so. You seem to be finding it easier to accept Tod's will.'

'Listen,' Wulfgar said hotly. 'I had a vision of a good place but I didn't see myself as some latter-day Tod sorting out the clan's problems with a flick of my brush.'

They made scats together and pretended the conversation had not occurred.

Larks were singing when Wulfgar came to Sherberton, and mist in shapes like strange animals passed low over the moors. From the brambles that hedged the larch plantation fresh buds had erupted, and in the coombs by Hexworthy children were plucking lambs' tails off the hazels.

Tiny leaves had hidden Swart's nest in Crow Thorn and pink apple buds softened the walled gardens of Holne.

He ate St George's mushrooms on the turf where the sheep had been. Then the gleaming path fell through

97

dark masses of furze and whortleberry and the mist was swirling away.

'Teg,' he said, like a creature addressing a ghost.

A jay spread its blunt wings and jumped into the sky. Pollen drifted down through the hazel branches.

'Fox-ox-ox-ox-ox-ox,' the jay screeched.

'Idiot bird,' said Wulfgar. He shook himself and clenched his teeth on a flea that had been living dangerously in his chest fur. The jay's manic cry doused him like cold water. He returned to the moment and used his nose to fathom the mysteries of the morning air.

Rabbits were squatting close to the ground or sitting on their hindlegs watching him. Among the hawthorn roots were many runs and burrows, and the turf all around was beaded with droppings.

Wulfgar walked in a circle and rose on his hindlegs and began the rabbit-stalking ritual …

'Aren't you hungry?' he said, nudging the carcass towards her with his nose.

'No I'm not,' she snapped irritably.

The damp, earthy smell of underground mingled with her own strong scent and the less attractive odours of decaying flesh. Teg shifted restlessly about the den, scratching first in one corner then the other. When he came near her she lifted her back and showed her teeth in a savage snarl.

'What is it?' he said.

Anger flashed in her eyes and while she continued to turn and twist like an animal with worms, Wulfgar dragged the rabbit carcass to his corner and began to skin it. A little light filtered through the roof boulders.

'Come on – move,' Teg growled.

Wulfgar's hackles rose.

'Move,' Teg said. She was puffed out with unmistakable rage.

'And don't look so surprised. Maybe you'll end up like Stargrief delivering prophetic incantations to daft dogs, but this is real fox stuff.'

She drove her muzzle into his haunches and he could feel her whole body quivering. Clamping his jaws on the rabbit he shuffled to the far side of the den and ate quietly, keeping his thoughts to himself. With a couple of pounds of red meat in his belly it was easy to sleep.

Across his dream the blackthorn squeaked. Swart sat on the top branch opening and closing his wings. He was very black against the dark sky and there was something else in the spiky black tangle of twigs and boughs – something blacker than the crow. Then a terrible mouth was gaping like a gin trap and the thorns kept on squeaking and wailing in the wind that had no other voice. Thin and insistent the squeaking followed him into consciousness. He opened his eyes and shivered. The squeaking sounded too real to be the shard of a dream. He moistened his nose with his tongue. The squeaking smelt of newly minted life.

'We have four cubs,' Teg murmured. 'I'm sorry I was so bad-tempered. I just couldn't think of anything except giving birth to these.'

The blind cubs whimpered faintly and Teg licked away the birth-membrane from their fur and nostrils. The licking not only sent the blood flowing briskly through the tiny creatures but made them aware of their mother and her love. Wulfgar watched silently from the warmth of his own feelings.

After the grooming Teg tucked the cubs under her body and laid her chin on her forepaw.

'Is there any rabbit left?' she whispered.

'No, but lie still and I'll see what I can get.'

'You won't have to go far,' she said. 'I've buried some lamb under the stone by the entrance.'

She greedied on the scraps he brought her. Every now and then a cub squeaked and was silenced with gentle licking.

'The cubs are our love, Wulfgar,' she said drowsily.

'My spirit and your spirit,' he said.

'Stargrief shall name them. I'm too full of them to do it sensibly.'

Teg breathed a score of ridiculous endearments onto the tangle of little bodies that lay beneath her. She called the cubs her catkins, her morning dew, her primrose buds, and names silly enough to make Wulfgar grin.

On the ridge above Wistman's Wood he sniffed out the old dog fox. The sunlight of late afternoon lit the abutments of Longford Tor and a contented flock of ewes and lambs grazed the slopes of Beardown Tors. High over the North Moor a kestrel was taking winged insects in flight.

Wulfgar said, 'Three little dogs and a vixen. She had the lot while I slept.'

'A healthy litter?'

'I suppose so – yes, or Teg would have said.'

The dog foxes decoded the calm air and walked south to the scattered boulders of Littaford Tors.

'She'd like you to name them,' Wulfgar said.

'Only if I can hunt with you tonight,' Stargrief smiled.

'Where?'

'At the larch wood by Little Two Rivers.'

They crossed the road swiftly and trotted over marshy land to the foot of Laughter Tor. The pearly haze of day's end had given way to twilight and a single star hung low in the sky.

'The dog cubs shall be known as Oakwhelp, Nightfrond and Brookcelt,' said Stargrief. 'I name the newborn vixen Dusksilver. May Tod keep them safe.'

The western sky remained bright for a long time. Grass and whortleberry leaf glinted on the steeps that took them down to the larch plantation of Brimpts beside the East Dart. Four crows flapped noiselessly over the treetops and vanished as the foxes paused to examine the wind.

'An omen?' Wulfgar said in a strange bloodless voice.

'Why should it be?' said Stargrief. 'It's only your anxiety for Teg and the cubs that makes you see doom everywhere you look. Four crows, four blackthorn trees, four frogs crushed on the road – you could go on for ever reading runes in this and that.'

But his words lacked sincerity.

Creeping through the wild blackberries on the borders of the plantation Wulfgar felt fear performing its cold, colic tricks in his stomach. 'Stargrief is right,' he thought. 'I'm acting like an old vixen.' He recalled his father who after being caught in a snare could think of nothing else but snares for the rest of his life. The sick fox saw wires all around him but he did not see the car that flattened him to the tarmac. 'No,' Wulfgar thought. 'I won't let a pack of stupid worries drive me to madness.'

He rounded his nostrils and took the measure of the shadows that reached out for him.

STARGRIEF

Vega twinkled in the tawny owl's eyes and minute noises scratched the darkness. Insects ticked against leaves and stems; earthworms came slowly out of their burrows with a whisper of tiny bristles. Little escaped the ears of Wulfgar and Stargrief.

They dug out a nest of young rabbits and ate their fill. River song crept up through the trees, and the tawny owl looked out upon the universe from his perch in the larch. Gemini and Orion added their soft fire to the glow of the western sky.

Wulfgar gave a bark of joy.

'There's something of the wolf in you,' said Stargrief. 'You are well named.'

'No, you're wrong,' said Wulfgar. 'I'm all fox. I snatch at the meat the wind brings me. I nose out mysteries.'

In the half-dark he saw the glitter of Stargrief's teeth as the old fox grinned.

'What if there's no such thing as fate?' Wulfgar went on. 'What if there's only a life to lead?'

'It would make a mockery of your visions,' said Stargrief.

Wulfgar sighed.

'What song does the wind sing when I'm not here?' he said.

'Tod alone knows such things.'

'Isn't it wrong to keep on using Tod as a refuge and an excuse? Shouldn't we shape our own destinies without appealing to a lost age – to a fox with our dreams in his veins instead of blood? We say Tod wants this and Tod wants that, but how do we know? And is it important? We are here, now, under these trees.'

'Tod is as real as the trees. The heart has eyes.'

'But don't you understand,' Wulfgar said. 'If there is a Star Place for us there must be a Star Place for rabbits and everything else including Man.'

A breeze stirred the tree tops.

'You look back to the First Dusk, Wulfgar,' Stargrief said. 'But I look further, into the Great Night from which Tod came. There are truths beyond truths.'

'Does my ignorance and conceit upset you?'

'No. Curiosity isn't vanity. In my thirst for knowledge I was very much like you.'

'I'm a cub in your presence.'

'I've been through a lot of seasons,' Stargrief smiled. 'The wisdom of Tod is hard earnt.'

'But the unanswered questions – '

'We can't know everything. If we lived for as many summers as we have enjoyed sunsets we would still have a river to drink dry. But cheer up. Birth and death always make us look beyond self for things to illumine the experience.'

They parted company at Stargrief's suggestion. Wulfgar did not ask the old dog fox where he was going but he guessed and it made him uneasy. Then he thought of Teg and the thought was liquid sunshine in his belly.

He returned along the West Dart at moonrise. The stars had lost the gem-like brilliance of winter and did not shine in great clusters. On the slope above Dunnabridge Farm he came out of the scrub oak and saw the ponies standing perfectly still where the river mist had risen. They were very big in the soft tranquillity, adding their breath to the crumbling greyness; and if it had not been for the slow rise and fall of their flanks they could have been mistaken for statues. Wulfgar passed among them carefully for he sensed their reverence. Even the wind had died to a hush. All the animals were staring up at the horizon, to the dark curve of the earth and the swelling brightness above it. A huge moon rolled into view and silver ponies stood motionless like pilgrims at a shrine waiting for a miracle.

Wulfgar ran over the dewy moors full of the beauty of the night.

In the rick-yard at Prince Hall he discovered roosting fowls and snatched a plump Rhode Island Red before it could squawk. The gut-constricting scent of the bird had him wild with excitement but it was a gift for Teg and he would rather have died of starvation than eat it.

Lapwings sprang from the darkness and their sad cries pursued him to the Moretonhampstead-Tavistock road.

Meanwhile Stargrief was trotting in the opposite direction. He was recalling his own cubhood as he approached Runnage Bridge on the Walla Brook and the collie bitch took him by surprise. Like most farm dogs Queenie had been brought up to hate foxes. Two springs before she had worked the flocks of Swincombe Farm but had always shown a preference for a wilder life. Her habit of wandering off for days, even weeks, had not alarmed her master. Then one morning she had met and mated with a stray mongrel and never returned to the farm. The mongrel had been shot for sheep-worrying but Queenie survived and lived as her ancestors had done before Man claimed them for servants.

Crashing through the reeds the border collie flung herself at Stargrief but he rolled on his side and under her. The animals squared up to each other. Stargrief puffed out his fur and swished his brush while his blood stiffened the hackles on his back. The cold fire of moonlight danced about him and stars splintered his eyes with diamond points and twinkled on his fangs.

Queenie had chased a few foxes in her time but she had never been confronted by one who seemed totally fearless. Her growling lacked conviction and she had difficulty in lifting her own hackles. She froze on stiff legs and tried to pretend she was not afraid of lighting the fuse of Stargrief's ferocity.

The blood banged against her eyes and she swallowed noisily.

'I am Stargrief,' the fox said, speaking the simple canidae argot. 'If this is your hunting ground I'll go. Fox don't want to fight dog.'

'Maybe you go. Maybe you stay,' Queenie said slyly. 'Maybe Queenie kill you.'

'Maybe Queenie grow wings and fly,' Stargrief grinned. 'Maybe Stargrief rip off one of Queenie's ears.'

'You're too bloody small to do that.'

'And you're too wise to chance it. Let me pass.'

'Maybe.'

Stargrief squatted close to the ground and shook his head.

'Look, Queenie,' he said. 'You don't belong to Man any more. Why do bad things that Man taught you? There's plenty of room on the moors for dog and fox. Plenty of rabbits. Plenty of mice. Plenty of birds.'

'True.' Queenie sank on her rump and twisted in a vain attempt to lick a place on the nape of her neck.

'Are you hurt?' said Stargrief.

'Bloody barbed wire. Big cut but I can't get at it.'

'Let me.'

'How do I know you won't go for me throat?'

'What good would it do me? I don't eat dogs.'

'OK, then, but Queenie ain't slow. If you play foxy tricks I'll have your throat out before you can blink.'

The cut was deep and festering. Queenie bowed her head and Stargrief gently licked away until the wound was open and clean and the swelling had gone down.

'I'm sorry I gave you a bad time,' the collie bitch said. 'You're a good animal. Queenie will never forget. You and your tribe can use my hunting ground any time. Are we friends?'

They stood nose to nose for a moment.

'Friends,' Stargrief said. 'Now I go. Man is coming to my homelands to kill foxes. Stargrief must warn all.'

'Man no bloody good,' said Queenie. 'Man killed my mate. Man took my puppies away. No bloody good.'

The old fox reached Leighon Woods with a few hours of darkness left. There was a lot of snuffling and grunting at the mouth of Thorgil's sett. The great one-eyed boar greeted the fox amicably.

'Have men been around with dogs and guns?' Stargrief said. The badger said they had not.

'They will come,' said Stargrief. 'The lurcher killed a sheep and some lambs. We will be blamed for it.'

'It always happens when we have young,' said the sow.

'No matter,' Thorgil said gruffly. 'The terrier that can get me out of the heart of my sett hasn't been born yet.'

'Have you any lodgers?' asked Stargrief.

'Foxes? Only one. I think it's Wendel.'

'Will you let him stay?'

'Does Wulfgar wish it?'

'Yes.'

'Well, there's room – so long as he does as he's told.'

Stargrief ran on, visiting the earths and clitters around Hay Tor, taking in a wide circle of moorland and in-country. But one vixen with cubs refused to move. She was called Redbriar and her stubbornness was well known among the clan dogs. Her mate had been killed by the hounds on the last hunt of the season. The earth was on a tree-clad hillside in Crownley Parks.

'When are the men coming?' she said, looking down her muzzle at him.

'Today, tomorrow – three sunrises from now; does it matter? I'll help you carry the little ones to a safer place further south.'

'And what if they decide to visit that "safe place" instead of my earth?'

'They never have in the past. It is the trapper. He is as much a creature of habit as the hare and the badger.'

'I suppose the runes told you,' she sneered.

'Surviving for eight summers tells me.'

She would not be persuaded and Stargrief was too tired to argue at length. He dragged himself to the top of the hill and kennelled under a holly tree. He was asleep almost before his eyelids shut out the world.

ALMOST A FOX SHOOT

Things went wrong from the start.

Yabsley arrived at Emsworthy with the sun, and his mates who had been standing around for nearly an hour were not amused.

'It'd be easier to separate a wasp from jam than to lever your butt off the mattress,' said Farmer Lugg.

'My missus is a heller for her oats,' Yabsley grinned. 'I got to sneak out of bed mornings, maister, or her would have me at it all day.'

'We come to shoot foxes not to jaw,' said Scoble.

'A few minutes either way idn goin' to matter, Len. Foxes don't carry watches.'

Scoble lit a cigarette and his eyelids slowly descended. Leather cut into his hand as Jacko strained at the leash. The lurcher whined and glared at the terriers who were inspecting Farmer Lugg's border collie.

'Right then,' the farmer said. 'Let's make a start. Better late than never.'

Scoble was already striding down the hillside with his twelve-bore on his shoulder.

'Miserable bugger,' Yabsley said under his breath.

A cock pheasant whirred up from the bracken and the iridescent head shone against the sky. The crash of Yabsley's shotgun sent flat echoes skipping across the valley.

'Are you mazed?' cried Farmer Lugg. 'You've told every bloody fox this side of Widecombe we're coming. One day they'll have 'ee certified, Yabsley. You idn sixteen ounces. There's more sense in a cowpat than you've got between your ears.'

'But old pheasant didn know that, did he?' Yabsley said gleefully.

He hoisted the bird aloft by its feet and swung it round his head. Scoble was speechless, and all he could do was screw a forefinger viciously into his temple and spit.

'Don't fret, Len,' Yabsley bawled. 'You can have the foxes and I'll make do with these little beauties.'

The sun vanished behind a cloud and a shower fell. Then it passed and the last raindrops glittered down. A rainbow arched over Leighon, and along the edge of Seven Lords Lands the fence posts were steaming.

They put Tacker in Holwell Clitter. The terrier went down on all fours and squeezed under the stone that blocked the crevice. Urged on by the men, he explored the maze of runs and galleries to the centre of the clitter. A muffled yapping marked his progress. He met fox smell and bolted a few rabbits that were shot, but eventually he had to admit defeat. Some of the passages ran far underground into blackness and from their depths came the ghostly chittering of stoats and weasels.

Every so often Tacker nosed through a warm pocket of air heavy with the reek of mustelid. The stoats mocked him as they flowed in and out of the boulders.

'Coo-ee … cooo-eee … Over here, dog. No, not there – here, stupid. Yoo-hoo … I see you-oo. Stoaties chew out dog's liver, yiss – snik-snak! Dog crazy to come alone into Stoatland. Get out. Get out, crow's guts, or you'll stay here forever.'

Tiny pointed fangs nipped his hindlegs and he yelped, but the narrowness of the tunnel stopped him turning. Above him was a small aperture, and scrabbling furiously he shot out of it into the sunlight and stood panting on a boulder.

'I bet there's half a dozen foxes lying up in this place,' said Scoble. 'Your terrier idn all that smart, boy, or he'd have 'em out by now. He's a bit like you, Bert – all wind and pee.'

'Get home, do!' said Yabsley. 'If a fox was in there Tacker would have flushed 'im out. Tacker's flushed more foxes than you've had hot dinners.'

'If some daft bugger hadn let off his gun there'd be a few foxes round here to shoot,' Farmer Lugg said.

'They usually goes to ground when they'm scared,' said Scoble. 'It idn right for the clitter to be empty.' He fingered his wart and frowned.

'Still us have got a couple of brace of rabbits,' Yabsley said.

'Rabbits don't kill sheep,' Scoble grated.

'Big ones might,' said Yabsley, shaking with laughter.

Scoble showed him a saturnine face and marched off towards Leighon Woods.

The terriers were let loose in Thorgil's sett but found the way to the chamber where the sow and cubs lay blocked by the boar. The passage was wide enough for two dogs to attack at the same time. Thorgil was not impressed. Bristling and growling he bowled Billy over and crunched Jan's left forefoot like a hazel nut.

The terrier bitch squealed and struggled to reverse past Tacker. Thorgil thundered into them. His jaws snapped shut and locked on Billy's stump of a tail. The dog let out a howl of agony as the badger's teeth severed a part of him that had never been his noblest attribute. Jan and Billy collided with Tacker and their panic filtered through the rocks to the men above.

'Fox?' said Yabsley.

'Badger,' said Scoble.

'Where's Old Blackie to, Len?' Yabsley said with a wink. 'Here, that fox is leadin' you a bit of a dance, boy. Dang me if he idn.'

Scoble stared through him into the past and kept quiet.

'Tidn natural,' Farmer Lugg said. He wedged himself between Yabsley and the passenger door of Scoble's van. 'Not one bloody fox. Last year us were shootin' them in job lots.'

'There's still the woods round Bagtor,' said Scoble in his frosty voice.

'Not for me,' said Yabsley. 'Drop us at Halshanger Cross. My little dogs need the vet.'

'I'd have the sods put down,' Scoble said. 'They idn up to much.'

'Careful I don't put you down, Scoble,' Yabsley said.

He knotted his handkerchief on Billy's bleeding stump, while Jan whimpered softly from the back of the vehicle.

'Soddin' old badger,' Yabsley growled. 'If I had a stick of dynamite I'd blast 'im out.'

He fixed his eyes on Jacko and said, 'Does that tripe hound do anything else other than whine and piddle?'

Scoble was too wise to bite ...

The trapper and his dog came alone to Crownley Parks. Lugg had departed in disgust with Yabsley, the farmer trying to be philosophical. If they had not seen a fox there were no foxes about and his lambs were safe. It was an opinion Scoble did not share, for he had a feeling

the foxes were one jump ahead of him. The hair stiffened on the back of his neck. They had never behaved
like this before. Blackie was responsible – he had to be.

'You're a sly old boy,' Scoble murmured.

Stargrief heard the van pull up on the bridge over the
River Lemon and within seconds his nostrils were full of
the smell of oil and petrol, gun metal, trapper and lurcher.
He hurried down the hillside into the earth. Redbriar
bared her teeth and snarled at him, but there was an
urgency about the old dog fox that could not be ignored.

'How many cubs?' Stargrief said. 'Quickly – the trapper is coming and Tod help you if his lurcher gets in here.'

'Three,' Redbriar said. 'But what – '

'One each and hurry,' Stargrief snapped. 'I'll come
back for the third. Follow me.'

He grabbed the nearest cub by the scruff of the neck
with his teeth and darted outside.

The foxes ran through the beech trees to the narrow
road. Stargrief crossed it in four strides and wriggled through the hedge. The cub squeaked as a twig
scratched its nose. Stargrief tightened his grip and trotted down the slope behind a derelict cottage. He could
hear the river surging past the mill on the other side of
the clearing. Lowering his head he dropped his cub.

Dog and vixen were standing under an ash tree that
was growing outwards at an angle of forty-five degrees
from the bank.

'Now what?' Redbriar said breathlessly.

'Do exactly as I do,' said Stargrief.

He gathered up the cub again and climbed the tree, running up the bark like a squirrel, until he reached a great branch about eight feet from the ground. The branch shot out horizontally over the cottage roof. Stargrief walked along it and jumped onto the thatch, then he scrambled to the top of the roof and vanished down the other side.

Redbriar found him squatting between the thatch and the chimney.

'Wait here and keep them quiet,' Stargrief said.

'The cub is called Gorseflame,' said Redbriar.

The journey back to the earth seemed to take a long time, but Stargrief was in and out of the bolt-hole before Swart could spread his wings a dozen times. The crow flapped through the tree tops and said 'craark-craark'. He had seen the man and the dog creeping up through the ramsons and ash saplings. A little earlier he had been sucking eggs in the nest a thrush had built low in the ivy of a hazel bush.

Scoble dug a fingernail savagely into his wart and drew blood.

'Blackbird, black fox; black bloody day,' he said.

Jacko tugged so hard on the leash he nearly strangled himself.

'Can 'ee smell fox, boy?' Scoble said. 'Go get 'im. Go on – good dog. Good Jacko.'

The lurcher was away like a snipe but he had seen nothing and merely wanted to stretch his long legs. He barked excitedly to con his master and pretended to be on the fox trail. Blindly he smashed through brambles, primroses and ramsons, loving his freedom.

Scoble clenched and unclenched his fists. He reached the earth, smelt the hot stink of fox and for a moment could not catch his breath. There seemed to be a tight steel band round his lungs. He coughed and retched and brought up an oyster of phlegm.

'Soddin' fags,' he wheezed, fishing out his cigarette tin.

The England's Glory match rasped and a whiff of sulphur cancelled out the fox smell. He inhaled deeply and felt better as Jacko trotted out of the trees looking alert and keen.

'Get down the hole, boy,' Scoble said. 'Go on, Jacko – chase 'im out.'

The lurcher stared mindlessly up at him and wagged his tail.

'For Christ's sake!' Scoble snorted.

He gripped the dog's collar and dragged him to the earth.

'In,' he said, planting the toe of his boot in Jacko's rump.

The dog nosed around the passages and yelped and barked to show he was busy. Then he emerged wearing a morose expression and slunk up to Scoble.

'It don't matter, boy,' the trapper said. He crouched and ruffled Jacko's fur.

'There was a fox in here and that's certain sure.'

He shifted the scats with a stem of dead bracken and retrieved a scrap of wool from among the beetles' wing cases and the beak of a chaffinch.

'The sod's had a lamb too,' he murmured. 'Well, Jacko, us will till a few gins round here at dimpsey. Yabsley and his lap dogs can go to hell.'

The cigarette end fell from his lips and lay smoking in the primroses.

'If we don't make a noise we're safe,' Stargrief whispered. 'When the man goes I'll take you and the little ones to another earth downstream. It's in a thick wood where men are never seen.'

'Why bother with me?' Redbriar said. 'I've made a fool of myself again. I'm always doing it.'

Stargrief smiled.

'Better a live fool than a brave corpse,' he said. 'Suckle the cubs and rest. We're not in danger. I've used this hiding place before.'

'You look very pleased with yourself,' said Redbriar.

'Do I? Well, we've beaten the trapper and that doesn't happen every day.'

Redbriar grinned and licked his muzzle.

Stargrief suddenly felt an intense sorrow, as though an old wound had opened inside him. For a while the sensation puzzled him, then he realised what it was. He was in love with life of which he had so little left.

A WOODPIGEON CROONING

The wren's mutes splashed white on the fern frond. The little bird dipped through the deepening light of the wood into greenness that had the luminosity of an aquarium. Wulfgar did not raise his head from his outstretched forelegs even when the brimstone came to cling to the nettle. A faint breeze lifted the dust from the butterfly's wings.

Wulfgar cocked an ear and yawned.

A lizard's length from his nose a cuckoo pint was poking out of the ground-ivy and ramsons. The plant's arrowhead leaf had uncurled four sunsets ago to reveal the stiff purple spike of the flower stem. The flowers were at the base, protected by the spathe and ringed with bristles to trap insects. Wulfgar could smell the frail odour of decomposing animal matter given off by the spike to attract flies and tiny beetles. At a signal from the bristles the leaves would shut, holding the victim in a green envelope. Its efforts to escape would lead to the collection of dust from the male flowers and the pollination of the female flowers. When the spathe withered the insect would escape.

In Princetown the children called the cuckoo pints 'Wake Robins' and 'Lords-and-Ladies', but they did not pick them.

The dog fox looked up. Beyond the tree trunks was a close horizon glimpsed through fern fronds and the dark leaves of wild garlic. The pale evening sky was stamped with the outline of hills and tors. It was a soft sky to complement the soft colours of blossoms and flowers. Cockchafers clacked against the ash saplings. It grew darker, and a woodpigeon began to croon from her platform in a solitary fir. Gradually the universe flickered and glowed, and just east of the meridian a curving group of stars bloomed for Tod's glory. The bottom star was pale Regulus. Lower in the sky the constellation of Virgo shone beneath the dim star cluster known as the Hair of Berenice.

Alert for a detailed picture of his Good Place Wulfgar had seen his dreams climb out of the darkness, shaping his joy. For a little while longer he lay staring into the night with the heightened sensibility of the predator. The thin days of winter were forgotten. He stretched and sat up, and his eyes tasted the rabbits feeding on the sward where the wood ended. Their smell was a hot knife turning in his belly – red meat to hold death at bay.

O Teg, he sang from the silence of his thoughts. Your head is a brow of bracken in the autumn. Your body is sweet like the flow of sunset on a gentle hill. He shuddered, recalling the warm part of her from which the fox future issued in blind, mewling cubs. It was not merely the ache that coupling dulled but a choking happiness.

She growled as he entered the den but accepted the young rabbit and made a noisy meal of it.

'Down by the river the night is calm and full of scents,' he said. 'You wouldn't have to be away long and it isn't very far.'

Teg rose and shook the cubs off her nipples. They lay in a quaking mass while she silenced them with her tenderness.

'I would give ten seasons of my life to have a complete set of legs,' she said. 'If anything happened to you we would starve.'

'There's Stargrief,' Wulfgar said. 'He wouldn't neglect you.'

'What about silly little Redbriar?'

'She's taken a more active mate.'

Teg smiled and allowed him to cover her on the star-speckled leaves.

They lingered a long time at the mouth of the earth before departing. Teg moved her head from side to side, testing the wind. Then they dashed into the darkness and shared again the joys of their courtship nights.

The cubs' eyes were open. Large and bright they stared from snub-nosed faces. Their coats were chocolate brown and woolly; their tails short and pointed. Teg fussed over them as if they would perish without constant grooming, and it amused Wulfgar to see them staggering under the force of her busy tongue. All of a sudden they had felt the urge to leave her belly-fur to explore the den, but as fast as they waddled off the vixen retrieved them and let them taste her displeasure.

Wulfgar was rarely permitted to remain in the earth after he had delivered food.

'I'm as servile as a farm dog,' he told Stargrief. 'I bring her a coney and she eats it and turns her back on me.'

'You don't sound too upset,' Stargrief grinned.

'I'm happy for her.'

Morning light was slanting across the valley, falling on the scalloped hawthorn leaves and the broken surface of the river. A sparrowhawk rushed past trailing thin, yellow legs, and larks climbed high on their song. The thrill of the living world hummed through Wulfgar's body.

Things soon lost to the eye remained trapped in a fine mesh of ganglia and the musky scent of gorse filled his mind. All round him the season burgeoned. Whinchats had returned to nest on the railway embankment near Moretonhampstead and a nightingale sang after dark in Yarner Wood. Swifts circled the church tower of Holne and cuckoos spoke above the open heathland.

Several dawns had flared since the sluice at Slapton Ley was clogged with elvers. Spawned in the Sargasso the young eels had drifted on ocean currents for three summers before reaching Devon. Herons trod the shallows and fed well, alongside gulls and waders.

He went alone to Cherrybrook Farm and ate curlew chicks on the boggy ground. At the foot of the dwarf elm in the goyal by the old quarry the leaves were like a mouse's ears.

Golden lichens plugged the cracks and chinks in the wall, and the countryside was the colour of a firecrest. The day had been hot enough to ripple distances, but after sunset the temperature dropped rapidly. Curlews and lapwings fluted across the dusk and he hunted field corners where the rabbit runs were furrows in the dew.

Teg's reluctance to have him around permanently had forced him to bivouac on the west side of Longford Tor. From a couch of whortleberries and ling he could watch over the valley and the earth, but sometimes the purring, bell-like cry of the vixen was almost too much to bear.

During his hilltop vigil he saw Isca the roebuck eating bramble leaves on the edge of Wistman's Wood. The small, red-brown deer crept through the shepherd's crooks of new bracken, curling his black, velvety upper lip to tug the shoots off the tendrils. The doe sat under an oak, her ears flickering and her nostrils opening and closing. She had dropped a stillborn fawn and was still mourning the loss. From a hole in a dead limb of the oak came the soft lisping of infant birds. Eight naked marsh tit nestlings crowded together among the pony hair and down. The hen scolded the deer, crying 'chickabee-bee-bee-bee', and shaking her head with its glossy black cap.

Teg hesitated at the earth's entrance and gathered the scent of roedeer, crow, rabbit, woodpigeon and the myriad vegetable smells of the wood and moorland. The pigeon, who had nested in one of the few rowans that survived amid the oaks, started her song, 'Cooo-coo, coo coo, coo', repeated three times and ending abruptly on a crisp 'coo'.

Teg was satisfied. She led the cubs into the sunshine, and while she suckled them on a mossy boulder, they kicked their back legs as they drew the milk out of their mother. Teg breathed a sigh of contentment and let her tongue dangle. The woodpigeon gazed at her for a moment then eased the nictating film over its eyes.

After the feeding the cubs played the Life Game. They hissed and spat like kittens, grappling each other and rolling over and over in balls until the one underneath squeaked for Teg to release him. The vixen was keenly interested in all they did. She remembered how she had learnt the tricks that had honed her own hunting skills, so she twitched her brush and the cubs pounced on the tag as they would pounce on a fieldmouse.

Wulfgar brought them toys: the skull of a fitch, a grouse's wing, a moth, beetles, dead frogs – things for them to carry around in their mouths or strike with their paws. They brawled over the treasures, playing tug-of-war and pretending to disembowel with a feline raking motion of the hindlegs. Teg answered their cries like a cat greeting its owner and her melodious trilling froze the hair on Wulfgar's back.

He laid a rabbit at her feet.

'There can't be many of these left,' she said cheerfully. 'You must have emptied a warren or two.'

The cubs bustled up to Wulfgar and rubbed against his legs. He touched each one in turn with his nose, for they smelt of Teg, but his stomach did not flood with tenderness as it did when he was close to her. The confusion of the wood seemed an extension of his own confusion. Sunlight felt its way through the massed twigs and branches, settling on the grey-green blister lichens and the yellow lichens, burnishing the luxuri-ant clusters of mosses and wood rush. Everything was tangled and lost within other things: whortleberries and brambles, filmy ferns, honeysuckle, hard ferns, fallen branches, polypody ferns, the carcass of a sheep, spiky tendrils worming into crevices, rock upon rock.

And his mind was in a worse muddle. He tried to concentrate on the Star Place but self-doubt clouded his thoughts. Shamefully he realised he had always been woolly-headed. The stages of reasoning were like stepping stones across a wide river, and he could never progress beyond the seventh. Never. But of one thing he was sure: the beauty of the living world stopped when it reached Man.

Stargrief's hooded eyes made him look very old and tired – a creature closer to death than life. He is already a tenant of the Star Place, Wulfgar thought. One life is enough until you near the end of it. Star Places are born out of despair and bitterness. Despite his love for the ancient dog fox he listened to the Tod Saga with mounting irritation. Stargrief squatted on a fallen tree and said: 'We must follow the Tod Saga in the flow of the seasons. Winter is the moors before Tod. Spring is the birth and re-birth of Tod. Summer is his doghood, and autumn his death and fulfilment.'

Dog and vixen had heard the saga countless times yet never before had it lacked relevance. The cubs were playing hide-and-seek among the boulders close at hand. Brookcelt and Nightfrond fought over a leg of hare and the woodpigeon continued to croon. This is our time and place, thought Wulfgar.

But his doubt had taken a new direction and he lowered his glance and sighed. Teg laughed softly, casting her eyes over the two dog foxes.

Stargrief had read her mind.

'Tod and the Star Place offer hope in a life full of fear and cruelty,' he said. 'If we give ourselves to –'

Teg stopped him with a cold chuckle and said, 'We all know that foxes must suffer and die. It has been so for ages. But I don't care about the Star Place – wherever that is. I'm alive and Tod's got nothing to do with it. He doesn't help, he just complicates things. There is me and Wulfgar and the cubs. Maybe I'll be a golden fox like Tod one night and chase golden rabbits over golden fields; and maybe I won't. I'm not interested in what happens when I'm crowbait. Get on with the Now of life is my motto.'

'And the visions?' Stargrief said wrinkling his nose.

'Visions, dreams, runes – rubbish!' Teg snarled. 'You bright pair have a lot in common with the lurcher.'

'And perhaps you are Redbriar's sister,' said Stargrief.

'O get out of my sight – both of you,' she sneered. 'I need more than sunset sagas to put milk in my paps.'

Wulfgar and Stargrief narrowed their eyes and pretended to find the cubs amusing. Dusksilver balanced on her hindlegs and gave Brookcelt a left hook with her forepaw. She had decided the stoat's skull was her property and carried it around in her mouth. The little dogs had given up trying to steal it off her.

'Cubs can be quite boring,' Wulfgar said one night.

'You must make allowances for Teg's condition,' said Stargrief. 'If she had all four of her legs things would be different.'

'I suppose you're right,' said Wulfgar doubtfully. 'But it's 'Nightfrond this' and 'Oakwhelp that' and 'Did you see Dusksilver with that frog's leg?' As far as she's concerned the moon shines out of their behinds. I'm no more than a glorified guest.'

'You sound as if she's your first vixen.'

'She's the first I've ever cared about. I really need her.'

He nuzzled the blackness that was scribbled over with scents. The hawthorns wrote a rounded script on the horizon, stars were scattered across the sky. The foxes walked over the dark moorland in the lovely silent hours before dawn.

Stargrief was panting when they reached the straggling copse below Beardown Lodge but he managed to jump up without warning to catch a moth in his forepaws. He grinned and crunched the insect like a child eating a sweet.

'Pretty good for a bonebag – hey?' he said.

'I bet it's knocked five sunsets off your life,' Wulfgar said.

The pleasant earthy smell of badger set his nostrils quivering. Perhaps if anything the nights of early May were too rich in scent and he recalled how they used to drive him crazy during the first spring of doghood. More pungent than the badger smell was the tang of freshly killed rabbit.

The foxes sat among the bluebells and watched the feeding badger. He was a young boar by the name of Rootscowl. Although he had fought desperately for a mate he was still a bachelor and this did not help sweeten his temper. Placing a powerful forepaw on the rabbit carcass he lifted his white head and grunted, 'Are you looking for trouble?'

The two black stripes that ran vertically from behind his ears almost to his snout made it difficult to see his eyes.

'That's a lot of coney for a small badger,' said Wulfgar. 'Maybe you'd like to donate it to a better animal.'

Rootscowl showed his teeth in a mustelid snarl and said, 'Try and take it – sheep's fart!'

'Well, let's see if you're as nimble as your wits,' Wulfgar said.

He swaggered up to Rootscowl while Stargrief sought a strategic postion behind the badger.

'Rootscowl idn stupid,' the boar said.

Wulfgar looked down his muzzle at him and smiled. But it was no longer fun. It was fox sport but it wasn't funny. Standing on the slope of bluebells waiting for the inevitable to happen he surrendered to emptiness. Briefly the shapes and sounds of the night ceased to be real. Then Stargrief was charging and the badger was swinging to meet him and there was no need for further thought.

Rootscowl lowered his head and rushed at an enemy who was swerving away into the shadows. The badger grunted and turned, slipping on the crushed white flower stems. Both the fox and the rabbit carcass were gone.

'Rootscowl is stupid,' he groaned.

Luckily there were bluebell bulbs to grub and more esoteric badger pursuits to blunt his disappointment.

'The trapper will come one day,' Wulfgar said.

Beneath the hawthorns and hazels the bluebells rose stiffly from a carpet of dead leaves. Stargrief was close to sleep. They had eaten the rabbit and dropped scats near a scenting post. Now Stargrief surfaced reluctantly from his catnap, sniffing the new day in the east.

'This isn't the trapper's hunting ground,' he yawned.

'He's like us,' said Wulfgar. 'He has our cunning.'

'But he doesn't know Rocky Wood.'

'If he wants me badly enough he'll find it.'

'In all my seasons no man has behaved like this.'

'Old fox, I speak the truth. When the cubs are stronger we will go to the Fastness. A man might die hunting us there.'

Birds awoke and gave voice. To begin with, the crows shook the dew from their feathers with harsh caws, then a robin burst into song followed by a woodpigeon and a blackbird. The cuckoo quickly joined in and as the volume increased a thrush poured out a clean torrent of music.

The foxes curled up side by side and sank into the mystery. The chorus was crescendoing. Wrens, chaffinches and coal tits opened up, but it soon became impossible to identify individual voices.

Stargrief was asleep, muzzle pressed between fore-paws. And in the river valley the mist hung pearl-grey, luminous, motionless.

Much of what the cubs did was instinctive, but important parts of the Life Game had to be learnt from their mother. The vixen asked Wulfgar to bring her a fresh cowpat.

'Beetles live in the cowpat,' she told the cubs. Lactation was finished and she had mixed feelings about the loss of intimacy with her young.

'Beetles are good.'

She turned the pat over and held the insect in her teeth.

'Chomp-chomp! – good. Now you try,'

Brookcelt took a big mouthful of dung and spat it out. His eyes widened, for his mother had never deceived him before.

'Beetles live in the scat.' Teg laughed. 'Beetles very good. Scat very bad.'

'Bad – ulk!' squeaked Brookcelt.

'Beetle,' said Nightfrond. His teeth cracked the insect's carapace.

The vixen had left the earth and was lying-up close by under some roots. She came to the cubs with great caution, her zig-zag approach bringing her into the wind and around the earth in a circle. She was suspicious of everything and would prick her ears to decipher the different bird calls and cover the ground with her nose before entering the earth. Beneath the boulder-jumble the chamber was untidy but not dirty. The floor was littered with bones, the skulls of animals and birds, wings, feathers, scraps of sheepskin and the odd putrified body of mole, shrew and weasel.

Wulfgar's gifts were dropped near her and wordlessly accepted. She broke up the carcasses and the cubs were given the vitamin-rich entrails and gobbets of masticated flesh. But Wulfgar was not content merely to provide. He was the bold warrior chieftain of an outlawed tribe, yet Teg treated him like a ga-ga vixen. The lizard basking on the dead bracken had more dignity.

The stalking exercises were simple and there was no need to teach the cubs to pounce stiff-legged. The rule was: 'Stalk it – don't charge at it'. Guile was the key word. A fox is born with a head full of cunning but it has to be developed.

'It's a waste of time to chase a flying bird,' Teg said. 'Grabbing them from the grass or the hedge is the fox way. A sleeping bird can be shuttled quickly from roost to fox's belly.'

'But it's hard to see a bird in the dark,' said Oakwhelp.

So Teg showed them how to use their noses, how to choose a thread from the web of smells that spread at darkfall.

One evening Wulfgar trotted in with an old Wellington boot from the rickyard at Cherrybrook. The smell of Man covered it like an unpleasant mould.

'Learn this smell, my little primrose buds,' Teg said. 'Learn and never forget. It is the scent of Man, our great enemy, the great killer of foxes. When your nose brings it to you, run, hide, disappear.'

Like most wild creatures foxes are born without the fear of Man.

'They are the Death Creatures, the bogeywolves,' said Teg. 'All animals and birds fear them.'

And Man set snares and tilled gins. Therefore it was necessary to teach the cubs to recognise the smell of the choking-wire and gin-metal.

'I lost my leg in a gin trap,' the vixen said grimly. 'One careless moment and I finished up a cripple. Many foxes die in the metal jaws. It is a bad death.'

At another mealtime she said, 'Never crawl under wire or roots or branches. Man puts his snares in these places. Wherever it is possible jump over or go around. Remember this and live.'

The cubs sat before her in a half-circle while she spoke the deathless words of the clan. The Fox language was sweet on her tongue. Wulfgar lay on his heather terrace high above her and let the music of her voice warm his blood. The days were long and green; the nights magical. He lived the invisible fox life, coming to Teg when the mist was blue-edged; and their talk was low and tender against the quiet chorus of the cubs' breathing. Then the thoughts that belonged to the kennel of old age were lost in her image.

SHADOWS

The hills darkened slowly. Leaves silvered and blurred again, heavily green. A raw wind swept along the valley. He turned into the evening and carefully sorted through the scents. His coat was drenched with a hard shower of rain. All day the showers had fallen, sometimes far-off, slowly, like shifting columns of smoke. Grass shone across hollows and everything smelt of rain. Then the cloud was moving on and the sun returned as the rain hammered down and died away to leave the moors glittering.

He presented the cock grouse to Teg and watched her clipping the wing feathers tight to the flesh. Nosing through the rough heath over Huntington Warren Wulfgar had surprised the chestnut-red bird in its jag amongst the ling. A peregrine had killed its mate on Easter Sunday and the crows had eaten all but one of her eleven eggs. The surviving egg was found by a stoat who rolled it off under her chin to feed her kits.

'I think we should take the cubs away from here, Teg,' Wulfgar said.

She gave him a quick sidelong glance and asked why.

'I've a feeling about the trapper. And I can't forget the crow omens.'

'Stargrief reckons you see too many shadows. Crows are crows – nothing else. I throw a shadow.'

'My gut tells it differently.'

'But we have everything here – a safe den, plenty of food, water, the lot. The cubs are happy.'

'Nevertheless we are moving,' Wulfgar said. His dark, triangular head tilted and his nostrils widened.

'When?'

'At sunset tomorrow.'

'We are not,' Teg said firmly.

'I'm not arguing,' said Wulfgar.

Teg lifted her upper lip and snarled.

'And where are we going?' she said.

'The Fastness.'

'Is that another of your gut feelings?'

'Yes it is.'

'But the cubs aren't old enough or strong enough to make such a long journey.'

'Very well,' Wulfgar said. 'We go seven sunsets from now.'

'It's so daft,' Teg snorted. 'We hardly ever see men around here.'

'You have my final words on the matter, vixen,' Wulfgar said.

'O I shall follow you, great fox. But you are as stubborn as a crotchety old boar badger.'

He smiled and licked her muzzle.

'You should have mated with Wendel,' he said. The darkness inside himself was diminishing.

They went onto the east slopes of the valley, where the wetness of grass and rock was turned to gold by the setting sun. Another shower fell, a swallow skimmed the river. The moors smelt like a living creature, and if they stood still and listened they could hear it breathing. Dog and vixen were content in each other's company. The bond between them could not have been stronger.

Running on the high ground was the perfect thing, for away from the cubs they could melt into the hush and enrich it with their silence. Her lovely form was all raindrop bright. Her hobbling gait on the steeper slopes made his heart lurch, and her sleekness, her beautiful ears, her delicate muzzle lit by the dying sun would haunt him for the rest of his days.

A few sunsets later he sat beside the West Dart while Teg and the cubs were hard at the Life Game. The vixen was hiding a rabbit's foot among the pebbles and encouraging the young ones to sniff it out.

'The thin fox is the fox with an uneducated nose,' she said. Nightfrond placed his muzzle in the river and got an earful of water.

'The river is alive,' laughed Teg. 'But it isn't an animal. You can't bite it, silly.'

The cub gazed into his own reflection and tried to understand. Brookcelt and Dusksilver came galloping up and bowled him over and a tangle of little bodies thrashed about in the shallows. From a grassy hollow between two boulders Oakwhelp turned a deaf ear and chewed the rabbit's foot. He was almost as dark as his father and half the time he had to be coaxed out of his daydreams.

'He's different,' Teg said. 'He's Wulfgar right down to the tips of his claws.'

The cub stretched and yawned, and a faraway look filled his eyes. Yes, Wulfgar thought with a pang, there I am. He flashed across the seasons to the first spring of his life. Shimmering flowers, birds freckling and blotching the sky, the famished way he loved the dusk. Lying under the fresh bramble leaves, his nose among the dog violets, he listened to the steady pulse of his blood. Back there the grasses bent in a thwack of wind but only if he conjured the memory to the front of his mind and excluded everything else. Then he would see the thick, heavy nests of rooks and hear the cawing. A hushed place and Oakwhelp the small liberated ghost of a lost forever cub.

He closed his eyes and floated calmly on the birdsong. He loved fine weather as all creatures do. The evening rushed into his knowing. A buzzard mewled. Oakwhelp dragged himself through the gap in the drystone wall and ran up the fox path to the boulders and trees. His brothers and sisters scampered after him and Teg leapt onto the coping stones for a better view.

'Don't stray,' she barked. 'Go to the earth and wait for me.'

The untroubled landscape faded and left an ache around his heart.

'They're hungry,' Teg said without looking at him.

The hunting-passion nagged away at her like tooth-ache. Soon she would visit the nearby vole runs and perhaps make a kill. But it was never enough. In her private moments she still made lightning rushes on rabbits and lapwings.

'If you were to die,' she said, 'I would die.'

'And what about the cubs?' he said carefully, drag-ging his hindquarters in a slow, stiff-legged stretch.

She dived into the shadows. The buzzard called again and between its keening and the murmur of the river came the low music of the pony fillies calling across the wilderness.

WHEN THE WHIMPERING STOPPED

The Devonport Leat followed one of the lower contours of Beardown Hill up the West Dart to the weir under Longford Tor, and from it a walker could look down into Wistman's Wood. But the blond boy had crawled on hands and knees through the shallow waters of the leat until he reached a spot a hundred feet above the foxes. Parting the reeds with exaggerated care he sucked in his breath and held it for a moment.

Three cubs were squabbling where the river curled narrow and low through the debris of last winter's floods. Another cub was just visible by the drystone wall.

The boy grinned and let the air hiss out between his teeth. Then the little red vixen glanced up and seemed to look directly at him and he froze again. A buzzard steered a high course over the valley and left its cat-calls on the breeze. Teg swung her head and sniffed at the noise. The shadow of the boulder came to life and stepped out onto the sward to become a large, black fox.

'Old Blackie,' the boy whispered. 'It's Old Blackie. I've found 'im! Bleddy hell! You're beautiful. Beautiful.'

Excitement loosened his bowels but he fought the urge until his stomach stopped growling. He was ten years old and moved about the moors like a fox. All day he had tramped the heights, robbing birds' nests and catching butterflies. At dawn he had pedalled from Middle Stoke Farm, south of Venford reservoir, to Postbridge where the bicycle had been left in a cottage garden. With his satchel slung across his back he had walked up the East Dart to the great marshes beyond Sandy Hole Pass. Here he had taken the eggs of curlew, mallard and snipe.

By noon he was jumping the black ditches of Cranmere Pool, and crows, larks, lapwings and golden plover had surrendered prizes for his collection. The egg box was full and he was happy, but while there was still daylight he was reluctant to leave the beloved places.

Returning over Cut Hill and Rough Tor he had heard the vixen bark and had come fox-wise along the leat.

'I idn ever going back to Paignton,' he murmured. 'I'm staying here always – for ever. Just me and the birds and the foxes.'

He had been sent to the farm on doctor's orders suffering from what his mother called 'nerves'. Before the end of spring he would be back in the seaside town eating his heart out for Dartmoor.

The clitter swallowed up the cubs, the shadows deepened and a last soft blaze of sunlight touched Longford Tor; then the vixen was gone, running awkwardly on three legs.

'A little cripple!' the boy said. 'Blackie's got himself a three-legged vixen!'

He shivered. The water filled his gym shoes and ran cold around his calves and knees.

'Trust him,' he thought. 'Any old animal could mate with a four-legged vixen but he's got himself a little cripple. He's a proper hero – a spitfire pilot.'

Wulfgar was swift and sure-footed over the boulders. He carried his pedigree proudly up the slope to the ridge, a noble black hunter blurred by the long shadows and the massed whortleberries.

'I can give 'ee a lift to Hexworthy,' said the cider-merchant.

He hoisted the bicycle into the back of his lorry and wedged it among the barrels.

'Idn you a bit young to be trapesing round the moors this time of night? You'm only a tacker.'

'I'm ten,' the boy said solemnly.

'You're him who's staying at Middle Stoke,' the cider merchant said.

The lorry crawled up the hill, coughing carbon monoxide, its headlights settling briefly on the eyes of sheep and ponies.

'Where you been today?'

The boy told him and opened the egg box.

'You gets about, don't 'ee!' the cider merchant said. 'If I was you I'd clean myself up a bit before I got home. You're grubby, boy. Dang me! If I didn think 'ee were a gypo at first.'

'I saw old Blackie,' the boy said.

'Old who?'

'The black fox – the one they can't catch. He's got a little three-legged vixen and some cubs.'

'You lying?' the cider merchant said. He grated down through the gear box and glanced across his shoulder at the boy.

'It was Blackie.'

'Where was he to?'

'Somewhere.'

'O yes,' the cider merchant grinned.

Outside, the darkness was complete. The sky had clouded over and the horizon was hard to detect.

The boy pressed his face against the side-window and said nothing.

'You got the price of a pint, Len?' said the landlord of the Rock Inn.

Scoble's face darkened and he lightly touched his wart, first with one finger and then another, like a man drumming a tune.

'Depends,' he said.

'Have a word with Ernie Claik.'

'Why?'

'It's about old Blackie.'

Scoble tugged at his nose while his flesh goosepimpled.

'The old black bugger,' he said hoarsely.

'He's around,' said Claik. And he tapped his empty tankard on the bar.

'Around where, boy?' Scoble said.

The shilling rolled out of his palm across the counter into the landlord's cupped hands.

'Mild and bitter,' Claik said.

'Around where?' Scoble persisted.

'That's for you to decide.'

The trapper frowned and tweaked his wart between forefinger and thumb. Claik grinned into his pint pot.

'Cheers, Leonard,' he said. 'First today. I don't hold with lunchtime boozin'.'

Scoble watched him drink.

'I hope this idn no trick,' he said in a low, dangerous voice.

'Old Blackie's been seen, I tell 'ee,' Claik said. 'I give a lift to the boy from Middle Stoke last night. Cor

144

bugger if he wadn in a state! Mud up to the eyebrows! Well, he swore he'd just left old Blackie.'

'The boy's mazed,' Scoble sneered. 'They say he walks round in his sleep, screaming his head off.'

'Maybe so, but he saw old Blackie. Loobies have got eyes, Leonard. Anyway I picked him up by Clapper Cottage and he said he'd walked from Two Bridges. Now, if his bike was at Postbridge he must have gone up the East Dart to Sandy Hole and across to the West Dart and down past Wistman's to Two Bridges.'

'And you believed him?'

'I did. His legs was all scratched and he had a girt box of birds' eggs – curlews, peewits, snipe. You don't find they by sittin' on your arse doing nothing.'

He drank slowly and deeply and added, 'Seems like old Blackie's got a mate – a three-legged vixen.'

Scoble closed his eyes and smashed a fist into the palm of his hand.

'Then he wadn lyin',' he crowed. 'The little sod wadn lyin'.'

'How do you know, Len?' said the landlord.

The trapper took something small, dark and furry from his pocket and slammed it on the counter.

'A fox's pad!' Claik said.

'Old Blackie's got a three-legged mate, right enough,' said Scoble with a pale grin. 'I made sure of that. Reckon I'll pay a visit to Wistman's after tea.'

Claik said, 'Why Wistman's?'

'Vixens bring out their cubs at dimpsey. You picked the boy up after dark and he'd walked all the way from Two Bridges. I bet he was under Beardown at sunset. That old wood is handsome for foxes. I'd bet money on it.'

He tossed the pad into the corner and said, 'Go get it, Jacko. Us will have more than a pad before dark.'

'You ought to have been a detective, Leonard,' Claik said, winking at the landlord.

But Scoble had forgotten him. He had some business to do with Bert Yabsley.

Between showers it was very hot and for some reason he could not fathom, Wulfgar was irritable. Teg and the cubs sensed his moodiness and kept away from him. He lay on a rock in the river while the gnats danced round his head and the shadows slowly climbed the hill to Longford Tor. Eventually he got up and drank.

'What's wrong?' Teg said.

He shook his head and yawned.

'Cubs have to be fed,' she went on. 'I told you it wouldn't be any fun looking after a cripple and four young ones.'

'O don't keep on about the cubs,' Wulfgar snapped.

Teg turned away, but Wulfgar ran to her side and licked her ears.

'Tonight I'll go to the chicken runs and kill the fattest bird,' he said remorsefully.

'A rabbit would be sufficient,' Teg smiled.

'You shall have both.'

'Run far,' she said, 'and shake off your mood.'

'At sunset tomorrow we leave for the Fastness.'

'Will that make you happy?'

He nodded and gently placed his nose against her own.

'Go, Wulfgar,' she said in her soft bell-like voice.

As he sped up to the ridge without a backward glance, Stargrief called to him but he did not answer. The sun was immense in the smoke of day's end and he ran on, keeping it on his right shoulder. Down the valley he went to the marsh by Powdermill Cottages, along the lane, over the road and into the dusk that was gathering around Bellever Tor.

Scoble switched off the van's engine at Crockem and put Tacker in the fishing bag. It had cost him thirty shillings to hire the terrier, but if Yabsley had not been drunk nothing would have persuaded him to part with the dog.

The trapper loaded his shotgun and clipped Jacko to the leash. The haze of late afternoon had rubbed the hard edge off distance. Jackdaws flighted in to Beardown Lodge. Rain fell, hissing above the babble of the river; but it did not last long.

Jacko shook himself and whined. His brain had cast its moorings and was nudging the ceiling of his skull. He dreamt the strange red dream of flickering red shapes on the broad delta between night and day.

Footprints on the red sands, and the slow curl of the blood-wave carrying him into a dizzy plunge through darkness.

Scoble crossed the river and trudged up to the leat. His old scars ached as day clotted into dusk. Another shower overtook him, pocking the water of the leat, trickling down his neck. Sweat glued his underclothes to his body, but he felt truly elated. There were no birds to sound the alarm and he was walking into the wind. He knew he was going to kill foxes, of that he was certain sure. Yet it galled him to think of their mind-lessness. They weren't like people, they weren't afraid of dying. Bloody vermin, he thought. God had an off-day when he made they buggers.

The clouds were blowing away, leaving a clear sky. Teg's chin went up and she smelt the sour reek of the thing she dreaded most. A short, harsh bark sent the cubs scuttling underground.

'Lie quiet,' she hissed. 'Man is coming.'

Dusksilver began to whimper but the vixen said 'hush, hush' and licked the cub's muzzle. The taint grew stronger and terrible sounds crept down through the boulders: heavy footfalls, the whining of the lurcher and the yap of the Jack Russell, the grating voice of the trapper.

'Tod, Tod,' the vixen cried silently from a corner of her spirit.

She was breathing very quietly. Her ears were cocked and her brush was twitching. Then she snarled and the stink of fear broke from her coat. The cubs could not stop whimpering and the loneliness of the sound was hard to endure.

Her eyes flooded with bitterness and she whispered, 'It will be all right. Just don't move.'

The nightmare was coming true but with a sluggishness from which she felt curiously remote. Tacker came at her and clapped down in the gloom and bayed. He was an excellent terrier, trained to locate a fox, not to attack it. Sometimes an animal turned and fought, and only then would the Jack Russell prove his courage.

'Come to heel, Tacker,' Scoble bawled.

The trapper had found two bolt-holes above the earth. The main entrance was big enough for Jacko to squeeze through. Scoble's plan was simple. When Tacker emerged he carried the terrier to the smaller bolt-hole and left him to guard it. Jacko watched him jealously and barked with the itch to be at the killing.

'Wait a minute, boy,' the trapper grinned. 'They foxes idn going nowhere yet.'

He scrambled up to the hole, which brambles and roots partly concealed, and thumbed back the trigger of his gun. The songbirds had stopped singing and Longford Tor was silhouetted against the moon. The dark-smelling wood withdrew into night and Scoble wiped the sweat from his eyebrows.

'Go find 'im, Jacko,' he cried. 'Go in, boy. Go in.'

The strength seemed to drain from Teg. She heard the lurcher growling as he flattened under the pointed boulder at the earth's entrance. Then the dog gave full, savage tongue and gulped the smell of fox. His belly dragged the ground until he blundered into the den and collided with the vixen.

Teg surfaced from her misery and showed him her teeth, but he brushed her aside, cracking his head on the roof. She gripped his cheek and bit through to the gums. Jacko yelped and screwed around, shaking her off with a twist of his neck, but the cramped space hampered his style. Blindly he seized a leg and jerked. Teg screamed and tried to reach the dislocated joint with her tongue. The lurcher closed his teeth half a dozen times on empty darkness. The situation was new to him and he was not happy.

As he crouched there swallowing his own blood, the fox clawed up his spine and ripped one of his ears. He tried to wriggle backwards out of the earth, leaving Teg free to take a neckgrip on Dusksilver and break away. The cubs were whining now. 'I'm not deserting you,' she wanted to say but the words caught in her throat. 'Trust me. Trust me.' She limped up the corridor to the nearest bolt-hole and suddenly Tacker's breath was on her face. The dog barked and sprang at her but she was squirming down again into darkness. A pure, shivering thrill of fear lifted the hair on her shoulders and back. She tightened her hold on Dusksilver and all at once the terror left her.

Jacko was wedged in the main hole, struggling between pain and rage. The vixen ignored him. With a damaged hindleg and a front one missing her movements were slow and deliberate. Up ahead of her was a small patch of moon-silvered sky. Using her back legs she pushed through her pain into the night where the breeze droned in the oak twigs. Sanctuary was close at hand, a deep hole in the clitter, and a vixen and her cubs could lie up on the dry leaves and face any dog. 'Yes,' she sang from that serene inner self that hope illumined. 'First Dusksilver, then Oakwhelp and – '

The trapper rose from the shadows and pointed his gun at her. Teg stared fearlessly into death, sorrowing through her quiet anger for the cubs. Dusksilver fell from her mouth and she snarled at the giant figure. Then there was a great noise and a searing explosion of pain and she felt the world slipping away from her. At the point of death her eyes glowed, but only for a little while.

The cub cowered beside her mother's body and buried her face in her paws. Scoble smiled. His fists clenched on the barrels of the twelve bore until the knuckles gleamed white.

The gun swung downwards and the whimpering stopped.

'That's better than chopping off Blackie's front legs,' he said. 'I'm danged if that idn better than killing 'im.'

'I'm glad you came this way,' said Stargrief.

The dog foxes confronted each other on the ridge path. The shrillness in Stargrief's voice disturbed

Wulfgar. He dropped the Leghorn and narrowed his eyes.

'The trapper has been to your earth,' Stargrief continued.

'Teg?' said Wulfgar.

'Dead. He killed her and the cubs.'

'All the cubs?'

Stargrief nodded.

'And I ignored the crow omens,' Wulfgar said. 'Tod sent me a sign and I did nothing about it.'

He raised his head and the pain burst from his gape in a long howl.

'My heart is breaking, Stargrief, and I'm … lonely.'

The old fox bowed and Wulfgar rested his chin on the grey neck. To touch his friend somehow made the misery bearable.

'We must go to them,' Stargrief said.

They waded through the grasses to the wood and approached the flat boulder where the vixen and cubs lay. Scoble had stretched them out neatly, like trophies.

Wulfgar stood over Teg, looking down at the cubs, unable to believe his eyes. They sprawled as if asleep, soft and beautiful in the moonlight. And Teg's eyes were two green tears. Tenderness welled up into a sharp ache, and his own tears broke and slowly plodded down his muzzle to splash onto the little vixen. He nudged her with his nose but she would not stir. Then he licked the bodies of his dead mate and cubs, trying to bring them back to life. All through the night he worked, whimpering low in the dreadful loneliness of his grief.

At daybreak he climbed to his feet and Stargrief helped him drag the bodies into the den.

'He has made things of them,' Wulfgar said.

'They are with Tod,' said Stargrief. 'You believe that, don't you, Wulfgar?'

'Yes.'

His face was screwed up with misery.

'O Teg, Teg, sweet Teg.'

'Tod helps us into death,' Stargrief said. 'We are never alone. He has many helpers.'

'Tod has cut out the living thing that was inside me,' Wulfgar said.

The marsh tit began to sing and he hated it for being alive.

'I killed the fat white hen for her,' he said absently.

But Stargrief had returned along some faint bardic trail to a past that was visible only to fox seers.

'She was like autumn,' he crooned, eyes closed, body swaying.

'Leaf-fall brightness
she took from the sky.
From the wind
the sun-sparkle she borrowed.
She has gone.
The leafing trees weep

on bare hillsides.
Leaf-fall brightness
gone with the sun
to the Star Place.'

'Words,' Wulfgar snarled. 'Come and bite the pain out of me, you old fool. Your words are like dead leaves.'

The morning swelled warm and giddy with insect chirr and lark song. Through the haze he ran, but his senses were still busy despite the pain. Despair pursued him like a shadow, and soon he was panting in the heat, drawing deep breaths of dry, windless air. Hunger and thirst were welcome, for they increased the emptiness.

And while he ran he thought he had dreamt her death and would wake up to the squeaking of the cubs. The barren North Moor echoed his distress. He had no love for the shapes and colours and sounds of life. The racing scream of hills ended in a gasp of rock piled on rock. The moan of grass slanting away on the wind was a threnody for Teg.

Part Two

'He who catches the joy as it flies
Lives in eternity's sunrise'

William Blake

LONE WANDERING

Clouds had gathered and as he swung onto the path the first drops fell in a patter. The distant hills stood grey and silent on the edge of a different world, then a sheet of rain was hiding the rowans. It grew darker and the sky roared. The path to the tor was lit by lightning flashes. He climbed at speed, easily keeping his footing on the wet stones.

And the running brought moments of oblivion. But the heart does not know how to stop loving. The voice of Teg would call back the pain as the landscape returned. Truly there is something that comes from beyond self to dull misery. Days fall and blur the moments of distress and joy, but the greatest love incurs the greatest grief, and to relinquish pain seems a betrayal of the dead loved one.

Yet Wulfgar belonged to the wilderness and he had to be on the move, running, taking food warm and alive. His ferocity was quenched by the act of killing, but only for a while. Teg was always waiting to step into his thoughts. The rabbit died silently in the manner of most wild creatures and he saw her breaking it up for the cubs. Sadness went through him and he squirted a mess of scats onto the heather.

The thunderstorm was spent, the clouds opened and the sky became huge. Rain powdered away in the south, leaving a glitter all down the valley. And beyond the Tavistock-Moretonhampstead road night was fretting like the sea.

He lay in the furze, waiting for darkness to take him.

Deserting the stream he cut across to Higher White Tor, but he was still tempted to go back to the earth and Teg. She is dead, he thought. The impossible had happened. He stood in the path of moonlight between two rocks where the scent of grouse and lapwing was strong. The bumble dors had taken wing to feed on cowpats and pony dung. He ate a dozen and left their shards in his scats.

But the running was a drug, and settling within himself he could float through time. Yet it was unacceptable to think of never returning to the wood.

'Teg,' he cried, seeing her lying cold and alone in the darkness beneath the boulders.

The wet weather passed and the east wind blew, drying the moors, making the hills good places to kennel. Soon Devon was enjoying a heatwave and nights were warm and scented. From dawn to dusk the drowsy hum of insects masked the heather and cotton grass, butterflies brought colour to the countryside and the rattle of dragonflies could be heard over stagnant ponds.

He went to the water and lapped slowly. For the first time since Teg's death he was aware of the evening's splendour. A bunch of ponies trotted along the ridge. Without raising his head he took the air, waiting for the ache to swell …

Mayflies were dancing over the river. They had laid their eggs and would die of starvation after dark. At daybreak they had emerged from the water without mouths. For three years the larvae had lived in the bottom of a pool under Hartland Tor waiting for the sun and the brief fulfilment of egg laying.

Wulfgar teased the odd furze-spike and bits of bracken from his belly fur, using his teeth. The grooming was meticulous, but all the time his yellow eyes with their narrow, brown pupils held the scene, and nose and ears completed the picture.

Skyglit the kingfisher and her mate Lazuli had their nest in a hole in the crumbling bank beside the East

Dart. The hen sat on her hunting branch. She was lovelier than a sapphire, her plumage a subtle, greenish-blue and her throat white. The minnow darted through the shallows and she belly-flopped and caught it in her beak, then she flipped back onto her perch and beat the fish against the bark before swallowing it head first.

The cockbird killed another fish and took it to the branch near the nest hole where five young kingfishers sat. He was teaching them to hunt, and although they cried for the stickleback he dropped it in the water and coaxed them to retrieve it.

Wulfgar stretched and walked on with his careful cat tread.

The moors were as hushed as an ocean and a red sun shone from the mist. He came to the farm below Whitehorse Hill and killed a duck. The duck had been sleeping near the stream that falls down Great Varracombe. Its death was silent and left its companions undisturbed.

Pipistrelle bats dodged and twisted around the farmhouse. He trotted up Mango Hill with the duck in his jaws. A dog yelped, a door opened and closed, and presently there was just the sound of his own quick breathing.

Sometimes grief clogged his mind and she would come running across the snow towards him, never to arrive, fading back into his dream of winter. Then he would push his nose into his brush and whimper until sleep washed everything away.

During the day he woke many times thinking she had returned. Larks sang and perhaps a raven would croak overhead. But he was always alone and sleep was the only refuge, and the nightmares were easier to live with than the truth.

One day with the rise of the sun he wandered down to the East Dart a little above Sandy Hole Pass. Marshes enclosed both banks of the river and walking was uncomfortable. It was a landscape of quaking bog where cotton grasses, rushes and asphodel flourished. Cross-leaved heath grew in patches amongst liverworts, sundews, lichens and mosses on the surrounding hills. The wet, acid soil was unkind to both wild flowers and creatures. Lizards and frogs could be detected by an animal with his nose close to the ground, and there was no shortage of dragonflies, dors and bumblebees. But rabbits and fieldmice were scarce, and the snipe were very alert.

Wulfgar ate carrion, sharing the carcass of a sheep with three crows. A welcome coolness fell upon him, and he glanced up and saw a cloud blotting out the sun. Then it was raining in one of those inconsequential showers that quickly give way to sunshine again. He trotted along the riverside while the clouds dispersed and the sky reached down to the horizon, clear and blue. Above the remains of the tin streamer's cottage the air was chilly, and the water sang through the wastes over a bed of rocks and pebbles.

As a yearling Wulfgar had come to Cranmere Pool in the company of Stargrief and they had lain on a peat hag and watched the stars gather round the top of the world. The old dog fox had found Tod there in his first vision and the Hay Tor Clan called it Stargrief's Mire. Even on a sunny day in late spring it was dreary. Many of the hags were taller than a man. They poked out of the maze of peat channels and where they had collapsed and crumbled away there were big ponds of black water.

After dark the lambency of the Star Place raised his spirits. He felt he was in the sky sharing Teg's happiness, warmed by a love too deep for his understanding, and he was ashamed of having doubted Tod's existence. The golden fox fell through the night with a blazing tail and vanished below the curve of the North Moor.

Wulfgar suddenly noticed he was not alone. Another fox sat on the hag across the gut.

'What do the stars tell you, Wulfgar?' the stranger asked.

'You know me?' Wulfgar said wearily.

'Wulfgar of the High Tor Clan of the Hill Fox nation. Who does not know you?'

'And you are – ?'

'I have no name. But I know what it is to run from despair. Once, long ago, I lost a vixen who was with cub.'

Wulfgar nodded but the pain of wanting Teg held back the words.

'I'm looking for Stargrief,' the stranger went on.

'Yes, Nameless,' Wulfgar said. 'You'll find him on the tor against the sunset above Rocky Wood.'

'I'm sorry I intruded.'

Wulfgar lifted his muzzle once more to the stars.

'There is no destiny without heartache, Wulfgar,' Nameless said.

'Words again,' said Wulfgar. He clenched his eyes. Starlight twinkled on his canine teeth.

'You'll get on with the old dog,' he added, heavily sarcastic. 'He has a brilliant way with hot air.'

'What do you want?' Nameless said. 'Someone to lick your muzzle and croon you a lullaby?'

'I want to be left alone,' Wulfgar snarled and he tensed to jump the gut. But the stranger had vanished and there were no tracks in the peat and no tell-tale stink on the air.

Wulfgar shuddered and ducked away and ran from Cranmere, bounding from hag to hag while the dream blazed at the edges and Teg's pain fed his body with a kind of explosive energy. Over folds of darkness he galloped, on to Cut Hill and Devil's Tor and the Cowsic River's source.

Through breast-high mist he ran chuckling at the memory of Stargrief's 'Tod Soliloquy'. Scraggy old fox! But he could rake up sermons better than a rickyard fowl scuffing up worms – and it was well meant.

He crossed Holming Beam giving a wide berth to the stacks of cut peat and raced on down to the Black Brook River, and followed it to the outskirts of Princetown.

The huge, featureless lump to the west of him was Dartmoor prison. Tiny squares of light gleamed from the main block, but Wulfgar was among newborn lambs, burning with blood lust.

The ewes bleated and fled before him. He was snarling now and the lamb leapt sideways in blind terror. Wulfgar pulled it down by the shoulder and transferred his grip to the neck. Strong canine teeth crushed the cervical vertebrae and the lamb died.

Wulfgar hauled the carcass to an ash grove and skinned it before sating two hungers.

RIVER'S END

The old man who lived in the cottage on the leat at Tor Royal came to the slopes of Royal Hill to cut peat for his fire. He used a triangular shovel called a budding iron. The turves were trimmed with a long knife after being lifted from the ground on the prongs of a turf iron. They were scattered along a terrace the length and width of a cricket square. Each day the old man carried several loads down to his stack. The 'vag' or top layer of peat burnt cleanly on a fire of furze and the smoke from the cottage chimney carried the tang of Dartmoor to Wulfgar's nose.

He watched the old man toiling up the slope of moor grass and bell heather, then he yawned and urinated on the nearest lump of peat. By the time the man had reached the turves Wulfgar was trotting through the bog cotton towards Foxtor Mires.

Hill foxes have a wide range, but Wulfgar was to wander further than any of his kind had dreamed possible. The good life was found in the pursuit of prey, in the running between sunrise and sunset. 'Living in the sacred manner', Stargrief called it, and he simply meant resisting the heresy of letting the mind lope ahead of the body.

Yet Wulfgar often felt a presence beside him as he ran, something more than his shadow, but he no longer looked over his shoulder to see if she was there.

At Foxtor Mire he stalked a green plover who kept a little ahead of him, dragging a wing. Whenever Wulfgar pounced the bird jumped out of reach. She had a nest full of chicks and was deceiving the fox. He snapped at her and rolled onto his side and pretended to groom the hindleg he had thrust into the air. He was embarrassed but had no intention of betraying it. He worked casually, clacking his teeth on imaginary ticks, eyes closed, ears and nostrils quivering. The green plover kept diving at him until he was sufficiently rattled to move on across blanket bog that quaked and oozed underfoot.

The merlin tiercel had spotted him but only as an unimportant peripheral object. The little falcon came corkscrewing low along the sinewy thread of water and overtook the meadow pipit. Neither bird made a sound in the death tangle. The merlin killed neatly and flashed Wulfgar an arrogant glance before hurrying upstream, the pipit in its talons.

Dartmoor rippled and trembled in the heat. Wulfgar drank the bright water as it glided over bronze-coloured rocks. The merlin was a quarter of a pound of feathered dynamite lost in a vast landscape. Among the cotton grass near his nest he had a plucking post and birds were brought to this stump of granite and butchered. The tiercel's name was Merelord. After decapitating the pipit he presented it to his mate in flight and sped over the sedges to search for more living snacks.

Wulfgar stood in the stream and let the water wash round his chest. The merlin cried kik-kik kik-kik from a blur of slate-blue, white and black. The morning paled. Midges enveloped his head, and he left the stream and crackled through a scimitar of reeds, his paws squelching into the sphagnum moss and lichen. He moved lightly and quickly, scattering meadow-brown butterflies from the grasses.

Two sunsets later, after quartering the Swincombe Valley as far down as the beehives of the Buckfast monks, he arrived at Huntingdon Warren. In the not too distant past rabbits had been kept on the hillsides in long banks of earth and stone to supply Man's table with fresh meat. The warrener's house was in ruins and the artificial burrows were hidden under grass, but the rabbits remained wherever there was a clitter, sharing the crevices with adders and lizards.

Wulfgar crawled into the tangle of dead bracken and furze. He was hungry. Drawing back his lips he squealed like a rabbit in pain, and a doe popped out of a hole and stared towards his hiding place. Soon several nursing mothers had assembled on the sward before Huntingdon Barrow, stamping their hind feet, anxious to know what was wrong. Eventually a buck hopped forward to investigate and never lived to see the new moon firming in the sky.

The track of Redlake Tramway marched down from the old china clay works to Bittaford, a distance of six miles as the raven flies. By dawn Wulfgar had left the track to kennel beneath the oaks of Piles Copse on the West-facing bank of the Erme. He slept soundly until the screeching of a jay brought him back with a jolt to the edge of another night.

He licked the tag of his brush and let the hurt have its way, but he could think quite calmly of her now. The panic that usually gushed with the return of consciousness never troubled him again. He walked to the river and lapped the surface of the pool. Through his reflection he saw the dim skeleton of a pony stirring in the current. The water was the colour of Teg's eyes.

The fox followed the Erme on its flight into darkness. He had no idea where he was going, the river would be his guide. Maybe it would carry him to Teg.

He grinned and wagged his narrow muzzle at the stars. Where the river ends a fox may find the truth, Stargrief had said. And the old dog had gone on to speak of the sea where the sun came from. Yes, he would go to it and eat the truth as a sick animal eats grass.

The cattle path beside the water hastened him into the shadows of a wood. He froze and pricked his ears. The otter's head glistened in mid-stream. The animals gazed steadily at each other, then the otter sank and became part of the rushing blackness.

Wulfgar trotted through the woodlands, the night sky broken between leaves above him. He went under the viaduct and cleared a fence to find himself in a vegetable garden. Houses crowded around him and a hen began to cluck. He crept along the wire mesh of the chicken run, filling his nostrils with the smell of the birds. Then they were squawking and flapping and beating against the wire.

Wulfgar jumped onto a high wall and ran along the coping stones. The river poured through the town of Ivybridge, passing rows of terrace houses and the paper mill, catching the glint of street lamps and the gleam of gaslights from kitchen windows. Wulfgar dropped down onto the footpath and was held in the beam of a torch.

'A fox!' the policeman grunted. 'God – you scared me, boy!'

The green eyes vanished. The policeman heard the splash of Wulfgar entering the water and tried to capture him again with his torch, but the fox was under the bridge, paddling downstream.

He was carried beneath the stone arches of two more bridges before he scrambled out and shook himself among the buddleia of some wasteland south of the Lower Mill. Once the town lights were behind him, he sniffed the breeze that was bending the cow parsley and charlock. Cars were roaring up and down the Plymouth Road.

The fox ran on.

He spent a couple of nights hunting the farmland around Ermington. Ducks were killed on the Long Brook and he chopped many rabbits in the fields by Modbury.

The Erme above Sequer's Bridge was a sleeve of clear moorland water, flowing shallow and fast, dancing on a stony bed. Trout dimpled the surface of the pools. They leapt to grab insects and flashed silver in the sunlight. Wulfgar eyed them as he quenched his thirst and inevitably he recalled how Teg had sipped the coolness of the West Dart. But too much was going on to permit brooding. He lay in the ferns while the water skaters moved jerkily on the surface of the pool. Other insects were creeping out of the larval form to enjoy the heat before the dragonflies bustled in and the wagtails came to hawk the quiet reaches.

Wulfgar yawned and revealed the armoury of the slaughterhouse. Without too much effort he could stretch and sniff at the spraint the otter had deposited on the rock below the alder roots. The fish smell did not please him. He glanced up at the leaf-dazzle and caught the eye of the sparrowhawk. The bird was so highly strung it would react violently to the snapping of a twig.

A blue tit cut a yellow and blue curve among the alder leaves. The hawk swished away and a leaf fluttered down and settled on the water.

The fox enjoyed the evenings beside the river. Although moulting had begun, his coat shone and everything about him had a healthy well-cared-for look from whiskers to claws. He was as sleek and lean as the torrent that caught the sun and tossed it about in blinding flashes.

He trotted at the easy hunting pace along the tidal reaches of the Erme to Clyng Mill. It was the green and golden time of late spring in that part of Devon, which is called the South Hams. Watered by five rivers the farmland of small fields, market towns and villages ran to the edge of the cliffs bordering the English Channel. The green was of thick new grass, leaves and flower stems; the gold was of buttercups and dandelions in the pastures.

That night he snatched conies from Torr Down and kennelled among bluebells and campion on the margins of the wood by the farm. An hour before dawn a pair of workdogs out rabbiting put him up and chased him through the trees to the river where he hid in a badger's sett. The bolt-hole led him to the bank above the water. The dogs were still barking but he was no longer concerned as he walked on soft sand. Birds were constantly coming and going. Gulls and shelduck fed in the distant marshes, mallard dropped from the sky. And he heard a new, exciting sound – the boom of surf.

The sky was dark and starry, and the emptiness of the universe made him sad. He had the feeling of swimming in space again. His bones and muscles and coat of thick hair had gone, and he had no more body than the wind.

A line of breakers separated the river mouth from the sea and on either side woods and fields sat in a grey mass on the clifftops. Wulfgar came to the estuary and lapped salt water.

The starlight was paling as the sky on the horizon slowly brightened. He climbed the cliff to a rocky outcrop and lay in a hollow of grass and thrift.

The light of the new day came stealthily. The stars disappeared and little by little things became substantial. The peaks of the waves lifted and fell, white water ruffled the estuary. Then the sun was rolling out of a sea that sparkled, and a great black-backed gull barked and a cuckoo winged across the bluebell slopes repeating its name.

Wulfgar laid his chin on his forepaws and waited for the divine revelation. But nothing happened. The sun climbed higher, the hoppers zithered and larks sang and the sea murmured. Presently he fell asleep.

The yaffle gave its crazed laugh and hopped from branch to branch. Brown-green oak leaves hid it from Wulfgar. He licked a paw and cleaned his muzzle. Above the copse in Fernycombe Goyal the herring gulls swooped, their primary feathers blazing with silver light.

Wulfgar had eaten gull chicks and eggs that he had found on the cliff ledges, and small crabs scavenged from Westcombe Beach. He had also gnawed bladder-wrack seaweed for the iodine.

The countryside was crying out for rain, but with the wind blowing gently from the continent the drought continued. Where the tiny green leaves of the turnip crop showed in the dusty soil the cockroach moved like a metal toy. The kestrel dropped and closed his talons on the insect, then he shrugged off the gulls who were mobbing him and returned to his mate and the nesting ledge at Beacon Point.

Running by night Wulfgar came to Loddiswell and the River Avon, where a poacher saw him sniffing round the pigsties. The man had taken a salmon from Reade's Pool. Crouching under the bridge by the mill on the Torr Brook he spotted the fox again as it waded the stream and dived into the darkness.

The hour of dusk pleased him most of all. He felt he had come to the frontiers of something thrilling. The wind had died and the air was loaded with scent. Along the grazing of Buckland-Tout-Saints dusk was gathering, and trees and houses had already been obscured. Cattle lowed, a lamb bleated, and the after-glow of sunset endured in the bottom of the sky. Mist hid the Kingsbridge Estuary and filled the creeks. It was almost dark and the coombs and lower fields were part of the night. Clusters of lights marked the towns and villages and an aeroplane droned against the stars. A shire horse stamped and snuffled and called to her foal. Wulfgar smelt the grassy fragrance of her breath as he descended the goyal.

The running took him in a straight line to the headland. He crossed four streams and many lanes before daybreak glinted on the duckpond of Start Farm. The muscovies paddled slowly through the shallows, dipping their heads into the brown water. Wulfgar stood on his hindlegs and stared at them. But someone in the house pulled the lavatory chain and frightened him. He sat back on his haunches and whimpered and swished his brush. The ducks crowded together and an old drake began to quack. Wulfgar slipped away where the hawthorns linked branches in a green shade ...

It was like Sunday morning in Eden. The farmland received the first sunlight. Every year there were young fields under old trees. Men came and went but the fields remained and never decayed.

A crow harassed him as he ran with the stream down the coombe that was dotted with sheep. The scent of the sea lofted from Lannacombe Bay. Wulfgar nosed through the dead fennel, jumped the barbed wire fence and took the path along the edge of the cliffs to Peartree Point.

Badgers had been rooting in the bluebells below Raven's Rock, a great grey crag rising steeply above the sea, and one of their trails led to a terrace high on the cliff face. A fox could crouch there unseen and sleep while the day flowed and ebbed.

And the blaring of the lighthouse foghorn woke him. The moon was full and yellow over Start Point and a thick sea mist stifled the sound of breaking waves. Only the top of the lighthouse was visible. The ridge leading down to the point was bare and serrated. The swinging shaft of light splashed the jagged outcrops like flashes from a welder's torch.

Wulfgar analysed the night air, drinking the smell of gulls' droppings and fish bones, jackdaws, seaweed, thrift and sheep. He was the first of the Dartmoor Nation to make such a pilgrimage. A wry smile creased the corners of his mouth, for Stargrief had got some of it right. The sea lay between all wanderers and the sunrise, but where was the vision of truth? Wulfgar had spoken to the stars and they had remained silent. He was alone, but a dog fox spent half his life without company. It was a good life. Then he thought he understood.

He had come to the sea like the river, shedding a part of himself on the way. The sea would provide no answers, no palliatives. The journey was the thing. In Man's terms he had run fifty miles. He was Wulfgar of Leighon once more and ached for the wilderness of his birth.

CONSPIRACY

The breeze lifted the speckled breast feather cast by Leaf-dancer the kestrel. It sailed across the bracken and foxgloves pursued by a butterfly. A cuckoo spoke and Wulfgar raised his head from the drinking. The morning was dull and overcast but warm. Above the waters of the Leighon Ponds the flags shook yellow flowers. It began to drizzle and there was the smell of rain on dry earth. A thrush sang, the dragonflies tacked and hovered and before very long the sun was shining.

The West Country had entered the third week of drought.

The ponds were the best place to be. Wulfgar lay up close to the water and fed well on young moorhens and ducks. Often he swam to the island of alders and willows when the sun had gone down and the ghost moths danced over the turf. Once he even caught a trout – more by luck than contrivance. Drinking at the slack water near the dam he had seen the fish lying in the shallows and had flicked it out with his paw.

The episode amused Romany. To him most creatures who were not water gypsies were dull-witted and clumsy. He hauled himself onto the dam and grinned at Wulfgar. Droplets of water fell from his whiskers. He had the head of a tomcat but his ears were small and flat and set far back.

'A fox with a fish,' he chirped. Like all members of the weasel family he spoke Fox with an unpleasant nasal twang. 'I missed the chase, Wulfgar. You can't beat a good chase – that's what I say. The bubbly, rushing thrill of speeding through the coolness. There's no excitement quite like it.'

'The trout came to me,' Wulfgar said. 'I'm not too bright at the underwater stalking. I got it with this.' He held up a paw.

'Lucky it was a trout. An eel would have given you the slip,' the otter said, and he winked. 'Eels are like long, dark streaks of water. You got to grab 'em with your teeth.'

'You're more fish than fitch,' Wulfgar said.

The animals smiled.

'And that trout's a fluke – if you get what I mean,' the otter said.

'Very droll.'

The fish was small and Wulfgar ate it quickly.

'Stargrief tells me you've been to the sea,' Romany said.

'He's back then?'

'Yes – on his hill. He told me about Teg and the cubs.'

'Going to the sea wasn't particularly thrilling,' Wulfgar said, hearing the metal jaws clang on Teg's hindleg. 'You follow a river and it takes you there. Nothing could be simpler.'

'What about the sea?'

'It's big and tastes bitter. The sun comes out of it.'

'Nothing else?'

'Nothing.'

'You have to swim in it to really understand it,' Romany said. 'I was there a couple of winters ago. The fishing was excellent.'

Using his tail as a third leg he stood upright and scanned the dimpsey. Water spilled over the dam in a cascade to fill the smaller, muddier pond.

Wulfgar said, 'Have the hounds been here?'

'Not yet,' said the otter and he dropped back onto all fours. 'They drew the river under the trapper's house but didn't kill. The trapper and his dog visited us back along. Ever since I took a chunk out of his leg the dog won't go near the water. It was very funny. I think they were looking for you, Wulfgar.'

'I wouldn't be surprised,' Wulfgar said. 'This trapper isn't like other men.'

'He caught one of my brothers on Little Two Rivers last spring,' Romany said. 'I fear him more than any living animal. I suppose you've heard about the lurcher?'

Wulfgar shook his head.

'He chopped a dog fox by Crow Thorn when the bluebells were opening. Stargrief said the fox was called Briarspur. It was an untidy death.'

'One day I shall kill the lurcher.' Wulfgar's words came through his teeth in a grating snarl.

'It isn't possible,' the otter said.

Water puddled under his thickset, short-legged body. His eyes were round and black in a pug face.

'Maybe we could learn something from the hounds and the bogeywolves,' Wulfgar said, sniffing the air that was rich with the dark, leafy smell of the ponds.

'Run and Live is our motto,' said Romany.

'And what if the lurcher could be persuaded to run into trouble?'

Romany shook himself and grinned. Perhaps this fox wasn't dumb. The dark one had always puzzled him. There was a light in his eyes quite different from the mere glint of intelligence. Then he considered another possibility. The death of the vixen and cubs could have unhinged him. Craziness took many forms and grief was one of them. Wulfgar was still fretting for his mate, but the pain was turning to anger. Romany was ten years old and he knew what it was like to nurse the ache of loss.

In the water the dog otter was a different creature. His body tapered away as he swam with swift undulations of the spine. The trout was caught up in the convulsion of underwater acrobatics and brought alive to Moonsleek.

Wulfgar heard the whistle and saw the sun twinkle on the wet head. The otter was stalking a moorhen. The bird was swimming on the far side of the pond and Romany took exact bearings before he sank. Closing his ears and nostrils he moved deep down, but the moorhen had sensed something was wrong. She gave a cry and dashed backwards and forwards. Then the otter had her by the foot and the surface was empty. An expanding ring of ripples broke the reflections of flags and trees.

Wulfgar rolled in the shallows below the alder branches. The night's hunting had yielded fieldmice and lapwing chicks but not in satisfying numbers. He soaked up the early morning sunlight and ran his teeth like clippers through the fur of his underparts. Wasps were snatching caterpillars from the leaves of Jack-by-the-hedges. In the fields of the border country the grass stood higher than a fox, and the clover was in flower. Occasionally rucksacked figures were seen on Holwell

Tor, although Man rarely came at dawn or dusk when the animals were busy.

The fox contorted his body and raked his neck with a hindfoot. His tongue lolled over his lower teeth as he scratched long and luxuriously. The wasps continued to devour the caterpillars, slyly searching the undersides of the leaves. Wulfgar's eyes narrowed. He would use cunning, not direct confrontation, so it would not be dog fox against lurcher. The clicketting Fight Ritual could not be applied. Foxes were masters of stealth but never hunted in packs. No, certain tactics could not be applied for hereditary reasons.

Teg's death was his own spur. Other dogs and vixens did not share this intense hatred. Fox would fight fox and any other creature in certain circumstances, but his instinct when confronted by overwhelming odds was to use cunning. There were extraordinary talents to be harnessed, yet how? If he could get the lurcher into the Fastness maybe the treacherous ground would swallow him, as it had swallowed sheep and ponies. He whimpered. In the open the dog would overtake and stop the swiftest fox, yet the animal had to die. The trapper loved it and it was his thing, an extension of his need to kill. The death of the thing would fill its master with pain. He would know the terrible ache that gnawed at the innards. And even if men did not have this capacity for suffering, the dog would be removed from their lives for ever.

He licked the long, black hairs of his brush and drew his teeth through the tag.

'And he's just a four-legged beast like us,' Wulfgar said.

'Not like us,' Thorgil grunted. 'He's got bloody long legs and a big mouth.'

'So has the heron,' said Romany, and Moonsleek sniggered.

'Listen, water weasel,' the badger said. 'You stick to moorhens and minnows. I don't like comedians. Give me any lip and I'll chew off your ears.'

'You take everything to heart,' Moonsleek sneered.

'I've lost cubs in the trapper's snares,' Thorgil said. 'The lurcher helped kill my first mate. I can't joke about it. It sticks in my craw.'

'I'm sorry,' Romany said. 'You're quite right, Thorgil. The lurcher and his master aren't funny. But what can we do?'

'We can kill his dog to start with,' said Wulfgar.

The animals stared at him as they crouched on the moss and lichen by the Becca Brook. The river tumbled through the Leighon Woods in a series of pools and little falls. The rosy glow of day's end stole through the treetops. Over the calmer water the damsel flies drifted and the brilliant blue dragonflies whizzed with the click and rustle of transparent wings.

'How is it to be done?' Thorgil said at last.

'I'm not certain,' Wulfgar replied. 'We can't bite him to death and even you, Thorgil, the toughest creature on the moors, wouldn't stand a chance in a straight battle, so we trap him. We let him destroy himself.'

'Poetic justice,' Romany grinned. 'Trapper's dog trapped.'

'Common sense,' the fox said. 'We don't know how to hunt in packs like bogeywolves or hounds but we could all be in at the kill.'

'Go on,' said Stargrief.

'If he were lured into a cave or a clitter, lots of animals could attack him.'

'And lots of animals would be maimed and killed,' Stargrief said. 'That dog is capable of slaughter on a grand scale. A mad creature is very difficult to destroy and in any case it isn't the way of foxes or badgers or otters.'

'Then we'll make it the way,' Wulfgar said impatiently. 'Once we hunted by day and Man shared the good places with us and took the game and passed quietly through the seasons. Now we skulk at night and this has become the way, yet when the flea bites we nip it from our fur.'

'Do you think the trapper would leave us alone if we killed his dog?' said Stargrief.

'Things couldn't be any worse than they are now.'

'O but they could! You've never seen a fox-drive with fifty guns and a hundred dogs on the hills.'

'Perhaps it's time to get rid of the trapper too,' Wulfgar said hotly. His voice rose to a shrill, high-pitched bark.

'Such an act of folly would mean the total annihilation of hill foxes – cubs, dogs, vixens. Man is lord of this world, Wulfgar. That's why we skulk and hide and run by night. The bogeywolves had the audacity to take man's sheep and cattle. And it is said they even attacked men, although this sounds too absurd to be true. But they are gone, finished, killed. Man saw to it and he could do the same for us.'

Wulfgar took a deep breath and said, 'I wasn't serious. Don't carp, Stargrief. It's so boring.'

Romany was a good-natured animal, clever but lacking imagination. The trout were ringing the surface of the pool and he itched to be in the water where the real world began.

'Look,' he said. 'Caves and clitters and chases and ambushes are a bit fanciful, a bit foxy if you don't mind me saying. But if you could con the lurcher into the pond, me and Moonsleek would do for him – permanent.'

'Are you sure this isn't a case of phony heroics?' Thorgil said bluntly. 'We want the lunatic dead but he's a more serious proposition than a rat or a fish. He's killed full-grown boar badgers.'

'If Romany can drag down an otterhound and all but drown him, I'm certain both of us could manage a skinny old lurcher,' Moonsleek said.

Stargrief gazed angrily at his fellow animals.

'Tell me I'm dreaming,' he said. 'Bite my brush and wake me up.'

The badger laughed and started to cough.

'We're fighting back, old outlaw,' he said.

'Honouring the ghosts,' Romany added.

'And this really is something we can fight,' said Wulfgar. 'It's not like the hounds or the poisoned rabbit meat or the gins and snares and guns.'

'But we live according to Tod's will. We take and are taken,' Stargrief insisted.

'The world changes with the seasons,' Wulfgar said. 'Surely Tod's will changes too? In the sunsets of long ago the old ways were perfect. Now we talk of the good death and the bad death as though Tod approves. We are hunters and warriors. We should live like hunters and warriors. Tod has spoken to me through the death of Teg. Tod lives in me. I know the lurcher will die.'

'All right,' said Stargrief. 'I'm convinced.'

'Marvellous,' Thorgil said in a tone that implied the exact opposite. 'So how do we get the dog to swim?'

'Leave it to the foxes,' Romany said. 'I'm hungry and the water looks sensational. Moonsleek has to return to the holt and I've got some serious fishing to do. When you come up with something let me know.'

After the otters and the badger had departed the foxes lay in the darkening woodland.

'To drown a dog you must first get him to the pool,' Stargrief said. 'Have you got a plan?'

'The beginnings of one. The lurcher hates us. Therefore a fox could lead him to the water and plunge in and head for the island. Naturally the dog will follow and the otters will do the rest.'

'Sounds fine. I suppose you've worked out how to get the animal to leave the cottage and run across the moors and land up here. Remember, he can outstrip us all – even you.'

'What if we used several foxes in relays?'

'It might work,' Stargrief said. 'But it's risky.'

'Do you know a better way?'

'Perhaps. Simplicity must be the operative word.'

'Tell me.'

'Not until it's clear in my mind and I've made a journey.'

'Do you have to be so mysterious?' Wulfgar said irritably.

'Mystery is my business,' the old dog fox smiled.

WHAT THE STARS SAID

The Becca Brook was actually more of a stream than a river and it was something he could understand and relate to. There were none of the tidal races of the estuary. The little beaches of grit and pebbles were created and destroyed by floods. Below Leighon it ran under a single-arched bridge and away into the trees. Flat reaches of silence lay in shadow and wherever the sky intruded the depths were honeycombed with sunlight.

Stargrief had left the river to meditate and sit on the hilltop night after night while the stars sang to him.

Approaching the old dog fox at times like this was quite useless, although Wulfgar fumed with impatience.

'For Tod's sake get going,' he muttered.

His nose was pressed to the brown sheaths of the rushes. The wind having gathered the scents of many flowers raked the water and made it shimmer.

But Stargrief took his time. From the darkness came the whistle of a curlew. The blood curdled into images behind his eyes and across the plain the golden animals ran, calling his name down the ages.

The restlessness would not be shaken off, and as soon as Wulfgar thought of Teg he did something wild – like jumping in the river or leaping up at songbirds or baiting fitches. And it took nerve to worry a stoat who was guarding a family of kits. Chivvy-yick and his tribe would have ripped the fox's throat out given half the chance, but like all the creatures on Dartmoor he was busy keeping his young alive.

For Wulfgar a visit to Emsworthy was too painful to endure. Time had not tarnished the vision of her running over the frosty grass, moon-silvered and eternally young.

One morning he left the ponds and stood for a while by the wall. The dog roses were blooming in hedges all down the road from Haytor Vale to Liverton, and although rain had fallen it was not enough to please the farmers. Now the fine, hot weather was back and the swallows were climbing high to attack the swarms of winged insects, and Wulfgar was happy. He dropped his head and tugged at his chest fur before moving off at the trot.

The moor had covered places where men had once worshipped animal gods. From Hamel Down the haze was setting hard like a far-off island and the hills swam into distances of heat. He had tried to reach them before, but they had retreated to reassemble on another horizon. Always there were the hills like waves that would never break, and he ached for that far-away place sunk in silence.

Slowly the shadows of the megaliths crept across the heather towards him. He lay on the sun-dried lichen watching a tiger beetle scuttle over the stone by his front paws to hide under a leaf of hart's tongue fern. The burring of the honey bees was comforting and summery. About his head hoverflies foraged through the slow drift of sunlight. Less than half a dozen tail lengths to his right a Galloway calf was curled up asleep in the heather under the watchful eye of its mother.

Wulfgar felt reality slipping away again. There was a sense of unbelonging as if he had never been a part of what was going on around him. He snapped at a fly before it could land on his nose. Many flies covered the mummified body of a crow where it rested, among the nearby ling. Sheep, ponies, cattle, crows, foxes – everything came to final rest under the sky. But he had never found the carcass of a man.

The swallow's beak clacked shut on a butterfly. Lower in the sky larks shrilled. He came back from the loneliness. The butterfly's wing settled on the lichen like the tom petal of a musk mallow. Gulls passed overhead, very elegant and white against the blue. Their wing beats were precise and unhurried. Mordo flew above them and cried cronk-cronk to his mate.

'I can find happiness on my own,' the fox cried.

Long after dark he ran up Black Hill and sat in front of Stargrief.

'What do the stars tell you, seer?' he said.

'They tell me Tod is holy,' said the old animal.

'Is he?' Wulfgar said coldly. 'Isn't he fox – like us? Perhaps we make him holy because we're ashamed of ourselves and don't want him to be like us.'

'Perhaps.'

'And the lurcher?'

'He will die.'

'Soon?'

'Yes. When the rain has fallen.'

'Will I be at the killing?'

'Of course,' Stargrief said.

'Do the stars say this?'

Stargrief nodded.

'Why must it always come from outside?' Wulfgar said.

'Why are we born?' the old fox replied.

It was midnight, but the great summer stars were still ghostly in the west.

HAYMAKING

Sheol flew to the ash tree before daybreak and worked at her wing feathers, lifting each rachis and drawing the barbs through her beak. She preened herself thoroughly, giving soft warbling cries and the occasional croak. Then she began her cawing routine that developed into craark-craark, repeated regularly and monotonously.

Swart had remained at the nest in Crow Thorn. He was unwell after eating a small portion of poisoned meat left near a sheep carcass by Farmer Lugg. The young crows peered vacantly through flat, black eyes and demanded food.

The lump under the blanket squirmed and groaned and an arm flopped over the side of the bed. Sheol continued to craark in her determined, manic way while a glimmer appeared above the tree tops of Yarner Wood. Scoble groped for the chamberpot, threw the covers off his head and waited for the ceiling to stop spinning.

'Craark,' said Sheol. 'Craark-craark'.

Scoble hoisted up his long johns and staggered to the window. Two crows lifted from two ash trees and settled again. The acid stew of last night's cider, pickles and cheese rose from his gut to his throat.

'Lord God no!' he choked. 'God no!'

He belched and waited for the nausea to subside. Jacko pushed out all four of his legs in a self-indulgent stretch and curled deeper into sleep. The trapper gripped him by the tail and yanked him off the bed.

Sheol said craark, and Scoble winced.

The stairs were steep and narrow. He went down on his heels in a rush and sat hard on the bottom step. The kitchen reeked of cider and tobacco smoke. Sweat stood out on his forehead. He passed a hand over it and shuddered. He had surfaced from the awful dream – fox mask, lips drawn back on the crimson froth, the gleaming skulls of sheep, the skeleton of a mule rising from the peat bog, and a hard brown fist pulping his nose. The crow went on laughing.

He rammed home the cartridges and thumbed back the hammers. Crows fluttered on the edge of trouble, bringing death, attending death – crows and rats and foxes.

Opening the door six inches he let in the weak, grey light. The whistle shrilled. 'Over the top, lads,' the sergeant cried. His arse hung out like the neck of a cider bottle. Silver seeds broke from the grass heads and clung to him as he ran. The twelve bore clapped twice and Sheol glided down into the blackness of the wood. A solitary pellet had passed through the secondaries of her right wing. Her heart raced but she was unhurt, and by the time she took to the sky at Drive Lodge she had forgotten the incident.

Jacko padded up to the trapper and thrust his muzzle into his hand.

'Yes, you'm a good dog,' Scoble whispered. 'You'm Leonard's boy.'

The dog slobbered over his fingers.

Using a Wellington boot Scoble wedged the door against the wall. The light was thin and pink now like rosé wine. Garden smells filtered through the crust of nicotine – dry, dusty smells. The dawn was too warm for comfort.

Scoble raked the embers and fed a handful of twigs and sticks to the fire. Then he put on the kettle and wondered how long the drought would last. He was lucky having the well just down the road, for it had never been known to run dry. He rolled the wart on his cheek where the stubble was grey and bristly. Luggy didn't mind the hot spell. His Galloways weren't going short of grub on the Emsworthy newtakes and there was always enough feed up on the commons to fatten the sheep. Watching the steam plume from the kettle's spout Scoble thought about the haymaking. Old Lugg would be in a good mood with the grass so high and the weather perfect. He wasn't tight with his booze or his money either, and they gave you your grub at Sedge Brimley.

It was the first year he could recall when it hadn't rained at haymaking time. He pulled on his corduroys, tightened his braces and buttoned his shirt to the neck. The foxes' masks stared down from the wall. Boiling water flooded the teapot and clouded into a fragrance that the dog could smell. Scoble selected a Gold Flake butt from his cigarette tin. They old foxes would be loving the hot spell, nights being so warm they could kennel anywhere. He used a twig to light up and dragged nicotine deep into his queasiness.

When he had finished coughing he put on his boots. The morning's glow had taken on a ruddy tinge. Scoble sat back in his armchair and waited for the tea to brew. And he thought about Wulfgar, assembling the familiar daydream, lavishing attention on detail until the creature stepped alive and glowing from his head. The black fox had been spotted at Ivybridge and down by Start Point. Scoble sighed tobacco smoke. But Old Blackie would be back round Holwell before long. Foxes were sly but not that sly. They had their roots – leastways, Old Blackie did. And I'll have the bugger stuffed, he thought. He can stand on the mantelpiece and listen to they vixens screechin' – only he won't be going nowhere no more.

He poured the tea and drank it without milk or sugar. The birch twigs flared and hissed on the fire. Down at Yarner Wells the cock was crowing.

The copse grew thick on the slopes. Along the lap of the coomb were good fields of grass, their hush held firm by hedges of may and blackthorn. Looking beyond Sedge Brimley Farm the eye was carried over great distances of hills and valleys to the mist guarding the sea. The faintest of winds delivered the hot reek of the piggeries and the kindlier smells of middens and shippens.

The lane to the farm followed Lansworthy Brook down to Horridge Copse and was overhung with old beech trees. Sedge Brimley was a forgotten place. A hound weather-vane swung above the thatch. The house was dirty-white, half-hidden in trees. Elderberry bushes shaded the dairy and behind the house stood an orchard thick with cow parsley and nettles. Logs and kindling littered the yard and fowls ranged everywhere.

Lugg emerged from the hayshed rubbing his hands together. For once things were going right. His three-year-old South Devon steers would fetch a proper price at Ashburton, and the sheep had dropped a big crop of lambs on the Duchy newtakes. Nothing on God's earth could prevent a bumper hay harvest. The three fields would see him comfortably through next winter. The grass was tall and silver-seeded, perfect for the cutting.

A cuckoo said cuck-uckoo in a lazy, idiotic way. Among the tiny, green-white flowers of the goose grass hanging over the hedge in curtains the honeysuckle and dog roses fumed. The whole of the border country was rich with wild flowers. Red sorrel and moon daisies waved in the hay fields but the real colour of early summer was green. The copse of oaks and beeches was as green as a sea cave.

Things went on in the hayfields that Lugg knew little about. Fieldmice with their blunt heads and short, hairy tails stole through the grass stems, avoiding the shrew runs. The barn owls killed many creatures there by night and the kestrels visited it daily. Members of Chivvy-yick's tribe also used it as a living larder, while Gnashfang the weasel hunted mice underground, in the galleries where the drought had not penetrated.

'There idn a lot of dew, dad,' George Lugg said.

He clamped his father's fist round a mug of tea. A haze covered the sun and Lugg squinted at the sky, noting the high-flying swifts.

'Best get they horses out,' he said. 'Scoble and Yabsley will be here soon and I idn payin' good money for them to stand round doing sod all.'

'Scoble must have had two gallons of rough last night at the Rock,' George said. 'I bet he's still got his head down.'

'You don't know him like I do, boy,' said his father. 'He's a worker. He'll drag Yabsley from between the sheets.'

'If Joan don't haul him in too,' George laughed.

'God! If her idn randier than a rabbit! Bert's getting more than his share of home comforts.'

'And so's a few others,' said the elder Lugg. 'Her was like it at Sunday School back-along – sweet as can be, hair done up in a pink ribbon, white frock and granny's Bible, and no knickers.'

The van was left under the beeches by the linhay. Scoble and Yabsley scuffed up the dust as they walked. Ahead of them the dogs parted the wayside nettles with their bodies to sniff the exciting smells and cock their legs. Scoble wore an old straw Panama that made his ears stick out. He moved heavily, the light sliding along the curve of his scythe and twinkling on the point. Every so often Jacko stopped and looked back to make sure he was still there. The strange, masked brightness of the morning had men and animals screwing up their eyes.

George Lugg led out the first pair of horses and the mowing machine. Another team had been borrowed from West Horridge. The farmer and his son would cut the two small fields leaving the large one by the brook to the hired help.

'Dew's light enough,' Yabsley said taking the reins.

'Reckon it'll be a scorcher when the haze lifts,' said George, and he opened the gate.

'Cuttin' grass is thirsty work,' Yabsley said.

'There's a barrel in the barn,' Lugg smiled. 'My brother down at Bickington let me have some of the rough he got from his Kingston Blacks.'

'That's cider sure enough,' said Yabsley with sincere reverence.

Marsh marigolds crowded in the corner of the field by the stream. Partridges whirred away low over the far hedge and Scragg the heron hoisted himself up from the water on his big, grey wings. The dogs, who were old hands at the haymaking, lay around and waited for the first swath to be cut.

'Before I forget it, Leonard,' the farmer said, 'I'm losing poultry and down at Sigford they'm missing a duck or two.'

'Old Blackie's got it in for you, boy,' Yabsley said. 'He's smarter than a commercial traveller. '

The metal bars were lowered and the cutting knives set about an inch from the ground.

'Was it the black sod?' Scoble said, pushing the wart into his cheek.

'Who knows?' said Lugg. ''Tis fox and a bugger that likes chicken. Red or black I idn happy with him on my place.'

'I'll look into it,' Scoble said. 'Fowls have been taken from Yarner Wells. Only I'm certain it idn Blackie. It's not his style.'

'Will you ever catch him, Leonard?' Yabsley said innocently.

'Yes,' Scoble said. The confidence in his voice impressed the men.

'Mind 'ee don't catch you, boy,' said Yabsley.

The trapper rubbed a handful of wet grass on his scythe blade and began honing, moving the stone firmly to and fro.

'It's just a matter of time, Bert,' he said. 'I got the vixen and cubs. One day Old Blackie's luck will run out and I'll have him – wire, gin, dog or gun, I'll have him.'

'Don't let Colonel Shewte hear 'ee, Leonard,' Lugg said. 'Us don't want to upset the Squire.'

Colonel Shewte lived at Lansworthy House, and like most of the local gentry he rode to hounds and respected the animal he hunted.

'He'll be round today,' Lug went on. 'He haven't missed a haymaking yet. Come dinner time we'll see him.'

'They'm all as wet as ducks' arses,' Yabsley said.

'Who?'

'The so-called bloody gentry,' Yabsley snorted. 'They don't know how to peel a spud or tie their own bootlaces.'

'At least they'm honest and fair to deal with,' Lugg said.

'And life can be hard if you cross one.'

The stone purred along the edge of the scythe.

They worked with the effortless rhythm of true peasants. The mowing machine sailed along behind the roans and the knives moved quickly from side to side, clipping the grass, laying it in a swath. When the knives became blunt Scoble put on a fresh bar and sat under the hawthorns sharpening the dull edges with a file. The haze endured for most of the morning to create a sticky heat, but as the sun climbed to noon the sky cleared.

'Christ it's hot!' Bert Yabsley said.

He left the mowing machine and came into the shade. Scoble swung his scythe at the grass growing tight against the hedge where the knives could not reach. Gnats hummed in to greedy on his face.

'I could drink a duck pond,' Yabsley continued. The terriers stood on their hindlegs and placed their front paws on his thighs. Their mouths were open and they were panting.

'They'm thirsty!' Yabsley said in a tender voice. 'Look at their little eyes. My kids look at me like that when they'm ill.'

'They're animals,' said Scoble. The sweat dripped off his nose.

'What about your Jacko?'

The lurcher lifted an ear and whined. He had sprawled in the white bed straw and foxgloves, but on hearing his name he arched his back and yawned. Then he shook himself. For the first time Yabsley saw the meanness and strength of the creature. It seemed to stare through him into places where thought had no right to trespass.

'What about that wicked bugger?' he said.

'He's a dog,' said Scoble.

'Dang me if you idn as cold as yesterday's mutton, Leonard.'

'Animals is animals. We ride them and work them, and hunt them and kill them and eat them. God intended for it to be that way. The Bible says so.'

'You idn a churchgoer, boy.'

'No, but I believes. Church is just another house. There's more of God in my garden than you'll find in Buckfast Abbey or Exeter Cathedral.'

'Get home, do! You're a bloody pagan, Leonard.'

Scoble pecked at his wart with a fingernail and lidded his eyes.

Presently the farmer's youngest son came down to tell them dinner was ready. The boy unharnessed the horses and gave them their feed. He was glad to be home from school for the mowing.

'Don't let 'em drink too much water,' Yabsley said.

'Want to give 'em some of your scrumpy, Bert?' the boy grinned.

'Mind I don't give 'ee a big ear,' Yabsley roared from the centre of a smile.

If was a short walk back to the barn. Normally the haymakers ate in the field, but Lugg had made the mowing a special occasion. His wife brought the pasties – or oggies as they were called in Devon – to the barn. Lugg drew off a half-gallon enamel jug of scrumpy from the wood and filled the men's pots. They drank in deep gulps and the fowls gathered round them waiting for crumbs.

'Bloody beautiful,' Yabsley whispered.

'The Kingston Black,' George Lugg said proudly.

'Agricultural wine,' the farmer said, smiling at his own wit.

Scoble ate slowly, cramming great wads of pasty into his mouth. Although the barn was cool the sweat still poured off him.

'You're giving that oggie hell, Len,' Yabsley said. He nudged George. 'I don't suppose you do a lot of cookin' at home.'

The trapper's eyes were becoming used to the half-darkness. He looked up and saw the barn owls crouching on the beam against the far wall. The soft keening of the owlets was almost drowned by the clucking of the hens and the leathery rustle of their feet in the straw.

'What did you say?'

'Mind you don't eat your fingers, boy,' Yabsley said. 'If you had a woman at Yarner's Cott you'd get oggies every day and somethin' better at night.'

George fluted through his nose into his cider pot making the pale yellow liquid bubble.

The old owls were clacking their mandibles. Why don't you fly off? Scoble thought. The young ones will grow on your strength, then desert you. If the vixen hadn't bothered about the cubs she could have escaped. He remembered the river and the liquid rustling of the grass, and the sky too hot and cerulean to be English. Half of him was scared and the other half excited. Then the noise and the filth and the death. And men died to save their comrades, strangers dying for strangers. They forgot their wives and families, forgot their sweethearts and took shrapnel for some stranger on the wire. His upper lip curled. Lose a leg, gain a medal – Shit! Shit on King and Country.

'Leonard.'

Scoble belched and drank another pot of cider in one go. The jug was refilled and went the rounds. The terriers dashed among the fowls, but Jacko sat beside his master and growled.

'Ever had a woman, Len?' Yabsley said.

Like a badger, Scoble thought, never lets go. Like to see him on the end of a Prussian bayonet, pig on a skewer, a big fat target.

'Why?' he said.

'Only askin'.'

'Women are like tapeworms,' Scoble said.

'We all had mothers, boy.'

'Us didn't have no say in the matter. Wives is different.'

'You have to earn your oats,' George Lugg said.

The farmer cleared his throat and looked down at his boots. Things had gone too far.

'Will it be gins or snares, Leonard?' he asked.

'Snares.'

'Idn it hard to get a fox in a wire?'

'Not if you know how.'

Yabsley glared at him and said, 'Give us some more of that scrumpy, maister.'

The trapper stuffed his face with pasty and shrugged.

The jug passed from hand to hand and the air was filled with the chaff of small talk. Scoble sat gazing at the owls.

Colonel Shewte and his daughter made a brave show of interest in Lugg's affairs. The workers sat at attention and their speech became as stiff as their backs. The gentleman's platitudes merged with the clucking of the hens and the softer more distant summer sounds. The tall, flat-chested girl wore a flower-print frock and sandals, and a tortoiseshell slide in her hair, which was the kind of dull brown that few men notice.

'Weather couldn't be better, Lugg.'

'No, sir.'

'Many partridges?'

'A few, sir – more than last year.'

'Good show.'

Weather's on our side, sergeant major, the subaltern said. Cricket weather, he smiled. And the sergeant major smiled, although he came from Liverpool and had never known anything but poverty and hard graft. Get the men away quickly, the subaltern said. His light, lounge bar accent had the flesh crinkling on Scoble's neck. Give 'em their due, Corporal Wellan said. They know how to die. Yes, Scoble thought, and they've got something to die for. Their England, their cricket, their woods and fields and rivers.

He glanced up at Shewte. He was his father's son, and no mistake. Scoble tilted his pot. Lieutenant General Shewte had been an even more imposing figure. He too had come down to Sedge Brimley for the haymaking. Leonard's father had been impressed. And the Lieutenant General had packed old labourers and their wives off to the workhouse, yet the poor had never condemned him or remarked on the inhumanity.

'Is the cider good, Scoble?' Colonel Shewte said briskly.

'The best, maister.'

'And the foxes?'

Scoble did not flinch.

'Out and about takin' lambs and chickens and things.'

'We'll let the hunt know. Foxes are the hunt's business.'

'Yes, sir.'

'We'll get Old Blackie for you, Scoble,' the colonel smiled. 'Stick to the small beer. No more cubs and vixens.'

'What do'ee mean, sir?'

'No more foxes.'

'Bible says we got dominion over the birds and the beasts. Don't that apply to foxes, sir?'

'This is Devon, not the Holy Land, Scoble.'

The trapper opened his cigarette tin.

'In Genesis it says there was a Garden of Eden. Well, I got a garden. The Bible don't say the Moors of Eden – just garden. And I reckon there was foxes in it.'

'We must be off, Lugg,' Colonel Shewte said, turning his back on Scoble and smiling now at the farmer.

'Will you have some cider before you go, sir?' Lugg said.

''Tis a pressing of Kingston Blacks.'

Colonel Shewte held up a hand and politely declined. Striding along the lane beneath the beech leaves, he said, 'What do you make of Scoble, Jenny?'

The girl frowned.

'He has a parochial imagination, Daddy.'

'So has God, my dear. So has God,' the Colonel chuckled. 'But never mind, we must look after the foxes.'

A goldcrest sang from the clustered white florets of cow parsley. It was seeking insects. Printed on the air behind father and daughter was the rasping chirr of the mowing machine, then Lugg's voice bellowing at his youngest boy, telling him to 'get out of the bloody seat and let the horses rest'.

'When's your American coming down, Jenny?' Colonel Shewte said.

'Soon – next week some time.'

'You like him, don't you?'

'Very much.'

'He's not too keen on hunting, I believe.'

'No, but he's not a crank. I suppose the war has put a lot of people off blood sports. Richard is just a nice human being.'

She smiled and suddenly looked very pretty.

Lugg wandered over to Scoble while the last swath was being cut.

'Best forget the snares, Len,' he said sheepishly. 'Shewte knows what you did at Wistman's.'

'So?'

'So I don't want no foxes trapped on my land.'

Scoble parted his stubble with a fingertip to get at the wart. The horses plodded towards him. He lifted a shock of grass on his boot and let it fall. The field was whispering.

BEAST OF THE EARTH

At last the drought ended and the wind went round to the west. It rained slowly in showers that cooled the air and made everything fresh and pleasant. Heavier downpours swelled the streams and raised the level of the ponds, and the hiss of raindrops hitting the water became a familiar sound.

There was a loneliness about the Leighon Ponds and the Becca Brook that surpassed all the country Wulfgar had visited. Often the hush enclosing them was intense, punctured by the cry of a moorfowl or the croak of a raven. It was the dream landscape and in the early part of the day he moved like a sleepwalker letting outside forces guide him. Everything conspired to create the timeless quality – the rise of fish, the fall of a leaf, the flags curling at the tips in the breeze.

'And God said, Let the earth bring forth
the living creature after his kind, cattle
and creeping thing, and beast of the earth
after his kind; and it was so.

And God made the beast of the earth
after his kind, the cattle after their kind,
and everything that creepeth upon the earth
after his kind; and God saw that
it was good.

And God said, Let us make man in our image, after
our likeness; and let them have dominion over the
fish of the sea, and over the fowl of the air, and over
the cattle, and over all the earth, and over every
creeping thing that creepeth upon the earth.'

Scoble shut his Bible.

'Over the beast of the earth, Jacko,' he said. 'That's foxes, boy – and idn I a man? It don't say gentleman – just plain, simple man. If the toffs can kill him with their bloody hounds I can trap him.'

He hacked a point on the stake of the heavy fox snare. He was happy, and Jacko, sensing his mood, became playful. When Scoble was calm the hot screw rarely turned in the dog's skull, but the visions of horror lay in ambush and there were times when he had to go and lie in the wood stack, tearing at the bark with his teeth, letting the madness escape through his nose in a whine.

Scoble put half a dozen of the heavy snares in the sack and ran an expert eye over the rows of potatoes. Under the ash trees at the far end of the garden he had a keeper's gibbet reserved exclusively for members of the crow family. The carcasses of magpies, jays, carrion crows, rooks and daws hung in decomposition. Scoble gathered maggots from the birds to use as bait for the illegal taking of pheasants.

The ferrets, which scowled at him from the wire netting of their hutch, were sleek and fit. He fed them on rabbits in fur, chickens' heads, entrails and birds in feather, but they were never permitted to overeat. Every thing and every creature in Yarner's Cott was put to good use, a lesson he had learnt from his parents in a home where he had been treated like a possession rather than a child. His character had been formed by those early years of drudgery and loneliness.

The jill ferrets clutched the wire and stood upon their hind feet to greet him.

'They'm worse than you for rabbits, Jacko,' Scoble murmured. And the dog thought he was growling and laid back his ears.

After the rain had fallen the night became still again, and an unknown living something moved through the rushes and plopped into the water. Romany was scrunching an eel on the dam, when his mate whistled to him from the margins of the wood.

Wulfgar came down Black Hill at speed trying to contain his frustration. Stargrief had gone off without a word like a true mystic. 'I'll give him one more sunset,' Wulfgar thought, 'then we'll take the dog my way.'

But he loved the old fox and was merely voicing his impatience.

The rooks in Holwell's beeches had finally stopped cawing. Softly burning Antares hung over Rippon Tor and a moon big enough and bright enough to please all predators rose above Haytor Down. Soon it was high over Leighon and mirrored in the ponds. A barn owl drifted along the brook and became one with the silence.

He lapped the current as it sped babbling over grit and pebbles. Tongues of silt and storm debris shaped the flow. Beneath the oaks were mossy boulders, uprooted trees and torn branches. Here the Becca ran in a freshet, moon-speckled. Eels flickered in the shadowy deeps, dragging their silver slackness over rocks that had been polished and rounded by water. The bends were thick with jetsam.

Having successfully stalked moorfowl he came to the pool below Leighon House. The deep belling of a hound carried across the lawn, then stopped as though someone had comforted the creature.

Wulfgar had reached a place where the river seemed to have fallen asleep. He made scats on a boulder that served as a scenting post and cleared the arching root of an oak in one leap. The wire noose jerked viciously at his neck and cut into his windpipe. His body was thrown horizontal and slammed down on the ground with a thump. A great surge of panic flooded his gut, spreading like frost through his nervous system. His feet scrabbled for purchase and he tried to leap up and out of the snare. The wire bit into his throat, dragging him back. His tongue showed between his teeth and he retched. The motion loosened the wire a little and he was able to take air in quick gasps, but any forward movement threatened to choke the life out of him. Slowly he inched backwards. Then the noose opened a fraction and he sucked in a deep draught of the night, which was now rank with the stink of his fear. The panic gushed out in a steady pumping of urine.

He lay and thought about the problem. He had seen many rabbits in the wire and their hysteria had always made matters worse. The harder they struggled the tighter the snare became until they blacked out and died.

Moving backwards on his belly he located the stake. It was as thick as a pony's fetlock and had been driven to the neck in the hard ground. Wulfgar gnawed at the wire, but it grated on his molars and would not part as the bramble snarls parted. Then he considered digging out the stake but any effort brought a savage reaction from the snare. Closing his eyes he gave a wail of despair that lofted to a full-bodied howl.

'Is there anything I can do, friend?' said a shrill voice at his side.

Chivvy-yick grinned and chittered and jigged about in the restlessness of his joy.

'Want me to loosen the wire with me strong little teeth?'

Wulfgar smiled despite the noose.

'Loosen my throat, more likely,' he said.

'Dear O dear! – don't old Canker Head trust Chivvy-yick? Ain't he grateful?'

'Don't play games with me, man's scat.'

The stoat laughed at this tremendous insult.

'You ain't in no position to be nasty,' he said. 'There ain't no foxes round to back you up, and that loud-mouthed vixen is just a kennel for grubs now from what I hear. Miss 'er, do you, Canker Head?'

Wulfgar growled and flung himself at the stoat but the snare plucked him from the centre of his pounce, leaving him choking and writhing in the grass.

'That was truly funny, Canker Head,' Chivvy-yick guffawed. 'Snares suit you. Rot my bones! – if you ain't more comical than a drummer in a wire! What a pity you crossed Chivvy-yick. Twice, if I'm not mistaken.'

'The third time could be fatal.'

The fitch rippled through the grass and sprawled before him and began to lick the black tip of its tail.

'How come a smart fox like you got his head in a noose?'

Wulfgar recovered his breath but was loath to waste it on the fitch.

'OK, Mange Bag,' Chivvy-yick said. 'There ain't no love lost between us but I don't do the trapper's dirty work like them ferrets. What do you want me to do?'

'No tricks?'

'No tricks. I spit on all foxes but Man is Man.'

He shut his eyes, drew down the corners of his mouth, shook his head and shuddered.

'There is a badger in the sett higher upstream,' Wulfgar said. 'He's my friend. He and the sow could dig out the stake.'

'Great diggers and burrowers and miners are the brocks,' Chivvy-yick agreed. 'And Thorgil is the best of the breed. I'll fetch him if you agree to one thing.'

'Very well,' Wulfgar said.

'No more coney-snatchin' off fitches. Never. Not ever.'

The fox nodded.

'Don't go away,' Chivvy-yick grinned. 'I won't be a jiffy.'

It was most unfitchlike behaviour and the stoat's departure left Wulfgar both perplexed and guilt-ridden. The short June night was nearly done. He yawned and the wire cut into his flesh. The stars had become feeble, like glow-worms.

He fell asleep without laying his brush across his nose.

The sharp stab of pain brought him back to consciousness with a jolt that nearly throttled him. Chivvy-yick had bitten the tip of his ear. Blood pulsed freely down the side of his head into his chest fur.

The fitch rolled around in the throes of help-less laughter and the rest of the stoat pack jeered at Wulfgar.

'O I do like foxy's collar,' Shiv cried.

'He looks like a rat on the keeper's gibbet,' said Flick-Flick.

'Like a ferret on a lead,' Snikker crowed.

'I bet three drummers to a dead dog old Canker Head really thought I was going to get his mate the brock,' Chivvy-yick gasped. 'Imagine – a nice bit of hope to brighten his misery. Heroic little me would arrange for Scat Stink to escape from the wire – despite all the aggravation he's given me.'

He bared his fangs and narrowed his eyes.

'O no no no! It could not be done. Never, no, not ever. Chivvy-yick went and got his nearest and dearest. A fitch can't gloat alone. Stoat gotta share a good gloat. A stoat gloat. Yik-yik-yik.'

Wulfgar gazed placidly at him. Day was breaking and he felt close to death, but he would not sacrifice his dignity in a slanging match.

> Though I may die
> the grass will grow,
> the sun will shine
> the stream will flow.

The words of the prayer came from the living world beyond himself. He felt he had drawn them from the air, like breath.

Soon the fitches grew bored with the mocking and taunting. At Slickfang's suggestion they played the Blood Game, darting in to nip an ear or a paw, or to close their teeth on the fox's brush. Wulfgar found it more difficult to endure the humiliation than the pain.

And lying close to the ground he dreamt of Teg and remembered how they had comforted each other. Oakwhelp and the other cubs would be waiting in the golden field. All the heroic dog foxes would gather and he would walk beside Tod through the radiant places. But not yet, another voice cried inside him. The sweetness of the new morning was too good to leave.

TREACHEROUS CONTRIVANCES

Higher up, the water frizzled in grit-choked runnels, and jets spurted between the boulders. He stirred and the pain pounced. Green leaves climbed in cliffs heaped with the noise of insects and birds. The light had broadened and distant things were visible. Briefly the rain soaked the trees, dripping through the foliage. The wind swept up on the shower and lifted the end of it as it would belly-out a curtain.

The stoats skipped around him, breaking the heads off the dandelions. The grass was full of the heavy, gold flowers. Wulfgar felt the familiar ache of regret. He had been careless with his life but now he cherished those little eternities of running on high ground. He pressed his nose to the earth, which smelt of the past.

'This one's got coney blood in him,' Chivvy-yick sneered. 'You'd get more fight out of a blind kitten.'

He jumped onto Wulfgar's back and cried, 'Behold, Mighty Fitch on the dung hill.'

The stoat pack hissed, then they were colliding with each other in a hotch-potch of limbs and bodies, but only for a second. Something landed in their midst and there was a silent explosion of fitches. Chivvy-yick departed furtively, avoiding the russet blur that streaked after Flick-Flick. The stoat twisted and screamed. The fox sprang, claws spread wide and fell on him, holding him pinned. Fetid breath was against his face. Once more he screamed, but the fox closed his jaws on the stoat's neck and the struggling ceased.

'Let the rest of the cowards run,' the stranger said. His words rumbled up from his throat.

He was a great, gaunt animal with a scarred head and a rip in his right ear.

'You are in a bad way, friend,' he added gently.

'It could be worse,' said Wulfgar. 'What do they call you, stranger?'

'Killconey. I've come from the country up beyond the Black Mire, near the sea that swallows the sun every evening.'

'I am Wulfgar.'

'Have you prepared to meet death, Wulfgar?'

'Yes – but it wasn't easy with the fitches swarming all over me.'

His heart sank and he whispered, 'Is it nearby?'

Killconey gave him a slow nod.

'A man is coming up the river. He has a dog. They will be here shortly.'

'I can smell them,' Wulfgar said.

'Has Tod been good to you?' asked Killconey.

'Nearly always,' Wulfgar smiled.

His blood ran thin and cold. The fear leaked from his fur and stank like sackcloth soaked in urine.

A stick cracked under someone's boot and a man coughed.

'I daren't stay any longer,' Killconey said.

'No. You must run. I'm grateful for what you did.'

'I won't be far away if it's any comfort.'

Wulfgar managed another smile.

'Go quickly,' he said. 'This is something that has to be done alone.'

And I won't die cowering like a rabbit, he thought. The hill foxes will remember me. His hackles stiffened and he grunted through his nostrils, sounding like a badger.

The dog scampered up the path and began to bark.

The young American was glad to get on the train and shake the dust of London off his shoes. He had done all the things he had wanted to do. He had seen the sights and eaten seafood at the street stalls and drunk

Guinness at the Prospect of Whitby, but the old city with its bomb scars and double-deckers was only an interlude.

The Torbay Express thundered across the shires, building up steam, pushing through the showery June day into the West Country. After Somerset there were small red fields among the greens of woods, corn and pasture, and as the train approached the cathedral city the foothills of Dartmoor were clearly visible.

He got out at Exeter St David's and collected the spaniel from the guard's van. The dog belonged to friends who were holidaying in the States. They had insisted he make Aish Cottage his home until the fall. On leave from the Air Force he had stayed in pubs and farmhouses. The moors were one of two good things to come out of the war. The other was Jenny.

Propped up in the back of the Shewtes' Humber Snipe he let her do all the talking. She still looked like a little girl. Sometimes the leaf-dazzle parted and sunlight flooded the car. Then he remembered her serenity back in those days when Dartmoor was the summer place on the edge of the nightmare. Now there were no more missions in Flying Fortresses so loaded with bombs they could hardly take off. But he had come through it all.

Looking out of the window he saw the River Teign glinting among the trees.

Aish Cottage stood small and whitewashed in the beeches above the Becca Brook. Up the hill was

Beckaford Farm and a mile to the north lay the village of Manaton.

The Shewtes drove away leaving him to unpack his gear and sort through the wildlife books he had bought in town. The spaniel romped on the lawn that needed cutting, birds sang and the beech leaves rustled in a low, watery way, like a stream flowing.

OK, his father had said – go to England for five or six months. Get it out of your system. He was puzzled and Richard never tried to explain. Montana was just about the greatest place on earth, but Dartmoor was the dream. It was like a piece of music and he wanted to hear it through to the end. Then he could go home.

Later he drank whisky and took his book out into the evening to catch the last of the sun. He wanted to sit in the long grass and read that passage from Anna Karenina where Levin mows the meadow with his peasants. The great literature went well with the sound of the trees and the solitude. Maybe he would put on the Berlioz seventy-eights, or maybe he would write a poem.

The dog came up to him wagging her tail. And after dark he sat on the sofa listening to the Fantastique while moonlight slanted through the window. It made him think of Walden and Thoreau and Wordsworth's poems of the imagination. Towards midnight he took the dog through the oaks to the river and walked its banks as far as Becky Falls.

The night was calm and starry. He knew the stars well but they looked fine without the flak or the white slashes of tracer. Antares glowed softly in the south, and all the obscene human deaths could not cancel out its beauty.

He sat on a boulder and the spaniel laid her chin in his lap. A cockchafer bumped against his forehead, once, twice, four times, and the water spilled white and loud over the rocks. Moonlight lay fragmented on the floor of the wood. Sitting there he thought about the things he had done. Being a survivor gave you an edge over your fellow creatures. His own company was enough. He didn't want anymore bullshit or dirty jokes or empty laughter. He wished to hell he hadn't promised to dine with the Shewtes the following night. Small talk was a kind of insult to the men who had never come back from the raids over Germany.

When the shower woke him he was lying on the moss beneath a holly bush, and day had broken. The sky above Great Houndtor was pale blue blotched with big grey clouds. Raindrops rattled on the leaves and hit his face. It was cold. He pulled the collar of his old tweed jacket up to the lobes of his ears and the dog planted a splathering kiss on his nose.

They went with the path up the side of the river. A blackbird alarmed and the shower petered out. Through the trees on his left he saw the house at the top of a sweep of lawn. The dog ran ahead of him and disappeared behind some boulders and gave tongue. Richard crouched to avoid the branches of the oak and saw the fox. The spaniel was barking furiously now and made token lunges at the trapped animal. Wulfgar faced her silently. He had encountered liver-and-white spaniels before. They were noisy but not too dangerous. The fox got to his feet and wondered how he was going to fight the wire and the dog.

'Stay, Meg,' Richard said.

The spaniel clapped down, whimpered, and looked over her shoulder at the man. Richard slipped out of his jacket and when he held it in front of him like a matador's cape, Wulfgar growled and fidgeted despite the wire. The fox leapt backwards in a contorted arc that fell apart in mid-air. He was choking to death. The noose had lacerated his throat. He beat at it with his paws, then the coat covered his head and the man was holding him tight between the knees, almost cracking his ribs. Fingers fumbled the wire and Wulfgar snapped and bit one of them clean through the nail.

'Easy, fella,' Richard grated.

He tugged open the snare with both hands and Wulfgar wriggled free. The fox ran blindly until the coat jagged on a root and was ripped off his head. He shook himself, laid back his ears and climbed the slope of oaks and boulders. The spaniel sent a single, defiant bark floating after him.

Using a rock, the American smashed the top of the stake and removed the wire.

'Away with your nets and traps and snares and treacherous contrivances,' he murmured.

Pythagoras knew his stuff. Someone ought to write it on the sky in letters the size of the Empire State Building. But he was no longer angry when he picked up the dead fitch. He examined it from fangs to claws before stowing it in his coat pocket.

Crouching at the pool he washed his damaged finger. Beneath the surface were pebbles of many colours – buzzard brown, rust, bronze, white, ochre. Close to the bank the shillets were half-hidden by drifts of grit. A little dark fish called a miller's thumb shot away, and above the water the midges and caddis flies rose in tribal dance. The morning was made for living things.

'I saw it but I don't believe it,' said Killconey.

He had finished licking the wounds on Wulfgar's body that the dark fox could not reach.

'Of course he didn't mean to free me,' said Wulfgar.

'Then it was an accident?'

'What else? Maybe he wanted me alive.'

Killconey shuddered. 'That would be worse than a bad death.'

'Stargrief says many animals are kept in captivity.'

'But why? Do they eat us?'

'I don't know. Men aren't like animals.'

They had come onto Hamel Down and were lying in the sun above Grimspound.

'I feel as if I've got a chicken bone stuck in my gullet,' Wulfgar said. 'Tod, it's sore!'

Killconey grinned.

'Will you stay to see the lurcher die?' asked Wulfgar.

'No. I'm not of your clan. It's your business.'

'Where are you going?'

'Here and there.'

'If you pass the ponds look out for me.'

'Run with your head high, dark brother.'

A TRUE ANIMAL

Under Greator Rocks was a meadow that always escaped the mowing machine. It was very small, bounded on three sides by woodland and on the other by the Becca Brook. Wulfgar visited it often for the mice and conies. In the wind the grass became waves of silver light, hollowed here and there with shadows that quaked and rocked and tossed out handfuls of larks.

On quiet days the rustlings betrayed mice and voles, birds, lizards and snakes. They threaded through the foxtail grass and meadow soft, making the field scabious and poppies shake. The scabious was a sturdy, lilac flower, a little lighter in colour than the meadow-crane's bill. When the wind laid back the grass the sun caught the flowers and set the goat's beard and buttercups glinting yellow. Sometimes the rustle among the packed stems was an adder swallowing a lark nestling.

The American had learnt to keep still for long periods. He came to the woods and river without the spaniel and waited for things to happen. Once he saw Wulfgar on hindlegs in the meadow catching moths, and near the end of June he glimpsed the otters fishing the big pond. He did not come frequently because he was afraid of alarming the wild creatures. He had also rediscovered the North Moor and its stretches of true wilderness.

The raven said cork in his deep, cheerful voice, while Stormbully and Fallbright soared above him to an immense height. Rain had beat down all day, but the evening was clear and warm. The moorfowl led their second brood across the pond. Romany had killed a few of their tribe but this family had nested safely in the lower boughs of an alder.

The dipper popped out of the Becca Brook and sat on a stone and watched the moorfowl. His nest was in the bank nearby. At dawn Romany had come close to seizing the dipper as the bird strode through the current like a tiny man walking with head bowed into the wind and rain.

'Have you seen the Yank?' Lugg said.

Scoble yawned and said he hadn't. The shearing crew had visited Sedge Brimley. The grey-faced Dartmoors from the border grazing, and the hardier Scottish Blackfaces driven down from the moors, had surrendered their fleeces. Lugg and his son were on the 'shorts', pouring double Johnny Walkers into themselves and trying not to look smug.

'Well, this Yank lives down Beckaford way,' the farmer continued. 'He was a bomber pilot, so they do say, and he's taken up with Jenny Shewte.'

'And he idn all there,' George cawed. 'Dang me! – if he idn more than a bit crazy.'

'Anybody who's sweet on the Shewte maid have got to have some thatch loose,' said Scoble. 'There's more tit on a grasshopper than her's got.'

'That's as maybe,' said Lugg, 'but Yanky's always trapesin' about the moors at night, talkin' to himself and singin' and what have you. That's what they'm sayin' all over.'

'He's against huntin', too,' said George. 'Bugger! – you should have heard un sounding off at the Kestor the other evening. He's against hunting, shooting, fishing, trapping – every-bloody-thing. He went white as a sheet when Ernie started jawin' about the otter hounds.'

'Probably a vegetabletarian,' his father growled. 'Bleddy foreigner.' He glanced slyly at Scoble and added, 'Be you goin' to have a short, Leonard?'

'I'll have a rum with 'ee, maister.'

Using the fat tip of his forefinger he stroked his wart and thought about the newcomer and the smashed snare-stake. The wisps of dark fur had been Blackie's, he felt it in his water. He recalled the stink of fox and the broken dandelions, and he had been worried in case it was hunt folk who had set the beast free. The rum was a trickle of warmth in his stomach. Thank Christ it was the Yank. His upper lip curled. Blackie had the luck of Old Nick. It was black looking after black, but luck only took you so far. Ted Yeo went right through the war – the Somme, Ypres, the lot – and not a scratch on him. First day back on the farm he slipped on the muck in the yard and cracked his head on the water-trough. Scoble snapped his fingers and smiled. Dead as a doornail.

Wulfgar sensed Stargrief's presence before the air confirmed it.

'I'm not alone,' Stargrief said.

He hesitated among the reed tussocks.

'I can smell dog,' Wulfgar growled, puffing out his fur and lowering his head.

Queenie the collie crept nervously from the reeds and crouched beside Stargrief.

'Calm down and let me speak,' the old fox said.

'Next time speak before you run off on your bardic quests,' Wulfgar said. 'I'm not interested in the ancestral stuff. I want the lurcher dead.'

'Would tomorrow morning be soon enough?'

Wulfgar sat up and glanced down his muzzle at the collie.

'And will "*it*" help?' he said pointedly.

'Queenie will help,' Stargrief said. 'Without her it won't be easy.'

'She has been Man's thing. Why should I trust her?'

'I trust her. She is an animal now.'

'But the lurcher is a dog. Could you betray a fox? Could you betray one of your own kind?'

'There are dogs like the lurcher who slave for men and there are dogs like Queenie who live in the sacred manner.'

'It's true,' said Queenie.

'Has the lurcher ever done you any harm?' Wulfgar said.

'Not yet – but he might. And Stargrief has been good to me.'

'Queenie will bring the lurcher to the ponds,' said Stargrief.

'What if she crosses us and joins forces with the dog?'

'What if I turn into a sheep and offer you my scats?' Stargrief said impatiently. 'What if the Tor got up and ran?'

'If the lurcher is mad I'll be in danger all the time,' Queenie said. 'He may kill me before we get halfway to the ponds. I'm gambling my life. For my sake I hope he sees me as a bitch, not a victim. Being an animal I don't feel safe with him loose.'

Her obvious sincerity brought a smile to Wulfgar's lips.

'Are you thirsty?' he asked.

The collie nodded.

'Come and drink,' Wulfgar said. 'The otters will be busy in the pond soon. It might be better if they met you now rather than tomorrow. The sight of two dogs coming down the hill unannounced would be a bit too much.'

He had eaten more than his usual amount of red meat, finishing off with a couple of frogs whose back legs had been devoured by a stoat. He sat cleaning himself beside the Becca while the dipper flitted in and out of the water.

The last remnants of daylight faded. Moonrise silvered the sky, and the moon edged up and cleared Holwell Tor. In the heronry below Great Houndtor Scrag tucked his beak under a wing and slept.

Wulfgar looked at Stargrief and said, 'If you had told me what you were up to I would have greeted Queenie with more than raised hackles.'

'I had to find her and speak to her,' Stargrief snapped. 'I couldn't prophesy her willingness to help.'

'Why not, you're a prophet aren't you?'

'He's not always this stupid,' Stargrief told Queenie as they came to the water. 'He gets irritated because I am what he will become. Sometimes he peeps at me and sees himself five years from now.'

'Only if Tod's got a weird sense of humour,' Wulfgar laughed.

Queenie certainly smelt like an animal and, unlike the lurcher, no Man odours clung to her. She settled as the foxes settled among the alder roots and told them about her life on the farm.

'I wasn't an animal,' she said. 'I really was a thing – like the mowing machine and the threshing machine, like the horse, the sheep and the cow. I was given very little to eat and worked from dawn to sunset. Then the farmer took away my pups and beat me when I howled for them at night. Now I make my own life according to the seasons.'

'It was the way when Tod stalked the moors,' said Stargrief.

They all spoke the canidae argot. Out in the pond the otters whistled and splashed.

'To walk in freedom is enough,' said Queenie.

'It's the only thing,' Wulfgar said.

'You were born to it,' Queenie smiled. 'I returned to it. It is my great adventure.'

Romany came lolloping out of the water and shook himself. Then he laid the trout at Queenie's feet.

'Dog eat trout?' he said.

'I eat anything,' said the collie.

'Trout isn't anything. Trout is otter food and otter eats only the best.'

'Damned good fish,' Queenie agreed, taking a mouthful.

'Later on I'll get you a coney,' said Wulfgar.

BY FOX CRAFT

Stargrief and Queenie left for Yarner Wood at daybreak. The collie bitch was fit and lean from living wild and Stargrief had difficulty keeping up with her. They ran along the old granite tramway as far as Haytor Ponds and cut across the heath to pick up the Manaton road. From Ullacombe way a dog barked incessantly, and the east wind that usually meant fair weather carried the noise far over the in-country.

The animals did not speak as they took up their positions. The vague, dark world of early morning opened to the flood of sunrise. Slates glinted on the roof of the cottage, and a glimmer of leaves spread over the wood. Birdsong swelled and the first bees burrowed into the foxglove bells.

Stargrief jumped onto the top of the hutch, surprising the ferrets who started to snake up and down, more curious than alarmed. Stargrief jerked back his head and let out a tomcat screech that seemed to hang on the air and fade away like smoke. Ceaselessly he repeated the cry until Scoble appeared at the bedroom window. The trapper ran his tongue over his lips. One shot would lift that skinny old fox clean off the hutch onto the collar of a lady's coat, but a few stray pellets would also take care of the ferrets. Stargrief looked up at him and barked. You're asking for it, boy, Scoble thought. A kamekaze fox, like them bloody mazed Japs.

'Us won't disappoint un, Jacko,' he whispered.

The lurcher followed him downstairs and stood raking fleas from behind his ear. The stiff hind foot moved in a blur.

'Fox, Jacko,' Scoble said, flinging open the door. 'Get 'im, boy. Show un who's boss.'

Dizziness climbed to the dome of Jacko's skull. He saw the fox on the ferret hutch like an object seen through the wrong end of a telescope. He flew towards it and leapt the wall as the white-tagged brush vanished into the leaves. A jay looped up through the branches, its sudden chatter perforating the dog's brain. Agony was driven hard into each tiny hole, making Jacko whine and bang his head on the trunk of an oak. The fox was running down the path where it curved and became lost in shadow. Jacko raced after him. He would bring the fox back dead to his master, lay it at his feet and get the 'Good Jacko – Lovely Jacko' treatment.

The bend surprised him. He fought the camber without success and skidded hard into the foxgloves and nettles. Anger screwed back his lips. Red is dead. When a creature turned red it had to die, it was the sign. The stars said so.

He regained the path effortlessly. A creature sat on the mud ahead of him. Jacko snarled and raised his hackles. The fox had changed into a collie dog.

'How you do that?' he cried.

'How I do what?' said Queenie.

'Turn into dog.'

For a moment Queenie was tempted to pretend she had magical powers, but maybe Jacko wouldn't be sufficiently impressed. If you are crazy a fox is a fox no matter what it looks like. Queenie shuddered. To think logically was to place her life in the lurcher's jaws. Keep it simple, she thought, think mad dog.

'I am dog – collie to be exact. I always have been,' she said.

'No,' said Jacko. 'You fox. Stars tell me. Stars don't lie.'

He crept towards her with the terrible, deliberate gait of a hunter preparing to spring.

'Stars don't lie,' Queenie agreed. 'But we don't always hear them correctly. There was a fox. He went down rabbit hole. You'll never catch him. Come and smell me, Jacko. I really am dog. Nose don't lie.'

'How you know my name?' the lurcher said. Queenie noted with relief that his hackles had dropped.

'Every dog on the moors has heard of the mighty fox fighter. You have killed more foxes than I've had bones. I bow to your bravery, cunning and speed.'

She inclined her head and Jacko trotted up to her and made a thorough examination.

'You dog all right,' he said, licking her under the tail. 'Why you come looking for me?'

'Stars tell me to. They say Jacko lonely. He need a good mate – a dog to give him plenty little Jackoes.'

'Lurcher mates with lurcher,' Jacko said haughtily. 'But you a good bitch. I let you be my friend.'

'It's a great honour. My name is Queenie.'

'OK – we run together, Queenie. Stars say we go to open places. You do as you're told and everything will be like the puppy time.'

He escorted her out of Yarner, across the tableland of furze and heather to the slope that swept up to Hay Tor. Jacko was happy. His master had given him freedom, and the stars were kind, not like white hot claws digging into his mind. Queenie was O.K. – maybe later he would kill her and send her to the stars. They'd like that, for he had never sent them a dog to play with. Endlessly the larks shrilled. The lurcher and the collie loped along, following the sheep paths through the deep bracken.

When they drank at Hay Tor Ponds they saw newts among the jumble of sunken roots. Swiftly a cloud passed over the sun, then another. Jacko cocked his leg against the rusty iron winch and watched the dragonflies whizz past his head.

'There was a black fox at the big pond before daybreak,' Queenie said. Despite her courage and sagacity her voice shook. Jacko flashed her a malevolent glance.

'He wasn't like ordinary foxes,' she went on. 'He sat by the water and just stared at me.'

'And you did nothing?'

'I was scared, Jacko. I'm only a simple collie.'

The red gut burst behind his eyes and inundated the world. The red dog stood shivering beside an expanding pool of blood. Not yet, the stars crowed. Wait, Jacko. Good boy, Jacko.

'Show me black fox,' he said.

'But he'll be gone by now.'

He uncoiled and caught her off-guard at the end of a spectacular leap. Queenie lay staring breathlessly up into his mouth.

'Stars tell Jacko what to do,' he growled. 'Jacko tell you what to do. Take me to black fox.'

The red mist billowed and gaped to reveal the sun. They climbed the path out of the quarry and ran shoulder to shoulder to Holwell Tor. A panic-stricken flock of Scottish Blackfaces stampeded before them, with the pale, embarrassed look of all shorn sheep. And quite casually the stars ordered Jacko to kill, so he cut his way through the animals, using his fangs like a saw-edged knife, making fierce, slashing strokes.

One ewe stood her ground to protect her lambs, and Jacko tore out her throat and grinned at Queenie. His lips were crimson with the blood that dribbled down his muzzle.

'Stars need lots of sheep,' he gasped.

A man shouted. The dogs turned towards the sound and saw a distant figure running though the whortle-berries under Hay Tor.

'Pity the stars didn't see the man before you killed the sheep,' Queenie sighed. 'Sheep-killing means plenty trouble.'

'I am magic dog,' the lurcher cried. 'No man will ever harm Jacko.'

'I believe you – but let's get out of here.'

'Now Jacko show you how to kill fox.'

From the reeds and marsh grass they were able to scru-tinise the big pond. A fish rose and ringed the surface. Fat summer clouds sailed over Greator Rocks, higher still were the mare's tails of stratus, but in between lay broad patches of blue sky.

'OK, collie bitch,' Jacko whispered. 'Where's fox?'

'He was down there by the willow,' said Queenie, feeling her innards slowly somersault. 'I thought he'd be gone.'

'If he don't come pretty damn quick Jacko send you to stars.'

The lurcher flattened his ears and grinned. The red collie grinned back, and red of many hues marbled the sky. Leisurely he gathered the cuckoo-spit off the grass stems with the tip of his tongue. The frog-hoppers had left small white gobs of it everywhere.

Queenie regarded him in disgust.

Rain fell hard and cool but the shower did not last more than a few minutes. Half the sky remained blue and sunny, and while the drops splattered on the pond the house martins visited it by the score, hitting the surface with a splash time after time.

'Maybe black fox turn into bird,' Jacko laughed. His mind was on fire, cooking in his skull.

The shadow grew legs and slid from under the trees. Small leaves silvered in the wind that blew away the last of the shower. The shadow had pointed black ears and a bushy tail. It stopped on the sward where the otters came to roll and play.

'Die, black fox,' Jacko snarled.

A jolt of anger numbed his brain, and ten strides brought him to the sward. The agony fell away from him and instinct measured the distance between himself and his prey, but the black fox was curving out over the reeds into the pond. Jacko splashed after him, the blood-lust eclipsing all his fears and anxieties. He knew he had the strength and the speed to overtake the fox who was swimming with head held high. O how his master would love him and give him the good tasty things off his plate, and the stars would sing lullabies and make the pain go for ever.

The water was soft and cool. The deep thrusting of his forepaws carried him closer to the fox. Kill the fox, kill the collie, kill the sheep. Kill-killy-killy. O Jacko do cracko the old foxio. Sharp and savagely relentless, like gin traps, the otters' jaws clamped on his hind feet and the sunny world vanished. Jacko twisted and fought to bite the animals as they pulled him down. Water filled his windpipe, and he coughed and writhed and tried to kick for the surface. Briefly the sunlight flashed like a shoal of silver fish above, then he was choking and gulping more water. One by one the stars exploded and vanished, leaving a warm and inviting darkness.

Jacko stopped struggling and sank into it like a puppy dropping into sleep, his mouth and eyes open wide. His legs no longer twitched. He stared from nothingness to nothingness, and the otters swam away trailing little bubbles.

'I thought it would take longer,' Wulfgar said.

The dim shape of Jacko's body was visible just under the water, grey and still.

'It probably wasn't so quick for him,' said Stargrief.

'I know what you mean,' Wulfgar said, remembering the snare. 'But one moment he was there behind me then he was gone. I had imagined a great fight.'

'Like the fights in the clan sagas?' Stargrief grinned.

'Yes.'

'When they turn this into a saga it will become a great fight.'

'Poor Jacko,' said Queenie.

The foxes looked at her.

'He was mad,' the collie continued. 'But perhaps I'd be mad if I had lived with the trapper. Don't misunderstand me – he had to die. If he had killed any more sheep we would all be wiped out. But he was born an animal. Man made him a thing. It saddens me a little.'

'He nearly had Moonsleek,' said Romany. 'His death makes me feel good.'

'Yes, he turned a lot of seasons red,' said Stargrief.

'He died by fox craft,' Romany said. 'Teg will be pleased.'

Wulfgar stared into the depths where the ghostly dog floated, and the old loneliness clenched round his heart. A martin hit the pond and cut through the sunlight again, trailing droplets of water, and as Wulfgar lifted his eyes to follow the flight the vision of his place appeared against the distance. He glided over the snowfield towards the mountains, a beautiful vixen trotting at his side.

'Teg,' he murmured.

But it wasn't her. He turned in desperation and said, 'I can smell approaching rain.'

Romany sniffed the morning.

'I believe you're right,' he said. 'Even though the wind comes off the sea it has a wet feel about it.'

'What's troubling you, Wulfgar?' Stargrief said quietly.

'Nothing. Go back to your bardic dreams.'

'Sometimes I wish I'd never wake from them,' said the ancient dog fox.

THUNDERY WEATHER

The cows were standing in a daydream. Scoble worked his way down the Becca Brook below Holwell and the cattle ignored him. It was a sticky day. On the roof of Holwell barn the swallows were sunbathing. Many young birds were on the wing, swooping over the massed foliage where the hush was silted with insects.

Scoble took off his panama and fanned his face with it. From a line two-thirds of the way up his forehead the skin was very moist and white, and he looked as if he were wearing a red mask. Bloody daft dog, he thought, sticking the hat back on his head. Idly he wondered if the lurcher had killed the fox, for Jacko had been missing two days. Funny old fox! What made un plant his arse on the ferret's hutch? Mazed four-legged vermin, you couldn't fathom them out. His fingers found the wart and stroked it.

The Becca Brook divided to enter the pond. Scoble stopped among the alder saplings on the island and checked the mud. Romany's spoor ran along the water's edge and the otter had dropped his spraint on a rock in midstream. The spraint and the tracks were fresh. Scoble squatted in the grasses, which the sheep and ponies had clipped, and watched and listened.

Above the reeds the crows fluttered up and down. Occasionally one or the other stayed down for a long time.

They said craark in thick contented voices. The glinting blackness of the birds belonged to the thundery weather. He saw the gone-forever crow gripping the mule's intestine with black talons and tugging off a strip with its beak, very clinically and powerfully.

'Christ!' Scoble breathed. 'Jesus Christ!'

He splashed through the shallows and broke into a run.

Swart and Sheol stopped worrying Jacko's carcass and retreated through the tree tops of the lower pond. The trapper was mouthing obscenities as he reached the patch of sward. Jacko lay almost totally submerged, with only the tips of his four feet showing above the surface.

Scoble waded into the pond and retrieved the bloated animal, then he sat cross-legged beside the body. The wounds left by the otters showed red and white amongst slate-coloured hairs.

'You went down fightin',' Scoble said. 'Jacko is a good dog – yes, he's handsome.'

Gently he trailed his fingers along the dog's muzzle. What did Yabsley know about love? It wasn't proper to jaw about it. Some things were spoilt when you talked about them. The dog knew he was loved, that was enough. Leonard and Jacko and all the good days after the conies. He sniffed and fumbled for a cigarette. Soddin' foxes. O yes, they were watching him, he could feel them out there. His flesh crawled. Between the leaves the sunlight twinkled as though on bright eyes. Old Blackie was across the water grinning at him, and a thrill of hatred had him gritting his teeth. As for the scrawny old fox on the ferret hutch, what the hell was he about, caterwaulin' like a vixen on heat?

'No,' he whispered, shaking his head in disbelief.

But if they could gang up to kill a coney they could do the same for a dog. Old Blackie was built like a wolf, and two or three foxes working together might do for a lurcher. Jacko was strong and fast but not too bright, not any more. He was like a windfall from the keeper's gibbet, buzzard bait. Scoble curled his upper lip. The crows had made mulberry smudges of the dog's eyes.

He placed Jacko in a hollow and collected rocks from the river bed to build a cairn over the animal. It was better than a hole in the vegetable garden, better than a grave in a military cemetery. He could lie close to things and sort of be part of what was going on. Why make it easy for the worms?

At last it was finished. He nipped the end of his cigarette between forefinger and thumb. A few shafts of sunlight hit the Holwell side of the valley and slowly faded. The wind had gone round to the west and a dark, moving curtain of rain hid Emsworthy. Swart and Sheol joined the daws on Greator Rocks.

The trapper walked across the boggy ground to the path that led up to Black Hill. As the rain swept in behind him, it drove through his shirt and vest and made the brim of his hat hang limply down over his eyes.

It was cool and quiet in the bar of the Star Inn at Liverton. A fly beat against the window that was open wide enough for the breeze to find its way in. The hedge beyond was buried under honeysuckle, and the scent clung to the tongue like the memory of a rich drink.

Richard Williams drew a deep breath and turned the pages of his bird book. The bar was West Country in a drowsy, guileless way. It had not been tarted up to lure the tourists. Small, low-ceilinged and clean it allowed the imagination to wander off undisturbed into reverie.

He sat at a bare, wooden table in the corner taking in the country scents and the smell of beer and cider. Summer lapped around the pub, and the bright hush of the July afternoon was riddled with the chirping of sparrows and the burring of bees.

On the table were some old copies of John Bull and Picture Post and a tattered Field left behind by a shooting gentleman. The cryptic taste of the scrumpy cut through his thirst. He was very hungry and kept looking towards the kitchen, thinking that perhaps he should have ordered more than half a mutton pie and peas. Meg pushed her nose into his hand. Dog and man had walked a long way with an eye on the weather. The farm labourers and unemployed standing at the bar had nothing to say to him. The book in front of him was a discreet plea for privacy, and the last thing he wanted was inane chat, although sometimes he could not help eavesdropping.

The sky darkened and there was a noisy downpour. He lowered his cider to the halfway mark. His enjoyment of Dartmoor had been tarnished by finding the fox in the snare. He had tried to tell Jenny about the brotherhood of the living and the dead who had dreamed of Utopia. It sounded odd and sentimental – the kindness and compassion that they had hoped would embrace the whole of creation – but the old ways continued, they couldn't change them. The jungle path meandered right back to the gates of Eden. Maybe he had returned to the company of men too soon. Rain falling on the extravagant greenness seemed appropriate. Hope was slipping from him again as it had done on grey days above grey, anonymous German cities.

A young woman brought the meal to his table. Her hair was darker than honey and piled on top of her head. She had a fulsome beauty with a suntanned face and large white teeth, and involuntarily he placed her beside Jenny. But the image of the Shewte girl caused no tremor in his blood. Not so long ago he had needed that bland, sexless quality just as some men had turned to the Virgin Mary. It was a war thing.

He quarried into the pie.

Lugg and his son George had taken a truck full of wethers to Newton Abbot market. They had met Yabsley, Claik and Scoble on a pub crawl and all five of them returned the worse for drink to the Star. The trapper had not said much throughout the morning, but Yabsley was in full song, roaring good humour and reeling off the jokes. They stood at the bar in their braces and shirt sleeves while the cider barrel tap squeaked. The rain had stopped and steam was rising from the stony forecourt.

'Old man Hannaford's gone, then,' said Yabsley.

'Get home, do!' said Lugg. 'When did un go? I was havin' a pint with un last Thursday up the Rock. He didn look poorly.'

'They called the doctor in Tuesday. Seems his heart was conkin' out. 'How long have I got?' old man Hannaford says. 'About five minutes,' says the doctor. 'Idn there anything you can do for me?' the poor old boy says. Doctor looks at his watch and says: 'I could boil you an egg.'

'You mazed bugger, Bert,' laughed the farmer.

'Is old man Hannaford really dead?' said George, wiping the tears from his eyes.

'Dunno,' Yabsley smiled. 'Should be. He's touchin' ninety.'

The trapper sat down and folded his arms on the table. He might have been invisible for all the interest he created among the farmworkers. It was a situation he relished. He was thinking of Jacko, remembering how he used to knead the dog's chest, absently, by the fireside, hour after hour. Yes, you'm a handsome boy, Jacko. Dead, shrivelled, wet, under a pyramid of stones. Bloody fox. Bloody murderous fox. He lifted a buttock and broke wind.

Yabsley guffawed and said, 'That's the most intelligent remark you've made all day, boy.'

Scoble swallowed cider and rolled his wart. The figure in the corner was silhouetted dark against the window.

'Poor old Leonard's lost Jacko,' Yabsley continued. 'Tell 'em how it happened, Leonard – go on, boy. Don't be shy.'

'Blackie killed un,' Scoble said. His voice was low and dry. 'Blackie and two or three other foxes.'

'Four foxes?' Farmer Lugg grinned.

'The same buggers who killed your ewe above Holwell,' said Scoble.

'Do 'ee say so?' Lugg said, no longer smiling.

'Ripped out her throat. They'm hunting in packs now, I tell 'ee. It's Blackie. He's regular bloody wolf.'

Richard Williams left his table and came to the bar.

'The sheep was killed by a dog,' he said.

Lugg placed his empty glass on the counter and looked down at his boots. The American gazed steadily at George.

'I was coming off Hay Tor. A big, dark grey dog was running wild with a border collie. The big dog attacked the sheep and put one down. The dog could have been a lurcher.'

'You'm a liar, boy,' said Scoble. The colour drained from his face.

'Jacko was a big grey dog,' Yabsley said.

'And he never killed no sheep,' said Scoble.

'I saw the incident clearly through binoculars,' Richard said.

'You idn a fox lover by any chance, be'ee, Yank?' Scoble sneered.

'Sure, I got an animal out of one of your wires, Scoble – and I'd do it again.'

'Maybe you won't get the chance.'

'It doesn't alter the fact that your dog was a killer. I watched it. It had done it before.'

'How would you know? You've only been in the country five bloody minutes.'

'We've got dogs like that in Montana.'

'Bigger dogs I expect, boy,' Scoble said. 'Everything's bigger and better over there, idn it?'

His face had turned grey.

Richard Williams shrugged and shook his head and turned to go. Lugg caught him by the arm. 'Was it the lurcher, sir?' he said.

249

'A long-legged, grey dog running with a collie,' said the American. 'Have a look at the sheep. Foxes don't go for the throat. And this creature wounded several others. The collie sat and watched him. '

'Jacko never went with no other dog,' said Scoble.

'How do 'ee know if you weren't there?' said George.

'There's a collie stray up over Challacombe,' Claik said.

'You're a clever sod, Yank,' Scoble whispered. 'You don't miss much do 'ee?'

'I'm glad I didn't miss the fox in your snare.'

'The black fox,' Scoble said.

'Yeah – old Blackie.'

The trapper was on his feet with surprising speed for a big man. His lower lip trembled.

'If you hadn't let that black bastard go,' he cried, 'Jacko would still be alive.'

The punch came up and over like the conclusion of a swimming stroke. Richard took Scoble's fist on the palm of his left hand and held it there. It was an old man's fist, with fingers discoloured by years of grubbing in the soil. Bert Yabsley grabbed the trapper's free arm. Scoble stood quivering, his jaw thrust out, his eyes wide and staring. Like a trapped savage, Richard thought. Is fortitude sufficient? What do we achieve by integrity and courage? Men crouched like this in the mouths of caves, growling at the night that had been deformed by their own fear. Nothing had changed. Only during the spate of human inner-ugliness and folly was nobility of spirit revealed – briefly, like a candleflame in a storm. And it wasn't snuffed out by an overload of horror but by the everyday ordinariness of life.

He went into the sunlight calling Meg to heel. Big John Constable clouds were piling up in the west, but the wind had slackened. Roses bulged on the white-washed walls. Game fowl scratched around in the orchard. At the bottom of the meadow was a gathering of lofty elms, and grasses and wild flowers pursued the stream he could hear babbling beside the hedge. The afternoon was very hot.

He walked the tension off, dredging up lines of Wordsworth as he tramped up the straight road to the village.

> For I have learned
> To look on nature, not as in the hour
> Of thoughtless youth; but hearing often-times
> The still, sad music of humanity …

Yeah, the old poet was on the ball, but reality had so many faces. The 'central peace subsisting at the heart of endless agitation' was his, now, in the lane whose hedges were heavy with convolvulus and honeysuckle. By Christ, he thought, I've earnt it.

A man came out of a field gate leading a couple of work horses. The great Shires with their chains clinking and rattling lumbered away towards the approaching storm.

KILLCONEY AGAIN

Dartmoor lay hushed beneath a sky overspread with banks of nimbus cloud. Thunder raced in a cracking boom from Hay Tor to Longford Tor, again and again. Sheep and ponies stood with bowed heads as the rain fell in great heavy drops, battering the heather and bracken. Spray danced around the birches and rowans, leaves were torn off, grass and flowers were flattened. In black columns the rain exploded on the surface of the roads, and the Becca Brook swelled, running white-clawed among the boulders and the colour of cider and ale along its deeper reaches.

By mid-morning the storm had passed. A multitude of scents rose from the earth, the sun shone, the road steamed. The dark masses of bracken glittered, and rivers ran fat and silent, their waters clouded with silt and dead leaves. Daws came to bathe at Dead Dog Pond, jumping into deep water, jacking continuously in the playful manner of their kind. Wulfgar watched them and thought of food.

Raindrops slid down the tall, flat-bladed spikes of grass that thrust in tussocks from the heather. He drank at the pond. A trout hung motionless close to the reeds, its black back dotted with red spots. Gold glistened on its flanks.

'Do you fancy the old otter fodder?' said a familiar voice at his shoulder.

Killconey shook the rain from his fur and grinned at him.

He was very dishevelled and muddy.

'You look like a newborn rat,' Wulfgar said.

'And you look better without the coney collar.'

They lapped water together while the daws continued to swim and jangle.

Later, Killconey said, 'So the lurcher got chopped.'

'Not far from where you're standing.'

'Yes, I heard. Stargrief told me. Tod! – but he's shrewd! How old is he?'

'He's coming up to his ninth winter.'

Killconey wagged his head and whistled through his teeth. He had a fresh scar on his upper lip.

Wulfgar frowned at it.

'You've as much chance of seeing nine winters as I have of flying to the moon.'

'The poodle came off worse,' Killconey laughed, caressing the scar with the tip of his tongue. 'It surprised me while I was asleep in a ditch by the road. Then I surprised it.'

'Have you eaten?'

'Beetles, a worm or two. If you can suggest something more exciting, I'm your animal.'

The dog foxes trotted to Haytor Down a little to the west of the Quarry Ponds. Shrews had their runs in the long grass and bracken. They fed on woodlice, harvestmen, spiders, beetles, moths and worms, eating their bodyweight of insects every day. The thick cover of high summer protected them from hawks and owls.

Wulfgar and Killconey took the ancient fox trail through the bracken to the whortleberry bushes. Moving leisurely up the slope under Hay Tor they ate scores of the blue-black berries, then flopped in the bell-heather, pressing their muzzles into the purple flowers. Insects zithered and chirred, and stonechats gave cries like pebbles being knocked together.

The day was climbing to the heat of noon. Ponies drifted between Saddle Tor and Hay Tor. And Wulfgar thought of Teg. To have ended such a morning beside her would have been ravishing.

'I saw something comical a few sunsets ago,' said Killconey.

Wulfgar closed his eyes against the glare and tried to forget the flies that were tormenting him.

'A hare attacked a dog – a spaniel, your spaniel, the one who had a go at you when you were in wire. I couldn't stop laughing. There was this great, over-grown coney practically hanging off the fool's arse. The man was waving a stick and bawling.'

'Did you find the leverets?' Wulfgar yawned.

'I had a peep but the man saw me and I ran for it.'

Returning to the Leighon Ponds they killed and ate some young rabbits in the rowans by Holwell Clitter.

'You'll be moving on,' said Wulfgar.

'Come dimpsey. I've got itchy feet. Why not join me, Wulfgar?'

'I don't feel the need. At the moment this place provides all I want. Perhaps in the winter.'

Moonsleek and her cubs were frolicking in the water by the island.

'Didn't you take a mate last winter?' Wulfgar said. Killconey nodded.

'The hounds got her. I found her in a ploughed field. They had cut off her pads and brush. Are those the only parts of us they eat? I don't understand.'

'Fitches will eat just the back legs of frogs,' Wulfgar said lamely.

Killconey followed the otters with his eyes as they swam into the reeds.

'The dog otter has wandered off,' Wulfgar said, happy to broach a new subject. 'Moonsleek was beginning to make life uncomfortable for him. Most she-animals seem to get like it when they've got young.'

Killconey curled up and hid his nose in his brush.

'Summer isn't a good time for otters,' he murmured. 'The hounds were on Big Two Rivers yesterday. I saw an otter take to the water.'

'And?'

'I don't know. Men come, we run, otters run, rabbits run – every animal runs.'

There was no more to be said.

CHANGES

The foxes settled contentedly into the flow of the season. It was still a time of plenty around Hay Tor. St Bartholomew's Day had passed and the barley at Sedge Brimley stood ready for harvest. The in-country was a patchwork of tawny and yellow fields cast haphazardly among the greens. On Dartmoor clusters of red berries hung from the rowans and the purple of bell-heather mingled with the rose and pinks of other heathers. Here and there the startling green of sphagnum clothed soft ground. The days were still hot but the nights had drawn in.

Now the wandering was good. Killconey had claimed a territory for himself on Hammel Down, but like Wulfgar he preferred to be alone. Once in a while the foxes' paths crossed and news was exchanged, though Stargrief came less often to the Leighon Ponds. Sometimes Wulfgar caught a glimpse of him on Black Hill, but he was difficult to approach. The abundance of insects meant he could feed close to his kennel and spend most of the night communing with the universe. To what end? Wulfgar thought.

Lately the vision of the pure white place had risen from many a twilight. He kept searching for Teg on the snowfields, but it was always the strange vixen running through the dream to greet him. Before anguish could set in he would recall Killconey's stoicism and clench his teeth and let the evening crowd his consciousness.

Since Jacko's death Scoble had become even more of a recluse. He came out at dusk and walked the high ground with his shotgun hoping to blast Wulfgar. Every so often he spent the night beside the Leighon water, which the animals called Dead Dog Pond to commemorate Jacko's drowning, and he left poison bait in the valley and tilled gins where the foxes ran.

But Wulfgar was hunting the border country that Scoble seldom visited unless there was farm work to be had. He laid up in the wood by Bagtor Mill and terrorised the duck who used the pool.

One of Moonsleek's cubs ate Scoble's bait and died painfully under the alders. The grieving otter bitch led her remaining young downstream the same night and made a new home on the River Bovey. Mordo and Skalla got at the cub's body before the trapper did his morning rounds, and by the time the man arrived the pelt was useless. The ravens climbed high out of gun range and beat up the valley.

Without a dog Scoble took fewer rabbits, and foxes who would not have stood a chance in Jacko's company slipped away unnoticed when danger threatened. Scoble brooded about it in his kitchen and drank scrumpy and became morose. He had to get another dog but there would never be another Jacko.

'Poor old boy,' he slurred. The cider loosened his teeth and his bowels, but his hatred remained firm-set.

One morning he found Meg the spaniel throttled in a wire among thick gorse close to Holwell. The dog had taken to running with the beagle bitch from Leighon and Richard Williams was used to her being out half the night.

Scoble's first impulse was to toss the animal in the pond but he had enough common sense to realise how stupid such an act would be. He couldn't afford to have every hand raised against him. So he took the carcass to Holwell Clitter and dumped it in one of the crevices. Then he smoked a Gold Flake and waited for his limbs to stop shaking. He had to be at Sedge Brimley after breakfast. Lugg's barley was ready to reap. He chuckled and tapped his fists together. If it wasn't sheer bloody poetry! The

Yank had got Old Blackie out of a wire but he couldn't save his own dog! Nature could play funny tricks.

He stretched and felt the hair stiffen on the nape of his neck. There was no need to turn and look up, but he did. The dark fox stood on the edge of the tor by the Scots pine that grew out of the quarry face. For a long time Scoble and Wulfgar stared at each other while the hatred crackled between them. Eventually the trapper gave a cry and covered his face with his hands.

'You,' he sobbed. 'You. You.'

His palms were wet with snot and tears. He snuffled and rocked to and fro. Charlie the mule and Jacko would help him. O yes, you bastard. He could see the two skeletons galloping side by side out of some foggy autumn night, hunting the fox to its doom, their white, fleshless jaws pulping the backbone, sending the vermin down to hell.

When he peered through his fingers, Wulfgar had vanished. The pine tree shivered in the wind that was pushing big innocent clouds across the sky.

'He ought to do it for nothing,' said George Lugg. 'I bet that wadn the first sheep his bloody dog's killed.'

'You've only got the Yank's word on it,' his father said. 'It idn evidence.'

'Us saw the ewe, father,' George said. 'Yank was right. Foxes don't kill like that.'

'All right, all right,' Farmer Lugg said soothingly. 'But the lurcher's dead and all this yap won't bring our sheep back.'

'No, and it galls me. I reckon Scoble knew all along and was takin' us for a ride.'

'Now why would un do that?' said his father patiently.

'Well, the great cake idn sixteen ounces to start with. He's scrumpy-puggled. All he can think of is bloody foxes.'

'I expect it's his didakai blood,' said Yabsley, hitching up his overalls.

The Luggs waited to see if he was serious.

'I idn leg-pullin', boys. His old mum got put in the family way by a gypo. I suppose her did more than cross his palm with silver.'

'Her should've crossed her legs,' George said and Yabsley grinned.

'Leonard's late,' said Farmer Lugg. 'It idn like him.'

'He'll be out after foxes, maister,' Yabsley said.

'Us had better start,' Lugg sighed. 'Pity though. I wanted to put a new bit of corrugated on the linhay. That storm back along nearly ruined the hay.'

The barley field shone in the sun and Scoble could hear the harvesting machine as he tramped down the long meadow by the copse. Whirling wooden slats were pressing the stalks against the blade. The barley was grabbed, bound and shuffled out in a line at the side. Yabsley crooned to the horse and gently flicked the reins. The Luggs stood the sheaves in stooks and the farm collies chased the rabbits, which were bolting in all directions.

Scoble stopped and put a match to his cigarette, and he had a clear mental picture of Yabsley perched on

261

the harvesting machine like an overweight Ben Hur. Endlessly taking the piss out of me and Jacko, he thought. Yabsley's never done nothing except flap his big lips.

He spun on his heel like a soldier and headed back up the slope to the lane. At dusk he would try the ponds again or maybe hang around Yarner Wells for the chicken thief. When I get Old Blackie I'll have un stuffed sure enough. He'll go to the Rock Inn and stand behind the bar among the whisky bottles. Caught by Leonard Scoble – that's better than havin' your name on the cenotaph. People looked at things in pubs, but cenotaphs were long forgotten except for one day a year.

Moonsleek slid into the water crying for her dead cub. Three small wet heads bobbed along with the current behind her. Romany shook the eel and dropped it at his feet.

'She doesn't come any more when I call,' he said. 'She carries an emptiness only the lost cub can fill.'

'I'm sorry, Romany,' said Wulfgar. 'The trapper has been busy lately with his snares and gins and poison rabbit!'

'We gave you the lurcher and Man took our cub. You foxes haven't brought us much luck.'

Wulfgar felt they had strayed into areas where words were redundant. Romany lowered his eyes, placed a paw on the eel and began to feed.

OLD BLACKIE DID IT

'Any luck, Richard?' Jenny said.

'She's gone,' the American said gently. He sank into the armchair and gazed up at the ceiling.

'I've looked everywhere. The whole neighbourhood's out searching for the dog. It's really odd. Meg's gone off before but never very far. I've been up the Bovey and the Becca Brook. I've been to places that aren't even on the map.'

Above the net half-curtains the first gleam of dawn showed in the sky.

'Has Scoble got anything to do with it?' Jenny said.

'I honestly don't know. Sure the guy's mean enough. I guess nothing surprises me anymore.'

'Look,' she said. 'I'll have to go in a moment. Would you like me to make you a cup of tea?'

'No, no,' he said quickly, as though he had pulled himself back from a remote thought. 'God, I'm sorry, Jenny! How long have you been here?'

'Since midnight.'

'What will your folks say?'

'They'll worry about the dog. Will you be at the meet?'

'Yes – if you can guarantee no otters will be killed.'

'They hardly ever see one, let alone make a kill,' she smiled. 'You won't do anything idiotic, will you?'

'I don't know. I guess I'm on the animal's side. The whole buiness of chasing it to death with dogs seems pretty obscene.'

'Perhaps you ought to reserve judgement until you've participated.'

'OK, Jenny. Thanks for coming over.'

He walked her to the door but did not kiss her good-bye. The bottom of the sky held the pinkish-silver light that he loved. A few birds were singing quietly. It was the sort of dawn chorus he expected at the slack end of summer.

Returning to the sitting-room he spun the 'Adagio e staccato' 78 from Handel's Water Music. The marvellous sound strode confidently into the twentieth century because it had been written to enrich eternity.

The hounds met at Parke, a large house on the outskirts of Bovey Tracey. The master and most of the field wore the dark blue hunt uniform: bowler hats, tweed jackets, knee breeches, heavy-knit stockings and black brogues. They carried ash poles shod with steel caps and notched to signify the number of kills they had witnessed.

The pack was led by a couple of pure-bred, rough-haired otter hounds called Bullrush and Mariner, and the rest of the animals were old foxhounds, too slow for the real job. Each had a watery name like Bargeman, Diver, Boatman, Navigator, Coxwain and Helmsman. But Bullrush and Mariner were the inspiration of the field with their good noses and the music of their cries. They were strong swimmers who could own a line better than the other hounds.

A day of slow cloud shadows and golden heat had Richard remembering occasions that seemed to have been stolen from death – excursions west in packed trains, a feeling of quiet desperation, sweat, blue and khaki uniforms, encapsulated, timeless.

'You didn't find the spaniel,' said Colonel Shewte.

Why did they make everything rhetorical? Richard thought. But he said, 'Meg's vanished off the face of the earth, sir,'

'Poor girl! The locals are blaming Old Blackie.'

'That's absurd,' said Richard.

'They're a superstitious lot,' said Jenny. 'Old Blackie's become a sort of Fox of the Baskervilles.'

'Thanks to Scoble,' Richard said.

The trapper was stooping over Bullrush, kneading the hound's chest with his fingers. He looked up casually and returned Richard's glance.

'There's something medieval about that guy,' the American murmured.

Jenny took his arm.

'He's coarse and a bit anti-social,' she said. 'Nothing else.'

'Salt of the Earth,' said Colonel Shewte. 'Try to think of Dartmoor as his factory. He's got the mentality of a ferret. Completely unsentimental.'

Richard made no reply. He saw the dark fox leaping again in the wire.

Yabsley came up with two of his terriers and the conversation swung round to dogs in general. The hunt moved off down through the parkland to the River Bovey. The water was cobbled with sunlight. Stubble glinted in the fields above the town and great dark mounds crowned the oaks and elms.

He was unhappy in that gone-to-seed piece of England where the undertones of decay were sharp and surreal. Banks of nettles, tall stands of cow parsley and foxgloves, the cloying green of the grass – everything was unnaturally still. The air was heavy. Only the water looked alive and optimistic.

He took off his jacket and rolled up his sleeves. The hunt jargon sounded as phoney as hell – 'half a couple of hounds', 'a good nose', 'grabbed him by the rudder' – like the bullfighting bullshit and the murderous monosyllables of Hemingway's Nick Adams.

'What are the terriers for?' he said.

'To worry a beast out of its holt,' said Jenny. 'I adore them. They're so plucky.'

The master was a nice, dapper little person; he trotted behind the hounds who were ranging upstream. They splashed through open, sundrenched stretches, over the gleam of shillit, stone and pebble into the glooms beneath overhanging boughs.

'If Scoble had his way we'd kill every otter we found,' Colonel Shewte said breathlessly.

'The hunt tries to take the dogs – not the bitches,' Jenny explained.

Richard struggled to think of something polite to say but he could only nod. More quaint, slaughterhouse small talk, he thought. Scoble and George Lugg were looking at him and laughing. He reddened and blew his nose. A boy of about ten tugged at his sleeve.

'You lost a dog, mister?' he said.

The boy's hair was the colour of corn stubble, his eyes dark and alert.

'Yes – a liver and white spaniel called Meg.'

'Is there a reward?'

'Would a pound note be OK?'

'Where do I bring the dog to if I find un?'

Richard told him.

'Got any gum, mister?'

'Sorry, I don't use it,' the American grinned.

'Off you go now,' Jenny said firmly.

They watched him overtake the leaders and fall in behind the master.

'Who was that?' Richard said.

'O a strange little character,' said Jenny. 'We call him Stray. He's never at school. You'll find him in the most extraordinary places. He earns a small fortune opening and closing the moorland gates.'

'I've seen him,' Richard exclaimed, snapping his fingers. 'A month ago, climbing Bowerman's Nose like a squirrel.'

By lunchtime no otters had been sighted. Several lines had been pursued by the pack, but neither Mariner nor Bullrush had given tongue. Richard and Jenny sat together on the bank above the weir. A buzzard wheeled over Trendlebere Down.

'Are you homesick, Richard?' Jenny said, unwrapping the sandwiches.

'No.'

'But something's wrong.'

He tossed a pebble in the water. Out of the corner of his eye he saw several hounds gathered round the trapper wagging their tails. Stray had started to wade across the river. Scoble cupped his hands to his mouth and cried 'cuckoo – cuckoo'.

'Why the hell did he do that?' Richard said.

'They think the child's simple,' said Jenny.

Richard hugged his knees to his chin and tried to think it out.

Presently he said, 'I'd like to go back to the cottage, Jenny.'

'Alone?'

'If you don't mind. I want to look for Meg.'

'This isn't to your liking, is it, Richard?'

'I guess not.'

She helped him into his jacket and placed a kiss on his cheek.

'You're not mad at me are you, Jen?'

'Of course not! Shall I come tonight?'

'I'd like that.'

He crossed the river clumsily and Scoble said 'cuckoo' again and Yabsley laughed.

Higher up, the Bovey glided black and silent through Houndtor Wood. Moonsleek and her cubs pressed tight against the bank, right in among the oak roots. Like all otter bitches with cub she had a nomadic nature and wanted no permanent holt. The Leighon Ponds had been convenient until Man had come, now he was coming again. She had smelt the hounds and heard the high notes of the horn. Moonsleek hissed and the cubs butted her with their noses, sensing her fear, fighting to get under her body.

Mariner let out his challenge. The pack responded with a deep-throated burst of music as they owned the line and picked up the drag of the otter bitch. They frantically seethed around Moonsleek's hiding place. The two pure-bred hounds were in the water, tearing at the roots. Moonsleek sprang at Bullrush and showed him her teeth in a fierce grimace. The master got down on his hands and knees and peered into the holt.

'She's got cubs,' he said. 'Whip the hounds off, please.'

A mile further on the valley deepened and rough ground climbed to the fields of Lustleigh. Romany had run up the hillside for a little way, changed his mind and doubled back to the river. He lay against the current for a while with just his nostrils showing. He had been hunted many times and knew it was fatal to seek out a holt. But the hounds weren't far off. He lifted his head and sniffed the air and had a look round. Sitting in the grass on the far bank was the dark fox.

'Moonsleek is safe,' said Wulfgar. 'The hounds will be here shortly. What do you intend doing?'

'I'll swim, run, hide, fight – what else?'

'Come with me. I'll foil the scent.'

'How?'

'Do as I say.'

Romany joined him.

'Get up through the trees and I'll follow you,' Wulfgar said. 'Take the badger path as far as the stream and wait for me by the fallen pine.'

The otter was ungainly but fast. Wulfgar kept on his tail, dragging his own brush. Back in the valley the hounds were belling again.

'Run,' Wulfgar cried. 'Run.'

He sat down and grinned at the fleeing otter. Bullrush had marked Romany's double and had returned to the water where the scent lay strong. Several foxhounds splashed past him and hunted Wulfgar's line up the badger path, but Mariner and Bullrush were reluctant to join them. The master and whipper-in jogged after the babblers who were running slowly on a confusing scent. Bargeman and Diver saw the fox high on the slope and mouthed their challenge. The master roared at them and they half turned, whimpering but still rebellious. The whipper-in brought the rest of the pack under control.

'It's that black fox,' the young man cried.

'Yes,' said the master, making a fuss of Bargeman and Diver. 'A beautiful animal but not much use to us.'

Wulfgar swung away unhurriedly into the trees.

Yabsley and Scoble were waiting below. The rest of the field had not braved the water.

'It was Old Blackie,' said the whipper-in.

'What happened to the otter?' said Yabsley.

The whipper-in shrugged.

'The old black boy's done you,' Scoble whispered. 'Christ! – if he idn the slyest thing on four legs!'

He pressed a forefinger into his wart like someone ringing a doorbell.

'Did un give the otter a piggy back, Leonard?' Yabsley said and got a laugh from the crowd.

The hot blood rose in Scoble's cheeks. He dug his staff savagely into the grass and climbed the badger path. A little beyond the spot where Bargeman and Diver had faltered the stones and grass gave way to mud. Amongst the fox's spoor were the broader, deeper tracks of an otter.

Richard Williams looked up and saw the fair head rising above the ferns. Stray came and stood in his path. The Becca Brook brawled over stones and fell noisily into the pool by the fallen pine. The wind swept through the oaks and birches shaking the brightness and the shadows.

'Old Blackie was here,' the boy crowed. 'When I left the big river I saw un watchin' us. He was up in the scrub. But he didn see me. Then he come up here and now he's gone. But he was there – by the fallen tree.'

He sucked in his breath with excitement and the American gazed at him solemnly.

'If us bide quiet,' the boy continued, 'he may come back. Animals do that. You don't like hunting do 'ee?'

'No. Do you?'

Stray shook his head and mumbled, 'Once I saw 'em take a dead otter that the dogs had killed and draw on the faces of some boys and girls with the blood. It wadn proper.'

'Why do you go out with the hounds?'

'To see things. Folk don't shout at 'ee if you're with the dogs. You can go all sorts of private places. But I idn looby, mister.'

'Looby?'

'Mazed, mad. Scoble say I am. But I bliddy well idn.'

'Hadn't we better get out of sight?' Richard said.

They sat in the bracken under the oaks. Stray's nostrils opened and closed. He's like an animal himself, Richard thought, then out of the undergrowth the otter emerged and the boy placed a finger to his lips.

Romany crouched by the pine tree and sniffed the wind that held the scent of green, living things. He was agitated and uncertain. Every so often he rose onto his hindlegs and peered back into the wood. All at once he detected something and remained upright watching it. Wulfgar slunk out of the shadows and joined him. The animals hesitated a moment then ran on, side by side, up the Becca Brook.

'That Old Blackie is a magic animal,' Stray said passionately.

'He sure is,' said Richard.

'They killed his vixen and cubs.'

'They would. It's a lousy world. People are lousy.'

'My mum's OK.'

'So's mine.'

'You sure you haven't got no gum?'

'Positive. Would half a crown buy a stick or two?'

'Bloody hell yes!'

Wulfgar and Romany continued along the stream on its climb to the Leighon Ponds. The fox travelled at hunting speed so the otter had no trouble following him. Within the woodland of the Leighon Estate their pace slackened and soon they were ambling.

'The hounds will go back and draw the deeper water below the town bridge,' Romany said. 'If Moonsleek stays put she won't be troubled. I'll join her tonight.'

He was plainly fretting for his mate despite the show of coolness. A strange little cry would escape from him at unguarded moments – a sort of low, nasal sobbing.

'Moonsleek won't be harmed,' Wulfgar said. 'The hounds could have taken her and the cubs, but the men called them off. I saw it.'

Standing erect Romany peered back into the coomb and let loose a long, soft whistle. Then he tilted his head on one side and listened. The tears trickled down his face.

'How can she answer?' Wulfgar said kindly.

'True,' Romany sniffed.

With amazing dexterity the otter brought up a hind-foot to scratch behind the ear. His fur, which had been grey and spiky from the swimming, was drying to a reddish brown. When he galloped on he did so noisily, thumping his hindfeet down together on the track.

No wonder you're always in the water, thought Wulfgar. The wind brought him the comforting, rotten smell of the ponds. A long way behind, woodpigeons were clattering out of the treetops that rocked above the junction of two lanes.

The boy and the American parted company on the Bovey Tracey road. Stray ran off to catch the bus to Newton Abbot and Richard marched cheerfully back towards Manaton. The kid was the closest thing he'd seen to a reservation Indian this side of Montana. What would the world do to him? But he couldn't be gloomy. The otter had escaped and he'd seen Old Blackie again. Sure, the kid would change but childhood was a separate lifetime anyway. It wasn't just the stifling of the pastoral instinct that dulled the vision. You couldn't endure that intensity day after day. You'd see everything too clearly, and all the mediocrity and stupidity would drive you nuts.

Woodpigeons rattled out of the ashes as he turned into the lane that led to Leighon and Beckaford. A coffee-coloured van was parked on the grass beside the brook. Scoble sat on the bonnet with his hands on his knees.

'Old Blackie did it, didn he, Yank?' he said.

'Did what?' said Richard. He stopped in the middle of the lane feeling curiously tired and helpless.

'Got the otter away from they hounds.'

'So?'

'Don't get the idea he's beat me.'

'Is he trying to?'

'They all are but that black bugger is the maister.'

Richard cleared his throat. 'Have you seen my dog?' he said.

Scoble slid off the bonnet and winked.

'Why, boy – idn her round no more?'

'I guess you know you're an evil bastard.'

'Old Blackie had the spaniel, Yank.'

'Like he had Jacko?'

'With your help. If you hadn't stuck your nose in he'd still be alive.'

'You'd better watch out, fella. The old black fox is after your guts.'

Scoble stood like a man in a trance. His fists were balled, his shoulders were rounded and his chin was thrust forward.

'No fox'll ever best me,' he breathed. 'Never.'

'But Old Blackie has bested you. Everyone says so. And they're saying he isn't an animal at all but a thing come up from hell to grab you and carry you off to the fires and eternal damnation.'

The trapper wrenched open the rear doors of the van and reached inside.

'He's just a fox, boy,' he grunted. 'Vermin – like this.'

He swung the stiff carcass high by the tail and drew his bloodless lips back in a grin.

'I shot un this morning when he came sniffin' round the hen coops.'

Richard lifted his eyes to the tree tops. Green and silver leaves twinkled and flashed against the blue. Scoble shook the lifeless body that had once been the dog fox Wendel.

'I gets 'em all in the end,' he crooned. 'They'm crafty buggers but I'm sharp as a knife.'

A calm evening brought Richard to the table in the window. Birds dashed across the sky. He opened his notebook and the pen nib scratched the silence. The cottage was like a clock that had stopping ticking.

'The war was the height of human frailty and viciousness,' he wrote. 'Yet I have seen the immortal psychopath in the shaving mirror. There is some awful, inherent, self-destructive, race-destructive flaw in man. We pretend we live in a state of history but we don't. We don't even live in a state of nature like the animals. We are outsiders – the prowling aliens against whom all the wolf fires have been lit.'

The stock doves were spinning their love song in the beech tree at the bottom of the lawn. They flew off when he stepped from the door to enjoy the sunset. Circling the house the birds climbed into a sky of softening indigo, and turning to plane down to the wood once more, they saw the dark fox leave Beckaford Farm and run across the field with a rat in his mouth.

THE WHITE VISION

The blackberries were fat and juicy along the edges of Colehays Plantation. The heavy dew of the September morning had given them a gloss. Wulfgar snipped them off with his teeth, carefully, having learnt at an early age to respect the prickles. Down on the plain the mist was lifting from the river valleys and the wind smelt of the sea and farmland.

A large flock of starlings fanned out over Kiln Brake and mantled the sheep field. They were birds from the Continent. Wulfgar made scats and trotted onto Haytor Down. His belly was full and he wanted to go directly to Holwell Tor and kennel above the Leighon Valley. On the slopes the bracken was yellowing and the heather was wine-dark.

The foxes of the Hay Tor Clan were more alert than usual. Summer was over and men were out in the border woods and fields with guns, and the hounds had visited the in-country for the cubbing. The air had a crisp edge to it and the clap of twelve-bores carried for miles. Grass in the valleys was misted with spiders' webs; martins and swallows congregated on the roof-tops and telephone wires. Where the flocks of sheep drifted across the heath the rams fought, clashing heads and horns. At Moretonhampstead the last game of cricket had been played and the goal posts were up on the Kate Brook soccer pitch.

Like shining breath the money spiders' webs veiled the ruts and hoofprints outside the midden. The day was warm and cloudless. Answering the call to migrate the tiny spiders released wisps of silk and sailed up into the sky to the high winds of chance that would blow them halfway round the world. Thousands would drift unnoticed across the Atlantic to spin new webs on American soil.

A little spider's lace stuck to Stargrief's nose as he loped through the deserted farm. He sneezed and ran a paw swiftly over his muzzle. The sleepy fade-out of summer had left him listless despite his age, but fresh morn-ings and cooler afternoons still excited him with their fragrance. There was a spring in his step. He bounded through the ancient trees of Leighon and drank from the Becca Brook. The river tinkled nut-brown under the footbridge.

'How are you keeping?' Thorgil said.

The one-eyed badger was dumping soiled bedding on the spoil heap outside his sett, and the sow was underground. Stargrief could hear the muffled bumping of her body going along a gallery.

'I'm fine,' the old fox said. 'And I'll stay this way if the hounds don't surprise me on my hilltop.'

'You'll see a couple more winters, I'm sure,' the badger said amiably.

'That would indeed be something,' Stargrief smiled. 'No fox – not even Tod – has lived ten winters.'

'Any news of Wendel?' the badger asked.

'None.'

'You know what that means, of course.'

'Yes – one chicken too many.'

'It is a foolish animal who fights lightning.'

They grinned at each other and read the air, holding high their noses. Despite the warmth Stargrief shivered.

'Can you feel it?' he whispered.

Thorgil nodded and said, 'Like ice in my blood and bones, like the feeling I got when I found the cub in the wire. What is it?'

'I don't know. Whispers from the future have troubled me a lot lately, but there are other signs. The wheatears have gone to the sun much earlier than they did last autumn, and the martins and swallows look ready to fly.'

'Wulfgar told me he's seen bramblings under the beeches where the rooks nest. What does this mean, Stargrief?'

'If I'm to know, the stars will tell me. But use the autumn well, Thorgil. Eat many mice and conies. Eat roots and berries but leave those nearest your sett.'

Thorgil bowed his head.

'I would be honoured if you'd share my home till the day is spent,' he said.

'Gratefully,' said the fox. 'Is Wulfgar back in his old haunts?'

'He was at the ponds two sunsets ago, but he's like the wind.'

'And the trapper?'

'He comes and goes, but he hasn't a dog and every animal except the mindless coney knows his trap lines.'

In the long shadows of evening he came to the meadow beside Dead Dog Pond, under Greator Rocks. Wulfgar was bobbing up and down in the grass. Sometimes he was at full stretch on his hind feet, closing his jaws with a snap or clapping his front paws together.

The leather-jackets were hatching into crane-flies and Wulfgar was grabbing them as they took wing. Stargrief joined him and they feasted until dark. Soon the stars were twinkling from a sky of deep blue. Gently and silently Isca the roebuck stepped out of the alders to drink at the pond. His nervousness reached across the night to the foxes.

They walked in the safety of their friendship, gathering the dew on their coats and whiskers. The bracken was limp and wet all up the hillside, and ponies stood or lay in it making velvety snuffling noises.

'I saw the white vision at sunrise,' Wulfgar said. 'There were no white birds or white hares or high mountains. It looked like the Great Tor over there. A beautiful vixen ran as always over the snow towards me. Where has my Teg gone, Stargrief? It is never her now.'

The sadness in his voice touched the old fox's heart.

'She is a Star Place vixen, Wulfgar. Loving the dead is hard. So Tod gradually takes away the pain.'

'But I still think of her.'

'Dutifully perhaps?'

'Yes. Much has faded.'

'You will never entirely forget her.'

Mid-Devon was strewn with hard, twinkling splashes of light. A sickle of orange flames flickered across the field by Whisselwell Farm where the stubble had been blazing all afternoon.

'I too have seen the white vision,' said Stargrief. 'It was this place – glaring white, dazzling like the lights of the Man places – and it made me think of death.'

'Often it is simply a feeling,' said Wulfgar. 'Or a strange darkness, like the look I saw in Runeheath's eyes.'

'Runeheath?'

'A sick old fox who died under the hounds last winter.'

'Today the last of the wheatears flew off to the sun,' Stargrief said. 'And while I slept in Thorgil's sett the lurcher invaded my dream. He was huge and white. His fangs were icicles and three foxes sat on his back. Then he tore a chunk out of the darkness and ate it.'

'Is it an omen?'

'Obviously,' said Stargrief. 'But dreams aren't always prophetic, as I've said before. Most of them are the images of our own fears and anxieties.'

He sighed and added, 'I'll consult the stars again from the Great Tor.'

'You could run with me to Quarryman's Cottage, old mouse.'

'No – go on alone, Wulfgar. The stars bring me joy. I have no present. I look to the future and the past.'

ON HAY TOR

Only in sickness was Stargrief lonely. The world was his mother and when he curled into her the love strengthened his spirit, for she was grass and rock and bracken, water, earth and snow. Her breath was the wind, the rain her tears, the night her sleeping. Age no longer seemed a penance, and Stargrief trotted joyfully to the foot of Hay Tor and scampered up the rock face from south to east where the scrambling was easy.

On the bald summit he lay among the autumn stars. The Milky Way dusted his fur with soft light. Buried in the brilliance of the star stream were the constellations of the Swan and Aquila, and below Aquarius the hard jewel of Fomalhaut glittered. Then Mira Ceti in the constellation of Cetus, and the four perfect stars of Aries.

But they were not individual foxes, they were great legions of animals ranging the sky – telling the sagas, feasting, fighting, enjoying the vixens. In the morning they would all come together to form the sun, a sphere of golden foxes rising from the sea to breathe life into the world.

The beauty of the night made him cry. The stars twisted, swelled, blurred and burst from his tears. He looked down at his paws until the bitter-sweet feeling had passed. Life droned gently through his body and all around him the night gave up its scents and smells – bracken crushed by hooves, sodden grass, furze, sheep, ponies, dying leaves. The silence was ancient and inviolable, and it helped the spirit rise to Tod.

Life itself is worship, Stargrief thought. By living I am praying, I am a prayer. His imperfections screwed into focus. He was insomniac, irritable, conceited. But the visions were divine. He had experienced them as a yearling and he had never questioned the authenticity of the blazing rowan. Sacred tree, the top half in flames, the lower part autumn leaves. It's the way the sun's striking it, Wulfgar had said. O no. The flames had become the ears and the muzzle of Tod. Words of fire had issued from the fiery jaws – golden words that burnt away doubt.

Once it hadn't been possible to live the pure, animal life. There had been too much ritual in Tod worship. Previous generations of foxes had suffocated under it. The Word, the bardic liturgy, the dances and saga-telling had eclipsed the simple vision: he had a dim folk-memory of foxes in unnatural, upright poses, strutting, as if Tod were not fox at all, only an object to bark at in self-pity. Then Tod's messenger came and cleansed the world. Nameless, the star that flew across the sky, visited the moors and spoke as a hunting fox would speak.

How can you say this is so and that is so if you haven't trod the Star Place trails? said the young vixen. But I have, Stargrief smiled. I close my eyes and I'm there. The vision doesn't come from inside me. It strikes the soul like a shaft of sunlight, flying from brightness to darkness. We are midnight wanderers but all paths lead to Tod. He is the silvery glow at life's end.

Starlight filled his eyes. The white vision swam out of the night and he stepped into it. Stars quaked and silently exploded. The snow was unbearably bright. Running over it came the giant lurcher – white, breathing frost, eyes of ice, fangs of icicles, tail of shattered snow, on a white field under a black sky full of stars. No paw prints, Stargrief noted. Now the dark Man-shape was rising from the field to stand like a megalith. The lurcher sprang and bowled it over, then the dog powdered away into snow and covered the Man-shape. Three foxes clad in hoar frost trotted slowly round the field, howling with joy.

He had come through many seasons to this moment. Most of the village lights had gone out and the darkness had grown bigger and deeper. But one tiny bright light flashed on and off, far away where the land ended and the sea began. He looked up into the starry mind of Tod. Many things had been learnt, but he had not mastered the mysterious language of birds, which was a music like running water, like grass sobbing in the wind.

Yet other small truths had been attained through loving vixens, by accepting love. And there really was a love more magnificent and profound than that of animal for animal. Love of the world of living things. Every morning he walked through to reach his kennel was the dawn of creation. Like Tod. He screwed up his eyes with happiness.

Was he within the star or the vision? The golden radiance was warm like the place inside his mother's body where he had drowsed. Many foxes were lying underground. Of course, he murmured. It's Wulfgar's vision. High mountains held back the sky. On the mountain snow were white grouse, white hares and white fitches. A great bird larger than a buzzard cruised down the valley. Now Stargrief was a spirit like the wind, gliding over the familiar moorland. Everything had changed. The towns were many, the houses were tall and roads ran wide and long where the fields had been. Only there weren't any people or cars. Under the Great Tor huddled the cattle, sheep and ponies. No foxes, he thought idly. Then a vast, blinding light filled the sky and all the towns were burning and the mushroom cloud was billowing up. And the darkness swept in on a mighty wind, heavy with the reek of death.

He moaned and drifted back to Wulfgar's vision. Several seasons had passed. The foxes were coming out to tread the silent, beautiful land. Great flocks of wildfowl shadowed the sky. Larks sang, the vixens screamed, the curlew called. Here and there a skeleton was slumped over the wheel of a rusting car or tractor. In the garden of the hillside farm the remains of a man, a woman and a child lay face down, reduced to bones, elemental – like the flints.

Was there something beyond Tod, concealed by the radiance? His mind could not take the same giant stride as his spirit. The dream was falling apart. 'The bards lope in full of bizarre mythology', he heard himself saying. Absurd. Looking into Tod's thoughts. Into my own. When we have crawled away from Death's jaws we may undergo a conversion. Thereafter vigils on the tors, vigils at the vole runs, mousing rituals, turning over dung for a meal, mesmerising conies.

He spun back into himself and drew a deep breath. The visions hadn't yielded their meanings, although one thing was crystal clear: the coming winter would be hard.

He yawned and stretched and lay perfectly still. The faint click in the darkness below was the trapper's cigarette tin shutting. Stargrief's ears pricked and his nostrils quivered. Dry tobacco and paper whispered between forefinger and thumb as Scoble prepared a Gold Flake butt for smoking. The overpowering stench of the man's body made Stargrief's gut heave. The old dog fox got to his feet and tensed to skulk down the path off the tor. It would not be easy. Scoble was half-way up the only possible route and smooth rock fell vertically on the other three sides. But Stargrief was not alarmed, for he possessed the amazing self-confidence of his tribe. In his early life he had done many daring things – like stealing unnoticed across a vicarage lawn during a croquet party to snatch a ham off the table.

He was creeping down the rough granite steps when Wulfgar barked. Stargrief closed his eyes and swore under his breath. The bark was one of those particularly inane contact calls that dogs exchanged to reassure each other.

Wulfgar barked again, much louder this time. He was running across the heath from Crow Thorn to Hay Tor, calling to Stargrief as he came. The hammers of the twelve-bore snapped back. O Tod, Stargrief thought, send the fool fox away.

But the next bark lofted from the turf very close at hand. Full of fear and dismay Stargrief cried, 'Run, Wulfgar. The trapper. The trapper.'

To Scoble it was no more than a tomcat screech of defiance delivered right under his nose. He switched on the torch and caught Stargrief in the beam, 'Shit,' said the trapper, struggling to find somewhere to put the torch while he used the gun. His hands shook. The fox shot straight at him and all he could see was a pair of brilliant, bluish-white eyes flying across the darkness. He dropped the torch and fired blindly – left and right barrels. Something hard and lithe hit him below the knees, throwing him off balance. Then Stargrief was away, his claws rasping on the rock, making the descent in wild leaps.

Running flat out round the north side of the tor he came face-to-face with an anxious-looking Wulfgar.

'Steady, old mouse,' the dark fox said, grinning sheepishly. 'You're far too old for these capers.'

'Don't "old mouse" me, man's scat,' Stargrief hissed. 'You nearly got me killed.'

'Next time make sure the coast is clear before you pop into one of your visions.'

The torch flashed in the night behind them and Scoble growled and rattled off some sharp four-letter words. He had broken the gun to reload it and had snapped it back on his thumbnail.

'Next time come quietly,' Stargrief said, 'or you'll end up as a maggots' snack.'

'I wasn't shot at,' Wulfgar said innocently.

He shouldered the old fox as they breasted the heather. Stargrief snarled and stopped abruptly to dribble scats.

DARTMOOR AUTUMN

And suddenly the sky was full of birds.

Hastening down from the north the hordes of foreign thrushes filled the dusks with their cries. Often the darkness above the Leighon Valley rang to the mellow chok-chok of the fieldfares and the softer more repetitive notes of the bramblings. Then one night the swirling drizzle brought in an immense cloud of redwings. The border country was raked by fall after fall of birds from north of the Baltic. Among the continentals were parties of songthrushes, blackbirds, woodpigeons, chaffinches and robins. Starlings rushed over the tors in dark waves to settle on the farmland of Mid- and South Devon. There was also an unprecedented south-western movement of lapwings.

Reading the signs the foxes were uneasy, but men went about their business as though no warnings had been scrawled on the skies. The children knocked the few remaining conkers off the chestnut trees at Trumpeter. The harvest had been sung home in village churches all over Dartmoor: Widecombe, Ilsington, North Bovey, Holne, Chagford, Lustleigh, Manaton, Peter Tavey – names like a peal of bells. Gifts had been brought to the Barley Man. Bonfires burnt in cottage gardens and the smoke climbed softly blue into thinner blue. Across the in-country the shires plodded, dragging the plough through dark soil. Browns and golds had crept into the woods, and rowan and silver birch were at their loveliest among the heather by the brook where Wulfgar lay.

He tested the breeze with his nose. The night was brilliant under the Hunter's Moon. A tawny owl hooted and received a sharp reply from his mate. The fox ran with the stream to the Manaton-Beckaford lane and singled out a strong thread of coney scent. He killed the buck swiftly on the lawn of Aish Cottage. There were no lights on in the building, for the American had gone home. While Wulfgar skinned the rabbit he dozed in the airliner high above the Atlantic.

The wanderlust possessed him again and he came down Ruddycleave Water through the thistles, ragwort and yellow spires of mullein to Elliott's Hill Farm. But the collie alarmed before he could grab a fowl and he ran on to the fringe of Bagley Wood. It was the late part of a typical West Country autumn day – soft, mild, drizzly. The hawthorns were full of winter migrants and leaves fell in a light patter. Exciting scents crammed the air.

Wulfgar sat in the clearing among the hazel poles and curled the tip of his tongue around his nose. The woodcocks tumbled down through the branches and began to hollow out resting places in the fallen leaves. The fox took one and put the others to flight. They had not fully recovered from their journey across the North Sea although they had rested two days by the coast before heading inland.

The night-running brought him through the cleave to the Dart and Holne Chase, to the river that was steep-banked and overshadowed in places by cliffs. Wooded hills rolled away on every side to the sky. Salmon ringed the surfaces of the pools and the stretches of deep water. A vixen passed him but did not answer his call.

The tawny owl dropped off the crag called Lover's Leap and released a tremulous cry. It sailed over the river and flopped down in the nettles and gripped the vole, pinching the little creature's scream into silence. Then it entered the darkness beneath the oaks and winged off to the Iron Age fort on the hilltop. A star left the Milky Way and slid across the sky. The moon surprised Wulfgar; it was so big between the boughs.

The next morning was misty, and Hay Tor soared remote and unearthly into fine, crumbling blue. Men and dogs came to the down and took away the ponies. The annual 'drift' began quietly, as colts and fillies were driven to Chagford fair. Dark streams of animals filled the lanes and roads. The drovers were happy. During the war similar ponies had gone to the horse-butchers for a few shillings, now they were to be sold as children's mounts. Those that did not come under the auctioneer's hammer would be branded and returned to the breeding herds.

Bert Yabsley loved the fair. He always drank best bitter and whisky chasers at the Ring of Bells. Afterwards he needed very little persuasion to do the broom dance on the wagon where the village ladies displayed their bottled fruit, jams and home-made wine. For his size he was amazingly nimble, and the crowd would laugh and cheer and egg him on. It was the highlight of the terrier man's year and he was King of Dartmoor.

Autumn delighted him with its sensuality. The last of the cider apples stood bagged in the orchards ready to go to the mill: Bloody Butchers, Slack-ma-Girdles, Grenadiers, Kingston Blacks – their poetry belonged to the season of windfall splendour. Drunken wasps, partridges in covey, blackthorn heavy with sloes, owl cries and dark, golden sunshine – they all suited Yabsley. Along the hedges, tiger-striped spiders were spinning their traps for the bees. The robin sang his autumn song and the ivy bloom was attracting insects and birds to the farmhouse walls. And after rain yellow leaves flashed as they fell.

The wind wrote long sentences in the grass and rubbed them out with the next breath. Cold-eyed thrushes spilled from the rowans. Wulfgar sat up on his haunches and watched them go down the coomb, flickering silver and grey. A flock of golden plover wheeled over Seven Lords Lands, then lapwings poured in and settled on the marsh. A calm, frosty night had vanished before a rising gale. The slow editing of the countryside for winter was well under way.

Wulfgar visited the trap line on Holwell Common and found Killconey filching the largest rabbit. The dark fox was hungry and bad-tempered and refused to get bogged down in idle chat. He came at the gallop and drove Swart off a strangled doe. 'Craark,' said the crow, fighting the gale to get a footing in the beech tree. The wood boomed, leaves and twigs littered the air.

Wulfgar gnawed the rabbit free and carried it to some reeds by Emsworthy. Swart had winkled out the eyes, but such delicacies did not constitute a breakfast. The rooks regarded the crow coldly. They rode the bucking tree tops with a kind of yokel exultation that annoyed Swart. Their rookery leader was an old hen bird named Elder, who was wise and peppery. Only her mate, Cawder, could stand up to her, and he was very popular with the other rooks.

'What does the crow want?' Elder asked.

'Ask him,' said Cawder.

'The last thing you get from a crow is the truth,' snapped his mate.

'Then don't ask him,' Cawder said, and the nearest rooks, who were picking up snatches of the conversation despite the gale, burst out laughing.

Elder glared at them.

'There is the business of Old Wintercaw,' said one of the younger birds.

'Yes,' said Cawder. 'He's been as miserable as sin for the last two nights. It has to be the Ring or something nasty and four-legged will get him.'

'That would be unthinkable,' the young rook bawled.

His deep cawing made Swart wince.

'Halfwits,' he muttered, marking Wulfgar's spot and dreaming of coney's entrails.

'Very well,' Elder croaked. 'Set to – set to.'

One day, she thought, I'll see the Ring from the inside.

Another winter, another spring and summer and then …

She swallowed. Her wisdom was as valuable to the rookery as a store of seeds, but the time would come when she could not participate in the nest building and stubble gleaning.

She fetched up a sigh.

'Let the Ring be made,' said Cawder, and the message was passed on to the rest of the commune.

Wintercaw could hardly fly, so some young rooks had to nudge him off his roost with their beaks. He was very feeble and his behaviour lately had disturbed the rookery. It was not merely age. Wintercaw's plumage was full of parasites and he could not keep down his food.

There were times too when his strange ways outraged the rooks. On several gleaning expeditions he had ignored the peck order, actually pushing past Cawder and Elder to get at the grain. The wrangling that resulted from this heresy had threatened the Holwell rookery. Elder had been unhappy to see the food-gathering time squandered on petty squabbles. The strongest and most sagacious birds had to eat the most if the commune was to survive. Wintercaw could not be tolerated.

'Him and his horrible ticks will have to go,' Cawder had said, but it was a situation the rooks did not relish.

Wintercaw stood on wobbly legs in the sheep-field encircled by his fellow birds. Four young rooks attended him, carefully keeping their distance because of the ticks. Swart was interested; he sensed carrion in the making.

The cawing ended when Cawder clapped his wings.

'The Ring has been called to decide the fate of the bird Wintercaw,' said Elder.

'What are his sins?' chorused the rooks.

'Abusing the peck order,' Elder said. 'Stealing nesting material, taking all and giving nothing to the rookery.'

'I am old and sick,' whispered Wintercaw.

'What did he say?' Elder shouted. The wind was lifting her feathers and shrieking in the grass.

'He said he's old and sick,' Cawder said.

'We know that,' Elder said sadly. 'He isn't bad – he's just a threat.'

'Exile could be cruel,' said Cawder, reading her thoughts.

'Must it be the beaks?' Elder cried.

'Let it be the beaks,' answered the Ring.

Elder nodded and the four executioners fell upon Wintercaw and pecked him savagely about the head. Then the Ring closed in and Wintercaw died under a torrent of blows. His tattered body lay like a black rag in the field and the rooks returned to the beeches.

'Nasty, nasty!' Swart said to himself. He battled against the wind and landed near the dead rook. His beady eyes missed nothing. The rookery appeared to have forgotten him and Wintercaw. He wagged his head. His seed-eating cousins had a dark side to their natures. Very crow-like. He hopped closer to his breakfast. There were depths of darkness that even he had not explored. Sheol would not believe him.

The thistles parted and the stoat dashed through them and flung himself at the crow. Swart leapt up on a black blur of wings and let the gale lift him over Holwell. His day had begun badly.

Chivvy-yick placed a paw on the rook and chattered at the sky. He would carry the carcass back to Emsworthy and the other fitches would think he had taken the bird alive.

A WET MORNING

Blood!

Chivvy-yick's whole body registered the fact. Warm blood leaking from a coney! He dropped the rook and let the drool roll down his chin. Bounding through the bracken he gave the long, thin staccato cry of a hunting fitch. Wulfgar raised his head and grinned at him and Chivvy-yick's heart froze.

'Keep coming, Long Scat,' said the fox. 'There's plenty of room in here for you.'

He opened his jaws.

Chivvy-yick crouched and hissed. He had stared death in the face many times but he had rarely out-foxed a fox. And he was clever enough to realise that bravado was not the answer. An irate fox was a dangerous animal.

'And where are all your brave brothers and cousins?' Wulfgar continued.

He lay with his paws across the kill and showed no eagerness to abandon it. The stoat fidgeted and blotted the gap in the bracken with his stink. The hot, musky smell of his fear pleased Wulfgar. The fox had shrugged off his black mood and was enjoying the rabbit. Drowsiness made him reluctant to get up. One night he would meet Chivvy-yick again and chop him, but now it amused him to torment the fitch.

The black buttons of Chivvy-yick's eyes never left the fox's face. Wulfgar ate some more coney and smacked his lips. Very slowly and carefully Chivvy-yick backed off.

'That's it – crawl, Long Scat,' Wulfgar scoffed. 'Crawl. Hug the dirt and go quietly. If you disturb me I'll bite off your head.'

His jaws slammed shut.

As soon as he was out of sight the stoat undulated away to the burrow by the drystone wall. He was quivering with rage. Next time he found Mange-Bag in a wire he would have his throat.

Shiv's head popped out of the rabbit-hole.

'Did you get a drummer?' he said.

'O yes,' Chivvy-yick said sarcastically. 'I got a drummer and a pheasant and a duck and a hen and a grouse and a hare and a bloody great turkey from the farm in the valley; and a goose. Take your pick.'

'Sorry I spoke,' said his cousin.

Chivvy-yick ground his fangs together.

The evening was hooded with rain. Out of the darkness rushed more flocks of birds. Wulfgar heard them calling low in the sky. At first light a thousand fieldfares covered the hawthorns of Bagtor Down. Then the rain was spent but the clouds looked ominous. Tawny oak woods and the rust of bracken sparkled. An underwater clarity and stillness prevailed. Cattle, sheep and ponies stood motionless.

The fox trotted up the headwaters of the River Lemon to the road. He was famished. The night had yielded half a coney. The rest of the animal had been eaten by a badger. Wulfgar's nose told him he was safe, but he ran up a road that led to Beckaford remembering the fowls of Yarner Wells. With Wendel long gone the old lady had grown careless and Wulfgar had seen hens scratching the wayside mud. His mouth watered at the thought of the warm, white flesh busy under wispy chicken feathers.

He caught the sound before he smelt the trapper. Darting off the road he clapped down under a gorsebush. The adrenalin jolted through his system. The piggish grunting continued. It was coming from the furze about thirty fox-lengths up the road. Wulfgar crept forward on his belly, ready to bolt at the first hint of danger.

Scoble was sprawled on his back, sound asleep. He lay on a mattress of heather and pony dung. His mouth was wide open and he was snoring. He was also soaked to the skin. Somehow he had managed to drink nineteen pints of rough cider at the Rock Inn from teatime to chucking-out time. It was a personal record. But the walk to Yarner's Cott had proved too much of an ordeal. He had staggered through the wet darkness with the uncanny homing instinct of all drunks, then he had stopped to empty his bladder and that was that. Etherised with alcohol he had crashed into unconsciousness, and if it had rained six-inch nails he would not have stirred.

The fox sat in the road and gazed down his muzzle at Scoble. The trapper twitched and mumbled and threw out an arm. How easy it would be to rip open his throat, Wulfgar thought. His guts constricted but he was mindful of Stargrief's warning. Killing a man would mean certain disaster for the Hill Nation. Yet he felt he could do it. The ghosts of Teg and the cubs cried out for Man blood. Maybe Tod had arranged this happening. Should he act as Wulfgar or as the leader of the clan? O Tod, he cried to himself. Send me a sign. Help me.

The trapper's stench curdled into nausea and Wulfgar vomited a mess of partly digested coney. Then he cocked his leg on one of Scoble's boots, but again fear of the ancient enemy held him back. His excitement threatened to ooze out in scats. Yes, he would go through his cowardice and grip that hateful throat. He would remain true to himself, true to Teg and all the other murdered animals.

The yell sent him hurtling down the slope to Yarner Wood and the relief of letting instinct take control. Behind him he heard pony's hooves on the road and wondered if it was Tod's sign.

The postman had rheumatism. He groaned slowly out of the saddle and hobbled up to Scoble. God, you're in a state, he thought, staring into the unshaven face.

'Leonard,' he said.

The drunk coughed cider fumes and rolled onto his side.

'Leonard.'

'Wha'issit?' Scoble gasped. The bed was sprouting toadstools and bracken. It had turned into a cold, wet compost heap. O Christ! he thought. I've pissed myself. The mattress would be ruined. On dilating ripples of giddiness the sky advanced and retreated. Why was it there? What had happened to the roof and the ceiling? Things tilted and squirmed, slowly, changing shape and colour like petrol stains in a puddle.

'Are you hurt?' the postman said.

'Where did you come from?' Scoble frowned. 'What you doing here? How did you get in?

'Get up, Leonard, or you'll die of pneumonia.'

'Never oldmonia,' Scoble wheezed, raising himself on his elbows. He growled up phlegm and spat.

'I thought the fox was going for your throat,' said the postman.

'Fox? The only foxes in my house are dead buggers.'

'You idn in Yarner Cott,' the postman said. The agony of his rheumatism made him grunt out the words.

'You'm on the moors. And by the look of 'ee you've been here all night in the pouring rain. I'd get out of it if I was you.'

'The fox?' Scoble said coming rapidly back into himself.

'Him they call Old Blackie.'

Scoble's teeth started to chatter.

'He was here,' the postman went on. 'He piddled on your boot and then –'

Scoble stroked his wart.

'Then he crouched down and started to move towards you ever so steady, like an old tomcat after a mouse.'

The last dregs of colour left the trapper's face.

'If you're lyin',' he whispered, 'I'll boot your puddens up round your neck.'

'I saw it. If I had'n yelled you'd be dead. Look – there's his marks in the mud.'

Scoble felt the life draining from his body. The postman's words had pulled out some sort of stopper in the bottom of his spirit and as his strength escaped darkness seeped in. He struggled to his feet. Hot and cold flushes swept over his skin, his head and eyes were on fire and he had a sharp pain in his right lung.

'Get on the pony, Leonard,' said the postman. 'You idn fit enough to walk to Yarner.'

'How long ago was the fox here?' Scoble said, and he coughed up more phlegm.

'Just now. But you ought to get home to bed with a hot water bottle. I'll phone the doctor.'

'No you bloody won't,' Scoble said. His teeth would not stop chattering and his kneecaps seemed to have melted.

'Look, Walter,' he added quietly. 'You done me a good turn and I won't forget it. But I'll be all right now. I'll make me own way home.'

'God, Len! – you're like death warmed up. If you don't hit the sack you'll be fillin' a box.'

'That's between me and the devil,' said Scoble with a grim smile.

He watched the postman canter away on the back of his New Forest mare. A cloud of rain rolled off Hay Tor and the horror rose in Scoble. What if the Yank was right? What if Old Blackie wasn't a fox at all but some sort of diabolical creature sent from hell to tear out his soul? The devil will get you, you little sod, his father had roared. He had dropped the basket of eggs, in the rain, in the winter long ago. The knuckles had pulped his nose. Yaas, the devil's got his eye on you, Leonard Scoble. Then another blow and another curse.

The trapper went down the road with the dawdling footsteps of a simpleton. The future gaped like a dark November evening and he had never really looked into it before. He groaned. The pain in his chest throbbed hot and insistent, like toothache. He was very cold, but the more he tensed his body the more he shivered.

Yet the fox hadn't got him, and they old foxes didn get me on the Somme, he thought. Something was watching over him. His dark eyes blazed. If the devil was on Dartmoor he'd have to work hard. O yes!

He piled his wet clothes on the hearthrug, then he lit the fire and boiled a kettle. The tea soothed his sore throat but he had no stomach for tobacco. He was shivering now in spasms and found it difficult to pull on his wellingtons and knot the baler cord round the waist of his greatcoat.

'Foxes run in circles,' he muttered. Old Blackie would go through Yarner. The Bovey would probably turn him and he'd come up Trendlebere, Beckaford Woods way, to Leighon. Scoble would hide by the bridge down from Aish Cottage. The fox had a choice of hugging the stream or using the lane. In the bank by the entrance to Leighon was a fox run that was well trodden. A man could sit among the trees and get a sniper's view of the whole scene.

The BSA bolt action .22 was wrapped in oiled sackcloth. Scoble had bought it second-hand, sacrificing precious scrumpy money. He kissed the butt.

'Dang me! – if you idn a little beauty!' he whispered.

He loved the feel and the balance of the rifle. And a good shot would bring down a roe deer. Rain rattled on the window. He coughed violently.

The cranking left him light-headed and weak, but a different sort of fever gripped him as the van sizzled along the lane.

With bouncing, catlike strides Wulfgar chested the rain that swirled along Trendlebere Down. The haunting desolation of the plains reached up to him. A hare broke cover and galloped off. Birds glided out of the gloom and flashed silently away.

In Beckaford Wood the hypnotic fall of oak leaves had him thinking the trees were on the move. He examined the air. It smelt of leaf mould, wet earth and flood water. The gap where the fox path began received his special attention. A wire or a gin might have been hidden there to take a tired animal, so he went cautiously, his nostrils crinkling at every step, his head constantly moving to the right and left.

Scoble squeezed the trigger. His eyes were watering and his hands were unsteady but Wulfgar was a big target. The crack of the rifle coincided with the zang of the bullet ricochetting off the rock. Wulfgar became a dark flare weaving among the brambles. The lead had scored a diagonal groove in the front of his left foreleg and blood seeped through the fur. He stopped briefly and licked it. The roar of the brook obliterated the sound of the bolt being drawn back. Scoble sent another bullet into the branches of the scrub oak.

Keeping low the fox sprinted up the cart track to Leighon, leaving only his stink behind him; and a couple of farm workers saw him run into rough ground below Hound Tor.

THE 11.35

He slept uncomfortably through the rainy night in a hollow under a rock. Whenever he woke he licked his wounded leg. Just after dawn the weather brightened and hazy gold smeared the grey. He plashed down to the barn on the edge of the wood overlooking Leighon House. Fieldmice were scarce and another fox had disturbed the conies. He made a few half-hearted attempts to stalk partridges before returning to the rock and his couch of dead bracken, and it was here that Lancer ranging ahead of the pack found his line and put him up two hours before noon.

The hound running by sight threw his tongue and was answered by a deep clamour. Above the music of the pack the yelp of the horn tailed away on a string of little notes.

'You saw him, sir,' said the huntsman, opening the gate.

'Yes – and I think we're in for a hell of a good run,' Claude Whitley said.

The news travelled back to Hound Tor and the foot-followers.

'They won't get un,' said Scoble. 'There idn a hound in Devon that can master Old Blackie.'

His face, turned to the light, was gaunt, pale and bristly. He planted his fists in the pockets of his greatcoat and began to cough, the tears streaming down his cheeks.

'He carried the undertaker's brand,' George Lugg told his cronies later. 'His clothes hung off un like a scarecrow's rags and he smelt like a polecat. I reckon it's T.B.'

As morning shrugged off the mist Wulfgar cruised into the wood. He was lithe and self-assured in his passage from sunlight through blotches of shadow and back to light again. At the deserted farm he ran along the top of the wall, jumped down and walked around the yard, and went into the shell of the barn before departing by way of the meadow.

For a while the hounds were in check, but Lancer had a nose capable of deciphering nearly all Wulfgar's tricks. He had bolted a huge breakfast of porridge and beef broth and was ready for anything. Quivering on tense hindlegs he sniffed the air. His arching back delighted the master who saw in him the perfect engine for hard going. The sloping pasterns of his feet gave him extra purchase on steep, difficult ground.

'Leu in – leu in, wind 'im,' cried the huntsman.

Dashwood the babbler was crying wolf amongst the trees but Lancer suddenly found the line and ran mute, so intent was he on getting his fox. The huntsman sounded the Gone Away and the pack spoke and came on the surge of their music. A wedge of hounds drove into the woods where Wulfgar had sought the path up the Becca Brook.

The fox quit the oaks without haste and climbed Black Hill. Drops of water flew from the bracken to bejewel his fur. Slowly a feeling of detachment stole across his thoughts. The living world was curiously indifferent to his situation and the starlings settling on the furze hardly noticed him passing.

'There he goes,' said George Lugg quietly.

Stray closed his eyes. Not Old Blackie, he prayed. Not today, God. Not now. The foot-followers, who had gathered on the eastern side of Greator Rocks, saw the pack roll out of the covert led by the badger-pied Lancer and swarm up the hillside throwing their cries. Then the silvery carping of the horn brought on the field in an untidy cavalry charge.

Wulfgar sprinted but Lancer closed the gap. His powerful, lolloping gait saw him swiftly across ground that was lumpy and bramble-snarled. Sweat splashed from his tongue and each breath captured the stink of warm, hard-running fox. Ahead Black Hill curved darkly against the sky and for a second or two Wulfgar was visible among a scribble of thorns on the horizon. The music of the hounds filled the valley below him. He heard the thump of Lancer's feet and the distant rumble of hooves, then the horn again, higher and more piercing than a vixen's cry.

Sunlight exploded in his face. He raced over the hilltop and down towards the road through furze and hawthorns. A flock of bramblings swooped low across Yarner Wood. Now Wulfgar's heart was punching out blood in loud blows. On the open heath he was much slower and weaker than the hounds. A train hooted, and gazing across the distant treetops he saw steam rising in white puffs.

The pack came over the skyline at full cry. Wulfgar crossed the road and traversed Trendlebere, running at times through the trees on the edge of Yarner Wood. The Manaton-Bovey Tracey road was crowded with Galloways and Wulfgar ran among them, back and forth, up one verge and onto the other. Then he made a loop, dashing in from the road and returning to it twenty yards further down to enter the wood. A zig-zag course brought him to a pond that he swam before trotting down through gloomy copses to the River Bovey at Pullabrook.

The hounds were breathing heavily as they quested below Yarner.

'Leu in, leu – wind 'im,' the huntsman cried, trying to lift them.

Dashwood gave immediate tongue and was rated by the first whip. The lemon-coloured dog Camper ran wide, making urgent but meaningless noises in the scrub, and there was a short-lived clamour when Lancer, Tickler, Trimbush and Witness showed the pack round the loop and back to the road. The cattle stumbled up the verge and galloped off, bellowing and tossing their heads. The hounds checked and feathered until Lancer nosed Wulfgar's line and belled. A swift, noisy run brought the pack to the pond and a sudden blank.

The huntsman took half a dozen couples to the far side and they found the line and their voices again.

'Old Blackie is a marvellous animal,' Jenny Shewte said in the breezy tone of a convent school girl. She had no trouble in handling her bay with its plaited mane and oiled hooves.

The Colonel's mare was less lively but she kept slugging her head straight out. He made little clucking noises with his tongue and tried to soothe her.

'You won't be going to America, I take it?' he said, smiling at Jenny.

'No.' She stood up in her stirrups. The field was moving off. 'I couldn't say goodbye to all this. I like Richard immensely and we're the best of friends. I suppose I've grown up a bit since the war. There's no question of marriage.'

'Has he proposed?'

She coloured and shook her head.

'He writes nice letters and says he's coming back next year. That's all.'

'Different worlds,' said her father.

The Bovey was a fluorescent strip of light between two high slabs of shadow. Wulfgar crossed the river and trotted up the path under the bridge to Houndtor Wood. He was still in no great hurry. His paws kicked up the damp smell of decay from the ground under the trees. It was good to run into silence, leaving the din of the hounds subsiding on the field beside the Bovey where he had forded it.

Cutting up through the trees he laid another loop, broad and far flung, running almost to the outlying cottages of Lustleigh and back once more to the river a quarter of a mile upstream. An old widow collecting acorns for her pigs saw Wulfgar pause to drink and trot on like a dog out for a stroll. She had seen scores of foxes but never one so big and dark. When the carrier bag was full she stepped briskly for home and presently met the pack as they were about to head up Wulfgar's loop. Her news enabled the huntsman to whip the hounds along the bank until they picked up the fresh line and gave tongue in a fierce clamour.

From Nutcrackers up Lustleigh Cleave to Foxworthy Copse the ground was tussocky and treeless. Lancer burst from the wood and caught a glimpse of Wulfgar a long way off. The heavy reek of fox clogged his nostrils and he threw a deep note that raced ahead of him to lift Wulfgar's hackles.

For the first time that morning the fox felt uneasy.

A jay scolded him and harassed him through Foxworthy out into the sunshine again. Tightening his muscles he sprang to the right and repeated the ruse every dozen or so strides until he had laid five false lines. The hounds were in the copse now but he was climbing the hill, keeping low among the boulders. On the summit he dropped scats inside the remains of a prehistoric fort, ran around the grassy mounds, which had once been earthworks, and set off for Barnecourt Spinney in the coomb below.

To have run straight through the trees and out into the field would have been too simple. He knew the brambly undergrowth would delay the hounds who were twice his size. Yet he moved swiftly, and once on the other side of the spinney, doubled back along the edge of the trees and entered it again. When he emerged and galloped through the cattle to the crossroads, the pack were coming off Hunter's Tor. The foot followers had gone by road to the clapper bridge beyond Langstone. They had seen Wulfgar slink into the spinney but had missed his exit.

Running along the lane was easy after the hard slog in the covert and the endurance test on the steeps above the Bovey. Although his tongue was flopped out Wulfgar carried himself as gracefully as ever, and he even allowed himself the luxury of chasing a rabbit that crossed his path.

The morning was sweet with all the shades of brown rushing in glittering array to a sky of palest blue. Passing a cottage he sniffed the aroma of baking bread and the crisp smell of washing drying on the line. In the fields he pushed his nose over partridge-scented hollows and trails taken by other foxes. Then he realised the hound clamour had grown louder. Obviously the dogs found the open country to their liking and were gaining on him.

A gang of labourers clamping mangolds under Narramore glimpsed him skirting the covert to hurry down into the Wray Valley. Less than two hundred and fifty yards adrift of the fox were sixty hounds crashing through the hedge and belling all the way.

'Thicky girt black varx,' the farmworkers called Wulfgar, speaking the Devon dialect. And 'that great black fox' took to the railway in the bottom of the valley, running on the nearest line so that the smell of steel cancelled out his own stink. But Lancer spotted him and spoke jubilantly, his long stride eating the distance between himself and the hunted animal. Wulfgar's lips were twisted back in a grin of exhaustion. Brambles had spiked his right ear and the blood had clotted thick and dark. He left the track and crossed the farmland to the allotment gardens at the back of Moretonhampstead station. The hounds were less than a field behind him and their clamour carried for miles.

Just after the war the Great Western Railway linked Newton Abbot to Moretonhampstead with a busy branch line. The little 'prairie' tank engine pulled a couple of carriages several times a day to the moorland town, climbing five hundred feet in the twelve mile journey.

As Wulfgar tore through the allotments and chicken runs the 11.35 for Newton Abbot was preparing to leave. The driver had opened the regulator letting the steam from the boiler to the cylinder. The noise muffled the hound clamour, but Wulfgar could hear the dogs as he trotted up the track and sprang onto the running plate of the moving engine. It was entirely an impluse thing, motivated by instinct and sixth sense. With the hounds on his tail a fox will run anywhere to escape and of all the Hill Fox Nation Wulfgar was the great opportunist.

He clapped down between the splash cover and the buffer beam and unloaded his smell in one final shudder of fear and excitement. The metal shelf shook and vibrated and the 'prairie' rolled on. Steam swirled around the fox and he pressed close to the boiler, his ears flattened and his brush twitching. An incredible acrid stench plugged his nose. Then the countryside was sliding by and the steam lifting. The wheels sang over the track and the pistons thudded below him. It was like riding on a stuttering peel of thunder but already it was too late for him to jump. The train was gathering speed with gasps of steam.

If he could have looked back he would have seen the hounds milling about on the line and platform. The tantalising whiff of fox had ended abruptly in a maelstrom of smells – the reek of engine oil, metal, coal and steam. Even Lancer was baffled. He gazed at the rear of the train, which was vanishing into the distance, but his simple brain remained blank. He turned and let his nose guide him up Wulfgar's scent to the railway workers' gardens. A man in blue overalls yelled at him and Lancer sat down and scratched, driving his right hind foot into his jowl. Coming hard through the cabbages on a horse flecked with froth and lather the huntsman knew the fox had outwitted them for the seventh time in three seasons.

Wulfgar's claws were buried in grime. The sooty smell of the plate distressed him but it was better than the death smell of the hounds. His body was jarred by the roar and rumble of the engine. He licked a forepaw. On the road between the trees were glimpses of riders and horses – a flash of scarlet, hunched black shapes, the arching neck of an animal. A farmstead flew at him and disappeared. Whenever he raised his eyes to the dark blur of branches he felt giddy and insecure. Many seasons seemed to separate him from the hunt, but he had entered a strange future and might never rediscover the autumn where Stargrief and Killconey lived. Excitement tightened his stomach. He had a vision of Stargrief mumbling and farting in his sleep.

The business of producing prophecy wasn't noble and grand. And why did the old dog fox keep on about order and beauty? Such things were conspicuously lacking in their lives.

He eased his chin between his forefeet. Where had Man come from? Where did he go when he died? – if he died? What was he? He wasn't an animal, for sure. He was as weird as this metal house that thundered along on wheels making smoke like the white winter breath of foxes. Man could discard his coat and put on a new one whenever he chose. Did the answer lie in the Star Place? But what if there wasn't a Star Place except in his head? He sighed. Every trail of thought brought him back to his own confusion.

Presently the train would slow down or stop and he would get off. He knew the valley although he had never seen it from that level before. His own world had shrunk and he did not belong to it. The engine hooted and passed under the bridge by Wray Barton farm. An alarming moment of darkness and noise blotted out the day, then there was sunlight once more, splashed and barred with shadow.

Scoble and Stray rushed across to the other parapet and watched the train pull away.

'You saw un, didn you, boy? I idn goin' mazed. You saw un?' the trapper whispered.

'On the side of the bliddy engine!' Stray said. 'Old Blackie on the bliddy train!'

George Lugg joined them on the bridge.

'What's up, Leonard?' he said.

'What's down, you mean,' Scoble wheezed. And he thumped his chest and coughed and rasped up phlegm.

'Old Blackie's just gone down on the 11.35 from Moreton – bold as bloody brass, squattin' on the plate above the engine wheels like he's always riding on trains.'

'Bugger off!' Lugg exclaimed. 'Tidn possible. Foxes is –'

Scoble stopped him with a glance and said, 'Us saw un – me and the boy. Us saw un.'

'He's magic, that old black fox,' Stray said. 'He can do anything.'

'But Leonard seen un – magic or no magic,' said Scoble. 'One day soon I'll blow his head off. His luck have got to run out.'

'Maybe it idn luck,' the boy said in a low voice.

Wulfgar left the 'prairie' when it stopped at Lustleigh. The number of passengers could be counted on the claws on his front feet so he was able to lope off unseen and come down to the Bovey to drink. He was tired, stiff and very dirty, and his pads were cut and swollen, but the water refreshed him.

Afterwards he crossed the river and lay in the bracken grooming his underfur and paws. The smell of the steam engine clung to every hair. He worked on them patiently with tongue and teeth. The breeze, which was bending the treetops, ruffled his brush and the keen beauty of Teg filled his thoughts. O foxes! O my blood brothers and sisters! Under the trees the shade was cold, the crisp tinge of autumn was on his nose. To live is to run. Always running – away from death, into death. Perhaps Man kills us to kill a memory. We are ghosts of Man the animal and he can't live with the knowledge. O Teg! Breath of my breath, spirit of my spirit, sister of the sun and moon. He stretched and groaned and moved up the great slope of oak trees.

In the evening the wind freshened and blew from the north. Wulfgar kennelled at Greator Rocks, in the cave under the holly tree. Throughout the night flocks of foreign birds whispered across the sky.

THE YEAR TURNING

The hunt returned a few weeks later and killed the vixen Redbriar. She died bravely under Lancer but her death did not go unnoticed by the Hay Tor Clan. The days were getting shorter and darkness fell quickly. There was bleakness in the light of the sky and in the country-side and in the hearts of the foxes. When the sun shone through the mists it was cold and yellow like a sparrowhawk's eye. Morning after morning the hedges were white with frozen fog and the mires were held rigid.

Wulfgar walked the banks of the East Dart above Dartmeet and ate salmon that had starved to death after spawning. Towards dusk a fresh wave of redwings dropped in the fields of Widecombe and huddled among the fieldfares and starlings. The blank sky darkened from time to time with new arrivals from the North. Then they were off again, heading for South Devon. A fall of light snow lifted and fumed on the wind, and at night the sleet rattled on the rowan trees, and the woods roared in a wind heavy with migrating birds.

The fox looked up at the lights of the universe. The swift little Becca cut across his thoughts but the stars danced on. He crouched and dropped scats and left his smell on the scenting post beside the stream. In a bottom window of Leighon House a fir tree decorated with fairy lights glowed softly. He crossed the bare meadow, feeling the night press cold against his eyes. The quieter reaches of the brook were iced over. He sat beneath the oaks listening for voles. An owl screamed and a vixen took up its cry, sending long grinding shrieks down through the trees. From far-off corners of the night dog foxes answered faintly but Wulfgar did not add his voice to the chorus. The emptiness in his gut suited him, for lately Teg had crept back into his dreams and he would wake up and think of the cubs. 'Oakwhelp, Nightfrond, Brookcelt, Dusksilver,' he murmured, as if their names were talismen.

Unlike the summer sun the stars were bright but cool. The dead are cold, he thought. It is the foxes, all the foxes – dead and reborn. Their spirits shine from cold bodies. The great field of the sky was full of foxes. Why did he ache for their comradeship and love yet flinch from joining them?

Stargrief's face parted the ferns. Stiff-spoked, the sun stood red between the treetops and the clouds. Daws jangled across the valley.

'The meadow under the old farm was full of rabbits yesterday evening,' said Stargrief. 'The buzzard was busy till darkfall.'

'You feel Redbriar's death like a wound, don't you, Old Mouse?' Wulfgar said. 'Every fox death hits you hard.'

The animals had been conducting a wordless conversation beneath the chat, reading each other's thoughts, deciphering the shift of images in each other's eyes. A mature vixen would be difficult to kill, she would carry her determination to live right into death's jaws. And the earth would claim her as it claimed all its children. Then the light would shine softly from the body of star gold, the new incorruptible fox-shape running the wilderness of eternity.

Stargrief closed his eyes and raised his muzzle.

'We are not more than shadows,' he chanted,
'flickering briefly on the moors.
But the flickering is beautiful.
Through drifts of hawthorn we pass.
We drink the seasons
and the seasons take us.

The seasons are hounds
and no earth or clitter-fastness
can keep that pack at bay.
We are no more than shadows.'

'The moors are crawling with young rabbits,' said Wulfgar before the Teg image could expand in a welter of melancholy.

'Were they as stupid when Tod ran the fox trails?'

'Rabbits are good at rabbit things,' Stargrief said. 'But perhaps their relationships are too intimate.'

Wulfgar laughed and the spell of misery was broken.

They trotted on to hunt the margins of the Becca Brook while Stormbully flapped over Holwell and held them with his intense gaze. The buzzard found the peak of his hill of wind and surfed down the far side to drop into the neck of the valley. But Shiv rippled away, sealing the entrance to the bolt-hole with the reek of mustelid. The year was turning. Frost, the woody breath of a bonfire, songbirds feasting on the hedgerow berries, a red sun in a white mist; nothing new yet enough refurbishing of the countryside to skin the eyes.

Wherever trees banded together the pigeons came and went, and the clatter of their wings ruffled the silence. Wulfgar looked up and sniffed them as they flew over the Leighon Valley. A roving peregrine had accounted for one of their number. The foxes examined the feathers and blood splatters on the rock, which still retained the delicate smell of falcon.

'Why does the summer die?' asked Wulfgar.

'Would you be happy in endless summer?'

'No. No, Stargrief.'

'What you really mean is why did Teg die.'

'How could Tod let it happen?'

'After all these seasons you can ask such a question? Teg's death was part of your destiny.'

'I'd rather have her than – than this.'

'We have no more control over our lives than the leaf that uncurls, grows green, yellows and falls.'

'I know,' said Wulfgar in a changed voice. 'But knowing doesn't help.'

'Grief is one of Death's hounds. He runs wide and takes us by surprise, never killing, simply worrying the soft inner parts.'

'I thought I'd lost him for good.'

'The sun sets and rises again. It is an indisputable fact. Draw strength from it.'

The hillside was the colour of a gull's wing. A flock of starlings uncurled in the sky and fell onto the slopes. At Seven Lords Lands the foxes put up snipe. Rabbit runs criss-crossed the grass and droppings were scattered about like black peas. Wulfgar was stepping carefully over them when his head jerked up and his ears quivered.

'Be still, Stargrief,' he whispered. 'There's a dog on the road.'

The dog, bounding along with the friskiness of a puppy, was a gangling creature, deep-chested and narrow round the shanks. Suddenly the starling flock rose in front of it and the dog barked and danced for a moment on its hindlegs like a bird trying to take off. Then someone whistled and it was gone. The returning hush had a cold ache to it.

The foxes' eyes met and Stargrief sighed.

'We could be wrong,' he said.

'About what?'

'The whistle.'

'It was the sound the trapper used to make to call his lurcher. No other creature makes it. It is his just as Romany's call is Romany's call and your bark is your bark.'

'Then he has another dog.'

'A young one. And I don't suppose it's crazy.'

'But he'll teach it to kill foxes.'

'That's inevitable,' Wulfgar said bluntly.

'You ought to get that cough seen to,' Bert Yabsley said. There was more irritation than compassion in his voice.

Scoble had surfaced from a great bronchial eruption to wipe his nose and eyes on his sleeve. A bushy grey beard and hollow cheeks had added twenty years to his countenance.

'The Luggs reckon you've got T.B.,' Yabsley went on.

'And they should know,' Scoble wheezed sarcastically. 'Dr Lugg and his young assistant, George – God's gift to medicine.'

He was panting like the lurcher pup that lay on the heap of dead conies and hares at his feet. White breath rose from man and animal. The morning was bitter but the wind was stealing round to the west.

Yabsley and Scoble lit cigarettes and stood smoking in silence while the terriers rolled on the carcasses and ruddy light spread over Haytor Down.

'They buggers in Palestine got Ernie Claik's brother Norman,' Yabsley said. It was not in his nature to be quiet for long.

'Who got un?' Scoble said, wrinkling his brows.

'The bloody terrorists. Norman was a policeman out there. They'm flyin' his body home. Atlee ought to pull out our boys and drop an atom bomb on 'em. That would make the buggers sit up sharpish.'

Scoble had closed his ears. The big man's words were as remote and meaningless as the cawing of rooks. Palestine didn't belong to the real world of tors, rabbits and foxes. Anyway, he had never liked Norman Claik – he'd had too much mouth.

The pain under his ribs swelled and he was suddenly bathed in sweat. When he coughed, his right lung kicked and hurt like it had been hit by shrapnel.

'For Christ's sake don't gob on me,' Yabsley grunted, turning away.

The trapper stooped and tugged at the young lurcher's ears.

'Norman's brother Perce is the railway rat-catcher, idn he?' he said.

'The one with the funny-tempered dog?' said Yabsley.

'A sour-gutted little Jack Russell,' the trapper said pointedly. 'But Perce is alive and Norman's dead as these rabbits.'

He dug his toecap into the pile of carcasses.

'Not many of they Palestine blokes gets up the Bovey-Moreton line,' Yabsley grinned.

Like a bank of rain racing low over the tors the fieldfares swept overhead and on down to the fertile lowlands of the south.

'Where do they come from?' Scoble said.

Bert Yabsley shrugged.

'I've never seen so many,' the trapper said. ''Tis like one of the plagues of Egypt – only 'tis birds not locusts.'

'Old Herbie Thorpe says it's the bloody atom bomb buggering up nature.'

'And the Bible foretold that too,' Scoble said.

BECKAFORD

The young lurcher did not last long. Scoble was in the habit of releasing it whenever he saw or smelt fox and soon it had grown accustomed to running wild on Haytor Down. Here late one January afternoon a farmer saw it disturbing his sheep. The man was out shooting crows and had no trouble in giving the dog the contents of both barrels. The body was dumped at the gate of Yarner Cott as a warning to the trapper. Scoble buried it by the ferrets' hutch and never mentioned the animal again, although he often thought of it on his treks across the moors. Everything that went wrong could be blamed on the black fox. When the vermin was dead his luck would change. The loss of the lurcher merely deepened his hatred.

With the rising of the moon the vixen began to cry and from valleys and hills all around Beckaford the dog foxes answered. A fall of heavy rain did not stop the caterwauling, and by dawn eleven dogs had assembled at the top of the lane leading to Beckaford Farm. The vixen sat on the boulder under the beech trees. The rain had powdered away into mist and the upsweeping wind brought the secrets of the valley to the foxes. Against the bank of rocks and moss celandines poked through the dead leaves, and here and there nettles grew in clusters no taller than an upright vole.

Wulfgar lifted a leg and watered the rowan stump. A wren sang from the thicket at the base of the ash and oaks. Cloudy and full the Becca Brook swept under the bridge. The dark fox fetched up a screaming wail that froze the fur on the backs of the other dogs, but Killconey's reply was high-pitched and not too distant. The unbelievably exciting scent of vixen saturated their beings. Now they were truly alone, sparking aggression, dead to everything except the fire in their bellies.

The hedge quivered under the passing wind. Wulfgar suddenly roused himself and stretched, curling his upper lip and crinkling his nose, his yellow eyes full of the vixen-madness. Setting off for Beckaford he thought of the lonely moments that assailed him every night and jerked up his head to tear loose the agony.

The nine dog foxes sparring on the open ground beside the beeches were called Thorngeld, Brackenpad, Furzegeld, Bramblewaif and Moonbreeze; Mireheath, Sundrifter, Copsewalker and Torsmoke. Killconey and Stargrief lay close to the boulder where the vixen sat apparently unperturbed by the skirmishing. But only Stargrief was at peace with himself. His companion had fought and defeated the boldest of the suitors, yet the blood still shot into his hackles.

'When Wulfgar comes,' Stargrief said, 'the rabbits will scatter.'

Killconey smiled and narrowed his eyes. He was more than a bit insane with lust.

'I've yet to lose at this game,' he said. 'In the fields of my homeland they call me Killconey-eat-Granite. I've killed five dogs in combat.'

'Wulfgar will drop you like a cub,' the old fox said quietly.

'Friendship has blinded you,' said Killconey.

'Yes, he is like my flesh and blood – like all the cubs I've ever sired. But when you tackle him you will be fighting seven foxes.'

'Riddles annoy me, Old Mouse.'

'He is Teg and her dead young ones. And he is Tod and Wulfgar.'

'Tod lives in us all.'

'Wulfgar has the strength of the great visionaries.'

'We'll see,' Killconey growled.

The dark fox was among them like a storm. A sputtering bark and the scream of an enraged tomcat hoisted him onto the boulder beside the vixen. He stood with his forepaws on the granite and swung his gaze across the gathering.

'Let the animal who is tired of living step forward.'

The racking, frenzied shriek silenced the dog foxes and brought the vixen to her belly. Then Killconey strutted into the little arena and the remaining animals sat in line along the edge of the lane, facing inwards. Killconey was puffed-out and stiff of leg.

'I piss on your words,' he snarled, flattening his ears and showing his fangs.

Wulfgar sprang, his forepaws spread, and bowled him over. But before he could be pinned Killconey twisted and wormed and bit one of his adversary's front legs. Wulfgar ran around him, reckless with anger, and dealt him a terrible wound with his incisors. The speed of the attack had Killconey gasping. Once more the world somersaulted. He hit the ground and rolled on his shoulder. The pain smashed through a blur of branches, rocks and sky. Fangs snapped and ripped the hair from his throat. He grappled the dark shape but Wulfgar held him down and raked his belly with hindfeet in a real attempt at disembowelling. Killconey screamed and broke free, then he lunged and missed and was floored yet again.

Wulfgar fought with unprecedented fury, killing the trapper for the marvellous happiness he had destroyed.

The hair along his spine had prickled and rage inflated him to almost twice his normal size. He whirled in his tracks in a flurry of fallen leaves and Killconey drew back, hunched and shaking. The screech paralysed him and he could only bare his fangs noiselessly before such strength.

But Wulfgar seemed to have lost interest. He sat down and scratched as if a problem had been solved.

'Seven foxes', Stargrief said.

In the dim light he looked greyer than usual. Killconey regarded him with respect, seeing for the first time the true prophet. The scar-faced fox had lived a solitary life and the doings of the Haytor Clan still puzzled him. Dark warrior, grey prophet, lovely vixen; it was the lost world of Tod. He recalled his mother's stories of the duels that lasted half the night. Was the Golden Age returning as spring returned after winter? Slinging a foreleg over his flank he pushed his muzzle into his haunch and licked the wound.

'Is it deep?' Stargrief asked. He shuffled up to Killconey and got to work with his tongue.

Behind him was a patter of departing foxes. The wind, gathering force, shook raindrops from the beeches and lifted Swart's feathers. The crow wobbled on the top twig and peered down through the branches. Only four foxes remained below but they were very much alive.

Spreading his wings Swart flew over the valley to the sheep field where a dead ewe lay.

On Trendlebere Down a second vixen was screaming. The shrill notes rose and fell three times.

Wulfgar's breathing had almost ceased and his brush no longer swept the ground. The vixen watched him placidly.

'You are the greatest of the Hill Fox Nation,' Killconey said. 'To be beaten by you is no disgrace. Call me and I'll come running – to the stars if necessary.'

'We are brothers,' Wulfgar said.

Killconey threw back his head and barked the double note of the courting dog. A missel-thrush began to sing. The vixen spoke again and Killconey and Stargrief hastened away.

'The Old Mouse never gives up,' Wulfgar said.

'Old Mouse?' said the vixen. Her voice was thick and tremulous with desire.

'Stargrief the bard. He lives on dreams. He mounts dream-vixens and sires dream-cubs.'

She jumped down and rolled in the leaves, her coat lustrous, reddish-brown, her paws black and neat. He tried to ignore Teg but for a little while her ghost stood between them. Yet the vixen was beautiful in the sleek style of her kind. The markings round her eyes were especially dark and the hair within her ears very white. Slowly Teg's phantom faded until there was nothing between them but the wind.

Rising on his hindlegs he danced around her, singing his love like a back-alley tom. Then her tongue was cool and wet on his nose and eyes. And it was good to leave thought behind at the estuary of being where many currents of emotion met.

Her name was Rowanfleet and her fur was the colour of autumn beech leaves. When she grinned she revealed teeth as white as hazel nut kernels. Unlike Teg she had very little to say.

They walked through Leighon Woods and he waited for the hunger to become something more profound, but only the lust endured and several nights later even that had diminished.

'It's every vixen's dream to be loved by Wulfgar,' Rowanfleet said one evening.

The raw desperation in her voice annoyed him. Snow was falling in big wet flakes that melted on contact with the grass. The sky above the valley was grey and white, goose feather – swan feather, drifting down.

'I'll carry your cubs but never your love.'

Her sorrow brought back a flood of memories.

'You don't love me, do you, Wulfgar.'

'I feel for you more than I feel for any living vixen.'

'Perhaps I should have given myself to Killconey.'

'Didn't he find a mate on the Down?'

'No, Leafsong went off with Sundrifter.'

Wulfgar laughed and licked her nose. He stretched his forelegs, then his back legs and shook the snowflake ice off his coat.

'The conies will be feeding in the field by the rookery.'

'Do you want me to come?' Rowanfleet said.

'Yes. The hunting will be easier.'

Maybe this is all I can ever hope for, he thought, crossing the Becca Brook in three bounds.

BLIZZARD

But the little joy there was soon vanished from their relationship and one evening she got up and left him. He made no attempt to stop her although her going weighed heavily on his conscience. Watching her zig-zag up the valley into the dusk he wondered if he would ever be free of Teg. In the past he had used vixens without regret, but Rowanfleet's sadness continued to reach out to him long after she had gone. For several nights the stale incense of vixen clung to his kennel.

From the rocks by Bowerman's Nose he could hear the bells of Manaton church. The blackness was as opaque as the emptiness in his gut. O Tod, he prayed, let me feel something, something good. Great, invisible flocks of fieldfares were passing across the moors, chacking their pebbly cries. The night was mild and laden with scent.

He came to Hedge Barton and killed mice. Stargrief answered his contact call at Jay's Grave and they walked down the road together. The old dog was talkative and spoke of the Golden Seasons, spinning his words into a bright acoustic drug, coaxing Wulfgar out of himself. Clouds opened above Hound Tor and the universe rushed into Wulfgar's head. Then he was entering the White Vision and the vixen ran to greet him, leaping high from the snow with every bound, catching the stars in her eyes.

'It's Rowanfleet!' he exclaimed.

'Where?'

'In the vision. In the White place. What does it mean?'

'I don't know.'

'But the mating had no love in it.'

'You're certain?'

'There's only Teg. There isn't room for any other animal.'

'What about this glorious Now of life you're always on about?'

'Teg comes and goes. I keep thinking I'm free but she returns to kennel in my heart and the suffering starts again.'

'In the vision are you chasing the vixen?'

'No. She runs towards me.'

'Then she'll come back to you and that's what you really want. She's part of your destiny. She is the future and Teg is the past.'

'But why did I reject her?'

'We know the past. The future is like a dark, scentless night.'

The mild weather ended with a week of January left. A cold snap filmed the edges of Dead Dog Pond with ice and freezing winds swept in from Northern Russia. Snow fell upon the moors and Stargrief and Wulfgar kennelled permanently at Greator Rocks, where the cave under the holly tree faced south-west. It was deep and dry and had been used by generations of dog foxes.

On a night of intense cold they visited Leighon House and killed two guinea fowls that had roosted low in an outbuilding. The deaths were quiet and the beagle bitch lying asleep in the kitchen did not stir.

The birds were lugged back to the cave and the foxes ate well.

'My nose is like ice,' Stargrief complained. 'And my pads don't belong to me.'

The dry bracken rustled as he twisted and turned and tried to get comfortable.

'Put your back against mine,' Wulfgar said. 'And stop whining.'

'This weather will finish me off.'

'Good,' said Wulfgar, curling his brush round his muzzle.

He woke at noon the following day. The cave roof gleamed brightly and looking outside he saw the fallen snow glaring against the granite. The wind carried clouds of little fuzzy grains, piling them in drifts, and above Greator Rocks the snow swirled and flashed against a leaden sky. Every so often the flakes were rushed in horizontal lines by the north-easter.

Wulfgar went out into the eye of the gale. The weird low-key drone made the landscape quake and undulate. As he sniffed the wind, which smelt of nothing but coldness, a shotgun blast of snow caught him in the muzzle. The furze and heather screamed and the rowan branches were flailing. He returned to the cave, which was quiet, facing as it did away from the wind. Stargrief shifted and groaned in his sleep, kicking his feet like a dreaming cub.

Throughout the afternoon snow fell and after dark Dartmoor experienced the worst storm in living memory. The roar of the wind filled the foxes with awe. Beyond the mouth of the cave the drifts were soon six foot deep and climbing higher by the hour. Most of the farm animals were caught in the open and some were buried where they stood against the drystone walls.

It was the coldest night Scoble could recall. He sat by the fire drinking Scotch and mulled cider. Yarner Wood was booming and snow was running up the hill to Haytor like white smoke. He had covered the ferrets' hutch with sacks and heaped the logs and kindling in a corner of the kitchen. The cold stabbed deep into his damaged lung, which ached in a dull, burning sort of way that no thumping with the fist could remove. Sweat poured off him and the bouts of coughing left him weak and gasping.

But the storm was welcome. You could track a fox easily in the snow, and animals did stupid things when they were hungry. It was heaven-sent white to defeat the blackness of hell and the black devil of a fox would leave his signature everywhere he went.

Scoble screwed the wart into his beard with the tip of his forefinger and saw off another tankard of hot, spicy cider. The taste of ginger and cloves seeped through the fur on his tongue. Dreamin' of home, Scoble? the corporal said. Scoble took off his boots and placed his feet on the fender, and after a little while steam rose from his socks. Young Leonard no longer seemed such a stranger; he wasn't just a faded, sepia figure patrolling the frontiers of a nightmare. Christ! How they prayed for bad weather! It was difficult to mount offensives in snow storms, in the winter mud. You could sit it out round a fire while the clock ticked away your life and Fritz crouched in his hole on the other side of No Man's Land. Dear Son of God, let me get wounded in the left arm and go home. There were whispers of revolution in Russia. All they had to do was bayonet the officers and it would stop – the cold, the shelling, the freezing filth of trench life. Cheer up, lads, Major Farjeon said. He had come from the bath via the breakfast table at H.Q. to boost morale. He was clean, portly and bored. Leonard wondered if the bayonet would penetrate all that Cafe Royal flab. But the hatred and resentment came to nothing. The bastards got their own way in the end – every time.

The balaclava had frozen to his lower lip. He peered across the waste of snow. The wind sang in the barbed wire and the skinny old fox hobbled towards him dragging an injured hindleg. It came howling with the agony of starvation and he put a bullet in its head. What the hell are you up to, Scoble? barked Corporal Wellan. Saw the enemy over by the wire, Corp. On a night like this! – the bastards deserve to have their arses blown off. Go and get a drink, lad. I'll take over for a while.

The Scotch dulled the ache in his chest. He leant forward and poked the fire. His socks were singeing. The fingers fumbling the cork of the whisky bottle trembled. Jacko looked up at him and grinned.

'You idn dead, boy,' Scoble whispered, reaching down to stroke the greatcoat that lay in a heap beside the chair.

It snowed all night on the north-easterly wind. Sometimes gritty handfuls swirled and rattled against the rock in the mouth of the cave. The foxes lay awake while whiteness grew outside, then towards daybreak the wind died and by morning the snow no longer fell. The hush was absolute. Dartmoor was completely isolated from the rest of Devon. The great drifts that blocked the roads and cut off the villages also brought the railways to a standstill. The Newton Abbot

– Moretonhampstead line was buried up to platform level at Lustleigh and even deeper by Wray Barton bridge.

Stormbully and Fallbright visited the Leighon Valley and loitered with intent above the coney runs. In many places the wind had made sure the grass was visible in tufts. Worried by cold and hunger the rabbits hopped out to feed and the old cock buzzard made a kill. The hawks wielded the gutting knives of their bills and let a little colour into the whiteness, but Wulfgar ranging across Holwell Down put them to flight and brought the dead rabbit back to the cave.

'That was quick work,' said Stargrief.

Wulfgar sat and watched the old fox eat. A sheep wandered into the cave, its eyes glazed with misery, but when it saw the foxes it turned and went slowly onto the hillside.

'Do you think Rowanfleet will be all right?' Wulfgar said.

'Why shouldn't she be?'

Wulfgar shook his head.

'I wish we had never been parted.'

'She'll be back.'

'Maybe I should go and find her.'

'Where? If you cry loud enough the trapper will come running. Watch the ponds. She'll return. Your visions have never played you false.'

'But this isn't the White Vision, Stargrief.'

The old dog glanced up at him.

'Where are the high mountains and the white grouse and the white hares?' Wulfgar said.

'Could it be the dream country of all foxes?' Stargrief said. 'The peaceful sanctuary, Star Place on earth? Or is it a bit of wishful thinking?'

'No, the country is real enough. I shall lead the clan to it some night. But it isn't here. It isn't the moors.'

'Will I survive to see it?'

'If you stop chatting and carry on eating there's a chance.'

'Maybe I'll reach your vision before you do,' Stargrief sniffed. 'Maybe it's the good hunting country we all tread after death on the way to the Star Place.'

'You look as if you might be there tonight.'

'Ho ho,' Stargrief said solemnly.

During the next few days the snow fell gently. In the lee of the rocks there were many brownish-yellow marks where the sheep had been lying. The ponies, too, had come down off the hills and a large herd roamed from Holwell to Emsworthy, their body steam floating above them. Stormbully filibustered down to rob the open grave of winter, slashing the silence again and again with his skirl.

During his vigil above the ponds Wulfgar saw flocks of birds flying over the moors on their way south. Often the sky was dark with them. Some tumbled to the ground and died of exhaustion but they were not worth eating.

After a night of fog that crisped on twigs, reeds and grasses the blizzard returned. Wulfgar and Stargrief lay in Holly Tree Cave while the wind raged and sculpted the drifts around the foot of the rocks, and when at last stillness returned the ponds froze over. Birds that made their customary flights to the water quickly perished, but Scrag the heron kept a hold on life by fishing the Aish Cottage reaches of the brook.

Pale light touched the treetops, the snow crystals sparkled. Every rut in the lane by Beckaford was hard-edged like iron under the snow. It hurt Scoble's feet through the thin soles of his wellingtons, but he pushed on and shot pigeons at the bottom of the wood. The walking had left him hot and close to vomiting, so he rested on the parapet of the bridge before checking his snares.

All but one was empty. Furzegeld, a young dog fox from Hayne Down, had died in the manner animals dread. Scoble kicked the stiff body. One morning it'll be Blackie, he thought. But I don't want him dead straight off, I want him to know that's goin' to happen. And after I've done with un the devil can grab his soul.

He knelt and loosened the wire. Something dark swooped by his head. Crows were settling in the trees, knocking off the powder snow, making it smoke.

'Seven black birds in a rowan,' he whispered.

Crows were good signposts. They pointed the way to carcasses, to wounded beasts, to fox kills. He had once owned a cat with seven toes on each paw and a temper like blackthorn. The mark of Satan was on her, he thought. Crows and black cats and foxes. The naked trees crowded in on him and the shadows soaked through his skin to chill his blood and take away his breath. The sky swam and he screwed up his eyes to fight the panic. Lying in the field hospital he had tried to tell the doctor about the foxes but he couldn't. The Germans were easy to fight. They came in lines across the field. You picked a target, squeezed the trigger and a gap appeared in the line. Foxes weren't like Germans. They were part of the dusk and only took on their animal shape at night.

He put the fox in his bag and marched up the lane to Beckaford. The crows followed him, hopping from branch to branch. At the entrance to the farm he lifted his shotgun, but the trees were empty. The sky was full of racing, grey clouds and flocks of plover. A fit of coughing took him by surprise and doubled him up. He slapped his knee while his lungs surrendered phlegm. If you cough like that, Leonard, said Corporal Wellan, every bloody Hun in Flanders will pinpoint our position. Best get down the line for a day or two. Where was Corporal Wellan now? Where was the sergeant major and all the other blokes who never took the piss? He wiped his mouth. A blurred brown streak paused in the middle of the field and became a hare. The plover were black bullet holes in the sky.

345

Stormbully's primaries buckled as he turned on the wind. The valley was brimming with light. The buzzard cut across the Western sky and reconnoitred the burrows of Emsworthy. Snow hissed over the tussocky slopes.

Shiv and Chivvy-yick dragged the coney from the hole and sat beside it grooming their whiskers.

'It ain't exactly the plumpest drummer what ever munched grass,' Shiv said.

'A skinny coney is better than a fat promise,' said Chivvy-yick. 'Things ain't goin' to get better and you'd better believe it.'

'What about the others?'

'What others?'

'Snik-snik, Thornwise, Wind-razor and – '

'They can eat pony dung,' Chivvy-yick grated.

Shiv sniggered and closed his eyes in blissful antici-pation of entrails.

'Have you ever tasted a goose egg?' he sighed, but his companion was no longer with him.

The buzzard had hit the fitch patriarch from behind, sinking his talons into neck and lower spine. For the first time in his life Chivvy-yick was speechless. In the split second the hawk required to get a good grip and flap skywards the stoat writhed. Then something cracked behind his ears and the living world vanished. Looking up Shiv saw the buzzard catch the wind and hurtle over Seven Lords Lands, the late deceased Chivvy-yick hang-ing from his feet.

'No more than a bird's snack,' Shiv told the family later, after he had gorged himself on coney.

'There he was and there he wasn't. The old buzzard grabbed him before Mighty Fitch could wink.'

'By tomorrow he'll be a smelly mess of hawk droppings,' Thornwise gloated.

'Yiss, and I an't sorry,' said Snik-snik. 'He was a greedy sod.'

Remembering the rabbit he had scoffed, Shiv struggled to pin an indignant expression on his face.

Servicemen were brought in to dig the trains out of the drifts along the edge of Dartmoor. The roads remained blocked and the villages were without bread and milk. Farmer Lugg made an effort to reach Haytor Down by horse-drawn sleigh, but the snow at Emsworthy Gate was piled ten foot deep and the clouds promised fresh showers. Driven before the wind his Blackface sheep had run up against a wall and the snow had covered them where they huddled. Most were starving and many were dead. The survivors chewed the wool off the backs of the fallen. The moors had become a vast deepfreeze packed with the carcasses of ponies, cattle and sheep. Songbirds sat quietly in the hedges and gave themselves to the cold. The waterfall at Leighon froze solid and the Becca Brook tinkled feebly under ice.

Starglit and Lazuli were both dead. The kingfishers lay together in the nesting hole above the pool that would never hold their blue reflections again. And on an evening of arctic dreariness Wulfgar found the dipper lying as hard as a nut beside the brook. He thawed out the little body on his tongue and ate it whole.

The foxes killed a brace of rabbits on Horridge Common but there was hardly enough meat off them to feed a cub.

'I think it would be wise to split up,' said Stargrief, turning his back on the rising easterly.

'You always look as if you expect the moon to drop on you,' said Wulfgar.

'It galls me to be a nuisance.'

'You're a selfish old mouse.'

'Selfish?'

'Your death would sadden us all. Keeping you alive isn't any trouble.'

He gazed affectionately at the ancient animal. It was too cold for jokes and banter. Snow and the noise of the gale sealed them off from the rest of night-time Dartmoor. They lowered their heads and walked back to Greator Rocks.

'She has returned,' said Stargrief, hesitating at the mouth of the cave.

Wulfgar's nose had also detected Rowanfleet. The vixen was curled up sound asleep in the corner.

'I'll leave when the snow stops,' Stargrief continued.

'No you won't. There's room here for ten foxes. If you go I'll hunt you down and bring you back by the scruff of your neck.'

The vigorous smell of fox softened the air of the cave, which had been hard and wintry. The animals lay with their fur puffed out, breathing gently. The night was loud but Thorgil the badger and his sow heard nothing in Leighon Sett, for they had passed from sleep into the coma of hibernation. Above them life had slowed and in many cases had stopped altogether like the frozen mill wheel at Bagtor.

'It isn't a good time to be alone,' said Rowanfleet.

'No,' said Wulfgar sadly. 'You look so thin. When was the last time you ate?'

'I had a cabbage yesterday from the garden of the house by the little river down there.'

They spoke in whispers for fear of waking Stargrief. The blizzard had passed and the morning had the dead quality of moonlight. A robin fluttered onto the ledge close to the roof. Its weak cheeping reminded Wulfgar of spring in Wistman's Wood and the voice of the first coal tit nestling. And Teg. But the memory was sweet. He found he could recall the joy to his heart easily, and it was gold-edged like a leaf catching the sun full on.

'I wanted you to come back,' he said.

They smiled at each other.

'Look,' Wulfgar said. 'The bird up there carries the sun on its chest.'

'It has risen for us,' Rowanfleet said. 'Out of darkness comes light.'

'Out of love comes life. You are the vixen in the White Vision.'

'What is the White Vision?'

He placed his chin on his forepaws and told her.

'Like the croodling of a constipated woodpigeon,' Stargrief yawned when the tale was finished.

'How long have you been awake?' said Wulfgar.

'Too long.'

'Wasn't I bardic enough?'

'You were plain and straightforward.'

'That's how I see it.'

Stargrief sat up and scratched.

'The snow's stopped,' he said, 'but more will fall.'

His gaze settled on the vixen and he sighed.

'The bones are poking out of your fur, Rowanfleet. We're all like leafless trees.'

'But we're alive and will be so when next summer is dead,' said Wulfgar.

'The summer doesn't die. It is stripped like the trees and gradually re-made so we never take it for granted.'

Wulfgar thought of this in the context of his feelings for Rowanfleet and did not argue.

'Give us a song, Old Mouse, and I'll go out and catch something fat to see us through the day.'

'What sort of song?'

'The Winter Song,' said Rowanfleet.

Hunger had silenced the robin. Stargrief shut his eyes and began to sing.

The Winter Song

Still are the trees at dusk,
Gold is the mist at dawn,
And the vixen softly walking
Leaves footprints on the lawn.

Gold are the winter lights
In the dark lake of the sky;
Breath of frost, kiss of snow,
And the vixen's midnight cry.

The stream bares white claws
And gold are the vixen's eyes;
Two pools where the heart may drink
The glory of sunrise.

Gold are the frozen tors
Flashing in the sun,
Then the Star Place radiant
Where dog and vixen run.

The robin fell dead to the floor but the foxes did not touch it.

'An omen?' said Rowanfleet.

'At night the clouds hide the stars?' said Stargrief. 'As if Tod doesn't wish to confide in me.'

'Is it an omen?' asked Wulfgar.

'It is a dead bird,' said Stargrief. 'The valley is full of them. If they're all omens I'd have to live another fifty seasons to unravel their mysteries.'

Wulfgar laughed and stretched.

'Come on, Rowanfleet,' he said. 'If we're hungry, other animals must be hungry. The rabbits will be out grubbing for rabbit fodder. They get very slow and daft when their guts are empty.'

'I supppse I'd better stay put,' said Stargrief gruffly.

'Yes, lie still. Get your strength back, compose another song, read the runes, doze,' Wulfgar grinned.

'Real dog fox stuff,' Stargrief said in a voice as cold as frost.

Rowanfleet moved like a cat and smiled at him with her eyes. She is already grooming the unborn cubs, he thought. Winter, spring, summer, autumn. The cry, the fighting, the coupling, the birth, the caring, the dying. And will the Star Place be so different? Will all the vixens we love become one perfect creature?

The icy morning made his teeth ache.

KNOWING THE ICE LURCHER

They went over the drifts with a faint, biscuity crunching of pads on frozen snow. The glare had narrowed their eyes to slits. Both Wulfgar and Rowanfleet were thin and dishevelled. The gales that raked the high ground on the eve of St Valentine's Day brought the Haytor Clan to the brink of disaster. Even the rabbits were dying of starvation and the foxes were forced to root for cabbages under the snow at Hedge Barton. A vixen and three dogs were shot trying to break into the hen houses of Widecombe. But Stargrief survived and remained cheerful on a diet of vegetables and carrion.

He was a great scavenger and rarely came home empty-handed.

'The trapper was hiding in the rocks near Crow Thorn yesterday evening,' he said.

'Did he see you?' asked Wulfgar.

Stargrief shook his head.

'I came up behind him.'

'And?'

'He was just sitting there coughing like an old sheep.'

'Waiting for me,' said Wulfgar. 'That one is truly strange. He has the patience of a cat.'

'He was alone,' Stargrief said. 'I've been asking around. His new dog hasn't been seen for ages.'

They patrolled the hedges by Kelly's Farm and ate the wasted bodies of sparrows, chaffinches and blue tits. Despite the weather Rowanfleet could not disguise her happiness. The wind had dropped and the air was sharp and exhilarating. Her breath escaped in little white puffs as she loped along, printing her scent on the starry night. When the moon rose the farmland became suddenly radiant. The silence had a silvery gleam.

'No matter what happens the stars won't stop shining,' Stargrief said.

They stared at each other through the stillness, their eyes twinkling cold and blue, like Vega. A vixen cried from the trees above Lustleigh.

'She is hungry and miserable,' said Rowanfleet.

Stargrief cocked a leg and left a wiggly, yellow signature in the snow.

The foxes hunted through the small hours and returned to the farm at dawn to kennel in the Shippen. Here they discovered Queenie under the straw eating a rat.

'We wondered what had happened to you,' Stargrief said.

'It's bloody cold on the open moor,' said the collie, making room for the foxes and nudging the rat towards Stargrief.

'I nearly died but I remembered how I lived before I became an animal. Farms mean rats and chickens. Tonight I'll lie here. Tomorrow another farm. Man ain't so busy in the snow and dogs leave me alone or bring me food.'

'Eat the rat, Stargrief,' she added quietly. 'Plenty more rats in the barn by the house. Wait here and I'll go and get a couple.'

'We'll come with you,' said Wulfgar.

'No. The dogs will bark and man will come. Dogs know me. They help me catch rats. Why don't you stay? I never go hungry.'

'We'd only bring you trouble,' said Wulfgar. 'Travel alone, Queenie, and may life always be good to you.'

The storm breached his sleep and roared in his dreams. The rocks vibrated and the woods went rushing away on the wind's spring tide to meet the new day. He lay still, imagining the sky choked with dead creatures and he the only fox alive. The flotsam of his thoughts danced on the surge and shift of light. He inhaled the cold reek of winter and subsided for a moment into Rowanfleet's warmth. Outside the drifts were higher than a pony and the wind had cut them in clean geometric shapes. Flurries of snow continued to dance across the mouth of the cave.

The foxes had not eaten for two nights; Stargrief's gut rumbled and gurgled as he stretched his legs and yawned.

'Tod! What a winter!' he gasped. 'In my long life there hasn't been snow to compare with this.'

'Perhaps it is the first of The Three,' Wulfgar said.

'The Three?' Rowanfleet said anxiously.

'Wasn't the story told in your mother's clan?' said Stargrief.

The vixen shook her head.

'Then I'll tell you about the end of the world,' the old dog fox said in the deep, slow voice he reserved for bardic occasions.

'And it will happen this way,' said Tod. 'There will be three bitter winters, one after the other. Rivers and lakes and even the sea will freeze. Snow will pack on snow and the wind will blow ceaselessly from the north. And the sun will give no more heat than the moon.

'After the three long winters the spring will forget its green promises and no summer will appear to break winter's spell. Ice and snow will endure for ever and all the stars will go out, and the sun and moon will vanish. The darkness will be blacker than the blackest peat mire. Loathsome and cold the night will last for ever. No scent. No warmth. No life. Eternal winter.'

'Must this happen?' asked Tod's companions.

'But Tod didn't reply. It was near the end of his life here and he was drifting in and out of visions.'

Rowanfleet shivered.

'The stars don't care if we die,' she said. 'When a fox dies they don't cry. The hills never sob.'

Wulfgar lowered his head and went outside. The vixen's words had conjured up a memory of the lone running on the bleakest part of the moor at the bleakest time of his life. Teg, Oakwhelp, Dusksilver –

'The snow's stopped,' Stargrief murmured, feeling his friend's sorrow.

A forbidding dawn brightened slowly into a day of pale, golden sun. They wandered down the snow slope to the ponds and crossed them on the thick ice, which was littered with the remains of redwings and field-fares. A pair of skinny, desperate-looking dog foxes sat by the solid waterfall. The Becca Brook had frozen to the bottom. The only sound breaking the hush was the swish and thud of snow sliding off the trees. Romany and Moonsleek had gone down the River Teign to the sea.

Chest deep in the recent drifts under Holwell Tor Wulfgar, Rowanfleet and Stargrief stood and sniffed the air. 'Nothing,' said Stargrief.

And they thought of The Three Winters and were afraid.

One by one the rooks left the beeches and flapped up the valley. They were like vampire bats with their long, heavy wingbeats, but Elder was not among them.

The arctic night had claimed her and half a dozen other members of the Holwell Commune.

The foxes climbed to the top of the tor. Ahead of them the white dorsal fin of Hay Tor cut the haze of blue, cloudless sky. It was like being on a snowy roof. Flying at two thousand feet Stormbully saw the three black specks moving across the down. The whole of the moor was filmed with light that hurt the eyes. He gave a cat-call and sailed over Yarner to quarter the farmland of Bovey Tracey.

'We could try for hens at the cottage on the edge of the wood,' Wulfgar said.

'The trapper would like that,' Stargrief grunted. 'He reasons as we reason. If he didn't get you there he'd track you to the cave and finish us while we slept!'

Wulfgar gritted his teeth and said, 'How he poisons our lives! I should have ripped out his throat when I found him beside the road.'

'But fortunately Tod sent a sign and you didn't kill him.'

'Get Tod to strike a blow for the Hill Fox Nation.'

'How can I?' said Stargrief.

'Ask him to hurl down a star on the trapper.'

'I read what he writes in the sky. I don't ask for favours. Our lives are our own affair.'

Fresh fox-spoors ran before them in the direction of Saddle Tor. They felt vulnerable and ill-at-ease out on the snowfield. Stormbully's faint, far-off skirl crept from the distance and lifted Wulfgar's hackles. Then a dog fox was howling the double notes that his kin found irresistible. Other foxes were on the move towards Saddle Tor and the three from Holly Tree cave joined the race. Where the snow had been exposed to the storm it was crisp and sparkling.

Wulfgar led the way to the rocks beyond Crow Thorn. His nose was bringing him the gut-warming smell of meat and blood and fox-musk. In the hollow beneath the tor a dozen dogs and vixens were milling round a dead pony. The animal had slipped from the crag during the blizzard and Killconey had laid claim to it. Now he was gorged and was willing to share the feast with the clan. Fox trails radiated from the carcass and a few early arrivals lay about grooming themselves and exchanging gossip. Those still busy at the meat snapped and growled in a tight scrum.

Killconey rolled onto his back and flashed Wulfgar a grin.

'Enough to feed the Star Place dogs,' he sighed.

All day they lingered by the carcass while the shadows lengthened and the sun became redder than the stains on the snow. The foxes were replete and drowsy but reluctant to leave the source of their contentment. It was fine to sprawl beside the frozen flood-pool while Stargrief mounted a nearby rock and gave them the verses and the sagas.

Such gatherings were memorable. The old prophet guided them through his visions. And as the sun crossed the western sky, bathing him in its glow, it seemed he had been turned to gold like a real companion of Tod.

Rowanfleet glided between the dogs in a cloud of musk. Brown and amber fires burnt in her eyes and her chest fur was the white of button mushrooms fresh with dew. She was mysterious and beautiful, and her words fell upon his knowing like water from a moorland stream.

'When I was a cub,' Stargrief said, 'the blood of the grass was on my teeth. My mother rested and licked my muzzle while I stood under her waiting for her to settle in drowsy song.

'We stood in the field close to the sky, two shadows on the summer, already forgotten and doomed like the grass. But we left a presence on the seasons.'

O sea of stars carry me through this winter, the old fox prayed. His haggard face was tilted to catch the last of the sun. How like a fantasy of all vixens was Rowanfleet. The snow blinked golden at her feet and something ancestral climbed through his blood to his brain. He was running with the dream of foxes before the ice that daily crept nearer. But the great rivers of ice did not carve and grind and stultify the moors. Bear and wolf, fox and man shivered in the arctic twilight. But they lived. In Rowanfleet's beauty was immortality and salvation.

The rich and bloody sunset flared and dimmed. Wulfgar, too, was watching the vixen. Her silence sang to him. It was satisfactory to lie beside her listening to the rise and fall of her breathing and exchange the love thoughts. When the sun set the fire remained in her eyes.

By starlight the foxes departed leaving the three to talk with Killconey.

'Why didn't you speak about the Ice Lurcher you saw in your vision?' Wulfgar asked.

'Because it troubles me and you know why.'

'I do, but destiny is destiny. Are you so uncertain of your prophetic powers?'

'As I get older, yes. It's hard to differentiate between vision and daydream. I'm afraid I'll send you on some errand dreamt up in a ga-ga catnap.'

'The meaning of the vision is crystal clear.'

'It turns my blood to ice.'

'But the winter will do it – this winter. And it isn't the first of The Three.'

Killconey gazed from one to the other and wagged his muzzle.

'Star Places and The Three and destinies!' he snorted. 'Go and sniff out a few more feasts. That's what the clan needs.'

'And the trapper?' said Wulfgar.

'Who knows about men? They aren't animals. They don't belong to the brotherhood of living things. The trapper is like the itching sickness, like the snares and the gun and the hounds. He is death and death is always with us.'

'You need a vixen,' said Stargrief.

'I've got one,' Killconey said. 'Leafsong. The trapper killed her dog, Sundrifter.'

'The Ice Lurcher will have its way,' Wulfgar said mysteriously.

'Ice Lurcher!' Killconey growled.

'Where are you kennelled?' Stargrief said.

'In the woods by the empty sett. There's a ruined cow house that keeps out the wind.'

The yawning vixen stiffened her forelegs in a stretch of well-being. Her face was livid in the light of the moon, in the reflected moonlight.

THE GREAT AMMIL

Scoble had pleurisy. He crouched by the kitchen fire and sipped the bitter juice of hoarhound. Silence pressed down on Yarner Cott. It seemed alive, as if Dartmoor had turned into a gigantic carnivore and was swallowing whole flocks of sheep and sucking birds out of the sky. He sent a forefinger burrowing through his beard in search of the wart. Snow slithered from the ash tree and he closed his eyes and saw the rats slithering over the corpses in the shell-hole. Crimp's bought it, the sergeant major said. The big one exploded with a hell of a noise and there was Crimpy – and there and there and there and there. The birch log banged and sent a shower of sparks onto the hearth. O the lovely bloody warmth and some long-dead soldier playing Roses of Picardy on a mouth organ.

He stared absently at the swollen joints of his fingers as they clenched on the cider barrel tap. It's all right for them bastards down at H.Q., Corporal Wellan said. Frost powdered his face. His eyes were dark and sunken. Just the morning to surprise the Allemands, Lieutenant General Shewte chortled, reaching for the bacon. The staff officers guzzled tea and grinned. But Lieutenant Gatty was OK. He cried when young Brannan copped it, and he shared the shit and misery. A machine gun nailed him to the Roll of Honour at some public school. Crimp was 'other ranks' but he got on the village cenotaph.

The trapper lit a candle and placed it on the table. The fox masks glared down at him from the wall and half a dozen pairs of glass eyes imitated the life-glint. Scoble swallowed cider and thought about Old Blackie. In the sky over Yarner Wood the stars shimmered and winked, and across Trendlebere Down a famished fox ran, fetching up a howl that hung unanswered on the stillness.

Snow fell again in the evening and by midnight another blizzard had arrived. From Moretonhampstead to Tavistock trees and telegraph poles were brought down. The muffling fall killed the last of Lugg's hill sheep. But while the wind blew and the snow swirled a whiteness endured that concealed the horror. Only in the spring would the piteous huddles of farm creatures come to light.

The wild night stampeded the stars and kept the foxes in their cave. At daybreak the blizzard was down to its last flake and Wulfgar led his companions onto the common. The strength of the wind took them by surprise. All along the ponds ponies were trampling the furze and eating it. The animals were emaciated, but unlike the sheep and cattle they knew how to survive. The easterly that was hurling flocks of thrushes over Yarner lifted their manes. They regarded the foxes from delicately lashed eyes, and continued munching. Light spread grey on the hills.

Later that afternoon the foxes raided a barn at Manaton and gnawed open a sack of meal. The white owls up in the rafters hissed at them but they gobbled the grain while the countryside creaked as the temperature dropped.

'Chicken food,' Stargrief grunted.

Rowanfleet smiled.

'Tod forgive my ingratitude!' the old dog fox exclaimed cheerfully. 'A full belly is a full belly.'

He stepped outside and the wind cut into him. Sirius glinted from the dusk. It grew dark very quickly and the lapwings started to scream in the fields under Bowerman's Nose. On the outskirts of the village they paused and looked up at the sky. The beauty of the world continuously filtered through their senses to feed their spirits. The stars were out in strength with Orion in the south and the Pleiades above it and the Great

Bear in the north. There were few things lovelier than the snowy hills set in the soft glow of the universe.

Winter spilled over into March and showed no sign of relenting. The wind rushing down the Leighon Valley flattened the reeds and ruffled Scrag's feathers. The intense cold had finally killed the heron and he lay like a badly wrapped parcel on the ice of Dead Dog Pond. The wind passed on, up and over Hound Tor, looping to add more snow to the drifts of Hamel Down.

At twilight Wulfgar emerged and lifted his muzzle yet again to the sky that was now calm and clear. A single bright star broke from the constellation of the Seven Sisters and flared through space.

'You've misgivings?' said Stargrief's voice behind him.

'None. Is Rowanfleet ready?'

The vixen joined them and they ran silently across Haytor Down. A mass of cloud spread from the east to meet them.

'Are you afraid, Rowanfleet?' Wulfgar said.

'Terrified.'

'Don't be. Nothing can happen to us. Tonight we are the great hunters full of Star Place magic.'

Where the moors fell steeply to Yarner Wood he said goodbye to the dog and the vixen. 'Wait here', were his parting words.

He went into the valley whisking his brush, raising the powder snow with his forepaws. Like a wolf, thought Stargrief. The sky was black and the lights along the coast were vanishing.

Wulfgar took the road to Yarner Cott. The frozen drifts made it easy for him to leap the wall and drop noiselessly into the yard. Light from the kitchen window yellowed the snow. He padded cautiously up to the window ledge and stood on his hindlegs and pressed his nose against the glass.

The trapper had drunk hard from the cider barrel until he was ready for the Scotch. Slumped in the armchair before the fire he laughed and scowled. Every so often he slid his tongue along his lower lip and let it lie in the corner of his mouth. Soon he was drooling and lidding his eyes and the tears dawdled over the mesh of broken blood vessels on his cheeks to vanish into his beard. His shirt and corduroys were stiff with sweat and grime. God, Scoble, Corporal Wellan said. You smell like a bloody compost heap. You never knew what was under the trench water. Rats were very good swimmers and they could sniff out a corpse. Softly through the fog of alcohol came the strains of 'Keep the Home Fires Burning'. The Cornish boy could really play the mouth organ. Ought to be on the halls. Better than the hymns. What had God done for them? But Church Parade was a holiday and 'We plough the fields and scatter' brought them back over the hills to Devon. The bloody padre spoilt it – spouting fat, posh words like we were suddenly important and not just the poor dressed up in uniforms. Not just yokels born to hold the horse and feed the hounds and drive the carts and carriages. Maybe it's really changed back home, Corporal Wellan said. Bands playing, lads marching, all the flags and bunting and flowers. And the girls stroking our medals and giving us great smacking kisses.

He groaned, coughed and clawed at the Johnny Walker bottle. Rationing never bothered him. The toffs were always ready to hand out the Scotch if you did them a favour. He wasn't old and sick. The medals were locked away in a box under the bed, but where the hell had the sergeant major gone? The slow-flowing gold of whisky pulsed in the glass. He turned to the window and lost control of his sphincter muscle. The dark angular fox mask stared back at him, eyes green and unblinking, mouth set in a satanic smile.

'Jacko,' Scoble wailed and his reflection wailed back at him. Like one of they shrunken concentration camp Jews, he thought, pulling on his Wellington boots.

'You won't have me. Lord Jesus you won't.'

The rifle kicked as he squeezed the trigger and splintered the window sill. But the fox had disappeared and Scoble was fighting to shrug off the dizziness. The devil sent you, you bastard, he thought, stuffing cartridges into his pockets.

You've followed me all the way from the Somme. Charlie the mule and Jacko weren't enough. Poor Jacko. Poor old boy.

Wulfgar's spoor led him across the road and onto the hill. The exertion brought him coughing and puking to his knees. There were three trails now. And that's how it should be, he mused. Three dark foxes under the flares, white swelling then fading into darkness until more flares lit No Man's Land. The rifle cracked but the foxes did not move until he had reloaded and struggled to the top of the ridge. Kamerad, the German soldier cried, but the bayonet was deaf. In, grunt, out, grunt. Scoble laughed. The snow came right over his wellingtons on the southern slopes of Haytor Down. The fresh falls had not had time to freeze. Dimly ahead of him the foxes kept their distance. Each gulp of icy air hurt his lungs and sweat beaded his body and trickled into his eyes. Tears and phlegm clotted his beard.

Wulfgar glanced back at the floundering figure.

'The Man-shape rising from the snow,' Stargrief whispered. 'We have become part of the vision.'

They groomed their fur while they waited. It was a casual business, like attending a sick cow or pony. Crow work, Stargrief called it. But they had a nose for death. When the bolt clicked they clapped down and waited for the bang before loping on into the darkness, which had thickened and grown colder. Every so often Rowanfleet gave a scream that carried to Haytor Vale and made Steelygrin hiss and draw back his ears. The feral cat lay in the garden shed of the Moorland Hotel and dined on dream voles.

Yeoman's been hit, Corporal Wellan said. That isn't human, Corp. It sounds like a horse screaming. Rats scurried out of their galleries to investigate. A shell droned by. Something legless was dragging itself from the gloom; something legless that screamed with the persistence of a spoilt child. Scoble fired and the noise stopped. The squad charged over the snow to the fortification. Bullets whined past his head. He scrambled up the hummock and saw the foxes vanish into the quarry. He was alone on a spinning battlefield. O Christ, the bloody lot are dead. The sheep path zig-zagged down the wall of the quarry. He dug his heels into the hard snow and leant on the rifle. Then he was coughing and jerking about and his feet were sliding away. The rifle clattered into the void and he joined it. A jumble of snow-crusted rocks flew up to meet him. He hit them with a force that jarred and twisted his spine and robbed him of breath and consciousness.

Wake up, Scoble, the sentry said. It's brass monkey weather. Best stand to before Wellan does the rounds. Dear God, wasn't it cold! What had happened to his tunic and greatcoat? You're a rum bugger, Len, doin' guard duty in shirtsleeves. He tried to get up but the pain in his left leg made him cry out. The kneecap was pulped. His fingers fumbled the mess of cartilage and blood. From the distance of No Man's Land someone was screaming. It isn't me, Private Scoble said. It can't be me. They were singing Land of Hope and Glory as the band marched them through Exeter. Old soldiers never die, they only fade away.

When numbness set in he surfaced from the agony. He couldn't move. His back was dead and cold. Through the reek of his sweat and filth he caught a whiff of fox.

'Black bastard,' he hissed, clenching his teeth to hold off the pain that had developed a tidal shift. The sweat turned to ice-water on his body. A hole appeared in the sky and released a flash of moonlight. The flare fizzed up and fell, bleaching the gloom. Beyond the shell crater the foxes sat cleaning their whiskers and paws.

'Get back to hell,' Scoble screamed.

His ruined knee poked from his trousers like a scavenger's tit-bit, something for the foxes to gnaw at.

Another flare plopped down and he saw all around him the bulging dead. His lung heaved and he siphoned up a warm gruel of blood and phlegm. The sniper's bullet had done disgusting things to Burdett's head. 'God moves in a mysterious way his wonders to perform', the padre sang, and Private Scoble was shivering. The tent was as cold as God's promises.

It began to drizzle. The temperature was well below zero and the fine rain froze on contact with everything it touched. Presently the wind came strong from the north-east turning the drizzle into an ice storm. Who will feed the ferrets? Keep your mind on the task at hand, Leonard, said Corporal Wellan.

A thin fox howled beneath the poplars. The lads were marching and singing the great songs. 'Roses are bloomin' in Picardy in the hush of the silvery dew.' But the life was leaving him as surely as if an artery had burst. Beneath the skin of ice it was warm and drowsy. The foxes had reached the mule on the patch of snow that grew larger and smaller, then unsteady and large again. He felt faint. The icy raindrops clung to his face and hands. Giddy with terror he heard the grinding squeal of the tank. Dear Christ don't let it come here. His fingers dug into the snow and stiffened.

'What have you done to the mule?' he slurred.

The shell exploded and he was falling backwards through his own darkness. Get out of the mud, Len, Corporal Wellan barked. Get up, lad – that's an order. But he was settling deeper, choking, drowning. It's Old Blackie, the boy on the bridge cried. Old Blackie's a magic animal.

He stared through his frozen eyelashes. Beyond the pool the foxes sat. And in the sickening moment before blackness swamped his mind he knew where he was and why he had been brought there.

At first the verglas formed on the windward side of twigs, grasses, wire, reeds, rocks and branches, but when the storm died the drizzle fell steadily like a dense fog, sheathing the entire moor. Twigs swelled to five times their normal circumference and became embellishments on the glass sculptures that had once been blackthorn bushes. Branches were torn off trees by the weight of the ice crystals; birches, rowans and beeches were brought down and telephone wires snapped. Reeds of ice stood beside the frozen streams and the snowfields ran sparkling to white and glistening tors. In the hedges of the lanes around Manaton and North Bovey the hazels bowed to meet in arches and tunnels of ice, and the oaks of Leighon seemed to have been carved from the same bright substance.

All night and for most of the next day the moors were glazed with frost, which Devonians called the 'ammil'. Scoble's body lying in Haytor Quarry was part of the savage beauty.

From his mask of ice the trapper stared blindly across the pond to the beam where the three foxes had sat watching him die.

'It's done,' said Stargrief.

'They do die, then,' said Rowanfleet.

'Like sheep,' Wulfgar said contemptuously.

The clouds were whirling away and Hay Tor sailed out of the murk like an iceberg. Mordo the raven soared above it to a place close to the fading Dogstar.

'Let's go back to the cave,' the black fox said.

'You two go,' Stargrief smiled.

'But the winter will kill you,' Wulfgar said.

'The winter is nearly over,' replied his friend. 'I feel the need to travel alone.'

They watched his slight, grey figure recede into the distance beneath the Tor.

'Stargrief,' Wulfgar cried. 'Stargrief.'

The ancient dog fox ran on and did not look back.

'I'm sure he understands the White Vision,' Wulfgar added. 'The white grouse and the white hares.'

'Perhaps it's not part of this winter,' said Rowanfleet.

Yet the mountain was there towering over Hay Tor, invisible to all other foxes. In his dreams it ran away from him to the edge of the sea at World's End. But he would set foot on its snow one day and he would not be alone. Of this he was certain.

LATE SUNLIGHT

Under the hedge behind Bagtor Cottages primrose buds had risen from the shrew's skull. Spring had come like a gasp of breath separating winter briefly from summer. But although the countryside looked drab and washed-out the grass was growing again beneath the dead bracken. The blackthorn was in blossom and the hawthorn's leaves were greener than young wheat.

Through the sunlight the Becca Brook flowed gently and the waterfall sang like a bird at the Leighon Ponds. Stray sat on the dam and watched the alders swaying against the sky. For a couple of hours he had hardly moved while daws came and went and trout dimpled the hush.

The American lowered his binoculars and smiled. Then he got to his feet and followed the edge of the pond past the cairn to the dam where the trees were thick and the water was spiked with reeds.

'What are you staring at?' he asked.

Stray frowned up at him and dipped his hand in the pond.

'Nothin' much – just the treetops and things.'

'You like watching the sky and water?'

'Not always. But some of what I see makes me feel good.'

'You've got a name I suppose.'

'It's Brian,' the boy said, colouring. 'I don't like it much.'

'I guess we can't help our names,' the American said. 'You could've been called Adolf and that would have been bad news.'

The boy laughed and said, 'You back at Aish Cottage, mister?'

'Yep. I've bought the place. All I need now is a dog to fill the basket in the parlour and I'm set up.'

'They say Scoble had your spaniel.'

'They're probably right.'

'Scoble's dead. He froze to death in the quarry last month.'

'I know. Jenny Shewte told me.'

'I idn sorry. He liked killing birds and animals.'

'What happened to Old Blackie?'

'O he's OK,' the boy said, his eyes sparkling with excitement. 'He's got a new vixen and her's lovely. I saw 'em up over Hayne last Saturday. They'll never have Old Blackie. Never. He's magic.'

'And he's won,' Richard Williams said quietly.

Snow still lingered where the goyals faced north, but the sheltered coombs were soft and green. Dartmoor carried the late sunlight on rounded hills into a haze ringing with the cries of plover and curlew.

The dark dog fox and the red vixen ran shoulder to shoulder over Conies Down to the tor above the Cowsic River. Mist rose from the valley and dimly at first Vega shone in the east where night waited.

This was Wulfgar's saga

A NOTE ON THE AUTHOR

Brian Carter was an artist, poet, columnist, children's author, naturalist and broadcaster who influenced a generation of nature writers. His six novels all explore man's relationship with nature, the first of which, *A Black Fox Running,* was published in 1981. His art was exhibited at the Royal Academy in London and at galleries in Paris, Germany, Holland and Canada, and he had a one-man show on London's West End. He fought and won many conservation battles for the English countryside and had a great love of the natural world, particularly of Dartmoor, within sight of which he lived most of his life, spending time outdoors there walking, cycling and playing football. He contributed to every edition of West Country newspaper the *Herald Express* from the early 1980s until his death in 2015. He is survived by his widow Patsy, his children Christian and Rebecca, and three grandchildren.

A NOTE ON THE TYPE

The text of this book is set Adobe Garamond. It is one of several versions of Garamond based on the designs of Claude Garamond. It is thought that Garamond based his font on Bembo, cut in 1495 by Francesco Griffo in collaboration with the Italian printer Aldus Manutius. Garamond types were first used in books printed in Paris around 1532. Many of the present-day versions of this type are based on the *Typi Academiae* of Jean Jannon cut in Sedan in 1615.

Claude Garamond was born in Paris in 1480. He learned how to cut type from his father and by the age of fifteen he was able to fashion steel punches the size of a pica with great precision. At the age of sixty he was commissioned by King Francis I to design a Greek alphabet, and for this he was given the honourable title of royal type founder. He died in 1561.